Jake saw a range *[of emotions flash]* **across Allison's face. Disappointment, worry, relief. He latched on to the last one. She wanted him gone.**

Then why was she here? Why did she insist on pushing past his caution when absolutely nothing good could come of it?

Jake wished for the thousandth time he could erase that one terrible day from their lives. He was comfortable with Allison, *liked* her, a dangerous thing, then and now. She made him smile. She even made him believe in himself. Or she once had. With everything in him he wanted to know this grown-up Allison, a dangerous, troubling proposition.

"You've grown up." Stupid thing to say, but better than yanking her into his arms.

She tilted her head, smile quizzical. "Is that a good thing or a bad thing?"

For him? Very bad.

Allison had definitely grown up.

And Jake Hamilton was in major trouble.

Linda Goodnight, a *New York Times* bestselling author and winner of a RITA® Award in inspirational fiction, has appeared on the Christian bestseller list. Her novels have been translated into more than a dozen languages. Active in orphan ministry, Linda enjoys writing fiction that carries a message of hope in a sometimes dark world. She and her husband live in Oklahoma. Visit her website, lindagoodnight.com, for more information.

Dana Corbit began telling "people stories" around the same time she started talking. She's continued both activities, nonstop, ever since. She left a career as an award-winning newspaper reporter to raise three daughters, but the stories followed her home as she discovered the joy of writing fiction. Now an award-winning author and member of Romance Writers of America's Honor Roll of bestselling authors, she loves telling emotional stories filled with honorable but flawed characters.

Cowboy Under the Mistletoe

New York Times Bestselling Author

Linda Goodnight

&

A Hickory Ridge Christmas

Dana Corbit

LOVE INSPIRED
INSPIRATIONAL ROMANCE

LOVE INSPIRED®
INSPIRATIONAL ROMANCE

ISBN-13: 978-1-335-28493-8

Recycling programs
for this product may
not exist in your area.

Cowboy Under the Mistletoe &
A Hickory Ridge Christmas

Copyright © 2020 by Harlequin Books S.A.

Cowboy Under the Mistletoe
First published in 2014. This edition published in 2020.
Copyright © 2014 by Linda Goodnight

A Hickory Ridge Christmas
First published in 2006. This edition published in 2020.
Copyright © 2006 by Dana Corbit Nussio

This edition published by arrangement with Harlequin Books S.A.

For questions and comments about the quality of this book,
please contact us at CustomerService@Harlequin.com.

Love Inspired
22 Adelaide St. West, 40th Floor
Toronto, Ontario M5H 4E3, Canada
www.Harlequin.com

Printed in U.S.A.

CONTENTS

COWBOY UNDER
THE MISTLETOE

Linda Goodnight

Now, however, it is time to forgive and comfort him.
Otherwise he may be overcome by discouragement.
—*2 Corinthians* 2:7

Chapter One

Someone was at the Hamilton house. Someone in a black pickup truck bearing a bull rider silhouette on the back window.

Curious, with a tremor in her memory, Allison Buchanon pulled her Camaro sports car to the stop sign in a quiet neighborhood of Gabriel's Crossing, Texas, and sat for a moment pondering the anomaly. She drove past this corner at least once a week on her way to her best friend's home. She hadn't seen any sign of life in the rambling old house for a long while. Not since before Grandmother Hamilton fell and broke her hip several months ago. And Jake had been gone so long no one even cursed his name anymore.

If Allison had a funny quiver in her stomach, she played it off as anticipation of Faith's bridal shower this afternoon. As hostess, she wanted to arrive early and make sure everything—including her dearest friend—was perfect.

She glanced at the dash clock. Three hours early might be overkill.

On the opposite corner, Dakota Weeks and a half-

dozen fat puppies rolled around in the fading grass while
the mama dog wagged her tail and smiled proudly, occasionally poking her nose into the ten-year-old boy's
hand for a head rub. Allison grinned and waved.

A boy and his dogs on Saturday afternoon put her
in mind of her older brothers. Even now as adults, rolling in the grass with a dog—or each other if a football
game broke out—was a common occurrence. And today
was a perfect day to be outside. The weather was that
cusp season when cool breezes crowded out the scent
of mowed grass, Dads cleaned out chimneys and Moms
stored away the shorts and swimsuits. Or as townsfolk
would say, "football weather."

Like many small Texas towns, Gabriel's Crossing
lived and breathed high school football year round, but
especially in the fall. Teenage boys in pads and helmets
became heroes, not only on Friday night but every day.
Golden boys. Boys of the gridiron.

Exactly the reason Jake Hamilton was no longer welcome at her mother's table or a lot of other places in Gabriel's Crossing.

Oh, but they didn't know the Jake Allison had known.
The Jake who carried her darkest, most humiliating secret, the one she'd never shared with another living soul.

Casting one last worried glance toward the Hamilton
house, Allison convinced herself the truck belonged to
a lawn service or maybe some long-lost relative looking
to take over the place, not Jake Hamilton.

She eased her foot off the brake and started across the
intersection. The front door to the house opened and a
man walked out onto the small concrete porch.

This time Allison's stomach did more than quiver. It
fell to the floorboard and took her breath with it.

Jake.

She slammed on the brake and stared. It was him all right. Trim and tight muscled in fitted Wranglers, dusty boots and black cowboy hat, he looked as dangerously handsome as ever.

His head turned her direction, and Allison realized she'd stopped at midintersection. She started forward again. At the last possible second, the steering wheel seemed to take on a life of its own because the Camaro swung into the Hamilton driveway and came to a stop.

With the spontaneity her parents considered impulsive, Allison hopped out of the running car and walked right up to the man, her pulse in overdrive.

"Hello, Jake. Long time." Funny how normal her voice sounded even when she stared into fathomless olive green eyes with lashes as black as midnight.

He hadn't changed much except for a new scar below one eye, and she fought off the crazy urge to soothe it with a touch the way she'd once soothed his football bumps and bruises. He'd also grown facial hair in the form of a very short, scant mustache above a bit of scruff, and his sideburns were long. She couldn't decide if she liked the look but then, when had Jake Hamilton cared one whit about what anyone else thought? Especially a Buchanon.

"You shouldn't be here, Allison." His voice was the same, a low note, surprisingly soft but steel edged as if to drive her away. The way he'd done before.

"We're adults now. We can be anywhere we choose."

Jutting one hip, he tipped his hat with a thumb. His nostrils flared. "Ya think?"

"You owe me a dance."

The reminder must have caught him off guard. Something flickered in his eyes, a brief flame of memory and pleasure that died just as quickly unborn.

Jaw hard as flint, he said, "Better run home, little girl, before the big bad wolf gets you."

Before she could tell him that nothing he'd ever done would change what she knew that no other Buchanon understood, Jake spun away from her and slammed inside the house, leaving her standing in the front yard. Alone and embarrassed. Exactly like before.

He had as much right to be in this town as the Buchanons. Maybe more. His great-great-something on his daddy's side had founded Gabriel's Crossing back in the mid-1800s when Texas was a whole other country and the adjacent hills of Oklahoma were wilder than any bull he'd thrown his rope over.

Jake banged his fist against the countertop of his family home. Right or not, being here would not be easy. Nearly broke, he needed to be working, and if that wasn't enough to move him on, the Buchanon brothers were. And Allison. Especially Allison.

But Granny Pat was his only living relative. Anyway, the only one that claimed him. She'd been his anchor most of his life, but now the tables had turned. She needed him, and he wouldn't fail her, no matter how hard the weeks and months ahead.

He'd wanted her to give up the Hamilton house to live with him in his trailer in Stephenville, but she'd wanted to come home. Home to Gabriel's Crossing and the familiar old house that had been in the Hamilton family since statehood. He understood, at least in part. There was history here, joy and sorrow. He'd tasted both.

Granny Pat had raised him single-handedly in this

house after his daddy died and his mother ran off. Grandpa was here, too, his grandmother claimed, and though her husband had been dead for longer than Jake had been alive, she missed him. Ralph, according to Granny Pat, had never liked hospitals and hadn't visited her in the convalescent center one single time.

As if that wasn't scary enough, who was the first familiar face Jake had to see in Gabriel's Crossing? Allison Buchanon. His heart crumpled in his chest like a wad of paper tossed into a fire pit, withering to black ashes. Allison of the dark fluffy hair and warm brown eyes. She'd always seen more in him than anyone else had, especially her family. Foolish girl.

Although as small as a child, Allison could hammer a nail as easily as she could back-flip from a cheerleading pyramid, an action that had sent his teenage chest soaring and turned his mouth dry as dust. And she'd broken that same young man's heart with one sentence. *My family would kill me if they saw us together.*

No, he'd said, *they'd kill me.* They'd have had every right, after what he'd done.

The rodeo circuit attracted plenty of buckle bunnies and if a man was so inclined; he could have a new girl every night. With everything in him, Jake wanted to put Allison and her family behind him, but he never had. They mattered, and the wrong he'd done lay on his shoulders, an elephant-size guilt. No matter what Allison said, he'd never been anyone's hero.

When he'd been a lonely boy living with his grandma, the Buchanons had been his dream family, a mom and dad, brothers and sisters. A boy with none of those yearned for the impossible. For a while, for those years when Quinn had been his best friend and Allison had thought he was the moon, he'd basked in the Buchanon glow.

Allison. Why had she pulled into the driveway? And why had he been so glad to see her? Didn't she remember the trouble they'd caused? That *he'd* caused?

He rubbed a hand over the thick dust coating the counters, coating everything in the musty old house with the pink siding and dark paneling.

He should have stuck to the rodeo circuit and stayed away from Gabriel's Crossing for another nine or ninety years, but sometimes life didn't give you choices. Four years ago, when he'd handed the reins to Jesus at a cowboy church in Cheyenne, he'd vowed to do the right thing from that moment on, no matter how much it hurt. Coming home to help Granny Pat was the right thing. And boy, did it hurt.

He didn't have enough money or time to be here. He needed to make every rodeo he could before the season ended, but Granny Pat came first. He'd figure out the rest. Somehow.

Once his grandma was up and going, he'd get out of Dodge before trouble—in the form of a Buchanon—found him again.

No one in their right minds had seven kids these days. Which said a lot about her mother and father.

The next afternoon, Allison pushed open the front door to her parents' rambling split-level house on Barley Street and marched in without knocking. Nobody would have heard her anyway over the noise in the living room. The TV blared football between the Cowboys and the Giants while her dad and four brothers yelled at the quarterback and each other in the good-natured, competitive spirit of the Buchanon clan. Her stick-skinny younger sister Jayla was right with them, getting in her two cents about the lousy play calling by the offensive coordinator while Charity, the oldest and only married sibling, doled out peanut butter and jelly sandwiches to her two kids.

"Home sweet home." Allison stepped over a sprawled Dawson whose long legs seemed to stretch from the bottom of the couch halfway across the room.

"Hey, sis," Dimpled Dawson, twin to Sawyer, offered an absentminded fist bump before yelling. "You missed the block, you moron!"

"I'll do better next time," Allison said, pretending not to understand. Dawson ignored that, too.

"Where's Mom?"

"Somewhere."

Brothers could be so helpful.

"Jayla?" she implored of her sister, who was scrunched on the dirt-brown sofa between Sawyer and Quinn.

Jayla, twisting the ends of her flaxen hair into tight, nervous corkscrews, never took her eyes off the game. She lifted a finger and pointed. "Backyard."

Backyard. That figured. Mom would rather putter in her flowers, though she'd wander in and out of the huge Buchanon-built house simply to spend time with her kids.

Before Allison made the turn into the kitchen, Brady snagged her wrist. Like Dawson, he was on the floor but propped against the wall with his dog sprawled across his lap. Dawg, a shaggy mix of shepherd, lab and who-knew-what, raised a bushy eyebrow in her direction, but otherwise, like the siblings, didn't budge.

"Aren't you going to watch the game?"

Allison's nerves jittered. Some things were more important than the game, although she would not share this minority opinion with any relative in the large, overcrowded living room.

"Later."

He tilted his head to one side, a flash of curiosity in his startling cerulean eyes. Brady, her giant Celtic warrior brother who bore minimal resemblance to the rest of the Buchanons. "Everything okay, Al?"

Jake Hamilton, one hip slung low as a gunslinger, imposed on her mental viewer. "Sure."

"Touchdown Cowboys!" someone shouted, and the room erupted in high fives and victory dances. His curiosity forgotten, Brady leaped to his feet and swirled her around in a two-step, as light on his feet as when he'd been chasing quarterbacks at Texas Tech. Allison, regardless of the worry, couldn't help but laugh. Her brothers were crazy wonderful, her protectors and friends, the shoulders she could always cry on, except that one awful night when she hadn't dared. Her heart swelled with love. What would she do without them? And how would they react when they learned Jake Hamilton was back in town?

Brady planted a loud smack on her cheek and turned her loose. Before he could ask any more prying questions, she high-fived her way through the elated sea of bodies and headed toward the kitchen. There she grabbed a bag of tortilla chips, one of several that yawned open on the counter next to upturned lids coated with various dips.

Allison skirted the long table for ten that centered the family kitchen-dining room to push open the patio doors and stepped out onto the round rock stepping stones installed by her brothers.

The yard was a green oasis, a retreat in the middle of a neighborhood of long time friends, of dogs that wandered and of kids that tended to do the same.

Karen Buchanon, matriarch of the rowdy Buchanon clan, looked up from repotting a sunny yellow chrysanthemum. At fifty-nine, she looked good in jean capris and a red blouse, her blond hair pulled back at the nape, her figure thicker but still shapely.

"There you are," Mom said. "You missed the first quarter. Are you hungry?"

Allison lifted the bag of chips. "Got it covered."

"Not very substantial." Her mother laid aside a well-worn trowel, pushed to a stand and stripped off her green gardening gloves. "That should brighten up the backyard."

"Mums are so pretty this time of year."

"Why aren't you watching the game?"

Allison crunched another salty chip. Her mother knew her too well to believe she'd abandoned a Cowboys game to talk about mums. Mom was the gardener whose skills served the Buchanon Construction Company. Allison barely knew a mum from an oak tree. Accounts payable was her area of expertise, such as it was, though Dawson often said, and she agreed, that Allison preferred all things wedding to construction.

But the family business was too important, too ingrained in her DNA to abandon in pursuit of some fantasy. Grandpa and Grandma Buchanon had built Buchanon Construction from the ground up before turning the business over to their only son—her dad. All seven Buchanon kids had known from the time they were big enough to toddle around in Dad's hard hat that they were destined to build houses, to provide beautiful homes for families. Building was not only the Buchanon way, it was their calling.

But construction was not on her mind at the moment. Not even close. "I have something to tell you. Something important."

Mom's eyes narrowed in speculation. Even in shadow from the enormous old silver maple that shaded the back yard, Allison could see the wheels turning. Her mother sat down in the green-striped-canopy swing and patted the seat. "Come here. Might as well get it out. You've been stewing."

"How do you always know?"

Her mom pointed. "That little muscle between your eyebrows gives you up every time."

Allison touched the spot.

She had been stewing. Since the moment Jake turned his back and walked away, a dark worry had flown in and now hovered like a vulture over a cow carcass. She'd told Faith, of course. Except for that one shuddery secret she never spoke of, she told her best friend since first grade everything. She'd even cried on Faith's shoulder years ago when Jake had packed a weathered old pickup and left for good.

Allison gnawed on her bottom lip. She was over him. At least, she'd told herself as much for the past few years. But she remembered, too, the terrible injustice done to a heartbroken boy.

Mom would find out anyway sooner or later. The whole family would. Then the mud would hit the fan.

She averted her gaze, watched a blue butterfly kiss a lavender aster.

"Mama," she said. "Jake's back in town."

For a full minute, the only sound was the bee-buzz of hummingbirds and the faint football noise from inside the house. Down the street someone fired up a lawn mower.

Allison could feel the blood surging in her veins—hot and anxious and so terribly sorry. Not for her family. For Jake. That was the problem, as the family, especially her brothers, saw it. Allison was a traitor to the Buchanon name. Back when the pain was rawest for everyone, she'd sided with Jake. They hadn't understood her loyalty. And if she had shared her secret, that singular defining reason for remaining loyal to Jake Hamilton, she would have caused an explosion of a different sort.

"Jake Hamilton?" her mother finally asked, voice tight.

The tone made Allison ache. "I saw him yesterday at the Hamilton house on my way to Faith's bridal shower."

"Why have you waited until now to tell me?"

"I stayed late at Faith's and then church this morning…" She lifted her palms, let them down again. In truth, she'd been a coward, putting off the inevitable unpleasant reaction and the feeling of betrayal that came along for the ride. "Faith said his grandma is coming home from the rehab center."

"Oh, Allison." Mom's tone was heavy-hearted. "The boys will be upset."

That was putting it mildly.

The *boys*. On the subject of Jake Hamilton, her sensible, caring, adult brothers behaved like children on a playground, the reason no one, even Quinn, had mentioned Jake in a very long time.

Mama pushed up from the swing and ran a hand over

her mouth, a worry gesture Allison knew well. Karen Buchanon was the kindest heart in Gabriel's Crossing. She drove shut-ins to doctors' offices and sat up all night with the sick. She provided Christmas for needy families and fed stray dogs, but her children's needs came first. Always.

"That was so long ago. My brothers are grown men now. Isn't it time to forgive and forget?"

"Some things go too deep, honey. I wish we could put all of that behind us—" she clasped her hands together and gazed toward the back door as if she could see her children inside "—but wishing doesn't change anything. Jake did what he did, and Quinn suffered for it. Still suffers and always will."

"I know, Mama, and I hate what happened to Quinn as much as anyone. But Jake was seventeen. A boy. Teenagers do stupid things." She, of all people, understood how one stupid decision could be catastrophic.

She went to her mother's side, desperately wishing to tell everything about that one night at the river. But danger lurked in revelation and she didn't. She and Jake had a made a pact, a decision to protect the innocent as well as the guilty. "I'm not asking them to be his best friend, but we're supposed to be Christians. The holidays are coming up soon, the time for forgiveness and peace. Don't you think the boys could find it in their hearts to forgive Jake and move on? Couldn't we all?"

But Mama was already shaking her head. "Don't do this, honey. Stirring up the past will only cause hurt and trouble. Jake may be back in town—and I pray his visit is short—but for everyone's sake please don't get involved with him again."

Allison thought of the young Jake she'd known in

grade school, though he'd been a whole year older and more mature, at least in her adoring eyes. Jake had been Quinn's best friend, a nice boy with sad eyes and a needy heart. The first boy she'd ever kissed. The one who lingered in her heart and memory even now.

Then she thought of Quinn. Her moody, broody brother. Her blood. Buchanon blood. And blood always won.

So she gave Mama the only possible answer. "All right."

But with sorrow born of experience, Allison knew this was one promise she wouldn't keep.

Chapter Two

He'd rather tangle with the meanest bull in the pasture than try to drive a wheelchair.

Jake yanked the folded bunch of canvas and metal from the bed of the pickup and shook it.

"How is this thing supposed to work anyway?" he said to exactly nobody.

Metal rattled against metal but the chair didn't open. He wished he'd paid more attention when the nurse—a puny little ninety-pound woman no bigger than Allison—folded the chair and tossed it into the back of his truck with ease. Getting the thing open and functioning couldn't be that difficult.

A hot summer sun roasted the back of his neck while Granny Pat waited patiently inside the cab with the AC running. She wasn't happy because he'd driven the truck right up next to the porch. She had fussed and complained that he'd leave ruts *with those massive tires* and ruin her yard. As if that wasn't enough, she'd been telling all this to Grandpa, a man who'd been dead for twenty years.

Jake's day had been lousy, and his head hurt. Last

night, he'd barely slept after the meeting with Allison. He kept seeing her smile, her bounce, her determined kindness.

He didn't want to remember how much he'd missed her.

Then today, he'd made the trip to the convalescent center, a place that would depress Mary Poppins. If that and Granny's running conversations with Grandpa weren't enough to make his head pound, he'd stopped at Gabriel's Crossing Pharmacy to fill an endless number of prescriptions, and who should he see crossing the street? Brady Buchanon. Big, hot-tempered Brady.

Seeing a Buchanon brother was inevitable, but he planned to put off the moment as long as possible. So like a shamefaced secret agent, he'd pulled his hat low and hustled inside the drugstore before Brady caught a glimpse of him.

He hated feeling like an outcast, like the nasty fly in the pleasant soup of Gabriel's Crossing, but he was here, at least through the holidays, and the Buchanons would have to deal with it. So would everyone else who remembered the golden opportunity Jake had stolen from Quinn Buchanon and this small town with big dreams.

Then why did he feel like a criminal in his own hometown?

Granny Pat popped open the truck door and leaned out, her white hair as poufy as cotton candy. "Grandpa wants to know if you need help?"

Jake rolled his eyes heavenward. The sun nearly blinded him. "Be right there, Granny. Don't fall out."

At under five feet and shrinking, Granny Pat didn't have the strength to pull the heavy truck door closed and it edged further and further open. She was slowly being stretched from the cab.

Jake dropped the wheelchair and sprinted to her side, catching her a second before she tumbled out onto the grass. "Easy there. That door is heavy."

"I know it!" Fragile or not, she was still spit-and-vinegar Pat and clearly aggravated at her weakness. "I'm useless. Makes me so mad."

"Let's get you in the house. You'll feel better there."

"Get my wheelchair."

"The chair can wait." Forever as far as he was concerned.

With an ease that made him sad, Jake lifted his grandmother from the seat and carried her inside the house.

"Where to, madame?" he teased, though his heart ached. Granny Pat had been his mama, his daddy and his home all rolled into one strong, vital woman. She'd endured his wild teenage years and the scandal he'd caused that rocked Gabriel's Crossing. For her body to fail all because of one broken bone was unfair.

But when had life ever been fair?

"Put me in the recliner." She pointed toward one of two recliners in the living room—the blue one with a yellow-and-orange afghan tossed across the back.

He did as she asked.

Granny Pat tilted her head against the plush corduroy and gazed around the room with pleasure. "It's good to finally be home. I'll get my strength back here."

Her pleasure erased the sorrow of seeing Brady Buchanon and the nagging worry over finances. Granny Pat needed this, needed him, and he'd find a way to deal with the Buchanons and his empty pockets.

"You want some water or anything before I unload the truck?"

"Nothing but fresh air. Open some windows, Jacob. This house stinks. I don't know how you slept here in this must and dust."

As he threw open windows, Jake noticed the dirt and dead insects piled on the windowsills. "Maybe I can find a housekeeper?" His wallet would scream, but he'd figure out a way.

"I don't want some stranger in my house poking around."

"Nobody's a stranger in Gabriel's Crossing, Granny."

"Grandpa says something will turn up. Don't worry."

A bit of breeze drifted through the window, stirring dust in the sunlight.

"Granny Pat, you know Grandpa—"

"Yes, Jacob, I know." Her tone was patient as if he was the one with the mental lapses. "Now go on and bring in my belongings. I want my Sudoku book."

Jake jogged out to the truck, eyeing the pain-in-the-neck wheelchair he'd left against the back bumper. Granny Pat needed wheels to be mobile, and as much as he wanted to haul the chair to the nearest landfill, he was a man and he was determined to make the thing work.

He was wrestling the wheels apart when a Camaro rumbled to the stop sign on the corner. Precisely what he did not need. Allison Buchanon. He refused to look in her direction, hoping she'd roll on down the street. She didn't.

Allison, tenacious as a terrier, rolled down her window. "Having trouble?"

He looked up and his stomach tumbled down into his boots. The soft brown eyes he'd never forgotten snagged his. A sizzle of connection raised the hairs on his arms. "No."

Go away.

As if he wasn't the least interested in the wheelchair, he leaned the contraption against the truck and reached inside the bed for one of Granny Pat's suitcases.

The Camaro engine still rumbled next to the curb. Why didn't she mosey on down the road?

"You can't fool me," she hollered. "I remember."

And that was nearly his undoing. He could never fool Allison. No matter what he said or how hard he tried to pretend not to care that he was the town pariah, Allison saw through him. She'd even called him her hero.

"Go home, Allison." He didn't want her to remember any more than he wanted her feeling sorry for him.

She gunned the engine but instead of leaving, she pulled into the driveway and hopped out.

Hands deep in her back jeans pockets, she wore a sweater the color of a pumpkin that set off her dark hair. He didn't want to notice the changes in her, from the sweet-faced teenager to a beautiful woman, but he'd have to be dead not to.

Her fluffy, flyaway hair bounced as she approached the truck, took hold of the wheelchair and attempted to open it. When the chair didn't budge, she scowled. "What's wrong with this?"

Determined not to be friendly, Jake hefted a suitcase in each hand and started toward the house. He was here in Gabriel's Crossing because of Granny Pat. No other reason. Allison Buchanon didn't affect him in the least.

And bulls could fly.

Something pinged him in the back. A pebble thudded to the grass at his feet. He spun around. "Hey! Did you just hit me with a rock?"

She gave him a grin that was anything but friendly. "I figured out what's wrong with the chair."

He dropped the suitcases. "You did?"

"Come here and see for yourself. Unless you're scared of a girl."

He was scared of her all right. Allison Buchanon had the power to hurt him—or cause him to hurt himself. But intrigued by her claim, he went back to the chair.

A car chugged by the intersection going in the opposite direction. Across the street a dog barked, and down the block, some guy mowed his lawn, shooting the grassy smell all over the neighborhood. Normal activities in Gabriel's Crossing, though there was nothing normal about him standing in Granny Pat's yard with a Buchanon.

Man, his death wish must be worse than most.

He crossed his arms over his chest, careful not to get close enough to touch her. He didn't need reminders of her soft skin and flowery scent. "What?"

She went into a crouch, one hand holding up the chair. Her shoes were open toed and someone had painted her toenails orange and green like tiny pumpkins.

"That piece is bent and caught on the gear. See?"

He had no choice but to crouch beside her. There it was. Her sweet scent. Honeysuckle, he thought. Exactly the same as she'd worn in high school. Sweet and clean and pure.

Jake cleared his throat and gripped the chair. He needed to get a grip, all right.

"I got it," he said, thinking she'd leave now. She didn't.

He reached in and straightened the metal piece with his fingers, using more effort than he'd expected. A deep rut whitened along his index finger.

"Pliers would have been easier," she said. Then she grabbed the oversize wheels and popped open the stubborn wheelchair. "There. Ready to roll."

Jake stepped around to take the handles. Allison climbed up on the truck bumper and started unloading Granny Pat's belongings.

"I can get those."

"I came to see Miss Pat." She handed him a plastic sack of clothes. Granny had collected a dozen shopping bags filled with clothes along with her suitcases and medical supplies. Where a woman in a convalescent center acquired so much remained a puzzle. But then, women in general were a puzzle to most of the male species and Jake was no exception.

"You shouldn't have come."

"Let her be the judge of that."

"You know what I mean, Allison. Don't be muleheaded."

She hopped off the bumper, plopped a bag of plastic medical supplies into the wheelchair and went back for another. When he saw she wasn't leaving no matter what he said, he joined her, unloading the items, much of which fit in the wheelchair.

"So, how have you been?" she asked, her tone all spunky and cute as if no bad blood ran between her brothers and him.

"Good."

"What does that mean?"

He squinted at her over the tailgate. "You're not going to give up, are you?"

"We were friends once, Jake. I believe in second chances."

Friends? Yes, they'd been friends, but toward the end, he'd been falling in love with his best friend's sister.

He shook off the random thought. Whatever had been budding between two teenagers was long dead and buried.

"How's Quinn?"

He hadn't meant to ask, hadn't intended to open that door, but he held his breath, praying for something he couldn't name.

"He's the architect for Buchanon Construction now."

"Granny Pat told me he went to Tech with Brady." He didn't say the other; that Quinn's full-ride football scholarship had disappeared on a bloody October morning. "Does he ever talk about—"

"No, and I don't want to either." She glanced away, toward a pair of puppies galloping around the neighbor's front yard, her eyebrows drawn together in a worried frown. "Quinn has a decent life here in Gabriel's Crossing. Maybe the path wasn't the one he'd expected to take, but he survived."

Jake slowly exhaled. "That's good. Real good."

Quinn was okay. The accident happened long ago. Maybe Jake was no longer the hated pariah. People moved on. Everyone except him and he'd been stuck in the past so long, he didn't know how to move off high-center. "What about you? Why aren't you married with a house full of kids?"

He hadn't meant to ask that either.

She shrugged. The pumpkin sweater bunched up around her white neck. "I've had my chances."

He was sure she had, and he wondered why she hadn't taken them. "Still working for your dad?"

"In the offices with Jayla."

"Little sister grew up?"

"We all do, Jake." She smiled a little. "I keep the books, do payroll, billing. All the fun numbers stuff."

"Put that high school accounting award to good use, didn't you?"

Her eyes crinkled at the corners. "You remember that?"

He remembered everything about her, his cheerleader and champion when life had been too difficult to live. "Hard to forget. You wore that medal around your neck for months."

"Fun times."

Yes, they were. Before he'd destroyed everything with one stupid decision.

"Faith's getting married," she said.

Faith Evans, her sidekick. The long and the short, as the guys had called them. Faith had grown to nearly six feet tall by sixth grade, and Allison had barely been tall enough to reach the gas pedal when she'd turned sixteen. "Yeah? Who's the lucky guy?"

"They met in college. Derrick Cantelli. I'm coordinating her wedding." She tilted back on the heels of her sandals, her warm brown eyes searching his. "Granny Pat told me you live in Stephenville now."

"Land of the rodeo cowboys."

"Do you like it there?"

"Sure." He glanced away, afraid she'd read the truth in his eyes. "We better get this in the house before Granny Pat starts hollering."

He gave the wheels a nudge with his boot.

"Unlock it," Allison said.

"It has a lock?" He poked around and found the lever, released the device with a snap, and incredibly, the chair rolled a few inches. "How did you know that?"

"Brady had knee surgery his last year at Tech."

Just that quick, the elephant was back in the room. "I watched him play on TV a few times. He was good."

But not as good as Quinn. No one in the state had been as good at football as Quinn Buchanon. Quinn, with the golden arm that had turned to blood.

He gave the wheelchair a shove and rolled toward the front door.

He'd gone quiet on her again. When Allison thought they'd moved past that awkward stage, past his determination to be the rude, don't-care cowboy, he had clammed up again. Between his reluctance and her brothers' animosity, she wondered why she kept trying.

But she knew why. Though she was a Buchanon with every cell in her body, her brothers were wrong to hold a grudge. Anger would not restore Quinn's arm to normal. Anger would not regain his chance at an NFL career. All bitterness had ever done was make them miserable.

Like now. If they knew she was here, her brothers would have a fit. Just as they would have a fit if they'd known about the other thing. They'd have done something crazy.

But she was as drawn to Jake Hamilton today as she had been in high school. He was her buddy, her first love, and foolish though she might be, she yearned to help him, to be his friend again, to repay a debt of love and loyalty.

If he'd revealed her secret nine years ago, maybe her

family wouldn't despise Jake so much. But he'd kept silent because she had begged him to. And he'd suffered for his loyalty.

He could walk off and leave her in the yard every time she visited, but she wouldn't stop trying. He meant too much to her.

If that was pathetic, so be it.

Grabbing a small black suitcase Jake had left behind, she followed him into the house. Her stomach sank like a brick in a pond when she spotted Miss Pat in the big blue corduroy recliner. The once vital, high-energy woman had shriveled to child-size in the months since her hip surgery. She looked a hundred instead of in her early seventies.

"Hi, Miss Pat."

"Look here, Ralph, it's little Allison. Isn't she pretty as a picture?"

Ralph? Who was Ralph? She looked to Jake for help but he'd moved around behind his grandmother and simply shook his head at her. Allison got the message and didn't press the subject.

She pulled a worn leather ottoman close to the recliner and plopped down. "How you feeling, Miss Pat? Can I do anything for you?"

"You sure can, sweetie. I am useless as a newborn." Her strong voice didn't match her body. "Get my purse over there on the table where Jacob stuck it, and then find my Sudoku book in all that mess of sacks."

"I can do that." Allison hopped up, amused but pleased that Miss Pat's personality hadn't faded like her body, a good sign she had the grit to stage a fourth quarter comeback. "Would you like for me to unpack and put everything away? I'd be pleased to do it."

"Now, there's a fine idea. See, Jacob." She tilted her head back to gaze up at her grandson. "Your grandpa said something would turn up and here she is. Allison will help get this place in order. Won't you, Allison?"

"Well, sure I will, if that's what you need."

"Good. This house needs a cleaning from top to bottom."

"I can do that." Never mind that her brothers would go ballistic to know she was in the Hamilton house with Jake. She was here for Miss Pat. Helping a friend was the Buchanon way. And yes, she admitted, she wanted to get to know Jake again. He was a memory that wouldn't go away. "I can't tonight, but I'll come by tomorrow after work. How's that sound?"

"She's a jewel, isn't she, Jacob? Just like in high school when she was sweet on you."

Jake looked as if he'd swallowed a bug. Allison's face heated, but she grinned. Miss Pat never minced words.

"Come on, *Jacob,*" she said, teasing him about the seldom-used name. "Help me find that puzzle book."

Reluctantly, and with his expression shuttered, he started crinkling plastic sacks. Allison fetched the handbag, handed it off to Miss Pat and joined Jake in the hunt for that all-important puzzle book.

Each time she looked up, their eyes met. Every bit as quickly, one of them would look away. She was acutely aware of his masculine presence, his cowboy swagger, his manly, outdoors scent. Aware in a way that disturbed her thinking.

She found the thick Sudoku pad in the bottom of an ugly brown plastic washbasin.

"Here's your puzzle book, Miss Pat. Need a pencil?"

"Got one in my purse." Miss Pat had already extracted

a cell phone and was scrolling the contacts. "No, Ralph, it's not time for my meds."

Jake glanced at a square wall clock hanging next to an outdated calendar, a sad reminder that no one had lived here for several months. "Another hour, Granny."

"That's what I told Ralph. I've got to text Mae at the prison and let her know I survived the ride home."

Jake rolled his eyes. "Carson Convalescence was not a prison."

"A lot you'd know about it." Using an index finger, she tapped a message on the phone's keyboard. "Ah, there we go. Poor Mae. Stuck in that prison through Christmas."

With a resigned shake of his head, Jake grabbed two suitcases and lugged them through a doorway. Allison followed with an armful of crinkling Walmart sacks.

"Do you know where everything goes?" she asked.

"No."

"We'll figure it out." Allison opened the closet and took out some empty hangers and then started unpacking the mishmash of belongings.

Jake edged around her, looking uncertain and a little thunderous. "You don't have to do this."

"Yes, I do."

"Why?" He paused in hanging up a dress to stare at her across Miss Pat's dusty dresser.

Every nerve ending reacted to that green gaze, but Allison refused to let her jumbled feelings show. "Because Ralph said I would."

He grinned. Finally. He had a killer grin beneath olive eyes that had driven more than one girl to doodle his name on the edge of her spiral notebook. Including Allison. But that was in high school. That was before the insanity of a football-focused town had heaped so much condemnation and hurt onto a teenage boy that he'd run away with the rodeo.

"Ralph was my grandpa. She talks to him a lot."

"Did the doctors say anything?" Allison folded a blue fleece throw into a neat square. "About her mental state, I mean?"

"No. I'm worried, though. I wonder if she'll be able to live alone again."

"You're not planning to stay?"

"Not long. Maybe until after Christmas." He jerked one shoulder. "I gotta make a living."

A massive wave of disappointment drenched her good mood. A short stay was better, safer, sensible, but Allison didn't like it.

A stack of nighties in her hand, she pondered her reaction. She was an adult now, not a dewy-eyed teenager in love with the only boy who'd ever kissed her.

Like that made one bit of difference when it came to Jake Hamilton.

Jake saw a range of emotions flicker across Allison's face. Disappointment, worry, relief. He latched on to the last one. She wanted him gone. Out of sight, out of mind. Away from the town that revered Buchanons and loathed Jake Hamilton.

Then why was she here? Why did she insist on pushing past his caution when absolutely nothing good could come of it?

He zipped open a tired blue suitcase, a throwback to the sixties, to find a stack of underwear. Not his favorite thing to unpack with Allison in the room.

His brain had a sudden flashback, a suppressed memory of pink and lace he never should have seen.

He glanced at her. Did she remember, too?

Allison was beside him in a second. "Let me do that."

She grabbed the stack from his hands as he crouched toward the opened drawer. They knocked heads.

"Ow!" Allison sat back on her haunches and laughed. "Hard head."

"I was about to say the same thing." In truth, her head was harder on the inside than on the outside. The woman never gave up, a trait that would leave her disappointed and hurt.

They were a foot apart in front of Granny Pat's oak dresser, on their toes, both holding to a stack of ladies' lingerie, and Jake wished for the thousandth time he could erase one terrible day from their lives. He was comfortable with Allison, *liked* her, a dangerous thing, then and now. She made him smile. She even made him believe in himself. Or she once had. With everything in him he wanted to know this grown-up Allison, a dangerous, troubling proposition.

"You've grown up." Stupid thing to say, but better than yanking her into his arms—an errant, radical thought worthy of a beating from the Buchanon brothers.

She tilted her head, smile quizzical. "Is that a good thing or a bad thing?"

For him? Very bad. But instead of admitting the truth, he tweaked her flyaway hair and pushed to a stand, distancing himself from the cute temptation of Quinn Buchanon's sister. "I'll drag in more of Granny Pat's stuff while you put this away. Okay?"

As if he wasn't already struggling not to touch her,

Allison reached out a hand. What could he do except take hold and help her up?

A mistake, of course.

Her skin was a thousand times softer than he remembered and smooth as silk. His rough cowboy hand engulfed her small one. He was nowhere near as tall as her brothers, but he towered above Allison. What man wouldn't understand this protective ferocity that roared in his veins?

Allison had definitely grown up.

And Jake Hamilton was in major trouble.

Chapter Three

Monday morning, Jake drove the dusty graveled road past rows and rows of fence line leading to the Double M Ranch two miles and a world away from Gabriel's Crossing. Multicolored Brahma brood cows grazed peacefully in this section of Manny Morales's pasture land. Not one of them looked up as Jake roared by and pulled beneath the Double M crossbars.

In the near distance, a sprawling ranch house sat like a brick monument to the success of a Mexican immigrant whose work ethic and cattle smarts had created a well-respected bucking bull program. Jake knew. He'd worked for Manny before the Buchanons and the rodeo had given him reason to leave Gabriel's Crossing.

Dust swirled around the truck tires as he parked and got out. Manny, short and stout and leathery, stood in the barn entrance, white Resistol shading his eyes.

"Manny!" Jake broke into a long stride, eager to see his friend and mentor.

"Is that you, Jake boy?" The older man propped a shovel against the barn and came to meet him.

With back slaps and handshakes, they greeted one another. "Manny, it's good to see you."

"Why didn't you tell me you was coming?"

"Why? Would you have cooked for me?"

Manny laughed. He could wrangle a cow, ride a horse and haul a dozen bulls all around the region, but he couldn't boil water. "Paulina will be crazy happy. She'll want to cook *cabrito* and have a fiesta!"

Jake laughed for the first time since his arrival three days ago in Gabriel's Crossing. "No need to kill the fatted goat. I'll be satisfied with some frijoles and her homemade tortillas."

"Sure. Sure." Manny clapped him on the shoulder again. "But first you got to see your bulls."

"How are they doing?"

Manny's black eyes crinkled at the corners. "You see for yourself. They're good."

Together they made their way inside the enormous silver barn where Manny's dark green Polaris ATV was parked. In minutes, they'd bumped across grassy yellowing fields to a pasture where a dozen bull calves grazed.

"I moved the big boys to the west pasture, closer to the house so I can keep an eye on them," Manny said as he climbed out of the Polaris. "Mountain Man is cranky sometimes so he has his own lot. You saw him buck in San Antonio."

Jake nodded. Chance meetings at rodeos were one of the perks of having a friend in the stock business. "He's a good bull. Some of the cowboys are afraid of him."

"Ah, he's not so bad."

Jake differed in opinion. Mountain Man, a white monster of a bull, was big and bad with the horns to end any discussion. He was also an athlete, hard to ride and keeping his owner in tamales. Manny hauled him to rodeos every week during the season.

"There are your sons," Manny said as he propped a boot on an iron gate and pointed toward the herd.

His sons. Likely the only ones he'd have for a long time. Not that he wouldn't love a family. A stray like him had dreams. A big ranch and plenty of money. Then a woman to love and a few kids. Maybe a lot of kids. If Allison Buchanon intruded on those dreams at times, he'd learned to shut her out and focus on the first part. A ranch. His bulls.

Over the past several years he'd searched out and bought the best young calves he could afford and partnered with Manny to finish and train them.

Their expense, along with the cost of the brood cows, meant a tight budget most of the time but eventually, he'd reap the benefits of his sacrifice. He'd start a ranch of his own and hopefully be able to retire from the circuit. The past couple of seasons had taken a toll on his body and his bank account. At twenty-seven, he was still fit, but a bull rider never knew how long before the constant pounding ended his career. Even now, his shoulder predicted rain before the meteorologists.

"How's the training going?" he asked. "Is Big Country about ready for the circuit?"

Though Jake had borrowed heavily to buy him, Big Country was the animal Jake counted on to make his name in the stock contracting business.

"You'll have to stick around Gabriel's Crossing for a while and find out for yourself, my friend."

"Can't stay long, Manny." He tried to keep the worry from his voice. "But I'm here until Granny Pat is better." Even if it meant dealing with the Buchanons and dwindling cash flow.

"Maybe you stay for good this time. Gabriel's Crossing is your home."

Jake looked out over the cattle—his cattle—and thought of how often he'd longed to go back in time before he'd ruined everything. Before regret and rodeo were his daily companions. Back when he'd been a part of this town and the big Buchanon clan.

"Water under the bridge, Manny. The rodeo can't get along without me." Which wasn't exactly true. Most seasons, he made a living, and arena dust got in a man's blood. But he was sick and tired of the travel and the loneliness.

Manny's dark gaze pierced him. "Still the bad blood?"

No point hiding from Manny. "Buchanons practically own this town. Coming back, even for a while, isn't easy."

Manny sighed and folded his brown, leathery hands on the iron railing. "The Buchanons are good people. By now, they will forgive you. Huh? You talk to them. Find out. Maybe you carry a burden for nothing."

"I don't think so, Manny. I talked to Allison."

"You still sweet for that Buchanon girl?"

Jake felt a lot of things for Allison Buchanon that he couldn't put a name to. Things he couldn't allow into the conversation. Now or ever. "That was a long time ago. Before I ruined everything."

If time healed wounds—and he prayed every night the Buchanons would heal—they didn't need reminders of him to rip open the scab.

He swallowed the taste of regret. He didn't like thinking about the accident, the worst day of his life, but the burden rode his back like a two-ton elephant. He could never forget it. Ever.

The accident *or* the girl.

Buchanon Construction was nothing more than a metal warehouse full of equipment with an office tacked on to one end. Inside that office at a U-shaped desk, Allison entered data for the Willow Creek project into her computer while blonde Jayla fielded phone calls and met with vendors selling ceramic tile or the latest eco-friendly appliances. The place was messy, practical and, other than the desk, bore little resemblance to a business office.

Not that she was thinking about business today with Jake Hamilton lurking in every thought.

Jake. The time at Miss Pat's had been fun and eye-opening. She liked the handsome cowboy as much as ever. His gentle concern for his grandmother tugged at her, but more than that, being with him reminded her of what they'd had, of what might have been.

Jake was unfinished business.

Her twin brothers, Dawson and Sawyer, ambled in from the warehouse, smelling of sweat and doughnuts. "Mirror" twins, her brothers were lady magnets with black hair, blue eyes and bodies honed by years in the hands-on construction business.

Dawson's dimple was on display because both men wore possum grins as if they knew a secret. Allison was relieved to see them smiling this morning. If they'd heard about Jake's return, they wouldn't be smiling.

"You can't hide those from me. I have a nose for fresh-baked anything." Allison held out a hand. "Gimme."

"Greedy, isn't she, Dawson?" Sawyer pulled a

doughnut box from behind his back and held the white container above his head. At nearly a foot taller than Allison's five-one, he had a distinct advantage.

"You want me to hop and jump and try to reach them while you laugh at me, don't you?"

"Torment is our game. Hop, little sister."

When she propped a hand on one hip and glared, he wiggled the box and said in a cajoling voice, "Come on. Hop. You know you want a hot, fresh doughnut from The Bakery."

"Well, okay, if I must…" But instead of playing her brother's ornery game, she poked a finger in his relaxed belly. His six-pack abs tightened, and when he curled inward with a "Hey!" Allison laughed and snatched the still-warm doughnut box.

"Greedy *and* sneaky," she said as she popped open the box. "Yum. Maple with coconut. Did you bring milk?"

"Quinn's supposed to be making fresh coffee in the back."

"He's so domestic." She bit into the sweet dough and sighed, her mouth happy with the warm maple goodness.

"Don't let him hear you say that."

"Those things will give you a heart attack." This from Jayla who held a palm over the telephone receiver. "I'm on hold about the Langley license."

None of her three siblings paid Jayla any mind.

"Hey, Quinn," Sawyer yelled toward the back of the warehouse. "What's the holdup on that java?"

Quinn's head appeared around the door leading into the warehouse. Golden haired and pretty, Allison thought he resembled a younger, bigger Brad Pitt.

"Some people work for a living." He gave them all a scowling once over and disappeared again.

"I guess I'll make the coffee." Dawson headed into the warehouse, returning a short time later with a full carafe and a stack of disposable foam cups. "He's in a happy mood today."

"Which means he's not," Jayla said. "The Bartowskis asked for changes to the plans he finished over the weekend. Major changes."

Sawyer snarled. "I hate when that happens."

"He threatened to let Dawg bite them."

"He *is* in a bad mood. Dawg wouldn't bite a hot doughnut. Well, maybe he would, but you get the point." Dawson leaned around the opened doorway. "Hey, Quinn, want a doughnut? Guaranteed to sweeten you up."

A muffled reply about exactly what Dawson could do with his doughnuts had the siblings stifling snorts that would not be appreciated. They were loud enough, however, that Quinn stalked into the room, hazel eyes shooting sparks. "Something funny?"

Dawg low-crawled from behind Quinn and collapsed at Allison's feet. "You're scaring Brady's dog. Where is Brady anyway?" She tossed the mutt a hunk of sweet roll. He snapped it in midair and tail-thumped in expectation of more.

"Open your mouth, Quinn," she said, "and I'll toss *you* a chunk."

Quinn fisted a hand on his hip and allowed a grudging lip twitch. "You'd miss."

"Can't miss something that big."

"Old joke, sis." But with his better hand, he took a chocolate-covered pastry from the box. "Pour me a cup?"

Dawson obliged, handing the steaming brew to his

brother. Quinn shifted the doughnut to his weaker right side to accept the coffee.

"Stinks about the plans." Dawson lifted his ball cap and scratched at his unruly black waves.

"Part of the job." As architect of Buchanon Construction, Quinn developed all their housing concepts, a recent turn of events, considering the slide into depression that had taken him away from home for too long. Even now, he wasn't the most social Buchanon. "Those plans were exactly what they asked for. Now they want changes. I have a feeling this project may not be our favorite."

"We could subcontract the entire project if the Bartowskis become a problem," Dawson said.

"That would only make things worse. If a sub messes up, we're responsible."

"Put Charity on them." Sawyer studied the Bavarian cream inside his doughnut. "This stuff is good."

The oldest of the siblings at thirty-three, Charity was the real estate whiz, slick as a used car salesman, a trait Allison found out of sync with the sweet-faced wife of a deployed navy pilot and the mother of a six-and an eleven-year-old.

"Nah, I'll make the changes. Once." Quinn ripped off a piece of his chocolate doughnut and tossed it to Dawg. Pathetically grateful, dog sat at his feet, begging for more. "Where are we on the Willow Creek project? Any news on the permits?"

Jayla's long hair swayed as she thumped the telephone receiver into its cradle and swung around to face them. "That was Brady. Permits are ready. He's at the courthouse now, and says he will meet you two—" she pointed at Sawyer and Dawson "—at the job site. Bring Dawg."

Quinn crossed the small space and kissed the top of her head. "You're amazing." He ripped off another piece of doughnut and held it in front of her nose. "Eat this."

She made a horrified face and squeezed her eyes closed. "Death in a doughnut. I'll pass."

He laughed and popped the bite into his mouth. "Don't know what you're missing, baby sister."

They were hassling Jayla about her rigid eating habits when the front door slammed open, and Brady strode inside.

"Weren't you going to the job site?" Jayla's question fell into the sizzling air and withered away, unanswered.

If a man could spit nails, Allison thought this might be the time to duck and run. With his warrior size, Brady was as dangerous as a rattler when stirred up. And something had definitely stirred him up this morning.

Allison was afraid she knew the cause.

The other siblings exchanged looks. The twins shrugged in unison. No one else had a clue to Brady's fury.

With a dread heavier than a forklift, Allison put her half eaten doughnut on a skinny strip of napkin and waited for the ax to fall.

Voice tight and low, steam all but pumping from his ears, Brady asked, "You haven't heard, have you?"

Quinn set his mug down. "Heard what?"

Blood rushed against Allison's temples. Oh, yeah, here came trouble.

"Jake Hamilton is in town."

Sawyer's jaw hardened. "What?"

"You heard me right. Jake's back."

"Where did you hear that?" Quinn's voice was quiet. Too quiet.

"Courthouse." Brady fisted huge hands on his hips. "I saw the lowlife with my own eyes. Miss Pat's out of the nursing home and Jake's moved in, supposedly to take care of her."

All eyes swung toward Quinn. Like the rest of them—except Allison—he looked stunned. A long beat passed while they absorbed the news. Then, without a word, Quinn spun on his steel-toed boots and left the room.

Chaos erupted.

As if the russet-haired Brady had announced an eminent asteroid collision with downtown Gabriel's Crossing, everyone talked at once. The general consensus was outrage. Outrage that Jake Hamilton would strut into town years after the fact and behave as if nothing had happened. As if he hadn't ruined a man's life.

"Don't you think you're overreacting?" As soon as the words were out, Allison clapped a hand over her mouth. Why had she said that?

Silence descended in a dark, pulsating curtain. Three pairs of eyes aimed at her like hot, blue lasers.

She swallowed. Let reason prevail. *Please Lord.* "Jake's been gone a long time. His grandma needs him now. We've moved on. Quinn's...okay. We don't even talk about the accident anymore. Can't we let the hard feelings end here and now?"

"You were always on his side." Sawyer's accusation hurt.

"That's not fair. We were all heartbroken for Quinn, even Jake. Quinn was his best friend! He's not some kind of evil monster."

Dawson slapped his cap against his thigh. "Tell that to Quinn."

Sawyer nodded in agreement. "I think the brotherhood needs to pay the hotshot bull rider a little visit."

Brady crouched to pat his dog. The shaggy mutt rolled onto his back, feet in the air. "I'm in."

Allison exhaled a nervous, worried breath. Her doughnut lay like a rock in her belly. "Just because a man you don't like comes to town to care for his grandmother is no reason for the four of you to go ninja grudge match."

Brady rubbed Dawg's belly, his eyes on Allison. "When that one man destroys my brother's future, I'm not likely to ever forget."

That was the problem. She came from a long line of grudge holders. Granddad Buchanon and his brother didn't speak for the last fifteen years of their lives. All because of a dispute over a used tractor. They were supposed to be Christians, but a Buchanon could sustain anger for a very long time.

Allison saw no point in arguing with her brothers. They were as immovable as a concrete slab.

"You should let sleeping dogs lie. That's all I have to say." She turned and headed around the counter to her computer. "We have work to do."

Brady followed her around the desk, Dawg at his side. His voice had calmed, but his tone held reinforced steel. "We'll handle Jake Hamilton this time, Allison. You stay away from him."

Allison gave him a mutinous glare. She was getting real tired of hearing that.

Chapter Four

The next morning Jake made the rounds in town. First, to the post office to redirect Granny Pat's mail where a friendly postal clerk he remembered slightly inquired about his grandmother. Then to the bank and finally to the grocery store.

Gabriel's Crossing was a lazy stir of business this early, sunlit morning. Townspeople wandered in and out of stores. Doors slammed. Cars and pickups puttered down a five-block main street still paved with the same bumpy red bricks put there eighty-five years ago.

A truck with a Buchanon Construction sign on the door rolled past. Jake watched it, curious and wary, though the morning sun blasted him in the eyes, so he couldn't clearly see the man at the wheel.

Allison had been at the house again last night. Her visits stirred him up and interfered with his sleep. Her and the musty smell of sheets he should have washed before bringing Granny Pat home. A man didn't always think of those things, especially a man who was accustomed to sleeping in his truck or cheap motels along the rodeo circuit.

He both dreaded and longed for evening when Allison would return. She'd promised Granny. Why had she done that? And why couldn't he find the initiative to be somewhere else when she arrived?

Heaviness weighed on his shoulders like a wet saddle blanket. That's what Gabriel's Crossing did to him. When he was on the road or in his trailer in Stephenville, he seldom dwelled on the tragedy. He'd learned to let it go or go crazy. But here, in Gabriel's Crossing, where memories lingered around every corner and Allison popped in unexpectedly, he thought of little else.

He felt as trapped as a bull in a head gate, unable to go forward, and he sure couldn't go back.

Inside the quiet IGA, Jake pushed a shopping cart down the produce aisle. He wasn't much of a cook but Granny Pat needed nourishing foods to rebuild her strength. A woman who'd cooked from scratch her whole life wouldn't stand for frozen dinners or pizza delivery either. He added a head of lettuce, some tomatoes and a bag of carrots to the cart. Salad. He could do salad. And steak. Big, juicy T-bones with loaded baked potatoes.

He tossed in a bag of potatoes and headed for the meat. The aisles were narrow, a throwback to earlier times, but he'd not been in the mood for the supercenter this morning. Too many people. Too many opportunities to run into someone he didn't want to see.

He wasn't afraid to climb into the chute with an eighteen-hundred-pound bull, but he was a coward in his hometown. The knowledge aggravated him so much Jake considered reshelving the groceries and driving out to the supercenter. If he hadn't promised to meet the home health nurse in an hour, he would have.

As it was, he threw a few more items into the cart

and headed for the checkout. A flaming redhead with a snake tattoo down one arm and a dragon from neck to chin rang up the purchases. Gabriel's Crossing had certainly changed. But then, so had he.

The redhead gave him a friendly smile. "Coach Hammonds brought in the football schedules yesterday. Want one?"

She offered a small cardboard card similar to the wallet schedules he remembered.

"I'm good." He would not be attending any football games.

"Oh, well. They're free." She tossed the schedule inside one of the grocery sacks. "You must be new in town. I don't think I've seen you around."

Jake was not about to make a fuss over a high school football schedule even though the red-and-white piece of card stock was a reminder he didn't want.

"Visiting my grandma."

"That's nice." The register beeped as she slid lettuce across the conveyer. "Are you a real cowboy?"

"Nah, I just found the hat." He softened the joke with a smile.

Her hand paused on the T-bone package. She giggled. "You're teasing me, aren't you?"

"Yeah, I am. Sorry. I ride bulls."

Her eyes widened. "No way. That is so scary."

If he lived to be a hundred, he'd always enjoy that kind of reaction, as if he was something special because he wasn't afraid to get on a bull. "Only if I don't stay on."

Which had happened way too often this season.

Another customer pulled into the lane behind Jake. Bolstered by the friendly cashier, he turned to acknowledge the woman, and his heart tumbled.

"Allison."

"Jake, hi." Her wide smile did crazy things to his head. "What are you doing?"

"He's visiting his grandma," Tattoo Girl said as the register beeped and plastic crinkled. "Isn't that sweet?"

Allison's eyes danced with merriment. "He's a sweetie, all right. Are you shopping for Miss Pat?"

"I'm not much of a shopper, but yeah, sort of. I wasn't sure what to buy."

"She made a list. Didn't you bring it?"

Ah, man. The note was sticking on the refrigerator. "Forgot about it."

Allison backed her cart out of the checkout. "I remember. Go ahead and pay out and then we'll go again."

He should refuse, but he couldn't. When it came to Allison Buchanon he didn't have a lick of sense.

Jake glanced at Tattoo Girl who hiked one shoulder and said, "Why not?"

He could think of a lot of reasons.

By the time he paid out and found Allison, an easy task in the small family-run store, she was pondering the brands of laundry soaps.

"I can't remember if she said Tide or Cheer."

Jake studied the detergent as though they mattered. "Pick one. I don't care. I'll be doing the laundry."

"Do you know how?"

"Allison." He grabbed a box and sent it thudding into the basket. "Single guys learn to do laundry or go dirty. I prefer not to smell like the bulls I ride."

"But you don't cook." So small she barely reached his shoulders, she gazed up at him through big brown eyes he'd never forgotten. Did she have any idea how pretty she was?

"How do you know I can't cook?"

"I saw your shopping cart." She made a cute face. "Steaks and salad are a guy's go-to meal. And then you're done."

Jake let a smile creep up his cheeks. "Wise guy." Though she was anything but a guy. Little Allison had grown up. "I don't suppose you'd take pity on a man for eating out a lot."

She tossed in a box of fabric softener sheets and pointed to the west. "Next aisle over. Come on. We'll stock the cabinets."

"Who's going to cook?"

Her answer nearly stopped his heart. "Me."

So much for avoiding Allison Buchanon.

Allison left the warehouse office at five-thirty, stopped at The Bakery to discuss Faith's cake with Cindy, the best and only wedding cake decorator in Gabriel's Crossing, and then headed toward Faith's house.

Jake's truck was noticeably absent as she drove past the Hamilton place, and if she was disappointed, she tried not to be. She'd see him tonight, though she questioned her sanity, as well as her family loyalty. At the same time, she wanted to be there for Miss Pat, a woman who'd taught all the Buchanon kids in first grade. And Allison loved to cook. Buchanon women were noted for their kitchen gifts.

Right. As if Jake had nothing to do with the buzz of energy racing through her system. A buzz that had begun the moment she'd seen him again and hadn't let up.

She passed two little girls pedaling bikes and pulled to the curb outside the faded red brick where Faith had lived alone with her mother since her parents' divorce twenty years ago.

"The topper is in," she said without greeting when her BFF pushed open the smoked glass door. Tall and narrow, Faith was a bleached blonde with a long face and gray eyes who could play the fiddle and clog at the same time, a feat Allison found both charming and hilarious considering her towering height.

"Did you take a picture?"

"Do birds fly?" Allison whipped out her cell and scrolled to the photo. "The next time you're not tutoring after school, you should stop by and check it out. The cake is going to be gorgeous."

"Ooh, I love this." A pair of silver and crystal hearts twined on a silver base engraved with the initials of the bride and groom. "That's exactly what I had in mind."

"Only the best is good enough for my bestie. How did the dress fitting go?"

Faith made a face. "Let's put it this way. Don't tempt me with ice cream or pizza until after the wedding. One more pound and Clare will have to paint the dress on."

"Tell that to Derrick. He's the one who wines and dines you like a princess."

"One of the many reasons I love the guy."

"Derrick is the steadiest, most dependable man in Texas. You'll be a princess forever."

Faith grinned. "From stork to princess. I love it."

Faith's superior height had made her the object of too many jokes through the years. Though Derrick was two inches shorter, he adored his fiancée the way she was.

Every girl wanted a man like that.

Ever present in her thoughts these days, Jake flashed into her mental viewer. He'd been entertainingly inept at the grocery store, and he'd made her laugh over a can of spinach.

"Stop calling yourself a stork. You know how many times I've wished I was tall enough to reach the second shelf in the kitchen cabinet?"

"I can change a lightbulb without a chair."

"Lucky duck."

Faith laughed and hooked an elbow with Allison. "Come on. I have a stack of RSVPs to go through. Let's see who's coming to the biggest party in town."

With the wedding in three weeks, time was running out for all the last-minute details. "I touched base with the band and the caterer this morning, and scheduled the final fitting with all the bridesmaids."

"And?"

"Everything's a go. The caterer even managed some vegan dishes for Jayla and her friends after I sent over some suggestions."

"She's a genius." They settled side by side on a fawn-colored couch. "So are you. How do you find time for all this?"

"The perks of working for family. When the office is slow, I make calls or run errands."

"Saturday for the bridesmaids, right? What time?" Faith chewed the edge of a fingernail.

"Stop that." Allison swatted her friend's hand. "Ten o'clock. Which reminds me, are you going for acrylic nails or natural?"

"Do you actually think I can keep my hands out of my mouth in the weeks preceding the most important day of my life?"

"Not a chance. Acrylic it is. Have you made the appointment? What about your hair?" Allison went down the list she'd checked and rechecked dozens of times. Faith had been known to forget the details. Allison was a detail girl.

A stack of wedding RSVP envelopes—in the same white pearl as the mountain of invitations the two of them, along with Faith's mother, had addressed weeks ago—waited in a box on the coffee table. "Have you opened any of them?"

"I was waiting for you."

"Good. I want to keep a list."

"And you know I'm lousy with lists."

"Part of your charm. You're marrying a statistician. You don't have to worry about lists anymore." Allison grabbed a stack and a letter opener. "Put acceptances in the white box, rejections in the blue one."

As they sorted the cards, they talked. About how hard it would be to live three hours apart. About the darling house Faith and Derrick had purchased in Oklahoma City. About the honeymoon in Saint Thomas. If Allison felt a twinge of envy mixed in with her absolute delight for her best friend, she didn't acknowledge it.

"Derrick's brother is pretty cute, don't you think?" Faith's voice was casual but she didn't look at Allison, a sign she was trying—and failing—to be subtle.

"Yes, and nice, too, like Derrick."

"And? He's the best man. You're the maid of honor. Maybe you could get something going, and we could be sisters-in-law?"

Allison laughed. "Marrying your husband's brother would not make us related. Besides, I like being single."

"You do not. We've both waited long enough. Now that I'm getting married, you should get serious about finding someone."

She'd found someone once-upon-a-fairy-tale. But her fairy tale had turned into a horror flick.

In self-defense, she said, "I went to the movies with Billy last month."

"Last month! Allison, do you know how pathetic that is? And you only went with him because his sister asked you to take pity on him." Faith put the stack of envelopes in her lap. "Jake's the problem, isn't he? Like always."

Was she that transparent?

"Maybe." Probably. "But that was years ago."

"You still have his picture in your wallet."

"I never got around to taking it out."

"You've changed wallets a dozen times since then. Which means he's still stuck in your head and your heart. So now that he's back you need to do something about him."

"And cause the biggest war since the Hatfields and McCoys?" Allison shook her head. "I only want to make things easier for him. Our teenage romance is long behind us."

Faith rolled her eyes. "Oh, please. This is me you're talking to. You have never—I repeat *never*—laid to rest the issue of Jake Hamilton. Every guy is measured up against your handsome cowboy, and then you kick them to the curb like a pop can."

Allison sighed. Faith was right. Even when she'd wanted to move on and forget her feelings for Jake, she never had. They'd been prematurely interrupted and she'd never liked unfinished business. It was so untidy. "I don't know what to do. I wish my brothers could get over themselves."

"If wishes were horses. Stop wishing and go for it. Your brothers should have nothing to do with your romantic life, so get to know Jake again and see what happens." Faith ripped open another RSVP. "I have an idea. Invite him to the wedding. We still have invitations."

Allison's heart jumped. "He won't come."

"You never know until you try. Sit right there." Faith pointed at Allison as she hurried out of the room, but stuck her head around the door facing. "Do you want anything to drink while I'm up?"

"Water would be great."

"Got it. I hear Mom in the garage."

While Allison opened, sorted and listed RSVP cards, a nervous pulse ticked in her temple.

The unresolved heartache of a first love that had crashed and burned pushed to the surface like a dead body in water. She had loved him as much as any teenager could. He'd seen her at her worst, her most humiliated, and had never judged her. On the other hand, he'd stood her up at the graduation dance.

Did she really want to revisit either of those places again?

She stared down at the vellum cards and thought of all the weddings she'd attended, of the tiny unacknowledged ache to find her own true love.

Faith was right. She needed to explore this thing with Jake and put the issue to rest once and for all.

"Hello, Allison."

Deep in thought, Allison jumped when Faith's mom, Ellen, trudged into the room wearing blue scrubs, a testament to her nursing job. She wiggled her fingers and padded on silent white shoes down the hall and out of sight.

"Your mom looks tired," she said as Faith returned, bearing a white invitation.

"Eight twelve-hour shifts in a row take a toll."

"Ugh. Poor woman."

"No kidding. I'm glad I went into teaching." With the teacher shortage in Oklahoma, Faith had easily found a new job in Oklahoma City for the spring semester. "I'm filling out this invitation right now, and I want you to hand-deliver it."

Allison returned Faith's grin, though hers was filled with trepidation. "That's easy. I'm going over there when I leave here."

"Cleaning Miss Pat's house is a great excuse to see Jake." Faith pumped her eyebrows.

"Helping an elderly neighbor is not an excuse to see Jake. Stop it!" Allison bit her bottom lip. "I would help Miss Pat even if Jake wasn't there."

"Yes, but you wouldn't enjoy your little trips nearly as much."

True. Painfully true.

She watched Faith write Jake's name in her beautiful script. "Do you think he'll accept?"

Faith slid the card into the envelope and held it out like an Oscar win. "Only one way to find out."

He shouldn't be here. He should get in his pickup and drive out to Manny's.

Jake looked at the spread of vegetables on the kitchen counter and considered sticking everything back in the fridge. Then he could shut off the stove and walk out. Allison would be here any minute.

"Jacob?" Granny Pat's voice wafted in from the living room. "Honey, did you buy cheese for the baked potatoes? Bring me a slice. I haven't had anything but prison food in so long, I'm hungry as a starved wolf."

At the request, Jake resigned himself to letting Allison help him cook dinner. Granny needed this, no matter how hard it was on him.

He took a chunk of cheddar to the recliner where Granny Pat had pretty much lived since coming home. Earlier, the home nurse had gotten her up and walked her to the bath, a trip that had worn her out and torn a strip from Jake's heart.

"Here you go." He went to his knee beside her chair. "Anything else?"

"No, baby." She patted his hand. "You're such a good boy."

The comment made him snort. "Is your memory failing you?"

"I remember everything I want to." She grinned her impertinent grin. "You were always a good boy with a big soft heart. That's why you acted up after your mama left. And you had a right. She broke your little heart in half."

Jake's muscles tightened. He didn't think about his mother much anymore. "I always wondered why she left."

"I know you did, son. Leaving you was wrong of her."

That was the only explanation he'd ever received. His dad was barely cold in the ground before his mother packed her bags and drove away in an old Buick. "Do you ever wonder where she is?"

Granny Pat's winkled face saddened. "All the time, baby boy. For a long time I thought, once she'd grieved your daddy, she'd come back for you."

But she never had. And he'd grown up with a big, gaping hole inside, waiting for his mama to come home and fill it with love.

"I'm not complaining. You took good care of me."

She'd done her best. In between work and her grief over the loss of a son, his grandmother had done all she knew to deal with a sad little boy and later, a wild teenager. Still, he wondered what might have been.

Outside a car door slammed. Jake shook off the uncomfortable nostalgia and jerked to his feet. "Allison's here."

"Ralph thinks you're still sweet on her."

He tried to laugh her off. "You want to get me killed?"

"You've been trying to do that yourself for years."

A man with nothing to lose made a good bull rider.

At the knock, he ignored his grandmother's keen insight to let Allison in. "Hey."

"Hey, yourself." She shoved a bag at him. "Put this in the kitchen while I bring in the casserole."

"Casserole?"

"Mama's chicken spaghetti."

Granny Pat's voice sailed across the room. "I love that stuff."

"I thought we were cooking." Jake looked over one shoulder. "I already put the steaks in the oven."

"For tomorrow," Allison said. "You know how Mom is. She still cooks for an army in case one or two of us kids drops in. She had an extra and I 'borrowed it.'"

Karen Buchanon had fed him for years when he'd tagged along with the four Buchanon boys. Now, he was as grateful as he'd been back then, and the throb of longing was every bit as raw.

He set the bag of what appeared to be cleaning supplies on a table beside the door and followed Allison to the Camaro. Wearing a tan skirt and crisp white shirt with a collar, her flyaway hair bounced as she walked.

He liked her hair, itched to touch the silk of it and wanted to kick his own tail for even thinking about her that way.

He had to stop this. Had to stop it now.

His longer stride caught up to her quickly. "Did your mother know you were coming over here?"

"She was going to bring the casserole herself. I volunteered."

"She must not know I'm home."

Allison shrugged. "She wasn't wild about me seeing you, but I make my own choices and she knows that. Besides, she and Miss Pat go way back." She handed him the still-warm container. "Mom takes care of her friends."

Right. Karen Buchanon would visit Granny Pat even if her grandson was Ted Bundy.

"Neither of you mentioned this little errand of mercy to your brothers, did you?"

"You're cranky today."

"Did you?"

"No. They might do something stupid. They've been threatening—" She stopped halfway to the house and slapped her hands on her hips. "I want this to stop. You got me to admit my brothers still hold a grudge, and I didn't want to go there. Does that make you happy?"

With her face tilted toward his and her brown eyes snapping, she was cute as a kitten. Adorable and off-limits.

"Happy? Hardly." But exactly what he'd expected. Not what he'd hoped for or even dreamed of, but exactly what he deserved.

She hadn't intended to discuss her brothers. He could see that and understood. Now, she was furious, both at herself and him, for opening up the sore topic.

Unlike Brady Buchanon whose temper was renown, Allison's fury wouldn't last long. She was too good, too generous, too kind. And she was tearing him apart.

Resigned to spend the evening fighting memories, he led the way into the kitchen where the smell of broiling steak overpowered the small space.

"Better check this," he said and peaked inside the oven. "Looking good."

So was Allison.

He watched her move to the outdated sink and glance out the window toward the darkened backyard.

"Remember that time we grilled steaks for Dad's birthday and the dog ate yours?"

He smiled at the memory. At the woman. "You gave me half of yours."

"I could never eat a whole one anyway." She gazed around the room. "Where's the steak sauce and all the fixings we bought?"

He wished she wouldn't say *we*. It sounded way too cozy. "In the fridge."

"Okay." Allison went to the refrigerator and pulled out sour cream, cheese, butter, steak sauce and bacon bits and set them on the small round kitchen table where he and Granny Pat ate their meals. The wooden top was scarred from the number of times he'd done school projects in this kitchen with Granny Pat's assistance. He never wanted to minimize what his grandmother had done for him. She'd been there when his mother had refused to be.

What was wrong with a kid that his own mother could walk out and never call, never even send a birthday card? For years, on his birthdays, he'd thought for sure she would remember him. She never had.

Memories were thick as swamp mosquitoes tonight.

To break his runaway thought train, Jake opened the overhead cabinet and eyed the questionably clean plates. "Should I rinse these off?"

"Have they been washed since you've been here?"

"First home-cooked meal."

"Better rinse." As he reached for three white plates, she moved from the table to his side. "I have something for you."

He set the plates in the sink with a clatter. "For me?"

Allison held a white envelope toward him.

Puzzled, he accepted the fancy envelope. As he did, Jake examined the rise of pleasure, the unspoken need to reconnect with things better left alone. Hadn't he just been thinking about a birthday card, though his birthday was long past? "What is this?"

"Open the envelope and see for yourself."

Curious, Jake removed a pretty scripted invitation and read. His belly dropped to his boots. "Are you serious? Faith is inviting me to her wedding?"

"Don't say no, Jake. Please come."

He shook his head, though his chest expanded with want and hope. "You're crazy."

"And your steaks are burning."

He whipped around to remove the meat, clattering the pan onto the stove top. Sizzle and fragrant smoke filled the air.

With a growl, he said, "I told you I couldn't cook."

"Which is why I'm here. Put the steaks in the warmer. I'll make salad and rinse the plates. You get Miss Pat ready to pig out. We're going to fatten her up."

There she went again, using the *we* word. He closed his eyes and gave his head a little shake. If Allison insisted on coming around on a regular basis, something was bound to explode. Either him or her brothers, and neither was a pretty thought.

He shoved the white envelope into his back pocket.

Inviting him to a wedding with all the Buchanons and half of Gabriel's Crossing? Was she insane? Did she want to ruin her friend's big day?

This new adult Allison was even more of a Pollyanna eager to fix the world than she'd been as a teen.

And she was killing him. Absolutely killing him.

Chapter Five

Jake's tenderness with his grandmother brought a lump to Allison's throat just as being here caused a twinge of disloyalty. Mom hadn't been pleased, though she'd relented for the sake of Miss Pat. Still, Allison couldn't help feeling guilty. Was Faith correct? Was Allison using Miss Pat as an excuse to see Jake?

The three of them sat at the scarred table with Miss Pat on a pillow to cushion her bony body against the hard surface. Jake had carried her to the chair with her hair freshly brushed and wearing a silky Dresden-blue bed jacket. She reminded Allison of a tiny snow-capped bluebird.

"Your robe is beautiful, Miss Pat."

"Jacob bought it when I first went to the hospital. I had to have something decent. Imagine a wrinkled old lady like me wearing one of those silly gowns with the naked behind." She made a face. "Better yet, don't imagine it."

Allison's mouth trembled with a smile. "He has good taste."

"That's what Ralph said. I have a feeling he was a

dab jealous of his own grandson. Ralph never bought me anything this fancy. But then, he was a skinflint." She whipped her napkin into her lap. "Yes, you were, Ralph. You know I'm telling the truth."

The conversation with Ralph brought a momentary lull as Jake and Allison exchanged glances.

"Well, Jacob. Are you going to pray or sit there and make goo-goo eyes at Allison?"

Goo-goo eyes? Oh, for crying out loud. Jake spent most of his time glaring at her and trying to run her off. Couldn't Miss Pat see that?

A dull blush darkened Jake's face. He rolled his eyes, but didn't respond to his grandmother's outrageous comment.

"Do you mind if I say grace?" he asked, his camo-green gaze holding hers steady.

"Really?" Jake Hamilton wanted to pray?

His sculpted lips softened into a smile as he shared the good news that he'd become a Christian. Allison's heart jitterbugged with the energy of a 1950s teenager. No wonder he seemed different.

"Changed everything," he said.

"I'm glad, Jake. Thrilled." Beyond delighted.

For Allison, faith had always been a given. She'd grown up in church, and though there were times she struggled to understand why bad things happened, she believed with all her heart in the goodness and power of Jesus. But Jake hadn't been raised to believe. The fact that he'd converted, and that his grandmother had noticed, was huge. As he said, it changed everything.

The one fly in her romantic fantasies about Jake had been his lack of faith.

Oh, my. This was wonderful and scary and promising.

And she was out of her mind.

Allison dropped her head and squeezed her eyes shut as Jake's low rumble asked the blessing on the meal.

Please, she prayed. *Let this make a difference to my brothers.*

She prayed this would change things between Jake and her family. The Buchanons had taken Jake to church on occasion, but he'd never embraced their faith. Until now. Surely, the brothers would forgive him now. Wouldn't they?

All through the meal, hope rode Allison's shoulders like a winged creature. Buoyed by the good news, she teased conversation out of Jake and relished Miss Pat's feistiness. The meal lingered for much longer than required to eat the simple food. Dishes were pushed aside and elbows propped on the table as they caught up on the years apart.

Something inside Allison centered. She'd missed their friendship, their talks and hanging out. She may have crushed on Jake as a teenager, but he'd been her buddy, too.

"You're tired, Granny Pat," Jake said when the older lady began to nod.

Miss Pat's head snapped up. "I know it. Silly old body of mine." She pointed a bony finger toward the cheese. "Cut me a slab of that, will you, honey? It's from IGA."

"You mentioned that earlier, Granny Pat," Jake said gently.

"I told *you,* not Allison. Stop acting like I've lost my mind. It makes me and Ralph both mad enough to spit."

Allison caught Jake's eye as she sliced the cheese. Miss Pat's body might be weak but there was nothing weak about her spirit.

"With your spunk, Miss Pat, you'll be back on your feet before Christmas."

"You got that right, honey." She waved the cheese at Jake. "Take me and my cheese to my room. I'm done in."

"Yes, ma'am. At your service." He scraped back his chair and tenderly lifted his grandmother. "You sure smell pretty."

"You sure tell tall tales." She patted his cheek. "Love you, Jacob."

He kissed her cheek. And Allison melted like chocolate on s'mores.

To get herself under control, she leaped up and began clearing the table. She hadn't intended to linger like a lovesick kid. Faith was to blame—Faith and her matchmaking ideas and her wedding invitation.

She glanced at the clock, saw the time was already growing late. She hadn't even begun cleaning the house, a promise she intended to keep.

Not that she minded another trip or two. As long as her brothers didn't know.

She scraped the dishes and put them into the dishwasher, thinking about the grown-up Jacob. In the years in between, he'd developed a cowboy swagger. He also hid his feelings better than he had as a boy, so that she was not quite sure where they stood. Not like before when she'd read him as easily as a Pre-Primer. The adult Jake was more controlled, too, not the wild, impulsive kid who'd vandalized a Buchanon construction site after the accident that had left Quinn with a crippled arm. And if his care for Miss Pat was any indication, he was even more tenderhearted, a trait he covered with attitude and silence. Beneath his rodeo-tough exterior, he'd always been a marshmallow, though her family didn't see him through her eyes.

From their dinner conversation, she'd learned about his rodeo career and the bulls he kept at Manny Morales's ranch. She'd also learned from a slip by Miss Pat of the Wyoming woman he'd almost married. Her heart had stopped beating on that one, though Jake had laughed off the reference and refused to discuss it.

"You should go on home."

She glanced over her shoulder to see the handsome cowboy enter the kitchen. He looked good in the faded-blue chambray shirt and old jeans, his dark hair trimmed and neat, his shoulders and arms muscled by hours of training. A lean teenager had gone away. A heartbreaker had returned in his place.

"I haven't cleaned yet."

"I'll take care of it."

"Don't push me out, Jake. You know I won't go back on my promise to Miss Pat."

"She'll understand."

"I wouldn't."

He came across the room and took the salad bowl from her hand, his voice low. "Why are you playing with fire when you know we'll both get burned?"

"Rebellion is in my blood." She gave him a perky grin and stuck the meat tray in the sink.

"Your brothers wouldn't like it if they knew you were here."

"Since when have my brothers run my life? You know me better than that. They didn't then, and they don't now. Especially now."

"I don't want to stir up trouble, Allison."

"Are you calling me trouble?" She took a step closer, challenging.

His nostrils flared. "What do you think?"

"I think we can be friends again. Like before."

His gaze dropped to her mouth. The air between them shivered with possibility.

Did the tough bull rider remember that night? That first and last kiss?

"I don't want to hurt anyone," he murmured.

The truth in his statement was a stark reminder that people had been hurt, including the two of them. "I don't either. That's the whole point, Jake," she said softly. "Hurt never goes away unless we choose to release it."

He was standing really close, and she could smell the faint scent of aftershave and steak sauce, a funny combination but pleasantly male. She wanted to walk right into his arms and see if they fit together the way she remembered. Though he'd only kissed her once, she'd never forgotten, and now she understood why. Faith was right. Every boy had been compared to that one defining moment. Compared and rejected. Jake had always been the one.

Oh, my. Life had suddenly become much more complicated.

"I wish letting go was that easy," he murmured, near enough that she read the wistfulness in his green eyes.

"Come to Faith's wedding." Suddenly, she wanted him there with all her heart. Somehow, together, they'd find a way to make things right again.

His laugh was a short bark. "Yeah, like that's going to fix everything."

"Being there might be a start." She touched his arm.

"Please. I want you to come. You have a right to be there."

He pressed his lips into a thin line and looked beyond her toward the window above the sink. When his gaze returned to hers, the green eyes held a look she didn't understand, but he said, "Let me think about it."

That was as good as she was going to get, and Allison decided to take hope and run. Let him fret over the invitation. Let him wonder what it would be like to be back among friends who'd helped shape his childhood. Let him yearn for something more, in the same way she had yearned for him, though until this moment, she'd not acknowledged that longing.

"Think about the invitation all you want as long as you show up at Faith's wedding with your dancing shoes on. Now, grab the Windex and a rag. These dirty windows are killing me."

He shook his head. "You're an impossible optimist."

"Yeah, but you like me," she said with a cheeky grin.

He tugged a strand of her hair. "Got me there."

And that little admission fueled her determination to make things right between Jake Hamilton and the Buchanon clan.

Several days later, Jake thought the freezer was well stocked with casseroles, the laundry was caught up and the killer windows gleamed. But Allison showed up at six-thirty anyway. As always, he made a halfhearted attempt to send her home but she called him grumpy and sailed right inside.

He had to admit her company was a welcome break from worrying over bills and his grandmother. And yeah, he looked forward to the moment each evening when a little bundle of sunshine lit up his day. As long as the Buchanon brothers didn't give her grief, he could deal with the other issues. He didn't want her hurt again, and whether she admitted it or not, she had been. He'd done enough damage in this town.

"What did you do today?" she asked, frowning around the somewhat cluttered room. He'd picked up his socks and put away the dishes. Wasn't that enough?

"Besides aggravating my grandmother until she ran me off?" He cast a look toward the chair where Granny napped. "I took a drive out to Manny's while the nurse was here."

"How are they?" Allison tossed a tiny shoulder bag onto the couch and made herself at home. "I haven't seen them in town in a while."

"They're good." He patted his pocket for his cell phone. "I need to give Paulina a call. She invited us out for dinner, but Granny isn't up for the travel."

"I will be soon." Jake and Allison turned toward Granny Pat whose sharp gaze rested on them. "Why don't you two kids run on out there without me."

Jake shook his head even though his heart had done a weird stutter step. Exactly the way it did each time he eased down on the back of a bull. "What about the casserole I set out of the freezer?"

"I'll eat it. You won't have to worry about feeding me." She shooed him with a skinny, pale hand. "Go on now."

"I don't think that's a good idea."

"This is my house and I want you out for a while. All this moping around gets on my last nerve."

Allison snorted. Jake shot her a scowl. "What are you laughing at?"

"You. Come on, cowboy, before she throws her Sudoku book at you. I want to see your bulls, and pig out on Paulina's enchiladas."

"Who's going to heat her dinner?" As much as he liked the idea of getting out of town, he was careful not to leave Granny Pat alone. And hanging out with Allison was like a death wish. A really pleasant one.

"Flo can use a microwave. Not much else, but she's a whiz of a nuker, and she's on her way."

"I thought she was in Florida on the beach."

Florence Dubois, which he was certain was a stage name, was Granny Pat's longtime friend, a former Las Vegas showgirl with legs like stilts, big hair, and abundant cosmetic surgery.

"*Was.* When she learned I'd finally escaped from prison, she fired up the Winnebago and headed back to Gabriel's Crossing."

"Carson Convalescence is not a prison." He'd made that statement so often, it had become as automatic as blinking.

She flapped her white speckled hand again. "Whatever you want to call my confinement, I've escaped, and Flo is coming over, and you're going to leave us alone for a while. Get moving."

"Well." He stacked his fists on his hips.

Granny Pat chuckled. "No excuses, Jacob. Go. Enjoy. Paulina cooked and a woman doesn't like to be stood up."

Jake turned to Allison. "What are you grinning about?"

She laughed aloud. "Grab your hat. You've been tossed out."

"Not the first time," he muttered.

The woman didn't realize what she was doing, or if she did, she didn't care.

"My car or your truck?" Allison asked.

"You gonna let me drive your Camaro?"

She snorted. "How about if I drive your big old truck instead?"

"Nobody drives my truck." But he grabbed his hat and followed her out the door.

The ride to the Double M Ranch was bumpy, short and quick. With country music as background and safely out of Buchanon radar range, he let down his guard and listened to Allison rattle about Faith's wedding plans, the big building project out in Willow Creek, a place he didn't even remember, and a hodgepodge of other topics. She jumped from one thing to another like a fluffy little bunny. That's what she reminded him of. Cute and full of energy and soft. He slammed the gate on the last thought. Allison and her softness were off-limits. She was way more than cute. Beautiful. Kind. Warm as a Texas summer.

They could be on friendly terms, as long as her brothers didn't get involved, but he wasn't about to think beyond friendship. As soon as Granny Pat was settled, he was out of here. Let sleeping dogs lie, and escape as soon as possible.

If he didn't get back to work soon, his bank account would suffer and he'd risk falling behind on his loans. Loans that pointed to his future instead of the mess in Gabriel's Crossing and a persistent past that intruded like flies at a picnic.

Occasionally, one of the other Buchanons seeped into the conversation. They'd been as close as family, and sometimes he yearned to be among them so much his

chest ached. Being back in Gabriel's Crossing messed
with his mind worse than a head slam to the dirt.

"Mom's already packing Christmas packages for all
the soldiers in Trevor's unit." Allison sat at an angle in
the bucket seat, the console open between them. He was
glad for the divider, or he might have done something
stupid like reach for her hand.

"Trevor?" he asked, instead.

"Charity's husband. He's with the navy in Africa."

Ah, now he remembered. "She married Trevor San-
difer, right? Didn't they have a kid?"

"Two." She opened the tiny purse and extracted a cell
phone. "Want to see their pictures?"

Before he could reply, she stuck the screen in front
of his face. He glanced down at a blond boy with blue
eyes and then back at the country road. Gravel spewed
out behind them, leaving a dust trail.

"That's Ryan. He's eleven."

"He looks like Charity."

"I think so, too. He's a mess sometimes without his
daddy here, but a cute mess. Charity has her hands full."
She ran her index finger over the screen and produced
another photo. "Amber is the dimpled princess of the
Buchanon clan. She's in first grade and learning to read.
You should hear her. Last night she read to her daddy
on Skype, and he got choked up."

"Man. That must be tough."

"Yeah." She put the phone back in her tiny, overstuffed bag. "But they're strong. Trevor will be home
in another six months."

"That's good." He'd considered joining the military
after the accident. If not for the rodeo he would have.
Anything to escape the daily censure, though he had

to admit, the inner condemnation had followed him for years.

Another pickup rumbled past in a wake of dust. He wanted to see photos of the other Buchanons, especially Quinn, but wasn't sure he was ready to face what he'd done, even in a picture. "Still have the big Buchanon get-togethers on Sunday?"

"Like always. You should—"

"Don't finish that thought." But the yearning hit him full force. He should come over, like before. While the smell of Mrs. B.'s pot roast or fried chicken filled the house, he could pile up on the floor with the guys and talk football and girls, cars and camo.

He gripped the steering wheel and strained toward the crossbars of Manny's ranch.

Camo. *God, don't let me think about hunting. Don't let my mind go there.*

But the pictures came anyway, flashing through his head like something out of a horror movie.

"Hey." Allison's voice broke through the ugly thoughts. "Earth to Jake."

"Sorry." He was sweating. He cranked up the AC. "There's the ranch."

"Will you let me ride one of your bulls?"

He offered a look meant to quell. "Not in this lifetime."

She snickered. "I was kidding."

"No, you weren't, you little hot dog. But I'll hop on one and impress you with my finesse."

"Remember when you took me to the rodeo in Sand Creek? I was scared to death you were going to get killed."

"That was one of the first times I placed in the short go."

"We had a great day."

"Until Brady found out and you got grounded."

"I wasn't grounded because of you, Jake. I was grounded because I didn't ask permission. I don't have to ask anymore. If I want to go somewhere, I go. We should do it again. When is your next rodeo?"

"You're kind of pushy, aren't you? What if I'm taking someone else?"

"Are you?"

"Maybe." He wasn't, but she was walking on dangerous ground.

His hedge bought him some time. She fell silent, and the turmoil that was Allison Buchanon stirred in his belly. He had no right to be attracted to her, any more than she should be attracted to him. He gnawed the inside of his cheek.

He wasn't attracted. He couldn't be. He'd put all that to rest the day he'd left Gabriel's Crossing for good.

"Hey." Her small hand touched the forearm of his shirt. He could feel her warmth seeping through, the warmth of a relentless optimist with the biggest heart in Texas.

"What?"

"Just hey. I'm glad you're here. I'm glad I'm here."

Oh, boy. "Granny's getting stronger every day. I have to get back pretty soon."

"I know. I know. You're only home through the holidays." She beamed a wide smile that did weird things to his head. "But we can enjoy today."

The truck rumbled to a dust-stirring stop in Manny's driveway. Jake shifted out of gear and with an arm looped over the steering wheel turned toward her. He didn't even want to think about how fresh and pretty she was.

"Yeah," he said, resigned. "I guess we can."

Chapter Six

Jake needed to be alone. He needed to pray. About Allison. About money. About his grandmother.

And so he drove to the Double M where he spent a little time with Manny and Paulina before taking the Polaris out to the bull pasture.

Beneath a leaden sky, a north wind coaxed leaves from trees and hinted at the coming winter, a normally toothless beast in warm-blooded Texoma. Still, something about the autumn pastures and tree-lined creeks brought Jake closer to God. He supposed he and the Almighty had a strange relationship.

He parked the ATV at the pond and, hands deep in his jean jacket, walked around the edge noting deer tracks in the damp red earth. Deer season was upon them. He'd not hunted since the accident. Probably never would again, though he enjoyed a good deer chili.

He squatted on a rock and thought about his job. He was floundering here, growing poorer with each sunrise.

But what was a man to do?

Last night with Allison at the Morales dinner table had been both wonderful and unnerving. He liked her more than he wanted to, more than he should, but every minute spent with her was pure pleasure.

He was one messed-up hombre.

Leaving the Polaris on the pond dam, he walked across the fields, praying and thinking, though no flaming banner from Heaven answered his queries.

Around him, the woods and fields smelled of damp fallen leaves. Thanksgiving was around the corner and then Christmas. Already, the town workers erected candy cane and snowflake lights along First Street, a jump start on the holiday season.

For once in many years, he wanted to be here for the holidays. Granny wasn't getting any younger, a fact that had slapped him in the face during her months in Carson Convalescence. He regretted the years of phone calls instead of visits, but then he regretted so many failures.

But more than Granny, he wanted to spend Christmas with Allison. He closed his eyes, fought the feelings that swam in on a current of warm pleasure. Allison was a ticking time bomb.

Between now and Christmas stretched a thousand miles of rodeos, and he prayed to make some of those events. A bull rider didn't draw a paycheck unless he rode, and Jake wasn't sure what to do about it. He couldn't leave, wasn't sure he wanted to, but being here cost him.

"In more ways than one, Lord," he said, looking up into a sky scattered with flat gray clouds. The money was one thing. The cost to his heart and soul was another.

He crossed a skinny trickle of water, a natural spring that fed the pond and led to the cross-fenced bull pasture. The sound of bawling calves reached his ears. He gazed into the horizon to where a young yellow bull bucked and jumped, his strong legs kicking out behind, a champion in the making. All Jake had to do was hold on a little longer and the bulls would make his living for him.

Then he saw something that jammed his breath in his throat. He stopped, squinted, hoping he was wrong. He wasn't.

Two boys ran around inside the gathering pen with a half-dozen young bulls. His bulls. Horned and dangerous.

Jake broke into a lope. "Hey, you boys, get out of there!"

Two heads jerked toward him, one blond and one dark. The blond looked uncannily like the photo Allison had shown him of her nephew.

The boys spotted him and bolted for the gate.

"Hold up!" Jake yelled, but the pair scrambled over the closed gate and ran like rabbits across the pasture in the other direction.

By the time Jake arrived, they had disappeared over the rise. He stood breathless, wondering if he should get the Polaris and give chase but decided against it. They'd be long gone before he could return.

He stared across the fading green pasture toward the gentle slope of land. The boys had disappeared from sight.

When he was their age, he would have pulled the same kind of dangerous stunt. Probably had.

But danger was the point. Messing with bucking bulls, even young ones, could be deadly. They all had horns and even snubbed ones were dangerous. They were all unpredictable. Even grown men with professional training were sometimes badly injured. A boy didn't stand a chance.

He wondered if one of the boys was Allison's nephew, Ryan, but he couldn't be certain. He'd seen only a photo of the kid.

The situation worried him, but he didn't know what to do. Without a positive identification, there were no parents to contact.

After checking his animals to be sure they were all right, he started back to the Polaris.

He'd better warn Manny.

Jake never saw it coming.

He was pushing a borrowed mulcher around the Hamilton yard filled with oak leaves when an unfamiliar Dodge Ram rumbled to a stop out front. Late model. Shiny red. Nice truck.

Though the autumn temperature was a pleasant fifty, sweat leaked from his body and dripped into his eyes. His damp shirt stuck to him like salty skin. He removed his hat, swiped at the sweat with a blue bandana and watched the doors of the Ram swing open. All four of them.

Everything in Jake went still. The roar in his temples was louder than the mulching engine. He felt dizzy. Sick. And the cause wasn't the sweaty job.

Four Buchanon brothers slid out of the truck and strode toward him across the lawn.

A wild mix of love and sorrow engulfed him.

From the stiff set of their shoulders, this was not a friendly visit. Not that he'd expected one.

Jake killed the machine and waited. Bits of dead

leaves and dry grass fluttered to the ground in the sudden silence.

Stride for stride they came like something out of a TV commercial. Not a one of the oversize men wore a welcoming expression.

He was tired and thirsty and about to have to fight four men at once. The old Jake would have lowered his head and, like a mad bull, gone on the attack. His motto had been: "he might go down but he'd get in a few good punches before he did." The new Jake understood. Whatever they chose to do, he had it coming.

Lord, I could use a little wisdom about now.

"Hamilton." Brady Buchanon was six feet six inches of muscles, a warrior on the football field and off, with a temper that had gotten him into a few scrapes over the years.

"Brady." Jake wanted to offer a handshake but knew he'd be rejected. Heck, he wanted to throw his arms around each of them in a man hug. But wanting and reality were as far apart as the earth and moon.

His eyes moved from one brother to the other. His friends. His enemies. How he'd missed them. "Dawson, Sawyer. Quinn."

The blue eyed, black-haired twins stood like bookends with Brady and Quinn in the center.

Jake's gaze centered on Quinn.

His former best friend was still built like an anvil with wide pro quarterback shoulders and a skinny waist. Standing before him was a champion athlete, the golden boy of Gabriel's Crossing, left fist clenched while the right arm curved at his side, smaller than the other. Allison said he was an architect now, but the lost dream hovered in the grass-scented air between them. Jake

Hamilton had destroyed Quinn Buchanon's arm and with it his dream.

If he could only go back...

"Nice to see you guys." What else was he supposed to say? He *was* glad to see them. He hurt with the pleasure.

Brady's nostrils flared. Though a good guy who'd give the shirt off his back to a friend, Brady Buchanon was a formidable enemy. They all were. Buchanons protected their own. "This isn't a social call."

"I didn't figure it was." Jake wiped his hands on the bandana and shoved the blue cloth in his back jeans pocket. His throat was dry as sand and he'd give a dollar for a drink of water. "So, why are you here?"

"To offer a warning. Stay away from our sister."

Jake heaved a weary sigh. He'd known Brady would say that. Though he'd managed to keep his friendship with Allison below Buchanon radar for a week, he'd also known this meeting was inevitable. "Have you discussed this with Allison?"

"What are you? A coward hiding behind a girl?" Quinn's lips sneered.

Quinn, his best friend. How many times had he wished the accident had happened to him instead of this man he'd loved like a brother?

"She's not a little girl anymore, in case you haven't noticed."

"Yeah, well, we don't want you noticing. That's the deal. Stay away from our sister. Stay away from *us*."

Sentiment only went so far. They were starting to get his back up. "I can't stop Allison from visiting my grandmother."

"We can."

Jake gave a short bark of laughter, incredulous. "Good luck with that."

Brady stepped closer, his massive size intimidating. Jake braced himself to fight or take a beating. "One warning, Hamilton. Back off."

"I'm not here to cause a problem, Brady. I'm here for my grandmother. I can't tell Allison what to do even if I wanted to. Believe me, I've tried. And neither can you."

"She was seen in your truck last night."

So that was the problem. The trip to the ranch for enchiladas. He wondered what they'd say when they found out—and they would—that Allison spent nearly every evening at the Hamilton house?

"I'll repeat. She's a grown woman, a fact she's made very clear to me."

Sawyer bowed up. "What does that mean?"

Jake shot the twin a narrow look. "You figure it out. Now, if that's all the good news you Buchanons have to share, I have work to finish."

He started to turn away but Quinn stepped forward and grabbed his arm. "We'll say when this conversation is over."

Jake shook him off. "Back off, Quinn."

"Or what, Jake? What are you going to do? Shoot me?"

As if the other man had sucker punched him, the wind went out of Jake. His shoulders slumped. He closed his eyes. In a voice ripped with pain, he said, "Do you know how many times I've wished I could change that day? It was an accident, Quinn. An accident."

"Yeah. What about the illegal booze you *accidentally* brought along?"

The truth was a chain saw tearing through him. Never

mind that Quinn had drunk the beer, too. Jake had the fake ID. Jake had bought alcohol on the hunting trip. In the misty morning, with a beer in his brain, he was the one who'd thought he'd seen a deer. *He,* and he alone, had been the one who'd pulled the trigger.

The memory of the report that blasted through the chilly autumn stillness, the thundering exhilaration when what he'd thought was a deer crashed into the brush. But it was Quinn's hoarse scream that haunted Jake, the electric realization that he'd shot his best friend with a deer rifle, a gun powerful enough to destroy bone and nerves and muscles.

He squeezed his eyes shut against the flashing video. Bloodstained grass. The weight of Quinn's much larger body as he'd carried him to the truck. The river of tears he'd wept.

"I was a stupid kid."

"So, don't be a stupid man. Leave the Buchanons alone, and we'll leave you alone." Brady tapped Jake's chest with his index finger. "Got it?"

Jake backed up a step, trying to hold his temper in check. Turn the other cheek. Walk away.

Dawson grabbed his brother's arm. "Come on, Brady. We've delivered the message. Let's go."

"Dawson's right," Sawyer said. "We've got work to do."

Brady stood like a towering giant, stretched to his full height. Intimidating seemed a mild word. Of all the Buchanon men, he was the biggest, and the rest were six footers or better.

With his eyes holding Jake's, Brady said, "You boys load up. I'll be there in a second."

Jake breathed a sigh of relief. One Buchanon alone,

he could survive, even if that particular Buchanon was eight inches taller and seventy pounds heavier.

Dawson, ever the sane voice, shook his head. "Not happening. Let's go. We're done here."

"He's right, Brady," Sawyer said, though none of them moved. "Message delivered, and I got a hot date tonight. If we don't finish the framing at the McGowen house, I'll be late."

Brady continued to hold Jake's eyes in a silent challenge, an old game of who would look away first. Jake didn't want to play. He backed down, looked to the side.

Turn the other cheek. Do the right thing.

A brown car puttered to the stop sign. The driver rubbernecked at the men in the yard.

As if satisfied, Brady spun away and walked with his brothers to the truck. Jake stood in the yard, sweating and sad, watching them leave.

Long ago, he would have leaped into the bed of the truck, whooped and pounded the heel of his hand on the cab top and gone with them. It didn't matter where. Anywhere with the Buchanon boys was a good time.

He watched Quinn and saw that the damaged arm was useful as Quinn reached for the truck door. Though weaker and smaller, the arm had function. *Thank you, Lord, for that.*

Throat thick, Jake desperately wanted to make amends. He'd forgotten exactly how desperately until faced with the man whose life he'd ruined.

"Quinn," Jake called, startled to hear his voice but certain he had to say something more, something that mattered.

Quinn turned his head, his injured hand braced against the open door. He didn't speak, only stared at Jake.

The other three Buchanons looked his way. Sun glinted off the truck, gilded them, especially Quinn, the golden boy.

A tumble of emotion rose in Jake's throat, words trapped inside that had no names.

"I—" What did he say? What *could* he say? He'd give his right arm in place of Quinn's? He wished he'd been the victim that November morning?

But he'd said all those things and dozens more, and not a one of them changed anything.

Tension stretched like a wire between Jake and the man he'd wronged. Stretched until it snapped, and the moment passed. Quinn slid into the truck and slammed the door, and the Buchanons drove away.

Allison's first indication that something had gone wrong occurred the moment she entered the office warehouse at nine o'clock Tuesday morning. All five Buchanon men stood in a huddle, voices raised as they talked in strained tones. Even the usually chipper Dawson wore a grim expression. Allison set a steaming caramel latte on the counter, tossed her keys and bag toward her computer and joined them.

She had a jittery feeling that this had something to do with Jake, though it very well might not. Lately, she thought everything related to Jake. Maybe because she couldn't get him out of her head.

"What's going on?" she asked. "Has something happened?"

"Trouble on the McGowen house." This from her Dad. At sixty-one, he still worked a full day, sometimes more and could build a house from the ground up single-handedly. At times, he was a hard man, and trouble on a job site infuriated him.

Allison's anxiety level decreased. Trouble on the job happened. It had nothing to do with Jake.

"What kind of trouble? Can we get Charity to take care of it?" Vendors and subcontractors sometimes caused delays. Materials were late or subs got tied up on other jobs and put the schedule behind.

"Someone vandalized the property. Spray paint everywhere. Kicked in some walls the boys put up yesterday," her dad said. Never mind that her brothers were grown men who towered over their father. To Dan Buchanon, his sons would always be "the boys." "Made a mess of everything."

"How bad?"

Brady growled like a dog. Dawg, who'd flopped at his master's feet, raised his head. Sawyer tossed him a chunk of muffin, which was deftly caught and swallowed in one motion. "Bad enough to put us behind for a week."

Allison grimaced. Like Dad, Brady ran a tight schedule, balancing more than one project at a time for optimal use of personnel. When the painters were in one house, the plumbers could be in another and the carpenters in yet another. At the moment, he juggled five different projects. A setback anywhere could disrupt the flow of work and seriously annoy her big brother.

Sawyer removed his cap and studied the Dallas Cowboys insignia. "We haven't had vandalism on a site in a long time."

"Years," Quinn said.

"I'm gonna knock some heads over this."

Her dad clapped a hand on Brady's shoulder. "You have to find them first."

"Oh, I'll find them. In fact, I think I know exactly where he is."

A warning buzz tingled up the back of Allison's neck. "You think you know who did this?"

"Yeah."

"Are you thinking who I'm thinking?" Quinn asked.

"I find it too much of a coincidence that Jake Hamilton is back in town and shortly after our unfriendly little talk, we have a project vandalized for the first time in years."

"What unfriendly talk?" Allison asked. "What did you guys do?"

Brady ignored the question. "He did before."

"Answer my question."

"Leopards don't change their spots." Sawyer slapped his cap on. "Maybe we should take another trip to see rodeo boy and see what he has to say for himself."

Allison's pulse jumped. "Another trip? What did you do? What are you talking about?"

"Buchanons take care of their own. Hamilton isn't wanted here. We warned you to stay away from him."

So this was her fault?

"Dad, talk some sense into them. Beating people up is not the way to handle a problem. It's also not the way Buchanon Construction does business."

"No one said anything about beating him up." Brady flashed his teeth in a shark's grin. "We'll only have a chat and find out where he was last night."

"Allison's right on this one," her dad said. "You can't go off half-cocked and get yourselves tossed in jail. Let the police chief do his job. You did call Leroy, didn't you?"

Brady shook his head. "Not yet."

Dad pursed his lips and gave his son a scathing look.

"I'll call him, Dad." Allison moved into the U-shaped desk and reached for the phone. Jake was innocent. He wouldn't do anything as juvenile as vandalizing property. Would he?

While she reported the incident to the police, her brothers and dad murmured among themselves.

By the time she'd hung up, Jayla sailed through the door, carting her blender and a bag of groceries. She looked like a runway model with her sleek hair and well-dressed, superslim body. Allison's jeans and sweater felt dowdy.

When Jayla learned of the vandalism, she ground her teeth. Like Brady, Jayla could be a control freak who expected business to run smoothly all the time.

"Leroy is out today with a stomach virus, but Jerry is on duty and said he'd take look at the site," she told them.

"Good. We'll meet him there." Sawyer shoved the last bite of muffin in his mouth. Dawg watched with big, sad eyes.

Brady scored a muffin from Dawson's white sack and juggled it in his massive palm. To Allison, he said, "Do me a favor, okay?"

"What is it?" If he told her to stay away from Jake, she was going to hit him.

He reached in his pocket and pulled out a list. "I won't have time to do this now and I promised. Will you take a run to the supercenter and get this stuff for me?"

She frowned down at the long list of groceries and household supplies. "What's this for?"

He hitched a shoulder, his expression abashed. "Ah, you know."

Oh. Okay. She got it. Brady's heart was as big as the

rest of him. He regularly bought groceries or gas or shoes or medicine for someone in need.

"Who's this week's recipient?"

"New family across the tracks. A woman and four kids."

Allison knew there was more to the story but didn't push. Brady, for all his temper and bluster, was a soft touch like Mom.

"Should I deliver?"

"I'll take it by later. The mom's kind of embarrassed."

"Consider it done."

He leaned down and kissed the top of her head. "Are you getting shorter?"

She bopped him on the arm. He rubbed the spot and grinned. "Mosquito bite."

The men started for the door when Brady looked back at her. "One more thing."

She reached for a pen. "Did you leave something off the list?"

Brady narrowed his eyes. "Don't talk to loverboy about the vandalism until after the investigation."

Allison's heart sank. Just when she thought her brother was the best around, he kicked her in the gut. "Are you going to tell the police about your suspicions?"

Brady's mouth shrugged. "If he asks, I'll answer." And then he was gone, swaggering across the parking lot with his big heart and hard head directly at odds.

Allison showed up on his doorstep at the strangest times.

Jake was in Granny Pat's flower bed digging up something Florence called an apricot bearded iris. She wanted a start for her garden and he was the elected shovel man.

He leaned on the shovel handle and admired the little bit of woman tromping across the lawn, her dark, flyaway hair like wings.

"Are you lost?" He tipped back his hat. "It's ten in the morning. Shouldn't you be at work?"

"Perks of being family owned. What are you doing?" She paused outside the flower bed, a messy thing that had gone wild in Granny Pat's absence.

"Digging. Want to help?" He was uncommonly happy to see her. Not that the Buchanons had scared him off. He wasn't scared. But in the time he had left in Gabriel's Crossing, he saw no point in making waves that might turn into a tsunami.

"Sure. What can I do?"

"When I dig, you get those little onion-looking things and put them in that bucket." He hitched his chin toward an empty white paint bucket.

"This is my mother's domain but I know my way around an iris."

He stuck his boot on the shovel and pushed. The rain-soft earth gave, emitting the scents of dying plants and fertile ground. He wiggled the spade carefully before levering up a clump of dirt and plant. "Are all women born with the flower gene?"

She reached into the dirt, heedless of getting her hands dirty. He admired that. A woman who wasn't afraid of dirt and work, two things he knew especially well.

"These are bulbs, not onions." She tapped the onion thing with a finger. "Lower the shovel into the bucket, dirt and all. No need to separate anything."

"You're brilliant."

"I am for a fact. Kind of late in the year to transplant irises. Who are these for?"

"Flo. She does things on her own timetable."

Allison stood and wiped her hands down the legs of her jeans. He was midtransfer when she said, "Take me to a movie tonight."

The clump of dirt hit the bucket with a sudden *thunk*. Where had that come from? Her brothers wanted to kill him and she wanted him to go to a movie?

He leaned the shovel against the side of the house. "Why?"

"Because I like you. We have fun together and I want to do something besides hang around your grandmother's house."

He didn't want to like the sound of that. "Not to spite your brothers?"

Her eyes met his and held. "Maybe a little. They had no right to confront you."

One of her strong suits was honesty. "I don't want to get between you and your family, Allison."

"Trust me, I know that. If you recall, I found that out the hard way a few years back. I don't always like your weird code of honor, but I appreciate the sentiment." She hoisted the bucket of iris bulbs, her focus on them. "I have to ask you something, Jake. Don't get mad, okay?"

"Starting a conversation that way is never a positive sign." He hunkered down beside the gaping hole in the ground and began to push dirt inside.

Allison set the bucket beside the porch and joined him, bringing along her honeysuckle scent. His heart began to misbehave.

"Someone vandalized a construction project last night."

His hand closed spasmodically on a gangly green stem. He tried not to let the implication sting. "You're asking if I had anything to do with damaging your family's work site?"

If he sounded incredulous, so be it.

"I don't want to."

He believed her. Those soft brown eyes were tormented as they held his with a plea.

"Will you believe me if I say no?"

"Yes."

With one small word and those big brown eyes, she had the power to make him feel better. Let the others think what they wanted. As long as Allison believed in him, he was all right.

"I told you I'd never do anything to hurt you. Not if I could help it." The little disclaimer was self-preservation. If they got involved again, if he followed his heart instead of his head, they'd both end up hurt no matter his good intentions. Hurt he could handle. Another Buchanon disaster would be his demise. "What happened nine years ago was the product of a scared, angry kid. I'm not that boy anymore."

"Good. Then you can take me to a movie tonight like a grown man."

He snorted. "Somehow your logic confuses me."

"Do you know where my apartment is?"

She'd never told him where she lived, but he'd made it his business to find out. He was still rationalizing that one. "Sure. Why?"

"Pick me up at six forty-five, and we'll make the first showing at seven."

"What if I want to feed you dinner first?" Oh, man, he was wading into deep water.

Her face lit up. "Really?"

"I could use the break. Flo's been here every day, driving me nuts, running roughshod over both of us. She's even convinced Granny Pat to get out of the recliner and use the walker. And she slapped my hand for carrying Granny P. around like a baby." He patted dirt around the filled hole. "Flo claims I've been coddling my dear grandmother when she is perfectly capable of carting her own bones around."

Allison sat back on her heels and rubbed her forearm over her cheek. The action left a streak of dirt. "That's fabulous news."

"Yeah. I agree." Extra good news because he had a rodeo coming up he desperately needed to enter and wanted Granny Pat up and around on her own before then. "Did you know Flo danced in Vegas?"

"Everybody knows that. The Daily Journal did an article on her." She put her dirty hands above her head and wiggled her fingers. "She danced with those giant feathered headpiece things."

"Exactly. Last night, she decided I should learn one of her routines. I was pathetic." He put his hands on his thighs and pushed to a stand. "I don't plan to repeat that performance tonight."

Allison popped up from the ground like a jack-in-the-box. "You danced with her?"

"I wouldn't call it dancing exactly. More like a trout caught in a fish net. Lots of flopping around."

"You never danced with me. And you owe me, buddy boy." She slapped an open palm on his chest. "I demand equal time."

"I just happen to have on my dancing boots!"

He grabbed her hands and began to sashay around the yard in a silly two-step. Allison stumbled on the edge of the concrete driveway but he easily held her up and kept dancing, scooting his boots on the fading grass and dipping her back and forth. He smiled at her laughter, enjoying the comfortable pleasure of her company, the ease with which they'd fallen back into old patterns of friendship, and this new something else that filled his chest with hope and made him pray for the impossible.

The memory of the dance that never happened was a heartbeat away, a bit of spun sugar that melted in the heat of his shame.

Enough. He was letting her get under his skin again. Or maybe still.

He whirled her up onto the postage stamp porch and into the single lawn chair he'd put there himself for watching the sunsets.

"There you go. There's your dance. Paid in full."

Breathless, her cheeks flushed and pretty, her eyes sparkling, she shook her head. "Not good enough. I want music and a pretty dress and the whole banana. Come to Faith's wedding. Dance with me there for real."

The fun was spirited away on the heels of memory, a morning in November, a gunshot that should never have happened. He crouched on his toes in front of her. Taking her small hand in one of his rough ones, he said, "You're special to me, Allison."

"I know. And you're special to me. So come to the wedding. Show my brothers the man you've become. Show them you have nothing to hide."

"Are you still thinking about the vandalism?"

"Hiding out makes you look guilty."

He dropped her hand. "I don't hide."

"You avoid."

She had him there.

"Better than causing trouble."

"You have to forgive yourself, Jake," she said softly, her sweetness twisting him into a knot.

"I'm working on it." He pushed to a stand and turned his profile toward her, focusing across the street where a pair of puppies cavorted. Looking at Allison clouded his thinking.

She came up beside him, touched his arm with the tips of her fingers. Voice soft, she said, "Let go, Jake. Heal from this and move on."

Was it possible? Or was he fooling himself to think he'd ever come to that point? God had forgiven him, but he needed Quinn's forgiveness, too, before he could let go and forgive himself. And Quinn's forgiveness wasn't likely to happen in this lifetime.

He stepped off the porch and reached for the bucket of irises. "I told Flo I'd bring these over to her house."

"I have a lot more to say on this subject, Jake."

"Not today, okay?"

"Will you come to the wedding?"

"I'm thinking." He started toward his truck, parked on the cracked concrete drive. A clump of grass poked through the cracks.

"A cheap way to say no."

His shoulders lifted in a sigh. "I'm leaving now. Are you going or staying?"

"Going. With you." Allison shot him her ornery, Pollyanna grin that let him know she was coming along and there wasn't a thing he could do to stop her. As if he'd even try anymore. "How else can I tell you about all the work I've put in on this wedding? You need to see me in action to fully understand how *awesome* I am." She laughed and did a silly wiggle dance, letting him know she teased.

Jake rolled his eyes and groaned, but his mockery was all for show. Allison *was* awesome. The cute little cheerleader had become a special lady. So special that he'd rather be stomped by a bull than see her sad.

But as long as she was a Buchanon, hurt was about the only outcome he could imagine.

Chapter Seven

Allison was nervous.

"You're being silly." She stood in front of a full-length mirror in her bedroom—the one Brady had hung on the back of the closet door—and assessed her outfit for tonight's movie date with Jake. She'd changed four times and now wondered if the skirt and heels were overkill. She was going out with Jake, for crying out loud, not Brad Pitt.

Allison looked in the mirror and saw the truth. She'd rather go with Jake.

Was she out of her mind? How else could she explain this twisted need to be with a man who'd rejected her once before and even now made no promise other than to leave her again?

She fluffed the sides of her hair. Her first official date with the grown-up Jake.

Impulsive. Foolish. And maybe stubborn enough to do the opposite of her brothers' demands. They were wrong about Jake.

As Mom always said, she led with her heart.

Allison grabbed the tail of her hot pink sweater, about

to pull it over her head for one last change, when a knock sounded at the door. She yanked the sweater down again and peeked out the window at the black pickup in the duplex drive.

So much for changing her mind. She went to let him in. "You're early."

He propped a hand on each side of the door facing. Oh, my. He looked really good. "I'm hungry."

"So you're all about the food? Thanks a lot. You're great for a girl's ego."

Green eyes danced. He pushed off from the door to gently tug her hair. "So needy."

She punched his arm. "Am not." But she was. Needy for him to be more than a friend, more than a guy she used to know.

Inside her small entry, a mere section of tile inside the front door, Jake removed his hat, a nicer one than he usually wore. "I like your place."

"Buchanon built to my specs. Jayla lives in the other side."

"I figured you for a girl who'd live with her parents until she married."

His comment about marriage offered the perfect opening. "When are you going to tell me about the woman in Wyoming?"

He gave her his most innocent look before his gaze dropped to her feet. "Aren't you going to wear shoes?"

"You can tell me, Jake. I won't judge. Remember how we could always tell each other anything."

Their long held secret buzzed in her ear like a gnat. She swatted it away.

"Not worth talking about. She and I didn't work out."

Didn't work out. Was that what he thought about the

two of them? They hadn't worked out so he had chosen never to come home again?

"You look nice." He stepped close and his voice dipped low. "Smell good, too. Like flowers on the wind."

Allison's breath left her body. She reeled back in time to another voice, another man who'd said she smelled good.

But this was Jake. A man she'd trusted as much as her brothers. Mentally, she wrestled the other voice back inside her locked box and found safety in Jake Hamilton's green eyes.

Beneath the cowboy hat lived a good and godly man. Somehow she had to convince her brothers of that.

"Thanks for believing me," he said. "About the vandalism. I wouldn't."

"I know."

Expression soft as a cloud, he reached for a lock of her hair and gently tugged. For as far back as she could remember Jake had tugged her hair. Yet, tonight was different. The action held a deeper meaning, a new tenderness that resonated deep within her. His eyes questioned hers. He must wonder, as she did, where this subtle shift would take them—if it could, indeed, take them anywhere.

Warm and pleasant as a baby's breath, a tingle danced over Allison's skin. She didn't know what might happen between them if given the chance, but she believed in the impossible. God could mend the rift between her family and the only man who'd ever mattered.

Jake Hamilton held her heart in his cowboy hands— probably always had. As she'd trusted him that long ago night to hold her secret, she trusted Jake to hold her heart with care.

For the briefest, breath-held moment, she thought he might kiss her. Then, as if one of her brothers had tapped his shoulder, he dropped his hand and stepped back.

What would it take to push him over the edge, to break through the regret into the warm and tender center Allison knew existed? To a man who accepted responsibility for wrong, all the while holding a secret that could change attitudes?

Flummoxed and a little disappointed, she reverted to safer ground, a tease, a joke, meaningless chatter.

"Are you going to feed me or not?" Her voice was throaty and a little breathy, a dead giveaway for the emotion Jake didn't seem ready to handle.

One eyebrow flicked. "Persistent as a buffalo gnat."

His words teased but his eyes were serious. They'd walked into his emotional danger zone, and he didn't know what to do about it. Allison didn't either, though she wanted to go there and find out. Apparently, Jake didn't. At least, not yet.

She understood. He was the one carrying the baggage, not her.

Taking her tiny handbag from the end table by the love seat, Allison kept her tone light, though her heart rattled with hope and possibility. "Let's get this party started."

"Sounds good to me. I'm starved."

Jake guided her out into the faded day and used her key to lock the house. Against a bruised sky, the sun cast an orange glow along the horizon. There was little wind but the air had cooled into the November fifties, and Allison was glad for the heavy sweater she'd second-guessed.

"Chinese?" Jake asked. Safe topics. Food and weather.

"Perfect. Feed me now, feed me later." The old joke about Chinese food brought a smile and broke the lingering thread of emotion. He didn't want to discuss the feelings flowing between, couldn't face them, but he couldn't hide them either.

Side by side, they walked the short distance to his truck. When his hand lightly touched her back, Allison smiled.

Peanut oil. Jake recognized the smell inside the Chinese Buffet, a restaurant that hadn't existed when he and Allison were in high school. Peanut oil and egg rolls and sweet and sour sauce. His belly did a happy dance.

It was either the smells or the crazy jitterbug he'd had all afternoon about this date. And then at her house. Man. He'd had the crazy urge to kiss her. He knew better. Knew he had no business making moves on Allison when he had nothing to offer but trouble and the memory of his taillights heading out of town.

But she looked amazing tonight. Gorgeous. He hadn't seen her dressed up in years and he liked the change. A lot. In jeans and sweater she knocked his hat in the dirt. In a skirt and heels, she blew all the common sense out of his head.

He had a lot more praying to do. They were playing with a powerfully combustive fire, and every time he stomped it out, Allison provided fresh fuel. She cared for him. He knew that. Knew and shuddered, both with dread and pleasure. Nothing good could come of a romance with Allison Buchanon. Nothing.

Then why was he here? Why had he agreed to this movie date?

Sometimes a man was his own worst enemy.

With his hand against Allison's soft hot pink sweater, he guided her into the restaurant.

From behind a cash register next to the entrance a young Asian man nodded a greeting. Above his head a red-and-gold calendar written in Chinese hung next to a panda photo. The place was humming with customers, always a sign of good food.

The restaurant's one concession to the approaching holiday was a tissue paper turkey above the buffet.

Beneath stainless-steel hoods, heat rose off the buffet in waves that reminded Jake of Allison's hair. But then, everything reminded him of Allison.

"Buffet or menu?" Jake asked.

Her pretty face creased in an ornery, Allison grin that made his heart light. She did that to him. Made him want things he didn't deserve and couldn't have.

"Oh, buffet, definitely," she said, "so we can try all the mysterious stuff."

"Chopsticks?" Jake reached into the cylinder and pulled out two pair. Chinese symbols decorated the red-papered sides.

"Are you kidding? I don't want to starve."

With a snort, he stuck the chopsticks in his shirt pocket. "Coward."

Grinning, they took their place in a busy line, and once they'd piled their plates to overflow and were seated, he quietly asked a blessing.

When he opened his eyes, Allison was watching him.

"What?" He touched his chin. "Do I have hot mustard on my face already?"

Her eyes went soft. "I love hearing you pray."

His insides spasmed. No one had ever said that to him. "Thanks."

He reached for his napkin, and self-conscious, made a display of shaking out the white square. His faith filled him with a peace he didn't understand, but he wasn't a preacher, not even close. He wasn't even that great at being a Christian, and he didn't deserve admiration.

"Any luck discovering who vandalized the property?"

"Not yet." Allison dipped an egg roll into duck sauce.

"The fearsome foursome still pointing at me?" He couldn't explain how much that had hurt, especially when history gave them reason to suspect him, but he'd fretted about the situation all day.

He reached for a wonton and crunched. Cream cheese. Not his favorite but he wasn't complaining.

"Not to my knowledge." She held the egg roll an inch from her lips. Pretty lips. He remembered how soft they were. How they trembled when she cried and how they tasted when she kissed. Like coconut. He dropped his gaze and fiddled with a pair of chopsticks. He shouldn't remember things like that.

"Can we please not talk about my family for one evening?" she asked.

Not that he could stop thinking about them or the shooting for one minute with her sitting across the table. "They're a part of you, Allison. A big part. Being with you brings everything back."

She touched the top of his hand with her fingertips. "I'm sorry. We have to find a way to move past all that."

"Why?"

"You know why."

His heart clattered like horse hooves against his rib cage. Coward that he was, he didn't ask what she meant. He was afraid she'd tell him.

To step away from the danger zone, Jake held up

a bamboo skewer. "The teriyaki chicken is amazing. Want a bite?"

As soon as he asked, he wished he hadn't. Feeding her a bite of chicken was too personal, too romantic. Already, he could imagine the moment. Allison's lips close to his fingers. Watching her nibble the bite, her breath slipping like silk over his skin.

His insides shivered at the unwanted image.

This is the way he'd always feel if he let her close again. A mix of pleasure and pain fueled by a past that drew them together while simultaneously forcing them apart.

Thankfully oblivious to his random thoughts, Allison wiggled her index finger at something behind him. "Charity and the kids."

Great. Another Buchanon.

Jake twisted on the chair, wary, anxious. He didn't want Allison taking flack over a Chinese dinner. Her older sister came toward their table, and when Charity saw him, she smiled, an encouraging sign. Unlike their brothers, the Buchanon women had shown more pity than anger.

"Charity," he said, tipping his chin, though he couldn't bring himself to smile.

"Jake." Up close, he noted that her smile was strained and didn't reach her eyes. She wasn't glad to see him, but he understood that, too. He was trouble with a capital *T* as far as the Buchanons were concerned.

If Allison noticed the tension, she played dumb. As chipper as a Christmas elf, she tugged the children close to her chair. "These little dumplings are Ryan and Amber."

Amber dimpled up, a dark-eyed charmer already. Like her aunt, he thought.

"Are you a real cowboy?" she asked in that big-eyed innocent way of little kids.

"As real as they get, I guess."

"You ride bulls, don't ya?" Ryan, as blond as his mother but with freckles on his nose, looked vaguely familiar. Probably because of the photo Alison had shown him. He hoped that was all. Having a Buchanon kid mess with his bulls was the worst possible scenario.

"I try to."

"I'm going to ride bulls someday."

Jake's gut lurched.

"No, you are not." Charity scuffed his hair.

Expression mutinous, Ryan shrugged her off but didn't argue.

"Your mother's right, Ryan." Jake figured the least he could do was discourage the boy, just in case. "Bulls are dangerous animals. Even experienced guys like me get hurt."

"But you still ride."

The kid had him there. "Maybe I'm not too smart. A boy like you can go to college and make money without putting your life in danger."

"My dad has a dangerous job."

"Yeah, he does, for a lot better reason than money. I heard he's coming home soon."

"A little less than six months. A hundred and seventy-one days to be exact." Charity offered a genuine smile this time. "But who's counting." She put her hands on Ryan's shoulders. "Come on, kids. Let's find a table or we'll be late to the football game." She looked to Allison. "Are you going? The Bears and the Tigers are a big rivalry and this is the season ender. Tonight is win, lose or go home until next year."

Jake's teriyaki soured in his stomach. He'd seen the Beat the Bears and All the Way to State signs slathered on the store windows with white shoe polish.

"Movie night for us. You all have fun." Allison bent forward and smacked a kiss on Amber's cheek. "Love you, princess. You, too, Ryan, though I know you'll gag if I kiss you in public."

Ryan made a gagging noise with a hand to his throat.

Charity hooked an elbow around his neck and as she led him away, she looked at Allison and said, "Could I see you for a minute? Privately?" She jerked her chin slightly away from the table.

Allison glanced at Jake before laying her napkin aside. "Be right back."

Jake watched her sister lead her a few steps away, studied the intensity of the brief conversation before Allison returned to the table.

Retaking her seat, she avoided his gaze. He was no fool. Charity, the polite, didn't like seeing her sister with Jake Hamilton.

"What was that about?"

Allison dipped the end of a half-eaten egg roll into plum sauce and stirred it around.

"Nothing important."

"You were never a good liar. She was upset about me being here with you. Wasn't she?"

Allison's glance flicked to him and then to her egg-roll. "We agreed not to discuss my family tonight. Remember?"

He remembered. But his appetite was gone.

Trying to avoid Buchanons didn't work. They were everywhere.

* * *

The movie was a real snoozer and the theater all but empty thanks to the football game. Allison and Jake spent most of the ninety minutes imitating the bad dialogue and mocking the overly dramatic story line. The rest of the time, they fed each other popcorn they didn't want and tried to pretend that sitting together in the dark theater wasn't a bit romantic.

The trouble was, the only other couple in the theater sat down front and used their ninety minutes as a make-out session. Once Jake murmured, "Get a room, Romeo," and set Allison off into a fit of muffled giggles. She laughed even harder when Jake put his hand over her mouth and in a stage whisper said, "Shh. Be quiet. Those people are trying to watch the movie."

Later, when they left the theater, Jake looped an arm around her shoulders and said, "That's the best show I've seen in a long time. Thanks for making me go."

"Are you crazy? It was terrible."

"I'm talking about the show down front, not the movie." He bumped her with his side and grinned.

Her belly did a flip-flop. "I had fun."

"Me, too."

Allison was relieved to hear it. The brief and terse exchange with Charity could have ruined the evening. Afterward, Jake had gone quiet and moody for a while.

Thankfully, the awful movie and ridiculous public display of affection down front had changed the mood to light and easy.

They sauntered down the sidewalk in front of the theater past the darkened storefronts. Other than a couple of convenience stores off First Street, Gabriel's Crossing closed up at night. A few cars puttered by including the local police car making rounds. Allison lifted her hand and waved. Jerry was a good friend of Dawson's which made him a friend of every Buchanon. The officer waved back and gave a soft honk.

Allison stopped in front of the Texas Rose Boutique, a shop of girly things and flowers owned by one of her friends, but then everyone was a friend in Gabriel's Crossing. Almost everyone.

In front of a snowy background, two flocked trees filled one corner of the show window. In the other, Angela had stacks of gaily-wrapped gifts, each with a product from the shop on top. Purses, perfume, scarves.

"The stores are already decorating for Christmas."

"Too early. We haven't had Thanksgiving yet."

"It's this way every year. Christmas crowding out Thanksgiving when we all have so much to be thankful for," she said. "What are you and Miss Pat planning for Thanksgiving?"

They stood side by side, peering into the pretty display. With his arm still casually slung across her shoulder, she could feel his warmth through his jacket. "No plans yet."

She wanted to invite him to the Buchanon feast. Instead, she said, "Maybe I could come over and help you cook."

He chuffed. "Help me? You'd have to cook everything except mashed potatoes. I've got those down."

She bumped his side. "Thanks to me. So what do you say? Thanksgiving night? I'll come over."

"What about your family dinner?"

"At noon. Mom's a stickler. Stuff your faces before you watch the Cowboys and the Lions."

Their breath made fog circles on the windowpane while Allison awaited his reply.

"I thought you'd jump at my offer."

He turned his face toward hers. "Can I get back to you on that?"

A frisson of disappointment dampened her mood. "Sure. No big deal."

The invitation, like Faith's wedding, was a very big deal. She wanted to spend Thanksgiving with him. But the ball was in his court.

They started on down the darkened sidewalk, pausing often to peek inside a window or chuckle at some outrageous item on display.

As they turned the corner, heading toward the parked truck, a yellow-white streetlight washed the sidewalk in shiny shadows. Hers and Jake's stretched out like dark clowns on stilts. In shadow was the only time she looked tall, a sight that never failed to amuse her.

Jake's hand slipped from her shoulder. Allison considered reaching for his hand beneath the cover of darkness, but she didn't. Jake had to find his own way in this relationship, as she had.

The damp scent rising from the distant Red River mingled with the chill of autumn. A half-dozen blocks south, the high school marching band played the Tigers' fight song, and Allison was almost certain she smelled grilled hot dogs.

She turned her head toward the music and the tall football lights visible from First Street.

Beside her, Jake was silent. The town's mania for high school football had ostracized him as a teen. No wonder he avoided conversation about the sport he'd once played with as much passion as her brothers.

He stared in that direction, his profile serious.

Feeling tender and sorry, she slipped her hand into his, a touch of comfort. When he glanced at her, questioning, she squeezed his fingers. His skin was rough, his grip strong, as he squeezed back. No words were needed.

Her heels tapped quietly on the bricks as they crossed the street.

Once inside the truck, Allison clicked on the CD player. The mood had shifted in that short walk from movie to vehicle. She couldn't quite put her finger on the emotion, but the feelings hovered in the warm cab and struck them both silent. Sadness, longing, regret, but something else, too.

With the heater at her feet and the CD filling in for conversation, they rode the few blocks to her apartment.

One hand on the door lever, Allison prepared to hop out with a cheery wave and a hearty thanks, but Jake killed the engine and got out, coming around to her door.

The step up into the cab was high for anyone but especially someone vertically challenged like Allison. Jake took her elbow and she jumped to the ground with a short laugh.

The corner streetlight cast pale light on her small front lawn, enough to maneuver to the doorway.

"I can walk to the door by myself."

"I know." But he walked her there anyway. His boots made soft padding sounds while her heels stabbed holes in the ground. Heels for a movie. What had she been thinking?

"Well," she said, "thank you for the fantastic Chinese and a stellar film."

She expected him to make some remark about being hungry again or about the awful movie, but he didn't.

Instead, he gazed down at her in the darkness, his face in shadowy relief, quiet again.

"What are you thinking about?" She didn't know why she bothered to ask. No male she'd ever known wanted to answer that question.

"You're something."

"So I've been told, though not in quite that tone."

His lips curved, and she was sure he moved a little closer though how he could get any closer on the small square slab of concrete porch seemed impossible.

"I wish—"

She touched his mouth with her fingertips. "No wishes. Reality is better."

He captured her fingers and pulled them away from his warm mouth, holding them against his chest. He stared, head bent, sheltering her with the brim of his hat. He was close enough that she felt his warm breath against her face. Longing rose in her throat, trapped there by a past they couldn't remedy.

His cowboy-rough fingertips stroked her cheek. His face moved closer. But then he kissed her on the forehead and stepped away.

"Night, Allison."

Before Allison could regain her composure and kick him in the shin, he stepped off the porch and strode away, leaving her in the dark.

Chapter Eight

Jake kicked himself all the way home and for the next couple of days, but no matter how much self-recrimination he heaped upon his Stetson, Allison was like a sweet perfume he couldn't wash off his shirt. Regardless of what he was doing, he thought about her.

As if that wasn't making him completely insane, every evening she popped in to see Granny Pat. And him. And every evening, he fought like a tiger to keep his distance. Still, she lingered, impressing him with her ability to make chicken dumplings that Granny Pat craved or convincing him to watch a sappy Hallmark movie that left him with a hot air balloon in his chest.

Matters got worse on Friday when he ducked into the drugstore for Granny Pat's prescription refill only to run into Allison's best friend. Faith, the long of it, was loaded down with sunscreen, lotions, cosmetics and a lot of other girly stuff.

"For Saint Thomas," she'd told Jake with a happy smile, a statement that led directly to the wedding and an effort to extract a promise that Jake would be there. He'd stuttered around and left the store without a com-

mitment but the date and time were imprinted behind
his eyeballs like a scene from a movie—a cross between
Cinderella and a horror flick. Allison would be the beautiful princess. Her brothers would inflict the horror. And
Jake Hamilton would be the bad guy who ruined the entire affair for everyone.

Better to skip the ordeal.

But when the Saturday of the wedding rolled around,
he was restless as a red ant.

"What is wrong with you, Jacob?" Granny Pat sat in
her chair knitting like a mad woman. The *click-clack* of
needles was driving him crazy.

"Nothing."

Granny Pat made a huffing noise. "Who was that on
the phone? Your woman in Wyoming?"

He scowled. "Bill Brown in Denton. We travel together some."

"Guess he wants to know when you're getting back
in the game?"

"I'm not worried about it." No use worrying at this
point. The die was cast. He was basically broke. "The
fall rodeos are winding down."

"What *are* you worried about? Allison Buchanon and
her big, burly brothers?"

He gave her a cool look. "Some things are better left
alone, Granny P."

"Umm-hmm. Tell that to Allison." *Click-clack. Click-
clack. Click-clack.* The needle speed increased. If she
could move the rest of her as fast as she moved those
needles, she'd be in the Olympics. Suddenly, the click-
clacking stopped. She rested the wad of knitting in her
lap. "Your grandpa wants you to know something, son."

Grandpa again.

"Sometimes a man has to step up to the plate and be a man even when he isn't sure."

"What's that supposed to mean?"

She picked up the knitting again. "Beats me. Ask Ralph. He said it."

Jake barked a short laugh. "I need to go somewhere." Anywhere.

"That's what Ralph said. Tell the boy to go on. Things can't get much worse and sometimes they get better."

Was she talking about the wedding? Ralph or not, she was right. Things couldn't get much worse with the Buchanons. So what if he showed up at the wedding long enough to give Allison a dance he'd owed her since high school and to offer his congratulations to the happy couple? What's the worst thing that could happen?

At that point, he got stuck. The worst thing would be ruining Faith's wedding.

But the Buchanons wouldn't do that. Would they? They loved Faith, and they loved their sister. Allison had thrown her heart and passion into planning a perfect day for her best friend. The brothers might seethe but they wouldn't cause a scene.

He bent to kiss his grandmother on the papery cheek. "Is Flo coming over?"

"I don't need a babysitter, Jacob. As much as I don't like toddling around on this walker like an old lady, I can if I have to. Go to the wedding. Take that gift on my dresser."

"You bought a gift?"

"Faith sent me an invitation so I asked Maggie Thompson to bring something over from her shop." Granny's face went nostalgic. "I remember when Faith used to ride her bike up here and I'd give her homemade cookies and let her talk about her daddy. That was after the divorce when she was hurting bad. Her mama was, too, but she was so busy trying to make a living for the two of them and hang on to her house. I know a little about that kind of worry. Bless her heart."

"I never knew we were in danger of losing our property."

"We've had some bumps in the road, but Ralph thinks something will turn up."

Jake was playing mental gymnastics. "Are we talking about then or now?"

Her needles paused. "Both. But don't worry. I'll handle Ned Butterman and his bank."

With a sick feeling, Jake asked, "You mortgaged the house?"

She waved a hand. "A while back. Before that silly fall. I needed a little cash. You were riding in Vegas and I wanted to be there."

"Vegas was four years ago. And I paid your way. I bought the tickets."

Granny Pat gave him the look of idiocy. "Jacob, I was in Vegas. I had to try my luck."

Jake's head fell back. He stared up at the hand-plastered ceiling. A thin crack ran from one corner to the light fixture. "You mortgaged the house for gambling money? Why didn't you tell me? This house means everything to you. That's the reason I brought you home!"

And the reason he'd been willing to deal with the Buchanons as long as necessary to see her well again.

"That's why I wanted to come home. I wanted to be here as long as I can. Before—" she sniffed "—well, you know."

"This is not happening." He rammed a hand across the top of his head. "I will not let you lose this house."

"You're a dear, good boy, but money doesn't grow on trees."

True. His money grew on grass. He swallowed thickly. His one asset was his bulls.

"How bad is it?" he asked grimly.

"I told you not to fret."

"How bad, Granny Pat?"

At his harsh tone, she looked him in the eye. "I have until after the first of the year to come up with the money. Ned doesn't foreclose during the holidays, which I think is mighty nice of him."

Foreclosure. Lord, help them both. "Exactly how do you think you can come up with that kind of money?"

"I buy lottery tickets every week."

Jake groaned. "Granny Pat!"

She rolled her eyes. "I'm joking. I learned my lesson on gambling. The truth is I don't know where I'll find the money." Her bottom lip trembled. "I don't want to go to the nursing home."

His grandmother's frightened, vulnerable expression jabbed at him. Jake took up her hairbrush and ran the bristles gently through her cloud of white hair. "You're not going to a nursing home." No matter what he had to do. "If worse comes to worse, you'll live with me."

"Darling boy, think on that. You're on the road most of the time. Besides, I don't want to leave Gabriel's Crossing. We're the last of the Hamiltons. We started this town, and this is where I plan to end."

The feathery wisps of white hair sifted through his fingers. *Aw, Granny.* Why hadn't she told him?

More than ever, he needed to work, but ranching and rodeo was all he knew. Manny would hire him in a heartbeat but that would lock him into Gabriel's Crossing.

All he had left were his bulls.

Not his bulls. Anything but that.

Granny Pat reached up and placed a white, spotted hand on his, stopping the motion of the brush. "You go on to Faith's wedding. Standing there worrying won't fix a thing."

"I'm not going." He put the brush on the end table.

"Yes, you are. Faith Evans is our friend, sweet as syrup, and never once turned her back or judged you when Quinn got hurt. The least you can do is put on your Sunday best and honor her wedding day."

Her words struck Jake like a cold rain in the face. He was as self-focused as a mule. This wedding wasn't about him. It wasn't even about Allison, though she played a big part in the day. Today was for Faith and her friends and family. "Tell you what. I'll go to the wedding if you'll go with me."

She put a hand to her cheek, her eyes wide. "Oh, Jacob, I don't know. Look at me."

"No excuses. You want to, and we owe it to Faith."

Granny tossed her skein of yarn into a basket at her side. "Well, I'm sick and tired of this house, I tell you for sure. I'd like nothing better today than to see Faith married to her Prince Charming."

"Then you're going." And so was he. Faith was a friend and a longtime neighbor, and the Hamiltons didn't ignore something as important as a friend's wedding. Even if Ned Butterman and all the Buchanons in Texas showed up.

Allison was halfway down the aisle of Jesus Our Savior Church when she saw him. Pachelbel's "Canon in D" faded though she managed to keep moving, past the swags of white tulle and kissing pomanders festooning the aisles in Thanksgiving colors.

Jake had come. She kept her eyes forward on the groom and his attendants, the flower girls and ring bearers, but her whole being wanted to do a happy dance down the aisle.

Nothing like making a fool of yourself at your best friend's wedding.

Her chiffon formal stirred around her heels in a swishing sound. She suddenly felt like a princess.

After taking her place across from the best man, Allison watched the bridesmaids file in exactly the way she'd rehearsed them. Then the organist launched into Wagner's "Here Comes the Bride," and the guests rose. Cameras flashed and the guests' collective sigh filled Allison's heart with pride and her eyes with tears. An elegantly beautiful Faith floated down the aisle of her childhood church on the arm of her grandfather, the only man in her life until now. Until Derrick.

Allison glanced toward the groom. Though he nervously swallowed, his eyes blazed with love for his bride. He smiled and Faith's answering radiance was all the pay Allison would ever want for coordinating this perfect day for them.

Someday she wanted a wedding like this with a groom who looked at her with the future in his eyes. A man and woman so in love that they saw only each other in this crowd of well-wishers.

Love was a beautiful gift that bathed the small church in an aura of light and hope. She wanted that with all her heart.

Teary and joyful, Allison glanced toward Jake again. She hadn't meant to, but her heart squeezed at the endearing sight of the cowboy in jeans and brown sport coat standing behind his grandmother's wheelchair. He'd brought Miss Pat.

Expression serious, his focus remained on the bride and groom. As hers should be.

He'd come. She couldn't get that thought out of her head. In spite of everything, he'd come.

She looked toward the pew filled with Buchanons. Mom and Jayla dabbed at their eyes while Charity whispered something to a restless Amber. The Buchanon men filled the rest of the pew like the front line of the Dallas Cowboys. Gorgeous, powerful, wonderful men with heads as hard as bricks.

They had better behave themselves.

Jake remembered why he didn't like weddings. They made him feel things he didn't want to think about. Bulls he understood. Rodeos, too. But weddings and relationships baffled him, filled his chest with a strange heat, like heartburn to the max.

He'd known Allison would look pretty, but he hadn't expected all the air to rush out of him like a deflated balloon. In a long dress the color of mint ice cream with her dark hair swept up on the side and held by a golden-orange flower, she'd knocked his eyes out. But then, the old guilt had returned with a sledgehammer to the brain, reminding him of the party he'd missed, of the promised dance he'd failed to deliver.

Failures. So many, and now he'd failed Granny Pat by not realizing sooner that the once strong independent woman needed his help in more ways than one. He didn't know what he was going to do about the mortgage. The worry rolled round and round in his brain and had no answer. For today he shelved the mortgage along with the many other problems and failures. Gabriel's Crossing made him feel like the worst failure on earth. No wonder he had stayed away.

When the emotional ceremony ended and guests moved like one body into the reception hall, he found a quiet corner to park Granny Pat's chair and make himself scarce. If the Buchanons had noticed him, none had reacted. So far. Might as well not press his luck since he was batting zero lately.

The reception hall was decked out like a New England foliage tour. Rusts and golds, oranges and yellows mingled with the mint green. In another rush of color, the attendants and the bride and groom came through the double doors to cheers and applause.

"Isn't she the prettiest thing?" Granny Pat said when Faith and her groom stepped behind a table to cut the three-tiered cake.

"Can't argue with that," Jake said, but he turned his gaze toward Allison as she crossed the room to hug her best friend. She looked as happy as the bride, a thought that generated mental pictures of Allison in a white gown standing beneath a lighted arch with candles flickering. She was the marrying kind of girl, and he questioned the manhood of every male in Gabriel's Crossing for not snatching her up. If she was married, he could stop thinking about her. He'd have to.

Cameras clicked and flashed, and a videographer panned the room before focusing on the fancy-looking cake table. Once the cake was cut, the newlyweds moved out onto the dance floor for the first dance. A romantic "Can't Help Falling in Love" swept them around the room, their eyes locked on each other in a way that kept the rest of the world out. Jake got that hot air balloon feeling in his chest again.

Granny Pat tapped his hand. "Get us some punch, Jacob. And some of those appetizers."

Relieved to have something to do, he left his grandmother talking to the postmistress and made his way toward the nearest table.

"Punch or mulled cider?" a smiling young lady asked, indicating a tiny glass cup that couldn't contain more than a swallow of liquid.

"One of each," he said to the woman who, like all the others manning the cake and drinks and appetizers, wore autumn colors. Jake gestured toward the corner. "One for my grandmother."

"Oh, that is so thoughtful. You brought your grandma."

"She brought me," he said ruefully.

The woman smiled. "You're Jake, aren't you?"

"That's right. You look familiar."

Her smile widened. "I should. We lived across the street from you when I was in grade school."

He pointed at her. "You're Maddie?"

She laughed. "I might have changed a little."

A little was a major understatement. She'd been around eight years old with big teeth and skinned knees. "You were about this high when you moved away."

"Now I've moved back, and so have you."

"Just visiting."

She tilted her head with a smile. "Too bad. But maybe we can dance later?"

The question caught him off guard. Was little Maddie coming on to him? "I'm not much of a dancer, but thanks for asking."

He would only dance once, and only with Allison.

Before the conversation could go somewhere uncomfortable, Jake took the miniature cups and went for the appetizers. He approached the table from one direction in time to see Quinn Buchanon approach from the other. Their eyes connected. Quinn's narrowed into a glare. His chiseled jaw hardened.

Jake got that sinking feeling, as if he'd been tossed over the head of a rank bull. He had plenty of reason to be at this wedding, but for Faith's sake, he wanted no trouble.

The sandy blond Quinn looked fit and strong in a black suit that hid his weaker arm. But Jake knew the damage was there. With a tight chin dip, he pivoted away from the appetizers and back to his grandmother on the periphery of the dance floor behind the food tables.

He handed her the punch.

"Where's my snack?" She sipped at the cup.

"Later."

One white eyebrow lifted. "Hamiltons don't wimp out."

He didn't ask her meaning. Granny Pat didn't miss much of anything.

By now, other pairs had moved onto the dance floor. "Are you ready to go yet?"

"No, I am not. After being stuck in that prison for months, I'm ready to kick up my heels." She tilted her face toward him. "If I don't starve to death first."

"You'll get your plate of food."

"And cake, too. Lots of icing with some of those pillowy mint things." She patted his hand where he held the wheelchair. "Go on, now. Remember what your grandpa said. Be a man."

"Were you always a troublemaker?"

She shot him an ornery grin as he once more wove his way through the people. His elbow bumped Allison's nephew, who looked miserable in a snazzy tux with his hair slicked to one side. Jake empathized. No eleven-year-old boy wanted to be trussed up like a penguin.

"Hi, Jake."

Surprised that the kid remembered his name, Jake paused. "Ryan, right? Nice duds."

Ryan tugged at his tie. "Mom made me wear this. I'm choking to death."

"I feel your pain."

"Bull riders don't have to dress up if they don't want to."

"Not much call for fancy clothes in the rodeo."

"Yeah, another good reason to ride bulls."

Jake saw an opportunity and took it. "Was that you the other day at Manny Morales's ranch?"

Ryan's eyes widened. "When?"

"Look, Ryan, if that was you, stay clear of those bulls. You can get hurt."

The boy's expression closed up. "I don't know what you're talking about. I gotta go."

With an inward sigh, Jake snagged a couple of plates and piled them high with food, paying little attention to his selections. Maybe he was wrong. Maybe Ryan wasn't the right kid.

A few old pals spotted him and stopped to talk, a nice moment that elevated his mood and made him glad he'd come. Les and Thad invited him to a fishing tourney. Some folks in Gabriel's Crossing had apparently forgotten his ugly past.

By the time he reached his grandmother again, he decided he'd made the right decision by attending the wedding. Things were going pretty well. Even the encounter with Quinn.

Granny Pat took the plate of food and balanced the fancy white china on her lap. "I could use more punch."

"I'm not making another trip, Granny. If you want food, we have a freezer full of casseroles."

She pointed a crooked index finger toward the floor. "That boy sure is cozy with your woman."

"I don't have a wo—" The word left his brain. The best man, a lean blond with a big smile and perfect teeth, held Allison in his arms. Taller than her by several inches, the blond guy held her in the usual way, nothing suggestive, but the look in his eyes and the smile on Allison's face started a slow burn in Jake's gut.

His grip tightened on his plate. Even though he thought Allison was the marrying kind of girl, he didn't want to watch her dance with some other guy. Yet, he couldn't take his eyes off them either. Allison's dress floated around her like a puff of mint smoke, a cotton candy fairy tale. The man said something and she laughed. Jake couldn't hear her, but he saw the flash of teeth and the cute way she tipped her chin up and squinted her brown eyes.

His gut clenched into a hard knot.

Mr. Best Man tightened his hold on Allison's waist.

Jake set his untouched plate of food aside.

When the other man pulled Allison's hand against his chest, Jake had seen enough. He owed her a dance. Time to pay up.

He was on the dance floor before his brain had time to think things through. He tapped Best Man on the shoulder. "I'm cutting in."

Best Man looked to Allison who nodded. "We'll dance later, Brian. Okay?"

Jake's back teeth ground together. Brian needed to stick his head in the punch bowl.

"Count on it." The tuxedoed blond gave Allison another of his dazzling smiles and evaporated from sight. Jake imagined him with green punch dripping down his face.

Allison tipped her head to one side and held out her arms. "It's about time."

Jake swept her into the dance, determined to maintain a respectable distance, to get this long-promised dance out of the way and hit the road. At least that's what he told himself. This dance was her idea. He hadn't even wanted to come.

"You look beautiful." He didn't know where the words came from. He hadn't meant to say them.

She beamed, and the smile she gave him radiated far more wattage than the one she'd given Brian. "My dress for the graduation dance was pink."

"I didn't want to stand you up that night."

"I know."

He doubted if she knew the full story but it was like Allison to simply forgive him and move on, to give him the benefit of the doubt. He wished her brothers had the same attitude.

"I thought leaving was the best thing I could do under the circumstances." He'd been young and heartbroken, and the months of finishing high school with the whole town mourning the loss of Quinn's golden arm had taken a terrible toll on his soul. He'd been shunned, beaten up and hated. Rodeo provided a much-needed escape, and he'd wimped out the night of the graduation dance to avoid more conflict. "I took the coward's way out."

"Life wasn't easy for you back then."

No, but life hadn't been easy for Quinn either. Or for any of the Buchanons. "Quinn looks good."

"Stop worrying about him."

Like that would ever happen.

He wrapped his hand around Allison's small fingers and pulled them against his heart. If blond Brian could do that, so could he. "You and me. We would never have worked out."

She gave him a long, sad look, and then laid her head on his shoulder. Her dark hair tickled the side of his neck, and he caught a whiff of the flowers in her hair… and cake icing, sweet and delicious.

His heart gave one giant *kaboom*.

Lord, help him. He'd fooled himself to think he could ever forget his little champion, his best cheerleader, this special girl who'd grown into an incredible woman.

He swirled her around the floor, as conflicted as he'd ever been and painfully aware that he was not doing her a favor.

One dance. One dance, and he was out of here.

His hand tightened on her waist. He wasn't about to pull her closer though the man in him wanted to.

She was such a tiny woman. Holding her made him feel manly and strong.

Couples bumped against them but Jake paid them no mind. He was too busy trying to keep his thoughts in order. From the dais, a band played "The Way You Look Tonight."

Beautiful. She looked so beautiful.

He kept telling himself he'd be glad when the song ended, but he was lying.

Someone tapped him on the shoulder. "Taking over, pal. I think you need to leave."

Allison raised her head. "Sawyer, go away."

Quinn appeared beside his brother. "Dance with Sawyer, little sister."

"I am dancing. Get lost."

But Jake loosened his hold and stepped back from her. He'd promised no trouble and he was keeping that promise. "Thanks for the dance, Allison."

"But—"

Sawyer grabbed Allison and spun her away, though he could hear her protesting before she disappeared in a swirl of mint green into the sea of wedding guests.

Jake's fist tightened. "I'm getting tired of your attitude, Quinn."

"Want to take it outside? Or are you afraid to hit a cripple?"

Karen Buchanon appeared next to her son. Her voice was low and conversational but held enough steel to get Quinn's attention. "Cool it, right now. This is Faith's wedding and you big lugs are not going to create a scene. You hear me?"

She shot her son a smile that, to the onlooker, appeared warm, but Jake saw the warning. Apparently, so did Quinn. He eased back, but his glare remained on Jake.

Everything in Jake wanted to resist. But he glanced at Quinn's right arm and then into Karen's concerned face and made his decision.

"Don't worry, Mrs. B. I won't cause a problem. I'm leaving."

She put long-nailed fingers on his elbow. "Thank you, Jake. Some things are for the best."

He'd been telling Allison that for weeks.

As he walked away from the dance floor and back to Granny P., he searched the hall for a small brunette in foamy green. He didn't see her. For the best, like Karen said. A man didn't start something he couldn't finish.

But Jake was tired of backing down, tired of turning the other cheek, tired of looking like a coward. Was this what it meant to be a Christian? Always slinking away with his tail tucked between his legs?

He took hold of Granny Pat's wheelchair and, with his jaw tight enough to crack iron, rolled her out into the evening.

Allison put on a happy face for the remainder of the reception but inside she seethed. After Faith and Derrick rushed out of the building amid a hail of birdseed and bubbles and into a waiting limo, she let the repressed tears slide down her cheeks. Everyone thought she was crying with happiness for her best friend. She was. But she was also crying for the incomplete dance, for the idiots she called brothers, and for Jake.

She slashed at the tears with the back of her hand. Someone offered a hankie. Through blurry eyes, she saw Brady.

"You're a jerk," she said.

"What did I do?"

"You know."

"That narrows it down." He put his powerful arms around her in a brotherly hug and lifted her off the floor like a child. "The wedding turned out great."

She sniffed. "Thanks."

He put her down. "I'm proud of you, sis."

"Then stay out of my life."

His blue eyes regarded her with something akin to sympathy. "So, that's what this is all about?"

"You had no right."

He held up both palms in surrender. "I didn't."

"You would have."

"True." He snagged a bottle of bubbles from a linen-covered table and blew through the wand. Iridescent bubbles glinted beneath the lights, now on in full power. "We're all heading over to Mom and Dad's later. The twins are bringing Bailey and Kristin. You coming?"

The twins always had girls on their arms. Usually a different one each time. "I have to finish up here."

"I could help out. Keep you company."

Allison looked at her brother with a mix of frustration and adoration. Brady, the big brother who'd carried her piggyback across mud puddles and up hills. The brother who'd taught her to ride a bike and to count by fives. He'd always been there for her. Until Jake.

Blood is thicker than water. The Buchanon way. Buchanons stick together.

Thoughts of Jake and their half dance crowded in.

But Jake had walked away and left her. Again.

Chapter Nine

Days later, Jake couldn't stop worrying about the wedding fiasco. He was glad he hadn't caused a scene but the Buchanons' attitude rankled him no end. He was a man, no longer a teenage kid they could kick to the curb. Worse, he couldn't get Allison and their slow dance out of his memory. Her soft skin. Her flippy, flower-scented hair. Her sparkly laugh that hit him right in the center of his chest.

With Allison, he lost his ability to reason. He didn't know what to do.

The longer he remained in Gabriel's Crossing, the more of a problem she would become. But he couldn't leave either. Granny had him in a serious bind, and he would not let her lose the house. No matter what he had to do. Though after speaking to the banker, he had come away more concerned than ever.

Maybe this was God's way of getting him to pray more. For sure, he'd done plenty of talking to the Lord since the moment he'd come home to Gabriel's Crossing. Take the issue with Quinn and the Buchanons. If God intended him to suffer for his wrongs, He was succeeding.

Granny, the house, Quinn and Allison. All of them kept him way more humble than he'd ever thought necessary.

If he wasn't with Allison, he missed her. Knowing she was in the same town, only a few blocks away, had him driving by her apartment like some lovesick cowboy even when he knew she was at work.

But he didn't love her. Couldn't. She deserved a man who wouldn't come between her and the family she adored. A man who could live in her town with his head held high, a man she and others respected, a man who wasn't growing poorer by the minute.

From the living room, he heard his grandmother's laughter, a good sound. She was getting better and that was worth everything and anything he had to endure.

Florence came over nearly every day to tease and cajole his grandmother onto her feet. She offered to teach Granny Pat to dance and mentioned a gig on *Dancing with the Stars*. Between Flo and Allison, his grandmother was bound to get better.

"Don't they hire celebrities for the TV show?" Jake asked as he sauntered into the living room, sipping a glass of orange juice.

Flo waved away his concerns. "I still have contacts in the business."

"I talked to Ralph about this crazy idea of yours, Flo," Granny said. "He says you're full of beans."

Flo laughed her bawdy laugh and pushed at her mile-high platinum-blond hair. Jake could imagine her dancing with fruit on her head and a train of feathers swishing behind her high heels, those long legs prancing around a stage with other over-the-top women. Granny's age, Flo's love of cosmetic surgery put her twenty years younger. He couldn't imagine Flo being anyone's granny.

"Maybe I am, but if not Hollywood, we'll head to Mexico. A cruise in the sun is what you need."

"I've always wanted to go on a cruise."

"Then, get your skinny self out of that chair." Flo whipped the throw from Granny's lap. "Quit acting like an old lady. You told me yourself the docs saw no reason why you weren't on your feet."

"Ralph and I had other things to take care of."

"Such as?"

"We'll talk later." Granny Pat cut a glance toward Jake who was folding a basket of towels on the couch. "Jacob, don't you have somewhere to go? I tell you, Flo, the boy has no social life. We fixed him up with that bouncy little Allison and he refuses to take the bait."

Jake's fingers tightened on his condensing glass. That bouncy little Allison. "Who fixed me up?"

"Ralph and me. I told you about that, but Ralph says we'll need dynamite to get you moving."

"Tell Ralph I have a life and I have a career that keeps me busy." He couldn't believe he'd responded to a figment of his grandmother's imagination. Again. "But you come first. If you want me out of your hair, you'll get well."

"She's going to dance, I tell you." Flo did a little soft-shoe with hands out to her sides. She was still good.

"You must have been something in your day."

She chucked him under the chin with a wink. "Still am, buddy boy. Now, if you have somewhere else to go, I'll be here all afternoon. Pat and I are going to plan a cruise, finish knitting that pile of yarn and talk about men. You don't want to be here for that."

He recognized a brush-off when he got one. "I'm headed out to Manny's to ride some practice bulls anyway." He downed the juice and clinked the glass on the coffee table. "I have my cell. Call if you need anything."

Granny Pat flapped her fingers at him. "We'll be fine. Don't stay out too late."

Smiling at a command he hadn't heard in years, he put on his hat and headed out the door.

He had more in mind than riding bulls today, but Granny didn't need to know his decision yet. He would ask Manny for a job on the ranch to supplement the weekend rodeos. If that meant sticking around Gabriel's Crossing a while longer, he would.

Somehow he'd keep Allison and her family out of the picture. Once the Hamilton house debt was resolved, he could kiss Gabriel's Crossing goodbye. Maybe by spring.

At the Double M Ranch, he'd parked and started toward the barn when Paulina's voice turned him around. She came out the back door and hurried toward him, urgency in her movements.

He went on alert. Something was wrong.

"Jake," she cried. "I try to call you. Where you been?"

He pulled out his cell and saw two missed calls. How did that happen? "What's wrong?"

"Manny. The big white bull pinned him."

Adrenaline jacked into Jake's bloodstream. The big white bull. Mountain Man. The image of an enormous set of horns and over a ton of muscle and mean sprang to mind. He broke into a lope, meeting her halfway. "Is he all right? Where is he?"

"His leg. He needs the doctor, but he is so stubborn."

Jake was through the back door and into the kitchen before she could say anything more. His mentor and friend sprawled on a kitchen chair, his head on the table, and one badly swollen leg stretched out in front of him.

His jeans were ripped and dirty. Sweat dampened his plaid shirt. His winter-gray Resistol lay discarded on the table next to his elbow.

"Manny, let's get you to the E.R. Let the doc check this out." Jake went to his knee next to the injured leg.

Manny raised his head. Sweat beaded his face. "*No es nada.* It's nothing."

"Better get that boot off while we can. You're looking pale, friend."

A hint of the Mexican's humor glinted in his eyes. "No one ever said that about me before."

Jake reached for the heel of Manny's boot. "This is coming off before your leg swells too much. Brace yourself. It's gonna hurt."

Paulina put her capable hands on the lower leg while Manny gripped his knee. "He is a stubborn man. That bull is no good for nothing."

The foot had already begun to swell but Jake carefully slipped off the boot. "Mountain Man got you good. You're lucky not to be in worse shape."

Manny didn't reply. He sat with shoulders hunched, holding his knee with both hands.

Pauline moved to his side and placed shaky fingers on her husband's shoulder. "You scare me this time, Immanuel. I could not close the chute fast enough."

Manny patted her hand. "Not your fault. The latch sticks."

"I'll pull my truck up to the back door." Jake stood. "Think you can hobble along with one of us on each side?"

Manny, jaw tight with pain, nodded. "I will try. The other leg is not so good either. The bull, he stepped on my ankle. I am not so fast anymore."

"We'll figure it out, but you're going to the E.R., either in my truck or an ambulance."

"I will get in the truck. No ambulance."

After a few harried tries and more groans than Jake had ever heard come from his old friend, Manny was loaded in the bed of the pickup along with a pillow and a quilt. The cab rose too high, so a windy ride in the back with Paulina at his side was the best they could do.

Driving more carefully than he had the day of his driver's exam, Jake grimaced over every bump and rut on the way to Gabriel's Crossing Hospital. Upon arrival, the medical team assisted Manny into a wheelchair and wheeled him inside the hometown facility.

Small and staffed by familiar locals, the hospital lacked the equipment of larger towns but did its best to serve the community with compassionate care. He'd learned of their kindness the hard way when he'd driven Quinn, bleeding and shocky, to the E.R. that long ago November day.

He swallowed down the memory and focused on the inside of the hospital. It hadn't changed much. Now, as then, shiny silver tinsel and multicolored lights swooped around the walls, a cheery contrast to a serious place. No one came here to celebrate Christmas.

Paulina hurried alongside her husband, hands fluttering in distress, speaking in rapid-fire Spanish as she often did when excited. Manny's voice, though pained, softly reassured his wife.

In rodeo, getting injured was a given. Jake had assisted lots of buddies out of the arena, into the locker rooms and even to emergency rooms. He was no stranger to the smells and activities involved in patching up a man in conflict with a bull. But this was Manny.

He plopped in a waiting room chair and checked out the magazines. *Country Hunter* caught his eye. A deer hunter in a camo jacket displayed his prize buck. Jake covered the reminder with an issue of *People* and turned his attention to the television in one corner. Opposite him, a woman sat beside a teenage boy in a boot cast. The boy's football jersey identified him as a Gabriel's Crossing player.

"Football injury," the woman said when she saw the direction of Jake's gaze.

This was not a conversation he wanted to have. "Bad deal."

"Yeah," The kid grinned. "But we won, and I made the tackle."

"Congratulations."

An hour passed before Manny reappeared. In the meantime, Jake listened to the boy tell of football exploits, checked his text messages and phoned his grandmother who, Flo claimed, was going to Mexico in January on her own two feet.

January. Precisely when foreclosure loomed. He understood. She wanted to escape from the terrible humiliation of losing her home. He wanted her to go. He owed her everything and had failed her completely. Somehow he would send her on that cruise, and he would stay here and fight for the house.

His stomach growled. He checked the time, saw he'd missed lunch and went to the vending machine for a bag of peanuts. A blue-clad orderly pushing an empty gurney clattered off the single elevator.

Jake hoped the stretcher wasn't for Manny. Pocketing the peanuts, he sat down again, propped his elbows on his knees and with clasped hands to his forehead, prayed that Manny's injuries weren't serious enough for surgery and for a quick recovery.

He thought about phoning Allison. She'd want to know about Manny's accident. After a few starts and stops, he decided against it. If he was stuck in Gabriel's Crossing, he'd need self-control. He couldn't call her or see her every time he wanted to. He had to learn to keep a distance, to steer clear of the Buchanons in order to keep the peace.

A hand touched his back seconds before the scent of honeysuckle wove into this consciousness. His heart gave one hard thud. Allison. Even in a dark room, he could recognize her presence. So much for keeping the peace.

"Hey," he said, looking up, painfully grateful for her presence.

"How's Manny?" She took the chair next to him.

He shifted toward her. In a red skirt and white, button-down sweater, she looked fresh and young, like the cheerleader she'd once been. "No word."

"Was he hurt bad?"

"Hard to tell. I don't think so, but he's in X-ray. I'm waiting for someone to tell me. What are you doing here?"

"Paulina called. I was on lunch break anyway." She shrugged. "She said you were here."

Which meant she'd come to support him and his friends. He shouldn't be glad, but he was. "Thanks."

"I could get us something to eat."

He lifted the pack of peanuts. "I'll share."

"Not enough. I want a sandwich." She started to the vending machine as a heavy door opened and a wheelchair bearing Manny rolled through. Both legs stuck straight out, a wrap on his ankle and a hard brace on his knee with ice packs on both.

Jake stood. "You look like a trussed turkey."

Manny laughed, but his eyes were glassy. "It is not so bad."

"So he says on pain medicine." Paulina smacked her lips in a tsking sound.

"I will be on my feet soon."

The nurse stepped away from the wheelchair. "Let me get your orders from the doctors and you'll be ready to go."

"What does the doc say?" Jake asked after the nurse left.

"Ligaments and muscles. Nothing too bad." This from Manny.

"No broken bones but his ankle and leg are not good for walking. If he takes care, no surgery. If not—" Paulina stiffened her posture. "He must stay off his feet for a few weeks, and I will see that he does."

Jake knew prolonged inactivity wouldn't set well with the busy rancher. He had cattle to care for, rodeos to attend. An outdoor man chafed at being stuck inside.

He thought of the job he'd planned to ask for, but now such a request seemed cold and callous. A friend helped a friend when he was down, the way Manny always had. He didn't expect pay.

"Crutches," Manny said. "The doc says I can use crutches."

"After a week when the ankle is better, you can use crutches. For now, you will hire that Winton boy to care for the animals." Paulina crossed her arms in a gesture that clearly indicated there was to be no argument.

"No need to hire anyone," Jake said. "I'll take care of the ranch until you're able."

"I cannot ask you to do this," Manny said.

"You didn't. I offered. I'm not doing anything but rusting and getting on Granny Pat's nerves."

Manny's head tilted back in a relieved sigh. "You are God sent, my friend."

He was nothing of the kind. Time at the ranch would keep him busy, away from the Buchanons and trouble. He cut a glance toward the pretty brunette. Away from Allison, too.

"We have bulls to haul on Saturday. Tim is good help but too young and inexperienced for this." Manny's face pinched in worry. He had a scrape near his ear, evidence that the bull had gotten closer than any of them wanted to think about. "I do not want a reputation as a stock contractor who does not show up."

Paulina put a hand on his shoulder. "They will understand."

But Jake knew how small rodeos worked. If Morales bulls had been advertised, riders would enter for that opportunity alone. Replacing advertised bulls was bad for business.

"Where?"

"Durant, a one night Bullnanza."

"I'll take them."

Manny perked up. "You will?"

"No problem at all." A full day away from Gabriel's Crossing? He jumped at the chance. "I'll ask Flo to stay over with Granny Pat."

Paulina clasped her hands to her chest. "*Gloria a Dios. Gracias,* Jake."

Jake hooked an arm around Paulina's shoulders.

She was still shaking. The couple had no children, and Manny was her world.

"Will you cook tamales when I get back?" he teased, hoping to ease her stress.

She patted his chest. "I have tamal in the freezer now. Come. Take us home." Suddenly all business and in her element, she motioned to Allison. "You come, too. I make plenty."

Allison shook her head. "Sounds so good, but I have to get back to work. Rain check?"

"Always you are welcome at my table."

"I'm glad you'll be okay, Manny." Allison hitched her tiny purse onto one shoulder.

"Gracias for coming."

To Jake she said, "What time Saturday morning?"

He tilted his head. "What?"

"To the rodeo. What time are you leaving?"

"Early. Probably six?" He shot a questioning glance toward Manny who nodded.

"Great," she said. "I'll see you then."

She was out the door before he comprehended her meaning. He started to follow her. "No, wait, Allison."

Paulina stopped him with a hand on his arm. "Save your breath, Jake. That one has a mind of her own. She will go." Paulina's hand patted him. "And you will be glad."

Chapter Ten

Allison disliked deceit, especially when she was the guilty party. She considered herself an honest person, but she was not about to tell anyone in her family that she was headed to Durant with a load of bulls and Jake Hamilton. Not after their behavior at the wedding. For once, the brothers four were not going to get in her way.

Jake, on the other hand, might.

She arrived at the Double M Ranch at five forty-five while the moon still hung flat and white against a bruised marble sky. Beneath a floodlight, a large stock trailer was parked outside the huge silver barn. Bulls moved against the metal insides in a series of thuds and clangs, their bovine scent strong in the chilled morning air.

Allison hugged herself against the cold and walked toward the truck. A gate clanged and Jake came around the side of the trailer. Her heart lurched.

"Hey, cowboy." She kept her voice low in case the Moraleses still slept.

Jake spun toward her on his boots, his hat shadowing his face. He didn't say anything for a second or two and when he finally spoke, the words were more resigned than welcoming. "You came."

"Happy Saturday to you, too." Was he disappointed? Mad? Had she pushed too hard? A sudden, uncharacteristic insecurity gripped her. "I won't go if you don't want me to."

Without answering, he reached inside the cab of the truck and took out a jacket. The dome light illuminated the sculpted angles of his face. Solemn. Serious.

She walked up to him, stuck her palms in her back jeans' pockets, jittery, unsure, and a little afraid she'd finally made the ultimate fool of herself. "Jake?"

"Did you tell them?"

"Who?" But she knew what he was asking.

"Don't play dumb. You snuck off, didn't you?"

"I don't have to tell anyone where I go."

"That's what I figured."

"Jake, stop. This is me and you, not my family."

His shoulders heaved once in a heavy sigh. He looked toward the purple sky and then down at her. "You don't know when to give up, do you?"

Not when it comes to you. Her confidence flagged lower. Since his return, Jake had kept her at arm's length, she thought because of her brothers. But were they really the reason? Did he simply not want her around?

She'd believed he needed forgiveness and healing and a second chance. She'd believed he'd walked away from their budding romance to protect her. Now she wondered. Had he been trying to let her down easy, and she was too dumb to know it?

"Are you trying to run me off?"

"Would it do any good?"

"Only if you meant it."

A soft huff escaped his lips. He removed his hat, studied the lining and slapped the Stetson back in place. "Get in the truck. I brought coffee and Ding Dongs for the road."

"You brought Ding Dongs?" A grin started inside her and spread all over her body. He'd brought her favorite morning junk food.

"Don't let a box of Ding Dongs go to your head. I eat, too."

Allison threw her arms around him in a quick hug. "You scared me for a minute. I thought you didn't want me to go with you."

"I don't."

Confused, she stepped away, but he caught her and reeled her in for a genuine hug—arms around each other, bodies close, the denim of his jacket pleasantly rough against her cheek. Allison's mood went from uncertain to happy faster than a bull could bawl.

"Stop worrying," she murmured to his chest.

"Easy for you to say." He tugged the back of her hair and stepped away. "Hop in, trouble. We're on our way."

The trip took a little more than an hour and by the time they reached the rodeo grounds in Durant, the sun shone bright in the east and Allison had succeeded in prying conversation from her companion. Talk between them was easy once the words started flowing. They could talk about anything—except the terrible accident that still affected their lives. For that, there seemed no resolution, though Allison prayed every night that God would show her a way to break the impasse.

After settling the bulls at the rodeo grounds, they roamed around Durant and found a café for a real breakfast. The bacon-scented restaurant housed a mix of college students and cowboys, some of whom Jake knew. Allison wasn't surprised that he was well liked. Her brothers didn't know what they were missing.

After fueling up on eggs and bacon, they spent most of the day either checking on the bulls who didn't seem to need them at all or talking to other rodeo people. Jake put her on some guy's horse and teased when her short legs wouldn't reach the stirrups. She rode around in a circle anyway, grateful that the horse knew more than she did.

Later, they strolled through the vendors' exhibits, tried on braided belts, admired beautifully tooled leather goods and Western Christmas ornaments and gifts. Allison considered a pair of dangly silver earrings while Jake donned a dozen different cowboy hats. When they walked with fingers laced, they pretended the connection was necessary to keep from getting separated in the growing crowd.

When the rodeo began, a woman with long flowing hair in a glittery shirt and hat rode out into the arena on a paint horse, the American flag held high. With the lights dimmed and the anthem playing, she loped round and round the dirt-covered venue in a throat-filling display of patriotism.

Allison sat with Jake on a hard wooden bleacher next to the bull pen. The bulls, docile now, milled quietly around, waiting for their chances in the spotlight.

"Want some cotton candy?" he asked.

"More junk food?"

"You don't want cotton candy?"

She grinned. "Well, yeah. Of course I do."

As they strolled to the concession, Allison saw the admiring glances Jake garnered as they passed groups of women. Naturally, women noticed him with his lean good looks and cowboy swagger. Jake seemed oblivious, and Allison felt ridiculously glad about that.

"Those girls are ogling you." She nudged him with her elbow.

"Yeah?" He ripped off a piece of blue spun sugar and stuck it to her lips. "They're like you, after my cotton candy."

She licked the sticky sweetness from her lips and reached for another bite. "*My* cotton candy."

"See what I mean?"

She poked a wad of spun sugar in his open mouth and grinned. "I'm glad I made you bring me along."

"Me, too."

Deep down, she'd known that, but hearing him say the words was a new high.

The bull riding event started with a whimper, and halfway through, Manny's bulls were ahead of the riders.

"Does Manny get paid more if the cowboys fall off?"

Jake nodded. "That's the plan."

"Can you ride that one?" she asked when Manhandler dumped a cowboy in the dirt.

"Haven't ever drawn him, but maybe. He has a pattern. Out of the chute to the right for two or three bucks before he goes into a spin in the other direction. It's that misdirection that gets cowboys off balance."

"You are so smart."

He laughed, tugged her hair. "You're cute."

Allison didn't mind being cute, but she wanted to be a lot more than that to Jake Hamilton.

Jake thought he'd done pretty well all day. He'd handled Manny's stock without problem and most of all, he'd enjoyed Allison's company without getting romantic. He'd worried about that, had prayed she wouldn't show up this morning, but when she had, he'd been way too happy to have her hop in his truck and go along for the ride. Yet, he'd kept a respectful distance and only held her hand. That tiny hand with the soft, smooth skin and the single mole beside the thumb.

Little Allison Buchanon had him in knots, but he knew his part and he was proud of how he'd handled the day. A man did what a man had to do to protect the people he lo—liked.

By the time they returned to Manny's ranch, they were both worn slick as river rocks. The long day had crept into early morning with another white moon and a splash of the Milky Way across a black sky.

She hadn't told her family. That part bugged him, even though common sense dictated the less said the better.

Still, she hadn't wanted them to know.

Was she ashamed of him? He wasn't a fool. Allison cared for him, always had, in her Pollyanna way of championing the underdog, but her family was her life and livelihood. As they should be.

"Can you handle the gates?" he asked.

She flexed her biceps. "I'm small but mighty. Tell me what to do and I'm your girl."

He refused to let his mind go there. She wasn't his girl. Never would be. She belonged here in Gabriel's Crossing with a good man and a couple of kids. A really good man. A man who didn't mess up, who was liked by the family she loved more than anything.

Choking on the thought, he hopped out of the truck and headed around to the back.

Still peppy at this late hour, probably due to the extra shots of espresso they'd had en route, Allison helped him unload the bulls, opening and closing gates on command. A light came on in the Morales kitchen and Paulina appeared in the doorway, a golden glow around her black hair. Jake went to her, assured her the bulls were secure and all was well.

"How's Manny?"

"Sleeping. Pain pills knock him out." Pulling her robe tight, she asked, "I make you coffee or food?"

Jake shook his head. "Too late. Go back to bed, Paulina."

The Mexican woman tiptoed up and kissed his cheek. "You are a good boy, the son we never had."

His chest tightened with affection. He patted her back awkwardly. "Good night, Paulina. I'll be here tomorrow."

"Sleep first. The cows will wait."

"Sure."

She closed the door, and Jake turned to find Allison right behind him in the darkness. The temperature had dropped and she shivered.

"Paulina's a nice lady." Allison's lips trembled.

"You're cold." Jake removed his jacket and wrapped the fleece inside around her shoulders. He tugged the collar close beneath her chin, his hands lingering there.

Someday a worthy man would stand in his spot and shed his jacket for the sweetest girl in Gabriel's Crossing.

Jake pondered the roil of emotion that came with that inevitable fact.

Inside the house the light went out, but he could see Allison's big brown eyes in the moon's glow. He could hear the soft puffs of her breath and feel her shivers.

Penned cattle moved about, mooing softly. Their restlessness resonated in him. He was restless, too, yearning for things he couldn't have and shouldn't want.

Allison rested her hands on either side of his waist. Through his shirt, he felt the coolness of her fingers against his skin. He moved in closer, sharing his heat. His brain pulsated with the thought that some other guy would hold her.

"I should get you home," he murmured, and heard the husky roughness of his words.

"I know."

But neither of them moved. They were cocooned there together on the Double M, and all day they'd been away from the distractions of town and family. A man's head could get muddled.

"Jake," she said on a breathy whisper.

"Yeah?" She lifted her face so the light reflected on her skin. Such a pretty, happy, caring face. He placed a palm against her cheek. "You're so soft."

He hadn't meant to say that.

She put her arms around his neck. His jacket fell away, rustled to the ground at their feet. He let it go.

He really wanted to kiss her. To hold her for a little while there in the quiet cold and absorb the essence of Allison. Before some other man took his place.

So he did. He had no right, knew he didn't, but he kissed her anyway.

Her lips were cold, her mouth warm as she sighed into him. He closed his eyes and held her face between his calloused hands, pulse thrumming in his head. A voice somewhere in the back of his brain tapped out a warning. Jake didn't listen. He kissed her, kissed the corner of her mouth, her eyelids, her hair. And when he was done, he rested his chin on her hair and held her close.

Allison. Her name reverberated through him.

"I love you, Jake." Her voice was muffled against his shoulder so that he could almost pretend he hadn't heard. But the slam of emotion shook him to his bootheels.

She couldn't be. He wouldn't let her be in love with him.

Fighting the wild exultation and the equally wild anxiety, he shook his head and tried to back away. Tried and failed. Allison was a sticky web of sugar holding him captive.

"Are you crazy?" His voice was a shaky whisper. Hadn't she admitted her brothers hated him? That she'd avoided telling her family about the rodeo because of him? And hadn't he reconciled to the idea that she'd find a better man?

"You took my heart when you left Gabriel's Crossing years ago." Her voice was soft and sweet with a tinge of hurt that set his soul aching. "I never got it back."

"We were kids." Jake kept his tone even, though his fingers touched her face and stroked her velvet cheek while he wished he was half the man she thought he was. "Too young to fall in love."

"We're not kids now."

"Ah, Allison." He shook his head, fighting emotion. Allison sucked his breath away, stole his last brain cell and filled him with such foolish hope. He pulled her in close and stared down into the most honest brown eyes possible. "We can't do this."

"Why?"

"You know why. Your family had a fit over a simple dance at a wedding. You didn't even tell them about today. That's meaningful." She opened her mouth to deny it, but he stopped her with a finger to her soft, moist lips. "Don't say it isn't. No amount of optimism will make the Buchanons accept me, and you're a Buchanon to the bone."

"We'll find a way. Give us a chance, Jake."

There was no chance for them. He'd known nine years ago. He knew now.

"I'll be helping Manny for a while and taking care of some other business, but I won't stay in this town forever. I won't do that to myself or your brother." *Or you.*

He didn't say the rest, the one thing he longed for but couldn't have. He'd never ask her to choose him over her family, because that's exactly what she'd have to do. And separation from family would break her heart more than his leaving ever could. She belonged with the Buchanons here in Gabriel's Crossing, not ostracized with a rodeo cowboy. Love between the pair of them was out of the question, no matter how much he cared for her.

She stared at him for a long, painful moment while he heard the earth crack around him. Or maybe that was his heart. Then, she bent to retrieve his jacket, holding out the now-chilled denim. "You shouldn't go around kissing a girl if you don't mean it."

She turned away and started toward her car.

He'd hurt her anyway—the last thing he'd intended, the reason he'd planned never to kiss her. He caught her elbow. She kept walking, and his boot toe stumped in the dirt in his haste to keep up with her.

"I do mean it. I did." Frustration laced his words. How did he fix this without saying too much? "You're special, Allison."

She stopped. "Am I? Really?"

She looked so vulnerable and those honest brown eyes were wounded.

"You know you are." He wouldn't kiss her again. He wouldn't even hold her. Nothing good could come of either.

She walked into his chest and laid her head on his heart. He tried not to put his arms around her but couldn't bear the thought that he'd hurt her more if he refused.

"I love you, Jake," she whispered again. And he bit his tongue to keep from saying the words back to her.

Chapter Eleven

Jake didn't like to miss church but he didn't want to see Allison. Not this morning. Not after he'd wrestled and prayed and tried to make sense of his life all through what was left of the night. She loved him. He'd known that, had probably known it for years, though he'd refused to let the information seep into his thick head.

What did a man do about a woman he couldn't have who loved him anyway?

He had no answer and apparently this morning, God wasn't sharing.

While he fretted, he phoned Manny, drank enough coffee to recharge a car battery and cooked flapjacks for himself and Granny Pat. When he offered to drive his grandmother to church, she refused, claiming they played the music too loud and gave her a headache. She always said that, but then, no one in his family had ever cared much for church. He was still amazed at the change in his own life even though he wondered why God had sent him back into the mess in Gabriel's Crossing.

After Granny Pat settled in the recliner with the

morning newspaper, Jake took his cowboy Bible and another cup of high-octane coffee out on the back porch.

He was glad for the excuse to escape to Manny's ranch this afternoon when Florence arrived. She was threatening to drag out Christmas decorations and send him on top of the house, but he wasn't in the mood.

He opened to a random page in Matthew and read:

You have heard that it was said, "You shall love your neighbor and hate your enemy." But I say to you, Love your enemies and pray for those who persecute you, so that you may be sons of your Father who is in heaven. For he makes his sun rise on the evil and on the good, and sends rain on the just and on the unjust. For if you love those who love you, what reward do you have?

With leaves blowing around his feet and the sun hiding behind a flat gray sky, he pondered the verses. What was Jesus saying? That he shouldn't love Allison if she loved him? Or that he should love her brothers regardless of their anger?

His cell phone vibrated against his hip. Expecting Manny or Paulina, he didn't bother to read caller ID.

"Hello."

"Hamilton, I think you know what this call is about."

"Who is this?" He held the phone out so he could read the display and didn't recognize the number.

"Brady Buchanon. I figured you'd be expecting my call."

Jake's mind raced through the possibilities and the only thing he could come up with was Allison and their trip to the rodeo. He didn't want her taking the brunt of Brady's animosity. Not because of him.

"What I do is none of your business."

"Trashing another Buchanon construction project *is* my business."

Jake's brain did a quick recalculate. So this wasn't about yesterday's rodeo? He didn't know whether to be relieved or shaken. "I don't know what you're talking about."

"Right." Brady's voice was thick with sarcasm. "We have an unfriendly little chitchat at Faith's wedding and then suddenly when the guys are off work yesterday and no one is around, a second job site is trashed. This time the Bartowski house. You trying to tell me that's *another* coincidence?"

Yesterday, while he was with Allison at the rodeo an hour away, something Brady appeared not to know. And Jake wasn't about to tell him. Allison had made her intentions clear. She claimed to love him, but she didn't want to get grief from her family. And who could blame her? He couldn't do much for her but he could do this.

"Can't help you, Brady."

"You're done messing with the Buchanons, cowboy. The first time might have been coincidence but not two in a row. I'm pressing charges this time." The line went dead.

So much for loving his enemies. They didn't seem too eager to receive.

With his stomach rolling, Jake stared at the cell phone. He wasn't worried about the law. Witnesses knew where he'd been. Allison knew. He realized then that she'd hear about the vandalism and jump right in the middle of the storm unless he told her to stay out of harm's way.

He punched in her number but the call went straight to voice mail. This was his problem and he'd handle it. Even if he had to confess to something he hadn't done.

He stuck his head inside the house and yelled, "I'll be back in a while, Granny Pat. Call if you need me."

Leaving his Bible and coffee cup on the lawn chair, he headed across town to the Buchanon Construction site.

The place was crawling with Buchanons. Every last one of the males and a couple of what he figured were contractors. Big burly guys in tool belts with clipboards and angry expressions. Nobody liked being called out on Sunday, especially for a problem of this nature.

He did a quick scan of the property to see what he was supposed to have done. Red spray paint covered the brick outside in graffiti. A couple of windows were busted out. Glass sparkled on the red dirt.

Jake's stomach soured. He wondered how bad the inside was.

Bad enough to skip church. Bad enough to call the cops.

A Gabriel's Crossing patrol car was parked next to the Buchanon trucks, and a uniformed officer he didn't recognize snapped photos of the damage. Nerves jumping, Jake crossed the unfinished yard and headed toward Dan Buchanon. The family father looked like an impending thunderstorm, a supercell about to spawn a F5 tornado.

One of the men saw Jake and said something to the Buchanon patriarch. Conversation stopped as all eyes turned on the accused.

"What are you doing here?" As tall as his sons and graying at the temples of his black hair, Dan wore a Buchanon Construction ball cap and a scowl aimed directly at Jake.

"Had a call from Brady." Jake stopped in front of the older man, never his favorite Buchanon, and chose his words carefully. "He seems to think I had something to do with his."

Before Dan could speak, Quinn appeared from inside the damaged house, eyes narrowed, face grim. "Where were you yesterday, Jake? Specifically last night?"

Though Jake struggled not to react to his former best friend, a tight fist clenched in his chest. "Durant. At a rodeo."

"You better have witnesses to prove that."

"I do."

"Don't be naive, Quinn." Brady's scowl was dark and threatening. "No one worked this site yesterday, and. Durant's not that far away. He could have hit the house before or after his rodeo and used the trip as an alibi."

"I didn't. I left early yesterday morning and returned early this morning."

A car door slammed. In his peripheral vision Jake saw Allison, in her Sunday dress, zooming across the dirt yard like a bumblebee. He whirled toward her and pointed. "Go home."

Her footsteps slowed. "What's going on?"

Jake's blood pressure ratcheted up a few notches. The last person he wanted in the middle of this mess was Allison. "Nothing that concerns you. Go home. Stay out of it."

But Allison, as Paulina had said, had a mind of her own. Brown eyes wide and concerned, she marched up to Quinn. "Jayla got a text that said someone vandalized another job site."

"Yeah, and cowboy here claims he was at rodeo all day," Brady said. "Isn't that convenient?"

"He was."

Jake's heart tumbled lower than a snake's belly.

Sawyer turned blue eyes on his sister. "How would you know?"

"Go home, Allison." Why couldn't she stay out of this? Jake took her elbow and glared down at her, telegraphing the message. *Keep quiet.* "Go. Now. You're not wanted here. Let me handle this."

"Let you handle it? So you can take the blame for something you didn't do? Just to keep my name out of it?" She gave her arm a jerk and pulled away. "I'm not afraid of my family, Jake. I don't need your protection."

But there was a time she had and the memory flashed between them like lightning. He had to get her out of here fast.

"Let me do this, Allison."

"You were going to lie for me, weren't you? You would have confessed to a crime because of me. Wouldn't you?"

Yeah, he would have. "Why can't you leave well enough alone?"

Five hulking men glared at Jake. "What is she talking about?"

Allison swung toward her brothers.

"I'll tell you what *she's* talking about." Allison slammed a doubled fist against her blue sweater. "*She* went to the rodeo with Jake yesterday. All day. From before dawn until early this morning. I was with Jake every single minute. He did not vandalize this property."

Her words rang on the Sunday-morning air like the ring of a hammer on steel. The Buchanons went from thunderstruck to thunderheads. Jake simply stared up into the sky and shook his head. His good intentions withered in the morning sun. She melted him, disarmed him.

"You agreed to stay clear of him, Allison." Quinn's voice was a Rottweiler growl.

"No, Quinn, you said that I should. I never *agreed* to anything. And I won't."

Quinn's glare burned into his sister with a mix of disbelief and anger. "You'd betray your own flesh and blood for a lying rodeo bum?"

"Whoa, hey, hold up." The usually quiet Dawson stepped between Jake and his brothers, his red fleece jacket like a stoplight. "If Allison says they were together, this conversation is over."

"The very fact that they were together for close to twenty-four hours says it's not."

"Come on, Brady, be reasonable." Dawson turned up both palms, persuading. "The man was willing to take on all five of us to protect our sister. He was willing to take responsibility to keep us off her back. That means something in my book."

"What it means to me is deception. Which proves how bad he is for her. He convinced her to sneak off with him—secretly."

Dawson shook his head. "Not the way I see the situation."

Quinn's left hand kneaded his right bicep as if the damaged arm pained him, an absent gesture that struck Jake to the bone. He'd caused all of this. The damage to Quinn and now problems for Allison.

Allison made a disgusted sound. "This is a ridiculous conversation. Jake didn't make me do anything and that includes sneaking off. My idea. My choice. Tell them, Jake. You didn't even want me to go."

Jake pushed back the sides of his jean jacket and fisted his hands on his hips. He wasn't going to make her look like the villain. "I've got one thing to say and then I'm out of here. I'm not responsible for your construction problems, Brady, and I'm tired of your finger-pointing, but you're right about one thing. Family matters more than anything. I learned that the hard way."

While the Buchanon clan absorbed his words, Jake spun on his boots and headed for the ranch.

Allison spent the afternoon at her apartment, opting not to attend the weekly family dinner and football game. She pulled out her tiny Christmas tree but didn't have the energy to put it up. She made a Skype call to Faith who was still in St. Thomas and from the joy on her friend's newly tanned face and the constant references to Derrick, Faith was one happy bride. In true best friend form, Allison didn't mention her problems with Jake and her brothers, though she wished she could talk to someone who would understand.

The problem was she didn't really understand herself. She was quite positive Jake loved her, but in his twisted viewpoint, love wasn't enough. To her, love was everything. But she loved her family, too, and loathed feeling like the odd man out.

She'd been too aggravated to go to Mom's today. Aggravated and unwilling to face the harassment about Jake and the ridiculous accusation. Again. Couldn't they understand that Jake Hamilton was a good, responsible man doing his best not to hurt anyone?

In her comfy gray sweats and fuzzy socks, she made a cup of cocoa topped with fat marshmallows and turned on the football game. She really should get a dog like Brady's, or a cat. Watching alone wasn't the same as watching with the rowdy Buchanons.

She blew on her hot chocolate. Was this the way things would be if she chose Jake over family? Would they really throw her out of the clan? Or would they include her in family gatherings but ignore the man she loved? Either option broke her heart but so did the thought of a future without Jake.

She wanted the man and she wanted her family. She wanted a happy ever after like Faith had found.

Settling in a tan easy chair—one of Mom's discards—she curled her legs beneath her and cradled the warm cocoa in her hands. The Cowboys were down twenty-one to seven, the offense struggling to move the ball. The brothers would be going crazy about now, yelling at the quarterback and formulating better plays while munching hot links or shoveling Fritos into Dad's ever-popular Ro*Tel dip.

She wondered what new green recipe Jayla had brought this week. And if Quinn was guzzling Red Diamond tea out of nervous energy. Brady and Dawg were probably sprawled like rugs on the floor, taking up way too much space. Dawg's big old tail would thump like mad when the Buchanons celebrated a touchdown as if he, too, cheered their favorite team. The twins, she knew, would be wearing blue-and-silver Dallas Cowboys jerseys, one of the few look-alike items they shared these days.

She sipped the sweet cocoa. This is what life would be like without family. Lonely. Missing them.

Was this how Jake felt after the accident? Was this how he felt now?

Someone knocked on the door and her heart leaped, hoping her visitor was Jake. It wasn't.

A gorgeous man in a Dallas Cowboys jersey stood on her square concrete porch. "Dawson."

He held up a bag of Fritos and a plastic container. "Delivery service. Chip and dip."

"I was hoping for barbecue weenies."

"In that case—" He pivoted as if to leave.

She snagged his jersey sleeve. "On second thought, chip and dip sounds great. Is that Dad's famous Ro*Tel?"

"Yep. Spicy hot. Guaranteed to take the hair off your tongue."

"The Cowboys are losing."

"Don't remind me." He set the foods on the coffee table, a chunky rectangle of distressed wood she'd bought at an estate sale. Brady and Sawyer had refinished the piece into a thing of beauty.

"Why aren't you at Mom's?"

"I missed my little sister. You seemed glum this morning after the—" he shrugged "—you know. Thought you might need a friend." His blue eyes were full of sympathy. "I could ask you the same thing. Why aren't you with the fam?"

"I wasn't up to it today."

"Jake?"

"I don't want to fight with them—or you—about him."

"Not why I'm here." Her brother ripped open the Fritos and offered her the bag. "This morning at the site, I saw something in Hamilton that got me thinking."

She took out a handful of chips but didn't eat; the salty corn smell lifted to her nose "Why do things have to be this way, Dawson? Why can't the family forgive and move on?"

"That's what I was thinking about. Prayed about it a little, too. We seem to be stuck back there nine years ago." He dipped his chip and crunched, chewing while he gazed at the television in a distracted manner. "Remember how things were before the shooting? Quinn's football picture was on posters in all the store windows. His name was in every Saturday morning coffee shop conversation."

Allison smiled, nostalgic. "I can almost hear Red Chambers reliving the play-by-play down at Darla's Doughnuts. *'Quinn back to pass. He scrambles, dodges a tackler. Then two. No one's open. But like a surgeon he slices through the defense and finds a receiver in double coverage. Twenty-five yard pass. No one could make more out of nothing than Quinn Buchanon.'*"

"He was grand marshal in every parade. Doted on by everyone in town. Recruiters, too. The rest of us should have been jealous, but I was so proud to call him brother. I idolized him."

"We all did, Dawson. The whole town did."

"He was going to put Gabriel's Crossing on the map. Heck, he was already doing it. News media followed him around like a rock star. *Sports Illustrated* did an article, comparing him to greats like Joe Montana." Dawson sighed, the chip in his hand forgotten. "Then the shooting happened and everything changed. We changed. Quinn changed. The town grieved, too."

"And someone had to take the blame."

"Yeah. We needed a scapegoat to focus our anger on. Human nature is an interesting thing." He grinned a little. "Psych 101 keeps coming back to haunt me."

Allison picked at the Fritos, remembering those terrible, painful days. "Human nature or whatever, Jake hurt, too. But no one cared about one stray kid who wasn't that great at football."

"No one but you." He popped the chip in his mouth, his blue, blue eyes on her.

"He needed someone." And she needed him. He knew her secret but never judged her, never spoke of it. Instead, he made her feel safe again.

Not that she could share any of that with Dawson.

She dipped into Dad's cheesy concoction and watched it drip into the container.

"You had a crush on him."

She hiked a shoulder, conceding the truth. No point in arguing. "I was trying to do the right thing."

"You infuriated the family. Even Mom and Dad were upset about the amount of time you spent with Jake."

"I didn't think they knew." Just as they hadn't known how badly she'd needed his friendship."

"They knew. We all did. Gabriel's Crossing is a small town and anything a Buchanon does is news."

Not everything.

"Or fodder for the grapevine." She reached for the remote and muted the television. The Cowboys, like her, were struggling.

"You have to remember, sis, it was a terrible year. Everyone was hurting, especially Quinn. Surgeries, rehab and the painful knowledge that he would never throw another touchdown pass. He had some bad juju going on. Still does."

"Are you saying Mom and Dad had their hands full without me consorting with the enemy?"

"I guess you could put it that way."

"Is that why you boys threatened him?"

Dawson tilted back into the nubby couch cushions. "Did he tell you that? Because it's a lie."

"No, he's said nothing negative about any of you. Jake isn't mad. He's full of regret."

Dawson pondered her words over a few more dipped Fritos that had him clutching his throat. "I gotta have something to drink. Dad went heavy on the jalapeños today."

"There's pop in the fridge. I'll get you one." She jumped up, returning with a cold can of Coke.

Dawson popped the tab and took a long pull. He swallowed and emitted a long sigh. "Ah, better. Man, that stuff's hot."

"You're a good brother, Dawson."

"I'm not taking sides."

No, he wouldn't. Buchanons didn't take sides with anyone but a Buchanon. No one but traitor Allison. "Do you think things will ever change?"

"Hard to say. Maybe. Maybe not." He set the can on the coffee table with a soft clunk.

"I love him, Dawson."

Her brother drew in a deep breath, puffed out his cheeks, and exhaled slowly. "Not the best news I've ever had, but I figured as much. You don't exactly hide your feelings well. What are you going to do?"

"I don't know. Nothing, I suppose. Jake thinks the situation is hopeless. I guess he's right." Hurting at the thought, she rubbed her forehead with her fingertips. "He'll be leaving as soon as his grandma and Manny Morales are well enough. Even if he didn't have rodeos to attend, why would he want to stay here?"

No matter how much she yearned to be the reason, she wasn't enough to hold him in the place that had hurt him so badly.

Dawson was silent, his elbows on his knees and hands

clasped under his chin, he turned his eyes on the football game. He was, no doubt, thinking, worrying, brooding over the bombshell she'd exploded.

She clicked the mute button and sound returned bringing the roar of a Dallas crowd at a field goal. Three points wasn't much, but "Da Boys" were making progress.

She observed her brother, the quiet one with the tender heart and the beautiful face. All her brothers were beautiful in a rugged manly way, but Dawson and Sawyer happened to be movie star quality. Not that either of them knew it. They thought of themselves as ordinary guys, Buchanons, and loyal as sunshine. She loved them so much. All of them, no matter their faults.

"Want a sandwich?" she asked, breaking the silence.

"I'm good." He patted his belly. "Too much cheese dip."

Outside car doors slammed. The siblings exchanged glances.

"Expecting anyone?"

"No." She went to the window and peeked out. "Oh, my goodness."

"Who is it?" Dawson rose and came to join her, standing a foot taller. As she opened the door and pointed, he laughed.

A gaggle of Buchanons piled out of trucks and trailed toward her small duplex like worker ants. Dawg leaped from the back of Brady's truck and ambled toward her with his usual tongue-lolling happy face and windshield-wiper tail.

"What are you all doing?" she asked.

Her mother stopped in the doorway for a hug. "We missed you."

Except for Brady, the rest of the family flowed into her tiny space and collapsed in front of her small TV. The biggest brother picked her up, his favorite way to annoy her, and with a wicked grin said, "You jinxed the ball game."

She giggled. Playful superstitions were as much a part of the Buchanon tradition as Sunday football games. The twins always wore their favorite jerseys. Brady wore his cap. Quinn ate exactly three pancakes before a big game and then there were the barbecued weenies and dips. It was the Buchanon way. "You're blaming me because the Cowboys are losing?"

He winced. "Don't say losing. Now that we're all together, there's still time to rectify this gross injustice to our favorite team."

"The Cowboy franchise will be forever thankful to know we Buchanons hold the key to their team's win-loss record."

"Got that right." Brady set her on her feet with a pat on the head. "Buchanons stick together. It makes things simpler."

She got the message. They were here. They forgave her. But Jake was still the odd man out.

Some of the pleasure in their appearance seeped out as Brady turned and picked his way over the bodies strewn about in her living room.

"Touchdown, Dallas!" Sawyer shot up from the floor in a victory dance and stepped on Jayla's leg. Jayla yelped. Dawg howled. And the rest of the family laughed.

"Did you see that?" Brady pumped his arm. "Did you see that interception? Linebacker, baby."

Allison stood in the doorway, watching the wild,

crazy, wonderful Buchanons with a sad smile. Faults and all, this was family. She loved them desperately, but as she listened to their conversation and watched their antics, she made a painful decision.

They were never going to back down, never going to change. The only person who could change was her.

Family mattered, but love was everything.

Chapter Twelve

Jake had meant to stay away but somehow his truck ended up outside Allison's apartment Sunday evening after a busy afternoon at Manny's. His friend was mending, stir-crazy and eager to be at work.

Through eyes gritty with the need for sleep, Jake saw the amber glow of light inside the duplex. He also saw the Camaro in the driveway next to a Buchanon truck. He shouldn't knock. He should go back home and forget this powerful need to be with her.

He parked at the curb and sat in the truck like a crazed stalker. Head tilted back, he talked to Jesus, who seemed to reside somewhere above the gray headliner. He'd never intended to love Allison Buchanon, never wanted to, but he finally had to recognize the secret he'd been hiding in his soul for too long. She was the reason he'd never married, the reason he'd tried and failed at the engagement in Wyoming. Like Allison, he'd given his heart away a long time ago. But he hadn't been as wise as little Allison. He hadn't known.

A soft melody of love came through the CD player, country music, the tunes of lonely cowboys everywhere.

He should go. He'd call her later.

His cell phone buzzed in his pocket. One look and he laughed. From Allison.

What are you doing out there? Casing the joint? You're not stealing my plastic Cowboys mug. I know you covet it.

He texted back, Spoilsport. I really wanted that cup. Heading home now. Good night.

Before he could return the cell to his pocket and start the truck, her front door opened and there she was. Hair dancing, she charged across the lawn and yanked open the driver's side door.

"Going somewhere?"

"Didn't you get my text?"

"I got it. Didn't like it. Come on in. I made soup and need someone with a healthy appetite."

He hitched his chin toward the other vehicle. "You have company."

"Dawson's alternator went out. Brady took him home."

"You're alone?"

"Not if you're here." She tugged his sleeve. "Come on, you didn't drive across town to park on my curb and send text messages."

He grinned and got out. "Sounds silly when you put it that way."

"I'm glad you stopped by."

He didn't know if he was or not. "Did your family give you any grief?"

"No."

"You sure?"

"All's forgiven. I'm okay, Jake, but thanks for caring."

That was the crux of the matter.

"Sorry I made you mad."

She shrugged. "You were trying to protect me. Like always. But these days I can take care of myself."

Jake wasn't so sure about that.

He pushed open the front door, and the bell on the cheery red-and-green wreath tinkled.

Inside, the scent of spicy Tex-Mex seasoning filled his nose. His belly growled. "That smells great."

"I won't tell you how long I didn't slave over that."

"Huh?"

She grinned up at him, cute as ever, and his whole being was happy.

"Did you catch up on your sleep this afternoon?"

"No. Went out to Manny's."

"How is he?"

"Annoyed, but I think he likes having Paulina fuss over him all day."

"You're sweet to take care of his chores."

Sweet?

"No big deal. Manny's done a lot for me. Why was Dawson here? Problems?"

She shook her head. "The family came over to watch football."

"Nice." He followed her into the kitchen where the soup bubbled on the stove top.

"When the Cowboys lost, they all crawled out whimpering like kicked pups. Even Dawg. They wouldn't even stick around for my taco soup." She took two red ceramic bowls out of an overhead cupboard and clumped them on the counter.

"Buchanons do love their football."

"Ain't it the truth? And guess what? The twins have tickets for next week's game."

"In Dallas?"

"Cowboys Stadium." She knew the venue name had changed but to loyal fans, whereever Da Boys played would forever be Cowboy Stadium. "Nosebleed section. It'll be awesome."

"Are you jealous?"

"Green as an avocado." But her eyes twinkled with humor. "They promised to bring me a foam finger."

Jake smiled at the mental image of Allison wildly waving a blue foam finger. "Everyone's favorite."

He wanted to take her to a game. He wanted to listen to her cheerleader voice yell at the refs while he bought her overpriced hot dogs and laughed at her enthusiasm. They'd have a great time. He knew as well as he knew she'd have to fight her family to make it happen. No point in putting her in a worse situation.

So instead of offering the invitation, he took the bowl of steaming soup to the round glass table in the corner of her tiny kitchen.

"How did all the Buchanons fit inside this place?"

"Wall-to-wall bodies. The house was rocking. Brady threatened to knock out a wall but was vetoed in favor of the game."

He remembered those times of crazy chaos with the Buchanons. Remembered and missed them. "Why were they here instead of your parents' place?"

"Long story." She sliced a spoon through her soup, gathering vegetables and broth which she held in front of her mouth. Steam curled upward. She took a sip and shuddered. "Hot."

"Go figure." But he sipped, too. "Do you have any

leads on who's vandalizing your properties? That's twice now. A pattern. Does someone have an ax to grind with your company?"

"I didn't ask."

"Some things are better left undiscussed?"

"Especially during a football game." She pumped her eyebrows, but he saw the truth in the worried way she glanced aside. Any conversation about the job site problems involved him, and Allison wasn't going there.

"How's your grandma today?" she asked instead.

"Feisty. She and Flo booked a cruise for January."

"No way! Will she be ready for that?"

"They think she will. She's coming along faster than I thought she would. Thanks to you and Flo. You've made her want to get stronger."

Allison put down her spoon. "Which means you'll be leaving sooner than later."

"Don't you think that's better for everyone?"

"No, I don't. And if you ask her or Manny and Paulina, I doubt they'll agree either."

She had that right. "Paulina wants to adopt me." He chuckled. "Joking, of course, but I appreciate the sentiment."

"They miss you."

"I miss them, too." *But I'll miss you, most of all.*

"Then stay, Jake. Put that one incident behind you and come home for good."

Home. He'd rambled the country for so long, home was a fantasy.

"I wish I could, but money doesn't grow on trees."

"You still haven't found a solution to the mortgage?"

He probably shouldn't have told her his concerns about the mortgage. She worried as much as he did.

"Not yet." He had enough money to live on but paying for Granny's house along with his own loan payments strained him to the max. The only solution was one he didn't want to think about yet.

She got up from the table and went to the window. She was slim as a child in her gray sweats and blue socks. Back to him, she said, "How much longer? You won't leave before January, will you?"

Jake heard the ache in her question and despised himself for putting it there. He followed her to the window, put his hands on her shoulders, massaged the fragile bones that framed the woman he loved. As much as he wanted to, he wouldn't tell her how he felt. Knowing would only hurt her more in the end, when he left.

Hurting her hurt him, though he didn't care about his own pain. He doubted she understood that either. He wasn't some melodramatic teenager anymore who thought only of himself. This was about her, about what he knew was right for Allison.

"Not sure. No longer than that."

"Not before Christmas. Please, not before Christmas."

Heaviness rode his shoulders with the weight of a Brahma bull. "I'll try."

He couldn't make promises, not with so much at stake.

Her breath made gray clouds on the windowpane. Beyond the glass, the navy blue evening pressed in, casting shadows and light through the trees. A soft mist fell, weeping softly against the pane.

"I love you," she whispered. "Doesn't that matter at all?"

He gentled his touch, stroked the sides of her slender neck. She was soft as air. He ached with wanting to tell her all that was in his heart, but knew better. What good could come of saying words that made promises he couldn't keep? Words that would only wound her deeper in the end.

In a whisper, he admitted the only thing he dared. "Yes, it matters."

He was humbled to be loved by someone as amazing as Allison Buchanon. Humbled and broken.

"I think you love me, too." Her sweet, soft voice throbbed with emotion.

"Allison." He closed his eyes, holding back the truth. The situation warred inside him. What was best for her? What was right? Was holding back his love a kindness or a stab wound? He didn't know, so he said nothing.

"I'm starting to feel like a fool, Jake, so if you don't love me, if I'm wrong, tell me now and I won't bother you about it anymore."

He opened his mouth to do exactly that, but the words tumbled out all wrong. "I could never lie to you."

Slowly, she turned, somehow ending up in his arms, until they were heart-to-heart. "You love me, but you don't want to come between me and my family."

What could he say? "As long as I'm in this town, especially if I'm in your life, there will be trouble."

"But you do love me, don't you? Please say it, Jake. Give me that much."

Only a stronger man could look into those soft brown eyes and deny her the truth. "I love you." He tapped his left chest. "You have me heart and soul."

The joy that lit her face was as bright as Vegas rodeo lights. Her soft fingertips stroked his jawline. "Love is all we need. The rest will work out."

He wanted desperately to believe her, at least for this moment. She tiptoed up, pulled his face down and kissed him with a tenderness that made his chest throb. He returned the kiss, holding her face between his rough cowboy hands, breathing her essence.

"I love you so much," she whispered between kisses and Jake's knees trembled with the honor she bestowed on him. To be loved by such a woman was beyond anything he deserved.

Deserved. He didn't deserve her. He couldn't have her. Her family would always be a wedge that would eventually come between them.

His brain, muddled by her nearness and the great power of her love, fought for clarity. Slowly, gently, he pulled back until he could breathe again, think again. Her sweetness lingered on his lips and in his heart.

She was starry-eyed and beautiful, looking at him as if he could do anything. That's the way she made him feel. Big and strong and worthy. But he wasn't, and somehow he had to make her understand.

"Allison, listen to me. Listen."

Her smile wobbled at the seriousness of his tone. "Don't. Please Jake, don't ruin this moment."

He stepped away from temptation but couldn't bear to turn loose of her hands. That simple contact sustained him to say what must be said.

"This is crazy. No matter how we feel, love won't fix things." He shook his head against the protest he saw coming. "We can't turn back the clock and erase what I did to your brother. To your family and this town. They don't want me here. They sure don't want me to have you. As long as I'm here, they'll keep up the pressure. They'll make you miserable. I don't want you hurt."

"I can handle my family."

"You shouldn't have to. We both know as long as I'm

anywhere around Gabriel's Crossing, you'll be caught in the middle. There's no solution other than my absence."

"Yes, there is." She slipped her arms around his waist and tilted her face toward his. "I'll go with you. We'll leave together."

Her sacrifice ripped through him like a bull's horn. "And say goodbye to your family? You can't do that, Allison. You wouldn't."

Soft brown eyes implored him. "Yes, I would. For you."

Because he was at a loss, he circled her with his arms and held her close. His heart in a vise, his chest exploding, he pondered what he'd done that someone as special as Allison loved him enough to give up everything that mattered.

Allison had made up her mind. When the time came, she was going away with Jake. Most of the time, she could ignore the anxious knot in her belly. The family would eventually forgive her. They'd have to. Wouldn't they?

The voice of her conscience said it was wrong. She should talk to her mother or sisters or even her pastor. But she didn't.

She had a savings account and some stock put aside. They'd be okay. She'd find another job. She'd help Jake pay off the mortgage.

Not that she'd tell him that. Not yet. His male pride would get in the way.

So with her mind made up, she prayed half-baked prayers and hurried home from work every day to see Jake. And if there was conversation about him at work, she ignored the grumbles. Brady and Quinn still believed he'd had something to do with vandalizing the property, regardless of her protests, and even though Dawson looked on her with sympathy, she'd learned to keep quiet and look forward to going home.

Today, she and Jake had escaped to the river outside of town where the muddy red waters lay like rippled stained glass and the cold front from up north had turned the grass a crisp brown and quieted the frogs and crickets. A few leaves clung for dear life to nearly naked limbs, heralding the coming winter, and a weak sun hid somewhere behind a gunmetal silver sky.

Except for waterfowl, this recreational section of the Red lay quiet and empty this late in the season, but in summer teens from Gabriel's Crossing fished and floated the calm waters on a lazy, winding five-mile stretch.

As a rule Allison preferred other places to this river, but in town privacy was impossible. She didn't like to think about that night when she'd been a foolish teenager, angry because her family refused to let her date Jake. She seldom thought about the other boy, the one Jake had slammed his fist into because of her. Or of the many tears she'd wept that night in Jake Hamilton's arms.

The past was the past. Let it stay there. Wasn't that what she always told Jake and her brothers?

Today, she and the man she loved walked along the sandy bank together, stepping over driftwood, content to be alone, holding hands while they talked about everything and nothing. The most important subject hovered like a horsefly waiting to sting. So they pretended to be a normal couple, in love, and planning for the future. Or at least Allison did. If Jake was too quiet at times, she understood. They'd never revisited her declaration, that she would leave Gabriel's Crossing when he did. She'd tried once to bring up the topic, but he'd sidestepped the issue. He was afraid for her, she knew, still insisting he would never take her away from her beloved family.

If she didn't know he loved her, she'd be hurt. But he worried about her, about how leaving her family would affect her. Allison was mature enough to know it would.

So she clung to each day they had together, praying it wouldn't be the last. Praying that when the time came, she'd have the courage to go with him, and that he would let her.

A ragged old rowboat lay on its belly on the riverbank. Jake gave the wooden structure a nudge with his boot. "Let's take a ride."

"Are you crazy?" She rubbed the chill from her upper arms and danced a little on the sand. "That old thing's been here forever. It probably leaks."

"I'm a bull rider. Crazy is my middle name." He flipped the small craft upright and found two splintered oars beneath. "What's the worst thing that could happen?"

"We could sink!" But she was already helping him push the boat into the shallows.

"I'll save you."

Like he'd done before.

"Remember the time we were all down here fishing and you fell in?" she asked. "You flailed around like a one-legged frog."

He laughed, a free, delighted sound that warmed her bones. She loved to hear him laugh.

"How do you remember those things?"

"A woman in love remembers everything."

"When you were ten?"

She stuck out her tongue. "Well, okay, I have a great memory."

The boat splashed into the water and bobbed there. Allison held the thin, muddy tie rope while Jake searched for leaks. "Looks sound to me."

"Like you're a boat expert."

"Hey, careful, little girl. You're insulting a man who once owned a twenty-foot bass boat."

"Really?"

"What? You thought all I could do was ride bulls and horses?"

"Of course not. You're a really good kisser, too." She wrinkled her nose at him. "Do you still have a boat? We could go fishing sometime."

"Nope. Sold it and bought a bull." He gestured toward the quiet river. "But we can go fishing here and now."

"We don't have any fishing rods."

"This is the Red River. Catfish." He held up both hands and wiggled his fingers. "Noodling."

"I'm not sticking my arm in a catfish's mouth!"

He laughed. "Had you going for a minute, didn't I?"

She whopped his shoulder. "Get in the boat, cowboy, before I push you in the river."

He stepped onto the flat bottom boat, wobbling a little until he found his balance, and then reached back to help her inside. They settled side by side on one of the two bench boards dividing the boat horizontally. Jake took up both oars, though one was chipped and broken, and pushed away from the bank.

They floated along, barely moving on the gentle current, leaving wide, concentric ripples in their wake. On the water, the air felt cooler and they snuggled together, grinning at the perfect excuse to be close.

"No leaks."

"So far." Allison wrapped her hands around his upper arm and leaned her cheek against his jacket.

Here on the river, alone without the censure of family, she felt such joy. She wanted to discuss their future, to dream of the life they'd have together. Here, on the river in an abandoned rowboat, anything seemed possible.

That Sunday night at her house had changed everything. Now that she knew he loved her, they'd find a way.

"Being with you makes me so happy," she said. Beneath her palms his biceps flexed with every sweep of oar. He tilted his face toward hers, ignoring the direction his oar sent the boat. She saw the worry in his green eyes mixed and mingled with the love.

Other than a few ducks waddling on the shore in search for food, they were the only beings for miles around. Thick trees, though essentially bare, blocked the river from the narrow road where they'd parked the truck before walking down the well-trod path to the sandy shore.

She wanted Jake to say she made him happy, too, but instantly felt childish at the thought. She knew she made him happy. It was there in his laughter, in the tenderness of his hand at the nape of her neck, in the way he perched his cowboy hat on her head and snapped photo after photo with his cell phone. As if he wanted to preserve every moment with her.

Sometimes that scared her, but they'd talked of the future, too. They both wanted a big family and a simple lifestyle. Jake would have a ranch, and in her spare time she'd plan weddings. And if the topic of their own special day never quite arose, Allison didn't worry. Much.

Jake loved her, and in the estimation of great philosophers and poets, but especially in her heart, love conquered all.

Didn't it?

On Thanksgiving Day, cheerful noise and generalized chaos reigned in the Buchanon household. The twins had invited their latest girlfriends. Jayla brought a guy none of them had ever seen before, and Brady arrived with a family he'd been helping to add to the five people their mother had invited, all with nowhere else to go for the holiday. The smells of turkey and sage and pecan pie had the noncooking parties roaming in and out of the kitchen like prowling wolves.

Allison savored the warmth of family more than ever this holiday, wondering if she'd be here for the next one. By the time the dishes were cleared and the crowd had settled in for the traditional football game, she was eager to head to the Hamilton house.

Alone in the kitchen with her mother while the other women checked the house for last-minute dishes and messes, she said quietly, "I'm going home, Mom."

Her mother turned from putting a pie in the refrigerator, her hazel eyes understanding. "Home? Or to Jake's?"

Her mother's tone held no censure, for which Allison was grateful. "Their dinner is tonight. I told Jake I'd help cook. I'm going, Mama." Regardless.

A beat passed while her mother studied her, and then Karen handed over a foil-covered pan. "Take this. Jake always liked my pecan pie."

The lump in Allison's throat melted into tears she swallowed. "I love you, Mama."

But she loved Jake Hamilton, too.

Later than night, full of roast hen, Stove Top stuffing and Mama's pie, Allison and Jake put up a Christmas tree in the front window of the Hamilton house. The artificial pine had been in storage so long they'd had to clean off cobwebs first, but once the lights were on the dust was forgotten.

Cooking dinner together had been fun. Decorating the tree together was even more so. Allison couldn't help dreaming that someday the tree would be their own.

Miss Pat bossed from her chair, which Jake had dubbed the queen's throne, but despite her sass, the older woman had grown quietly nostalgic at the appearance of certain ornaments.

"My mother—that'd be your great-grandma—gave us that little red wagon the year your daddy was born," she said. "His name is engraved on the bottom."

Reverently, Jake turned the ornament in his hand. "I wish I remembered him better. All I remember is how sick he was."

"You were the apple of his eye."

Allison's chest ached as she listened to the exchange between grandson and grandmother, aware they shared a sorrow she couldn't understand. Her family had always been there for her, completely intact, alive and well, and her memories ran deeper than the river.

She felt almost ashamed of how perfect her world had been.

Jake hung the ornament on a limb and reached into the tattered cardboard box for another. She joined him,

and soon the melancholy moment passed. When the tree
was decorated and the lights blinked a rainbow of colors,
she helped Miss Pat to bed, pleased when Jake's grandmother did most of the work herself.

She was on the mend.

When Allison returned to the living room, Jake sat
cross-legged on the floor in front the tree, cups of cocoa
on a nearby table. She sat down beside him.

"Will you help me with my tree tomorrow?" she
asked.

"Need my expertise, huh?"

"Something like that. I put up a real tree. They're
harder."

"Wouldn't know. Never had one."

"Don't you put one up in your trailer?"

"No. What's the point? If I'm home at all, I'm the
only one there."

"That's sad. I'm the only one in my duplex, but I'll
have a tree."

"You have someone to share it with."

The loneliness in that statement struck her. Jake, for
nine years, alone in his trailer at Christmas.

He must have read her expression because he said,
"Don't feel sorry for me, Allison. I'm not lonely. I'm not
sad. I'm usually working at Christmas. No big deal."

It was a big deal to her. And this year, he was home,
and she'd see to it that he had the best Christmas ever.

Thanksgiving had filled him in more places than his
belly. He'd loved every minute with Allison. Like a dry
sponge, he wanted to soak her up, to hold on for the
ride and pray the eight-second buzzer never came. He

knew he was being foolish, but he couldn't seem to help himself. He should let her go now and get it over with.

Yes, he loved her. But he'd lost enough people who were supposed to love him to know an emotion wasn't enough. His mama had proved as much long before the Buchanons had turned their backs.

So, he spent his days working for Manny, but as soon as the clock struck five, he started obsessing about Allison. Was she home from work? Would she enjoy a movie or a burger? Would she rather hang out at home or maybe take another drive down by the river?

He marked the last idea off his list.

Their last trips to the river had been dangerous. He'd kissed her too many times until he'd seriously considered a dip in the cold river to bring him to his senses. Neither of them could afford for things to get out of hand.

Allison. His whole world had turned in on that one little person with the big brown eyes and flyaway hair.

Since Thanksgiving his mood swung from joy to despair. Joy that she loved him. Despair that they would never work out.

As much as Jake liked the idea, he wouldn't take her with him. They would probably be ecstatically happy for a while in the full bloom of love, but eventually, she'd miss her home, her job, her loved ones. She'd grow to resent the man who'd taken her away from everything that mattered. If her family was broken like his, maybe they'd have a chance, but the Buchanons were different—a powerful, connected whole made stronger by the sum of its individual members. Allison was a link in that chain and she'd crumble without the rest.

He'd interviewed an older widow from elder services who, like his grandmother, could no longer afford to live alone. She seemed eager to move in with Granny Pat and the invisible Ralph, eager to be a companion and help-mate in exchange for a roof over her head. Jake hadn't told the woman about the mortgage. Saw no need. He was going to pay it one way or the other.

Granny wasn't too keen on live-in help, but she would come around. With Flo on hand as watchdog and general rabble-rouser, Granny Pat had come further in a couple of months than in all the months in rehab.

"I don't need some old woman living in my house."

"Melba's younger than you are, Granny Pat."

"What about my trip to Mexico? I don't have to take her along, do I?"

"She can keep the home fires burning while you're gone."

"You sure are eager to get away from your old grandma."

He knelt beside her chair. Her feet stuck straight out in front of her on the recliner, fuzzy slippers dangling on her skinny white heels. In a lot of ways his tiny grand-mother reminded him of Allison. Strong, sassy, small as a child and with the heart of a lioness.

"You know that's not true. If life had turned out dif-ferently, I'd never leave. I'd buy land here, close to you, and raise my bulls."

"Always running away. Like your mama. If things get tough, you run."

His hackles rose, shocked by the accusation. "I'm not running away." And he was nothing like his mama. "My being here causes problems. I hurt the Buchanons. They shouldn't have to look at me if they don't want to."

"What about Allison?"

Some of the starch leaked out of him. Allison. His biggest problem. "She'll get hurt the most if I stick around, and a man has to make a living. I can't do that here."

"She'll be hurt if you leave. Money comes and goes. Love's the only thing that lasts."

Now she was a philosopher.

"A responsible man does what's right regardless of what he wants." He was tired of this conversation. Tired of arguing with her and himself and Allison. Tired of trying to squeeze pennies, of dodging Buchanons, of tossing and turning half the night trying to solve the unsolvable.

No matter what his grandmother thought, sometimes a man had to cut his losses and leave the table.

"I'm sorry, Granny P., but the invitation to live with me is still open."

"And I still say no. You're not there half the time. At least here I have friends and neighbors to break up the monotony." She patted his head the way she had when he'd been a lonely, confused little boy clinging to her apron and wondering why his mama had left him. "I'll be fine. You don't get much finer than dancing the samba on the beaches of Mexico."

Jake's mouth twitched. "The samba?"

"Flo's teaching me, and if you're not real careful, I'll come back from Mexico with a new grandpa for you."

"What about Ralph?"

"Jacob Hamilton, you know good and well Ralph is as dead as a hammer."

Jake leaned back on his bootheels and laughed until he tumbled onto his backside. The fall tickled Granny so much she fell into a coughing fit that left her breathless. But the twinkle in her eye told Jake she was going to be fine without him.

He worried about her, but then he worried about everything these days. Granny. Allison. Manny. The confounded mortgage. So many of the people he cared about were here in Gabriel's Crossing.

He wanted to stay, a truth that surprised him. Though he'd never intended to return, being here changed him. Everyone he loved was here. Even his bulls were here.

Jake made a wry face. The bulls were here unless he sold them, a prospect that grew more real every time he spoke to Ned Butterman. Like this morning when the loose-jowled banker had shaken his head in sympathy and promised to hold off on foreclosure until after the New Year.

The trailer in Stephenville could be sold—it was just a place to hang his hat when he wasn't on the road. He warmed to the idea. The small mobile home wasn't much but a sale would bring enough cash to buy his grandmother some time at the bank.

He could move home with Granny Pat for good. She'd like that. And he could figure out a way to avoid the Buchanons most of the time.

Except for Allison. As long as he was in Gabriel's Crossing, he'd seek her out. He could no more ignore her than sprout wings and fly across the Atlantic.

The angst curled in his gut. He loved her too much to leave. He loved her too much to stay.

He sat down on the couch and put his head in his hands. What was he going to do?

Chapter Thirteen

Faith was back, and with enormous relief Allison talked to her friend about Jake and all the craziness with her brothers.

"You're glowing," Faith said while Allison bounced around her bedroom tossing clothes onto the bed.

"That was supposed to be my line." Allison spun in a circle. "Look at you. Tanned and gorgeous and wildly in love."

"True. At least the tanned and in love part. And Derrick thinks I'm gorgeous."

"He's a smart fellow. I'm so glad you came home for a few days while he settled the business in Oklahoma."

"I needed to pack up a few more things anyway. Besides, I miss everyone."

"You have to visit often."

"We will." She put her aqua handbag on a chair, folding the strap on top. "Why are you throwing clothes everywhere like a mad thing?"

"Jake's taking me somewhere special. He said to dress up because it's a surprise."

Faith squealed. "This sounds promising."

"I know! I'm so excited." A secret hope kept sprouting up like a dandelion, both beautiful and unwanted. She wondered if Jake would propose. "Up until now, he's stubbornly insisted we'd be miserable together."

"Would you be?"

"No, of course not." Allison chewed her bottom lip as she contemplated a brown skirt.

"Are you sure?"

"Now you sound like Jake."

Faith pushed away the skirt. "Try this red one with the lace top. The flared hemline is adorable, and you'll look amazing in red heels."

Allison held the garment to her waist. "Oh, yeah. This one."

"Any progress with the family?"

"About Jake? No. Except for Dawson. He's softening."

"Dawson's always been a soft touch where you're concerned."

"He's a good brother."

"They all are, Allison. They love you and they're afraid you'll get hurt. They're afraid of losing you."

Allison knew that. Sometimes she was afraid, too. Afraid of losing them, of losing Jake again. Both scared her no end.

"Love will find a way." She had to believe that to keep breathing. "Will you do my nails?"

Faith flexed her fingers. "Put yourself into my capable hands, my dear. I will make you beautiful."

By the time Jake arrived, Faith had headed to her mother's house, but not before she'd overseen every detail of Allison's beauty routine. With her hair flipped and fluffed, her nails sparkling red to match her skirt and shoes and her makeup carefully applied, she felt like a new woman.

Apparently, Jake agreed.

"Wow," he said when she opened the door. "Glad I brought these." He pulled a small bouquet of red roses from behind his back.

Allison squealed. "They're beautiful."

"So are you."

Okay, this was going to be a great night. In her heels, she almost reached his chin and with little effort, tiptoed up and smacked his lips with hers.

His grin widened. "Remind me to bring roses more often."

She liked the sound of that. Jake looked handsome in the same sport jacket he'd worn to Faith's wedding and a pea-green shirt that darkened the black circles around his green irises. "Let me put these in water."

He plucked one rose from the many and held it beneath his nose for a long sniff. "One for the road."

While she placed the flowers in a vase, they flirted and teased. Allison could barely keep her eyes off him and she knew he felt the same because every time she glanced his way, he was staring at her with a half smile.

There was mystery and romance in the air, a night of possibilities. And Allison couldn't wait to discover what was on his mind.

Jake was aware of the quiet conversations going on at the nearby tables and the quieter swish of waiters moving through the dining room. He was glad he'd chosen this restaurant even if it strained his weeping budget. Allison deserved nice things and beautiful places.

He loved her, and he wanted to give her the world,

but he had little to offer. Nothing really but hard work and heartache. A man of courage would get in his truck and drive away, but Granny Pat was right. He was afraid. Not of the Buchanon brothers, but of shriveling away to nothing, a broken down rodeo bum whose heart had withered and died without his one true love.

He looked across the table at her. She was beautiful in the amber glow of candlelight, this woman who'd begun healing him at seventeen and never stopped.

By the end of the evening, Jake was fighting both his head and his heart. He'd known this date would take a toll, but after all the times he'd failed her on so many levels, he wanted to do this right. Splurge a little. Buy her roses and treat her to a beautiful dinner and a good time. Show his love in the only ways he could.

During his times away from her, the situation was clear. He had to leave. He loved her too much to separate her from her family. But being with her muddled his thinking. Her Pollyanna effect seeped into him and had him wondering if there was a better way.

She reached across the flickering candle and dabbed a napkin against his cheek. "Cheesecake."

"I was saving it for it later."

"Ha. Funny." She leaned back in the chair, fingertips on her stomach and tried for a deep breath. "That was amazingly good. I'm too stuffed to breathe."

"Me, too. Want to take a walk?" He tossed his napkin beside his plate. "There's a park not far from here. The Christmas displays are supposed to be nice."

"Walk? I don't know if I can move!" But she rose when he came around to hold her chair. "You know I'm a sucker for Christmas lights."

Yeah, and he was a sucker for her.

In the foyer, he helped her into her coat and guided her through the parking lot, relishing the soft warmth of her hand in his. He was a Texas boy, raised with manners, but a long time had passed since he'd taken such pleasure in doting on a woman.

He wanted it to always be this way. He wanted her to be his forever, and the wanting clawed a raw place in his soul.

The park was Christmas in all its glory, though the night was cold and their breaths froze in puffs of fog as they strolled through the displays. Allison snuggled close to Jake's side, breathing in the pleasure of his woodsy cologne and the frosty air. Every naked tree lifted its branches in a lace-sleeved welcome of white lights beneath a starless sky overwhelmed by the earthly radiance.

Though others braved the chill, Allison felt cocooned in a world that included only the two of them. No outside problems. No family conflict. Just a man and woman in love. Was this the way it would be if they lived away from Gabriel's Crossing?

"Faith is back from her honeymoon," she said.

"I guess they had a great time."

"The best. She says Saint Thomas is a fabulous place, especially this time of year. Her photos are incredible. I can't imagine water that blue or beaches as white."

"Our water is red and so are the beaches. We're river rats."

Allison shivered, though the cold was only part of the reason. She didn't know why the memory pressed in on her tonight. Maybe the mention of the reddish sand or the fact that they'd not spoken of that awful event at all.

Now, here, miles away from her volatile brothers, she wasn't afraid to bring up the subject.

"I should have told them what happened that night at the river with Terry," she said softly. "Maybe things would have been different for you."

Beside her, Jake stiffened. He paused in midstride and turned toward her. "I'd hoped you'd forgotten."

"A girl doesn't forget a lesson like that. If you hadn't been there…" She shook her head. "I never should have gone off with him. I knew he had a wild reputation."

"Why did you?"

"You." She hunched her shoulders, recalling that night on the river. A group of them had built a bonfire and were hanging out after a football game. She didn't realize Terry was drinking until it was too late. "I was angry at my parents because of you."

"I was pretty angry myself." He took her hand and chafed it between both of his. "That's why I was there in the first place."

"All by yourself at the river." Regret and sadness poked at her. He'd been so alone back then after the accident, when no one wanted to hang out with him. Except her, and she'd been forbidden. After the incident that night she'd refused to listen to her family on the subject of Jake, but sneaking around had never been her style either.

"I didn't know your group of friends would show up," he said. "When I heard the voices, I moseyed on down the riverbank and around the bend, away from the bonfire."

"You must have despised all of us, down there having fun while you were left out."

"I deserved it, Allison. The same way Terry deserved a busted nose."

The images had stayed with her, as vivid now as ever. Her torn clothes, the struggle there on the red sand, her pleas for mercy that only made Terry more aggressive, the wrenching sobs she couldn't stop. And always the image of her hero, of Jake taking on the bigger boy, of throwing his coat over her exposed body and carrying her to his truck.

"I don't like to think what would have happened if you hadn't been there."

"I was scared of what he'd done."

"Me, too." She touched his cheek. "Thank God, as ugly as it was, it wasn't the worst. I was terrified of what my brothers would do if they found out."

Jake captured her fingers against his chilly skin, brought them to his lips and kissed them. A thrill raced through her.

"That's the only reason I agreed with your idea to keep the whole mess a secret. You were so upset. The way you cried for hours scared me. I would have agreed to anything to make you feel better again. Your family had been through so much with Quinn, and he was still recovering. Knowing what Terry tried to do might have sent them over the edge."

"I was afraid they'd do something terrible and end up in jail. Especially Brady with his temper."

"They might have. I certainly wanted to."

"I think I should tell them now."

He tilted his head to one side. "What good could possibly come from that?"

"You. I know my brothers. They'd respect what you did. The way you helped me."

"No." He gripped her fingers tighter. "Don't go there, Allison. Don't rip open a hornet's nest at this late date. Not on my behalf."

"I want them to accept you, Jake. As the man I love, the man who was there for me when they weren't."

"And what if you tell them and nothing changes? What if you open up a can of worms and they do something crazy. Aren't you concerned about that? Terry has a wife and family and seems to be a solid citizen now."

"You checked him out?"

He shrugged. "Had to. Didn't want that to happen to any other woman."

Jake's strong arm came around her. "As much as I wanted to drown the guy for hurting you, you were right when you asked me to keep the secret. Your family didn't need more grief."

"I thought so then." Now she wasn't so sure. Now, she worried her humiliation had been the motivator, not her concern for her brothers.

Jake bundled her close to his side. "You're freezing. Come on, let's head for the truck. Want to stop somewhere for hot chocolate?"

"Jake," she said, frustrated.

He touched his lips to the top of her head and in a quietly pleading voice, said, "Not tonight, okay? Just let it go."

She got the message. He wouldn't let her try to make him a hero in her brothers' eyes.

"Okay. For now." She put her hand over his heart and whispered. "You've always been my hero."

"Ah, Allison." His chest rose and fell in a quiet sigh. When she tipped her chin up, he kissed her. With the cold air swirling and a snowman display singing "Frosty the Snowman" in a tinny, animated voice, Allison let herself revel in his embrace.

Jake bewildered her at times. If he loved her, why wouldn't he do whatever he could to make things right with her family? Why wouldn't he take a chance when their future together hung in the balance?

But of course, she didn't have answers any more than she ever had. That had been their dilemma for nearly ten years.

Jake thought his chest would crack open with love for his special lady. He was no hero, but she made him feel like one.

He didn't understand why Allison had brought up the subject of that night on the river, an incident he'd buried as deeply as possible. No man wanted pictures in his head of the woman he loved being attacked by another man. Thinking about Terry Dean still had the power to infuriate him to the point of combustion. Didn't she understand that her brothers would feel the same?

Telling them wouldn't resolve a thing. It would only cause more trouble.

Slowly, he pulled away from the tender embrace, holding her perhaps an extra moment longer than was wise. If he had his way, he'd never let go. He'd stand right here in a Sherman, Texas, park until he turned into a Popsicle.

"What do you want for Christmas?" he asked.

She cocked her head and her dark hair took flight in a fickle puff of arctic air. "Are you going to buy me a present?"

He could see she was delighted. "Depends on my wallet and the size of what you want."

"A Mercedes-Benz."

"Done. With a big red bow on the hood."

They both laughed. A Mercedes was as unlikely as paying the mortgage on time.

"What would you like?"

You. But he didn't say that. "To take you to church on Christmas Eve."

"Jake, that is so sweet. I'd love to. But I still want to buy you a gift. Tell me something."

"You can give me your accounting medal. I think I may need it."

Allison's hitching laugh rang out. Glad they'd moved away from the unpleasant topic of Terry Dean, Jake took her hand and they sauntered on through the park sharing silly gift ideas. They admired the displays, laughed at some, including a moving dinosaur wearing a Santa hat.

"That's what I want for Christmas," Jake declared.

"What? A wire-framed dinosaur?"

"No, the Santa hat!"

By the time they reached the truck, chilled to the toenails, lips frozen and teeth chattering, their mood was light and fun and Jake almost believed in the impossible.

While he fished in his pocket for the truck key with Allison dancing around him and peppering him with silly ideas and quick, cold kisses, a cell phone rang from inside her tiny clutch bag.

"Hold that thought," she said and then giggled as she whipped out the device and answered.

"Oh, hi." Her smile faded. Her energetic bounce calmed.

"Who—?" he started to ask, but her eyes flicked a warning and she turned slightly to the side. That one little motion jabbed like rejection.

What was that all about?

Tense now, his bubble of joy burst, he busied himself with unlocking the truck. The dome light illuminated them, a weak spill of white that turned her lacy blouse ghostly pale.

"Looking at Christmas lights," he heard her say. Then the air quivered with hesitation. She glanced at him again, and this time her brown eyes pled for understanding as she said, "Just a friend."

Those three little words ripped his heart out and left him bloody and beaten and as cold as the winter night. She wanted to free him with her brothers, but she wasn't ready to tell anyone they'd had dinner together.

Jake started the truck. He shouldn't be upset. He had no right to be, but his heart hurt just the same.

Allison knew the phone call had hurt him. With her throat thick with regret, she put her phone away and climbed inside the truck.

"I should have told him." She touched his arm. A muscle flexed, tensed, held rigid.

"You did the right thing, all things considered."

Had she? Was hiding her love for Jake to avoid confrontation the "right thing"?

They'd had a perfect evening, full of special moments and romance and wonderful food. For this brief spell of time the future had been theirs.

Why did Dad have to call anyway? But worse, why hadn't she had the courage to simply tell her father the truth? That she was on a date with Jake and loving every minute with him.

Because she was a bigger coward than she'd thought.

Because she didn't want to rock the boat. Because her family's disapproval wore on her.

Every reason shamed her. Jake was a good man, worthy of the words *I love you*. Yet, what kind of love turned away in the face of adversity?

During the drive home, Jake said all the right things in response to her chatter, but he was different. Wounded. Because of her and her family. As usual.

No wonder he wanted to get away. All they'd ever done was hurt him.

Long after midnight they arrived at her duplex. Jayla's side of the home was dark, and Allison was relieved, another reason to feel ashamed. Allison didn't want to have that discussion. More than once, her younger sister had warned her to be careful.

Right. She'd been so careful she'd stabbed Jake in the back in a simple phone call.

"Want to come in?" she asked, huddled in her coat, wishing he'd hold her.

In the dark yard with little more than a pale wash from the corner streetlight, Jake's face was in shadow. "It's late."

"Are you mad at me, Jake?" She stepped closer, toward the warmth of his breathing. "I'll tell Dad we were together."

"I'm not mad. You did the right thing."

"No, I didn't. I hurt you and that's never right. I love you, Jake."

He was silent for a bit, his hands deep in his pockets, the brim of his hat tilted out toward the darkness.

"I wanted to give you tonight," he finally murmured.

Something in his tone set her nerves jumping. "Tonight was wonderful. I had the best time."

"Good." He brought his gaze down to hers and nodded once. "Good."

"Jake, are we okay?"

He didn't answer and her anxiety increased. He tugged his hands from his pockets and caressed her face. "You deserve the best, Allison. The very best."

While she grappled to understand his meaning, he kissed her forehead, his lips lingering for a long moment. Then he stepped off her porch and disappeared into the darkness.

Goodbyes stunk. Jake vowed to remember that the next time around.

Hat in hand, he stood inside Manny's big silver barn. While he'd told his friend of his plans, Paulina had fed him, and then Manny had insisted on riding with him to check on the animals. The rancher refused to stay down. He forked hay with the tractor, mixed the special brand of feed reserved for the bucking stock and continued ranching with few exceptions. A bum knee would never keep Manny Morales down for long.

"The only thing I can't do yet is fix fence and load bulls. Soon, though. Soon."

"Tim should be able to handle that until you're ready."

"*Sí.* He's a good hand. Reminds me of you at that age."

"Tell him to keep his nose clean and not to be stupid."

Manny's teeth flashed. "You tell him yourself. He comes every day even if I don't need him."

"You're good for him. Like you were for me."

"You're staying through Christmas, aren't you? 'Cause if you don't, you gonna break Paulina's heart."

"I'll do my best."

"What you got in Stephenville that's better than here?" Not a thing. "The neighbors like me better."

"Paulina and me, we pray for you about this. We pray for the Buchanons, too. They are a fine family but they have a burr in their saddle. Only God can pluck it out."

"Maybe this is my cross to bear, Manny. My penance for the stupid things I've done."

"Maybe. But my heart says no. Why you think they call Jesus the Prince of Peace. Huh? He tells us not to have bad feelings toward others. You keep praying."

Jake clapped his old friend on the back. "I'll do that. Fact of the matter, I thought I'd take a walk down to my bulls. I pray better with the smell of manure in my nose."

Manny let out a hearty laugh. "Well, go on. Go see your sons. This weather won't last much longer."

Jake raised a hand in agreement as he stepped out into the afternoon. The early December sky was as gray and shiny as a new nickel. He considered driving the Polaris but opted for a head-clearing walk. The air held a chill, but he didn't mind. His coat was warm and forty acres wasn't far for a man with a lot of praying to do. Boots scuffing the dead grass, he opened one gate after another until the house disappeared from sight. About a dozen brood cows saw him and ambled along behind, bawling when he had no feed bucket.

With the cows in hot pursuit, he stopped at his favorite little pond where Jake spotted deer and turkey tracks. The water reminded him of Allison and their day in the borrowed boat. A sweet day, a day that would linger in his memory like the taste of sugar.

"Give her every good thing, Lord," he murmured.

As if in response, one of the cows stuck her wet snout against his back and snuffled. Jake jumped, then laughed at himself. The others ambled away, bored with a human who didn't feed them.

He settled on a rock and prayed a little but no revelations flashed from the heavens. He started on, feeling defeated. He considered writing Allison a letter to tell her everything that was in his heart, but perhaps a phone call would be better. No, not a call. Hearing her voice would ruin him.

Head down, he prayed as he walked, searching for answers that didn't come. Granny Pat said he was running away like his mother. But she was wrong. He was doing the Christian thing. Turning the other cheek. Walking away from the fight. Wasn't that what Jesus had done?

Something Manny said nudged him. Jesus was all about peace and love and caring for each other. Did that mean he wasn't being punished for the bad choices he'd made as a kid? He wasn't sure and even if he was, it wouldn't change anything. The Buchanons would still despise his name. Allison would still be caught in the middle. But pondering the idea encouraged him.

As he neared his bull pasture and the loading pens where Manny worked the cattle, he heard excited voices. Going on alert, he strained toward the sound. Had those kids come back here after being warned away more than once?

Hurrying now, he drew nearer, and his suspicions were confirmed. Only this time the situation was far worse. The two young boys, one dark and one fair, had maneuvered several bulls into the loading corrals, and one of the boys had climbed atop the iron gate preparing to step onto the back of the bull. Jake's blood ran cold. For a second he froze, too afraid for the kid to think. But then his bull rider training kicked in and adrenaline jacked into his system so fast his vision blurred.

"Hey, you boys!" He started to run though his legs felt like Jell-O. As in a dream, he seemed to run without making progress. "Get out of there. Now!"

But the boys either didn't hear or refused to listen. They were focused on the bulls and the exciting adventure.

Jake was less than twenty yards away when the blond boy—Charity's boy, he now saw with terrible clarity—slipped his leg over the bull and disaster broke loose. The bull, feeling the presence of a human for the first time, went ballistic, thrashing and slinging his massive, horned head.

Fear slammed Jake, a metallic sting that tore through his blood vessels.

"Oh, God," was the only prayer he had time for.

The boy lasted two seconds before the big Brahma, nearly grown and ready for the ring, kicked out from behind and made one mighty jerk. In other circumstances, Jake would have been proud of his young bucking bull.

All he could think of was getting to Ryan before the bull did.

His boots slowed him down. His breath came in short gasps.

One of the boys screamed, his jubilance turning to a cry of terror. Jake didn't know which boy had cried out but Ryan lay facedown on the ground inside the small pen… And a massive, angry bull headed straight for him.

The next moments occurred in slow motion. Jake struggled to move faster. His heart hammered against his ribcage.

He yelled, trying to startle the bull away from the boy, but he was too late.

As he reached the gate, the bull hooked Ryan's inert body and tossed him high into the air.

Jake knew that feeling of going airborne. He also knew the crash was not worth the ride. His stomach sickened.

The other boy, clinging to the top of the corral, screamed again. Ryan's body hit the hard December ground with a terrifying thud and he lay still.

"Ryan. Move!" Jake yelled. "Crawl toward your friend."

But Ryan didn't move.

The bull, enraged now and probably as frightened as the boys, charged the injured Ryan again.

Fueled on reaction and adrenaline, Jake bolted over the gate and ran toward the bull. Yelling, he flailed his arms. The animal ignored the man in favor of the child. He pushed his fierce head against Ryan's body.

As he'd seen bullfighters do dozens of times in the arena, Jake grabbed the mighty horns to divert the bull's attention away from the fallen child. The angry animal whipped around and came for him. Jake dodged, but the bull caught his side. He went down hard, tasted blood and dirt, but popped up again. His side burned like a welding torch. But as long as the bull focused on him, Ryan had a chance to get away.

He ran toward the bull again.

"Get up, Ryan," he yelled. He didn't have time to consider the alternative. Maybe Ryan couldn't get up.

He yanked his hat from his head and slapped at the massive head. The bull turned on him.

The smell of dust and manure choked him. His ears rang and his head swam. He shook off the sensation, fighting for clarity. Fighting for Ryan's life. And his own.

"Mister. Mister! The gate."

Thank God.

Escape.

The dark-haired kid had the presence of mind to provide an escape route.

Though breathless and hurting, Jake loped toward the open gate with the bull too close behind him. One misstep, he'd go down and the bull would be upon him. The moment Big Country passed through the opening Jake leaped up on the iron railing beside the kid and slammed the gate onto its latch. His bull was loose in the wrong pasture but that could be rectified now that the boys were safe.

The thought no more than hit his brain than Jake leaped down and raced toward Ryan. The boy remained on the ground, inert.

Jake fell to his knees beside the child. "Ryan. Ryan. It's Jake Hamilton. Can you hear me?"

The boy didn't respond. A new terror, far more frightening than the Brahma, ricocheted through Jake. What if Charity's boy died?

He put shaky fingers against Ryan's throat and nearly collapsed with relief to feel a pulse. The boy was alive. For now.

The adrenaline rush pounded through him with such power, he trembled like a wet Chihuahua. He shook his head to clear away the fear and dust and dizziness.

He ripped his cell phone from his pocket and punched 9-1-1. In this remote town, the call went straight to Gabriel's Crossing's fire and rescue. He identified himself and explained the situation.

What he learned shook him even worse.

"All the emergency vehicles are out on a call. It'll be a couple of hours."

"Two hours!" Two hours when a boy's life hung in the balance. "He can't wait that long."

"Sorry, Jake, there's a big car wreck out on Highway 7. We can't get there any faster. If you can move the patient, you'd best bring him to town yourself."

He was forty acres from his truck and three miles from town. His side screamed and he was dizzy.

But Ryan was bleeding from his nose and mouth.

After a quick call to Manny, he gently braced the child's neck as much as possible, scooped him up and began to run. Once again, Buchanon blood was on his hands.

Jake paced the emergency waiting area of Gabriel's Crossing's hospital. The car accident victims had come in about the same time he'd arrived with Ryan. One harried doctor and a handful of scrub-clad nurses rushed in and out of rooms while techs pushed carts bearing machinery and IV tubes in a mad dash against too many simultaneous disasters. Their little hospital was unprepared for this much action.

The single elevator pinged so many times, Jake stopped looking that direction. A small tabletop television next to a Mr. Coffee machine rolled *Fox News,* but the only news he wanted was that Charity's son would be all right. So far, all he'd done was pace and worry. The Buchanons, alerted by the hospital less than five minutes ago, had yet to arrive. He was thankful he'd not been the one to call them.

The acrid smell of Ryan's blood burned in his nostrils. Still-moist blood stained his blue shirt. Jake looked way from the sight in search of something, anything to take his mind off the memory of Ryan's terrible stillness, his limp, pale form and the free flow of warm, sticky blood.

His gaze landed on Chet, Ryan's cohort. The dark-haired boy had sat in Jake's truck cab, his lower lip trembling, his skin almost as white as Ryan's and said nothing during the short, but endless, drive to the E.R.

Ryan's cohort. Subsequent attempts at conversation resulted in shrugs and crossed arms, trembling lips and a mulish glare. Jake recognized the symptoms. The kid was scared out of his mind. Jake's attempts at reassurance fell flat. After all, what did he know? Ryan was unconscious and bleeding. He couldn't promise Chet that his buddy would be all right.

He felt for the kid, though he wanted to blast him, too, for pulling such a dangerous stunt. But pity won out, and Jake cut him a break and left him alone. Time enough to sort out the blame. Jake knew plenty about that, too.

Being in this waiting room with an injured Buchanon flashed him back to that horrible day when he'd brought Quinn in, bleeding and pale as death. Like Ryan.

He shuddered. No use going back to the worst day of his life.

But the images kept coming. The Buchanons' frightened faces. Karen and the girls in a huddle, crying. Dan threatening to tear the place down brick by brick if someone didn't tell him something fast. Then there were the brothers, the men he'd come to think of as his own siblings. They'd stood together near the women, brawny arms crossed, faces tight, blocking him out. Even in those first moments they had blamed him, though no more than he'd blamed himself.

He'd sat with his head in his hands talking to the sheriff, alone and scared spitless, sure he'd go to prison forever, sure his best friend would die. Wishing he was in that exam room instead of Quinn.

He raked a hand down his face and shook his head to dispel the images. So much tragedy, all with his name attached.

Now there was Ryan, another member of the Buchanon family, though Jake thanked God that, other than owning the bull, he'd had nothing to do with this incident.

Suddenly, Chet leaped from his speckled plastic chair and rushed across the room. Jake looked up to see Charity, Brady and Quinn hurrying down the hallway with Karen and Dan not far behind.

Charity rushed toward the intake window with Karen at her side. Jake could hear them murmuring to the familiar-looking receptionist in hushed, frantic tones. He wanted to go to them and tell them what he knew and offer reassurances. He didn't. Couldn't. He wouldn't be welcome, just as he'd not been welcomed into the tight circle of Buchanons the day Quinn was shot.

He considered a trip to the restroom to check out the pain in his side, but opted against it. He'd been tossed around in the ring before. He'd survive.

He prayed Ryan did.

So, he took a seat at the far end of the waiting area and kept out of the way, letting the family take care of the necessary paperwork he'd known nothing about. When they were ready, they'd ask and he'd tell them what he knew.

Like the outsider he was, Jake watched them talk to the doctor, ached when Charity fell weeping into her mother's arms, and longed to ask what was going on. But he didn't. Though he couldn't leave until he knew something, he wasn't welcome in their conversations either.

More families, apparently from the car accident, crowded into the waiting room waiting for news of their loved ones. Jake gave his seat to a woman holding a small baby and went to stand against the wall. The hushed, tense conversations unnerved him. Ryan's blood felt sticky against his chest.

Opposite him, Quinn and Brady talked to Chet, and from Chet's teary eyes and frightened expression, he was relating the incident. Better the boy told of the misdeeds than for the news to come from Jake.

When Allison burst into the crowded waiting room Jake's stomach lifted. Brown eyes wide with worry, she beelined to her mother and Charity for supportive hugs. She didn't see him standing apart, holding up this wall. Ryan was the focus, the one who mattered, not Jake and his tattered relationship with her family. Still, having her in the room buoyed him.

While Jake's focus was on Allison, Quinn stormed across the waiting room and pushed into his space. "You worthless scum. Chet told us what you did. You moron."

Tense and wary, Jake cut a gaze toward the boy. "Exactly what did he tell you?"

"Don't play dumb. You have no business teaching these boys how to ride a bull."

"Do what?"

But Quinn was in no mood to explain. Before Jake knew what was coming, a hard fist smashed into his jaw. Jake's head jerked back, slammed the wall. His hat tumbled to the gray tile floor. Dark stars exploded behind his eyelids. His knees buckled though he somehow managed to retain his feet.

Like a wounded prize fighter in slo-mo, he shook his head, hand to his jaw. The ache spread up the side of his head into his temple. With his brain rattled, he couldn't comprehend. "What—?"

"Quinn, stop it. Stop it!" From across the room, Allison's distressed voice rang out and called attention to the confrontation. A dull flush of shame suffused Jake. Simply by being here, he'd caused a problem for all of them.

If he'd needed confirmation to leave Gabriel's Crossing sooner rather than later, he'd just received it.

Jake refused to look toward Allison. This wasn't her fight or her problem.

Quinn bowed up, the quarterback with his game face on, serious and eager for contact. "Come on, cowboy, don't just stand there. Be a man."

Jake struggled to keep his voice low and even. The old Jake wanted to retaliate as he'd done that night to Terry Dean. He wanted to put his fist in Quinn's face and prove his worth. But the new Jake understood the truth. Every action had repercussions. The same as in bull riding. A slight move to the left or right and a man would end up with his face in the dirt and a no-ride.

He didn't need any more no-rides in his life. "I told you before, Quinn. I won't do this. Not here. Not ever."

But Quinn had no compunction about coming at him again.

Brady grabbed his brother's fist. "Not here, bro."

Fury reddened Quinn's face. His fist remained tight and upraised as he strained against his brother, eager to land one more blow to his enemy's face.

Enemy.

The reason was skewed, but his former friend had every right to take his anger out on Jake. Manny was wrong. Quinn's anger, even his fist, was Jake's penance for the harm he'd done.

"We'll deal with this later." Brady didn't remove his big hand from his brother's good arm, the only arm he could hit with. "Come on. Charity needs our support, not this."

Quinn took one step back, but his glare never left Jake's face. "You're not wanted here."

In his peripheral vision Jake saw Allison moving toward them along with the rest of the Buchanons. It was the Buchanon way. When one had a problem, they all did. In Allison's case, she was caught between the two, trapped as she would be forever if he didn't get out of her life once and for all.

He wanted to tell her to back off, to stay out of his problems but knew she wouldn't listen. There was only one way to protect her from these confrontations. The Buchanons would never let go. So he had to. For Allison.

"I understand." The admission hurt worse than the punch. He wasn't wanted, and yet he'd kept hoping things would change. His beautiful, optimistic Allison had given him hope. But now he accepted the inevitable. Nothing would ever change for him. Not here in Gabriel's Crossing.

His side and jaw throbbed but not as badly as his heart. It killed him to do this, to walk out and leave behind the only woman he would ever love.

"I hope Ryan's all right. I'll be praying for him." Holding his side, he stiffly scooped his hat from the floor and clapped it onto his head.

Then, while Quinn glared holes in his back and with Allison's stunned expression a snapshot in his memory, he walked out of the emergency room and away from everything that had ever really mattered.

Chapter Fourteen

The hospital parking lot, normally half-empty, was packed today. Allison stood in the E.R. entrance beneath the brick awning and frantically cast around for the slender cowboy in a gray Stetson. She hadn't seen his truck when she'd pulled in, but then she'd been so focused on Ryan she'd thought of nothing else. The lack of news about her nephew terrified her, but her brothers just plain made her mad.

What had Quinn been thinking to do such a stupid thing? Such a useless, macho thing as picking a fight in a hospital waiting room?

A north wind whipped a paper cup into noisy somersaults and set Allison's hair and scarf fluttering like wind socks. She searched the lot, finally spotting her cowboy, head down, hands in his pockets, walking in the other direction.

"Jake!" Weaving between tightly jammed vehicles, she sprinted toward him. "Jake!"

He kept moving forward as if her cheerleader voice hadn't carried above the engine noises coming from the adjacent roadway. When he reached his truck and fished for his key fob, Allison darted across the driving lane. A car honked. She squealed and ducked aside, laughing in embarrassment as she gave an "I'm sorry" shrug to the driver. The commotion turned Jake around.

Allison's heart tumbled in her chest. A dark bruise already spread along his jaw and over his cheek. "Oh, Jake."

Breathless from the mad dash across the parking lot, she caught up to him and touched his cheek with her chilled fingers. Expression solemn, Jake turned his head away.

"Go back inside, Allison."

"Quinn shouldn't have done that. I'm so sorry."

"He did what he's needed to do for a long time." He clicked the unlock on his key fob. "I had it coming."

"That's ridiculous. Hitting people resolves nothing." Although, right now, she'd like to knock both their heads together.

His chest heaved in a deep, weary sigh. "Allison, this is hopeless. Let me go. There's no use beating a dead horse. This is never going to work out."

His words packed a chill colder than the north wind. She shivered. "What are you saying?"

"I think you know. You. Me. This crazy notion that we could fall in love and love would make everything all right. I tried to warn you." He shook his head, looked away and back again. "This whole thing has been doomed from the beginning. I should have stuck to the plan, but you came charging in to Granny Pat's with your optimism and—"

A slow slide of fear crawled down her back like a black widow spider. "So this is my fault?"

"No, never. I'm to blame. I always have been. This isn't about you."

"You're scaring me, Jake."

As if her words pained him, he closed his eyes and pulled her against his chest. Relieved, Allison wrapped her arms around him. He gasped, a short suck of air that had her stepping back to look at him. "You're hurt."

"It's nothing."

"Yes, it is. You're pale. Did Quinn do this?"

He shook his head. "The bull."

"The bull that hurt Ryan? I don't understand."

"Never mind. I've had worse. Go back inside." He clenched his teeth. "Go now."

"You're leaving, aren't you?" He didn't have to answer for her to know. He'd had all of her brothers one man could be expected to tolerate. "Take me with you."

"Do you have any idea how much I want to do exactly that? Any idea at all? But I won't." He touched her cheek. His fingers were cold. "You belong with your family, not with me. Go back inside, support your sister and take care of Ryan. It's time for me to get out of the way. If I hit the road now, I can make the rodeo in Fort Worth this weekend."

Her knees started to tremble. "But Christmas…you'll come back."

"I love you, Allison, and because I do —" Smoldering green eyes sad, he smoothed a lock of her hair. "I won't."

Then while she reeled, heart shattering into a million pieces there in the concrete lot of a hospital, Jake stepped up into the cab of the big pickup truck, closed the door and drove away.

Allison stood in the parking lot with all her dreams tumbling down around her like a wobbly stack of bricks.

Her mouth dry, her stomach aching, she wanted to scream and rail against the unfairness. She didn't know who made her the angriest, her brothers or Jake. Men could be such idiots.

He loved her, so he was leaving.

Exactly how much sense did that make?

Oh, she understood his reasons. She understood the kind of toll her brothers' animosity had taken on him, especially when he kicked himself more often than they ever could.

She slapped at the tears burning her eyes. He'd made his choice. And it wasn't her. Oh, but why did her insides feel as if they were collapsing in on her like an imploded building? They could have resolved the problems with her family eventually if he would have given them a chance.

"Allison?" Brady came toward her, his work boots thudding softly against the concrete. "Everything okay out here?"

She, the one who'd told Jake that violence resolved nothing, wanted to kick her big brother in the shins.

Afraid of answering that question lest she fall apart here and now, she asked, "Any word on Ryan?"

He stopped next to her and turned his back to the north, his oversized body shielding her from the crisp wind. "They moved him to ICU. He's still unconscious."

"Oh, Brady." She walked into his chest and when his comforting arms encircled her, she rested against him in relief. Big brother had always been there with a shoulder to lean all, for all of them.

"Hamilton gone?"

She nodded, her cheek rubbing the rough corduroy of his heavy shirt.

"Good riddance. After what he did."

For once, Allison didn't argue or defend. What was the point? Jake was gone, and neither the tragedy from the past or her own heartache mattered in the face of Ryan's injury. "Do you think Ryan will be okay?"

She heard him swallow, felt the rise and fall of his big chest. "They're waiting on more tests. An MRI of his brain when the mobile unit arrives."

"Oh." She made a small whimpering sound.

"Until then, we wait and stay strong. Charity's a basket case."

Allison stepped out of his hug, shivering when the cold wind replaced Brady's sturdy warmth. "Should we try to contact Trevor?"

"Up to Charity. She needs his support, that's for sure, but if he's on a mission, by the time we get word to him, things may change. Better to wait until we know more."

"What can we do to help her?"

"Be there. Pray. That's what Buchanons do."

Of course. Brady was right. Buchanons didn't abandon one another, even when they were wrong.

Although he drove through Dallas traffic, Jake made the two hour trip with time to kill. He'd stopped at Granny Pat's, only to find her on the way out to senior bingo with Flo and Melba. She'd been laughing, more her old self, so he'd taken the coward's way out, deciding to call her later. She'd known this was coming, that he needed to work and, more than that, he needed to get away.

The ladies had asked about his bloody shirt and bruised jaw, but he'd made vague noises about an encounter with a bull, only half a lie. He'd changed his shirt, downed some aspirin for the pain in his side and face and aimed his ride toward Fort Worth.

He'd expected to feel better with each mile he put between himself and trouble. But he didn't. He'd wrestled with his conscience, with his heart and with the look of betrayal on Allison's face.

He was leaving a mess behind. The mortgage loomed like a black cloud, but he'd call Manny and ask him to sell enough bulls to pay off the house. A secure future was the only thing he could give his grandmother, even if doing so meant putting his own dreams on hold for a few more years.

He wished he'd had something to give Allison. Anything except a broken heart.

In between questioning every decision he'd ever made, he prayed for Ryan. Not knowing worried him. He kept remembering the blood on his shirt and the pale stillness of Ryan's body in his arms. He was just a young boy. A boy who'd made a foolish decision that had cost him too much.

Jake understood all too well.

He still couldn't believe the other kid had lied to the Buchanons about the incident. Why would Chet do that?

But he knew. Or at least, he suspected. Ryan and Chet were privy to Buchanon conversations. Kids were smart. They would know about the hostility between Jake and the Buchanon family. Everyone in Gabriel's Crossing did.

He parked at the Cowtown Coliseum and paid his entry fee to ride both nights. Then he roamed the stockyards and considered a meal at Joe T. Garcia's which only made him think of Allison again and her penchant for hot foods. He decided to save his money.

Frustrated and down, he went back to the Coliseum to hang out with other cowboys. He had to refocus, get his game face on and be prepared to ride. Riding was as much mental as physical. Sometimes more. Anything less could get him killed.

Afternoon turned to evening. Hospital shifts changed and a new group of nurses came on duty. Like the previous staff, most of them knew the Buchanon family who crowded the hospital room and overflowed into the hallway and waiting area. No one had the heart or the nerve to ask them to leave. They all understood the Buchanons would stay until Ryan was out of the woods.

A weepy, shaky Charity was hugged over and over by visitors who'd heard the news and who'd come to express their concern. Chet's mother arrived and sat with her son who begged to stay until he could see Ryan. Pastor and Mrs. Flannery arrived with prayers and words of encouragement and a bucket of Kentucky Fried Chicken. Such was the way of life in Gabriel's Crossing.

Allison alternated between Ryan's bedside and the window at the end of the hall overlooking the parking lot. Security lamps had come on, casting their stick-figure shadows onto the pavement. Jake would be in Fort Worth by now, in pain inside and out. Gone only a few hours and she missed him already.

The weeks and months ahead, especially this first Christmas she'd planned to spend with him, loomed dark and lonely.

Her mom moved toward her carrying two disposable cups, and Allison wondered how much coffee and cocoa and how many hugs and words of comfort her mother had dispensed today. "You look like you could use some cocoa."

"Thanks, Mama."

"Are you okay? You're very quiet."

Allison accepted the small cup and let the warmth spread into her cold fingers. She felt cold all over today, like a blast of winter inside her soul. "A lot on my mind."

"You want to talk about him? Or about the confrontation with Quinn?"

Mom's soft, accepting tone opened the door to spill out her sorrow, but instead she said, "No use talking. The boys finally got what they wanted. Jake's gone."

Tears pushed up in her throat. She swallowed them down but not before her mother noticed.

Karen set her cup on the window ledge and stroked her daughter's hair away from her face the way she'd done for as long as Allison could remember. A gentle stroke of comfort and caring that only a mother could give.

Had Jake's mother ever done that for him?

"I'm sorry, sweetheart." Mama didn't say the obvious. She had warned Allison that Jake would hurt her.

"Jake never had this."

Her mother cocked her head to one side. "Never had cocoa?"

Allison managed a smile. "He didn't have someone like you, a mother to stroke his hair and bring him cocoa when life stunk."

"Pat did her best and was good to him, but he was a lonely child. The way he tagged along with you kids tugged at my heartstrings."

Always on the outside, always alone. "Mine, too. You were good to him."

"I never minded an extra place at the table."

"I love him, Mama. I think I've loved him forever."

Her mother looked at her with a mix of sorrow and understanding. "I know, and my heart breaks to see you hurt. And don't try to deny it because I know you, Allison. Those soft brown eyes are like a puppy's. They reveal every emotion. You're hurting badly."

The tears she'd kept at bay leaped to the fore. Allison batted her eyes and turned toward the window. Beyond the hospital, a Buchanon-built housing addition glowed with the multicolored promise of Christmas.

Her mother tenderly rubbed a hand between her daughter's shoulders.

"I wanted to go with him." Allison batted her eyes, fighting the blur.

"Oh, honey."

"He wouldn't let me. He said I'd hate him someday if he took me away from all of you."

"He was right."

"How can this be right? I love him. He loves me. Nothing's right about any of this!"

Before her mother could respond, Dad's voice called to them from the door to Ryan's room.

Mom's hand spasmed on Allison's back. Allison spun around.

Her dad motioned. "Come on. Hurry."

The women exchanged looks. Fear streaked up Allison's back. "Is Ryan —"

A smile broke over her father's face. "He's awake."

Relief, like a warm flood, caused her shoulders to sag, but she quickly recovered and followed her mother down the hallway.

Inside the room, Buchanon bodies made a rectangle around the hospital bed. Allison pushed in between Quinn and Jayla.

Tears streamed down her sisters' faces at the sight of Ryan with his eyes open staring around at his relatives.

"I'm thirsty."

Charity stuck a yellow plastic straw to her son's lips. "How's your head, baby?"

"It hurts. What happened?"

"You got hurt by a bull. Don't you remember?"

His gaze fell to the white sheets. "Yeah. Is Chet okay?"

"He's fine. You were the one Jake put on the bull."

His head came up. "Huh?"

The adults exchanged glances, worried about Ryan's memory glitch. "Jake Hamilton, the one who was teaching you how to ride. He helped you get on the bull. Don't you remember?"

Eyes wide now, Ryan moved his head slowly from side to side. "Jake wasn't there."

"Yes, baby. You've hurt your head a little. The headache is preventing you from remembering."

"No, Mom, Jake wasn't there. He would have been mad if he'd seen us there again. He told us never to go near the bulls."

Charity's hand went to her mouth. "Chet said Jake was teaching you, that he helped you on."

"But that's not true!" As if he realized he'd said too much, Ryan stopped talking and slid deeper into the bed, his eyes squeezed shut.

A silent moment of realization hummed on the hospital-scented air before Quinn ground out, "Get Chet in here. Now."

"Whoa, whoa, this is not the place." Dawson hitched

his chin toward the door. "Let's take this conversation outside."

Mom and Charity stayed behind but the rest filed out into the hall to talk to Chet. When he heard the news that Ryan would be all right, tears formed in his eyes.

"Want to tell us what really happened out there today, Chet?" Brady asked gently as he went down on one knee beside the boy's chair. "Ryan says Jake warned you away from the bulls."

Chet hung his head. "Yeah. He did."

"Chet!" The boy's mother paled.

Allison put a hand on the woman's shoulder. "Tell us the truth, Chet. It's wrong to blame someone else. What happened?"

In a mumble with his chin low on his chest, Chet told the story of sneaking off to play rodeo cowboy. "Ryan went first, and then he fell and he couldn't get up and—" his lips trembled "—Jake saw us. He yelled for us to get away. And when Ryan fell, Jake ran inside the pen. He threw himself in front of the bull so it wouldn't horn Ryan anymore. Jake got knocked down. I thought for a minute he was dead, too." Two tears rolled down his cheeks and dripped on his jeans. "I thought they were both dead, but Jake got up and made the bull chase him. He was trying to save Ryan. Ryan was bleeding and—"

Brady patted Chet's knee. "I think we understand now. You don't have to say any more."

For a moment, quiet reigned in the small waiting area, as they each absorbed the news. Jake, the Jake they despised, had saved Ryan's life.

Allison's pulse hammered against her temples. Chet had lied. And the Buchanons had accepted the lie as easily as breathing because it implicated Jake.

"Is that why the two of you were brawling like Neanderthals in the waiting room? Because Chet told a lie to keep himself out of trouble?" She pointed a finger around the box of Buchanons, her voice rising. "And you *all* believed a little boy over a grown man? The man who saved Ryan's life!"

"Now, Allison," Jayla said. "This is no place for drama. Nobody likes Jake anyway."

The revelation was the final straw. She couldn't bear it any longer. Allison burst into tears.

"Whoa. Wait. Don't do that." Quinn patted her shoulder and looked completely out of his element. "Somebody make her stop. Allison doesn't cry."

"You. You mean-spirited, unforgiving cretins." She glared at the other stunned faces. "All of you. You claim to be Christians, but you don't have an ounce of forgiveness in your souls. You want grace for yourselves but you refuse to extend it to a man who's done everything he can to make up for hurting Quinn. You stubbornly refuse to believe anything good about him, and he's a good man. A man I love. And he loves me. So much that he left town rather than come between me and my family. What does that tell you about yourselves and him? Huh? Answer me that?"

She was so upset, she didn't quite comprehend all the words streaming from her mouth. The Jake she knew tumbled out and suddenly she didn't care about her humiliation or the secret she'd kept for years.

"I never told you because I was afraid. You had enough on your plate, according to Jake. You didn't need anything else to worry about. But he was there for me the night a boy tried to rape me."

Brady leaped to his feet. "Who?"

"Doesn't matter now, and I won't ever tell you. The point is Jake stopped him. He fought for me and got a busted nose for his efforts. And like the gentleman he is, he carried me to his truck and took care of me. Not once did he ever criticize me or make me feel less than a good person because I'd been stupid enough to go off alone with...that boy."

Brady's face reflected that of his brothers in a mix of horror and shock. "We never knew. How could we not know?"

"I didn't want you to know. I was afraid of what you might do, of the trouble you might get into if you knew. But Jake Hamilton is not the villain you've made him out to be. He made a horrible mistake nine years ago, but he's made up for it a thousand times over. First with me that awful night on the river. Today with Ryan."

When she finished, the group was as silent as an empty church. Shocked faces stared back at her, some ashamed, others suddenly aware of their collective misjudgment.

"Wow, sis," Sawyer said. "You're something when you're all fired up."

"Jake thinks I'm something all the time." But now, she was nothing but drained dry. "I never meant to tell you, but I'm so tired of Jake being the bad guy."

Dawson's face was a picture of remorse. "When Quinn was injured at Jake's hand, all of us, but especially Quinn lost something we valued greatly. Maybe too much. In our pain and loss, we forgot what Jesus taught about forgiveness."

"We didn't forget," Brady said. "We ignored it."

"We hurt, so we hit back. It didn't seem like such a big sin. To despise one person who'd caused us grief.

But I see now, we not only hurt Jake, we hurt our little sister. We hurt ourselves."

Quinn massaged his right biceps, voice distant and thoughtful. "I've hated Jake Hamilton for so long, I forgot what a good friend he used to be."

"He was. He still is. He loves all of you." Allison sniffed, wiping at her eyes with her sweater sleeve. "Do you know what he said to me, Quinn? He said you had a right to hit him all you wanted. He would let you. You could pound him into the earth and he wouldn't fight back."

"Ah, man." Quinn rubbed a hand over his eyes. "You all know Jake wasn't the only one drinking beer that day. But we let him take all the blame."

"Yeah." A chorus of agreement passed between the brothers.

Quinn touched Allison's shoulder. "You really love the guy, little sis?"

Her lips began to tremble. "With all my heart."

"I think I speak for everyone when I say, go get him. We need to have a heart-to-heart. This time without threats."

A glance at the other faces confirmed Quinn's statement, but Allison shook her head. "I can't. He's gone." The tears flooded in again. She swallowed, the knot thick in her throat. "And even if he was still in Gabriel's Crossing, he'd never believe the Buchanon brothers would forgive him."

"Gone doesn't mean anything these days. The roads run in every direction. Where is he?"

"Fort Worth. The rodeo. He needed to make some money."

Quinn glanced at Brady. "You thinking what I'm thinking?"

"It's a long drive."

"Then we better get started."

Behind the chutes, Jake leaned against the far wall, dejected. He'd lasted less than two seconds before his side gave out and the Badlands bull slammed him to the ground. He shouldn't have tried to ride after everything that happened today. His head wasn't in it.

Now his wallet was thinner than ever, but the sale of the bulls would pay off Granny Pat's house and tide him over until he could find a regular job.

"Tough break, Hamilton," another cowboy called as he passed by.

"Yeah." He rubbed a tired hand down his face. Might as well head for the truck. The cab would be his bed for the night and he was bone weary and sorer than he wanted to be. He'd laid off too long.

The trouble was his heart wasn't in bull riding anymore either.

He missed Allison. He missed Granny Pat. He missed his friends, his bulls, his hometown. Not everyone there hated him.

He ambled back to the locker room to collect his gear, thinking as he went.

Granny Pat's words kept coming back to him. Did she really think he was running away like his mother had?

Praying in his heart for guidance, he took his belongings from a locker, slammed the metal door and started back out into corridor.

He could move his trailer back to Gabriel's Crossing. Or maybe sell it and move in with his grandma. The paper mill might hire him. He wasn't afraid of hard work and in a few years he could rebuild his herd.

Nah, none of that made sense. The problems would still be there.

So would Allison.

He wasn't sure if he could keep going without her. The temptation to bring her along had ripped through him like a chain saw.

Jake chuffed. Or maybe that was the bruise on his side.

With his navy blue duffel bag over one shoulder, he headed down the corridor toward the exit. Cowboys passed, nodded or spoke. The smell of the arena and animals drifted to him, as natural as sunrise.

Working in a factory wouldn't be easy. He was an outdoor man. But he'd do whatever necessary to get by.

As he approached the perpendicular hallway, four men rounded the corner. His stomach lurched. Stride for stride like old west gunslingers, the Buchanon brothers came toward him in a wall of muscle and mad. Jake stopped in his tracks. Was Ryan—?

Please no. Let the boy be all right.

But why else would the Buchanons be here?

Wary, he dusted a hand down his chaps and prepared for the news and the inevitable confrontation. He was too sore and heartsick to fight with the Buchanons tonight.

As the men came closer, their big bodies filling the corridor from side to side, he asked, "Is Ryan all right?"

Quinn spoke first. "He'll be fine. A concussion. And a confession."

Jake briefly closed his eyes. "Thank God." When he opened them again, he noticed something he'd missed before. The expressions on the Buchanon boys' faces.

Not anger, but something else. "You came all this way to tell me?"

Quinn shook his head. "Partly, but we mostly came with an olive branch."

"An apology," Brady said when Jake stared at them, dumbfounded.

"I don't understand. You don't owe me an apology. I'm the one—" He bit down on his back jaw, felt the pain of Quinn's punch, the pain he deserved.

"We were wrong, Jake. We've been wrong for a long time but we want to make things right."

Jake couldn't believe what he was hearing. "You do?"

"Chet told us the truth about today, and Allison told us some other things." Brady clapped Jake on the shoulder. "Thank you for taking care of our sister."

"I love her. I'd do anything for her." The words came out on their own, but they were true. If the Buchanons took offense, so be it.

"Even walk away?"

"I already did."

The four brothers exchanged glances.

Brady spoke up. "Well, we kind of took offense to that. You running off on our little sister. Her crying. Right here at Christmas. We thought you wanted to make her happy."

"I do. She'll move on, find someone good enough for her."

"I think she already has."

"We brought you an early Christmas present, Jake. Don't mess it up this time."

Bewildered, his heart hammering like a jackhammer, he watched as the wall of men separated and there stood his love.

"Allison." Before he could finish the thought, she launched across the small space like a linebacker after the sack, and into Jake's arms.

His duffel and bull rope fell with a thud as he caught her, holding on for dear life, hardly able to believe this was happening. Afraid that any minute, he'd awaken and discover he was dreaming.

But then Quinn spoke one final time and set him free to love.

"Go on, brother, kiss her. But wait until I turn my back. I don't want to have to hit you again."

Laughing, the four brothers turned away in unison, sharing a round of high fives.

Reality slowly seeped in. They'd forgiven him. He and Allison had the Buchanon blessing. She was here.

"I can't believe this."

"Believe it. Come home."

"Tonight I knew I could never stay away forever. I'm sorry, so sorry for hurting you."

"Will you shut up and kiss her, already!" A chorus of laughs came from the wall of backs turned toward him.

Jake needed no further invitation. As the world around him righted, he lowered his face to Allison's.

And finally, after nine long years, he could breathe again.

Epilogue

The Buchanon house was a zoo on Christmas Day. With the smell of turkey and sage stuffing lingering on the air long after dinner, Jake stood in the divider between the dining and family rooms. The house was jammed with Buchanons, friends of the Buchanons, neighbors with nowhere else to go for Christmas and he and his grandmother. Miss Pat, who'd made the trip on her walker, insisted on helping with the dishes, a sight that thrilled her grandson who'd despaired of her ever functioning on her own again.

He couldn't believe the changes since that night at the rodeo. As awkward as the initial days had been, the Buchanons were a family who kept their word. He was welcomed, forgiven. Though they were no closer than before to discovering who was vandalizing Buchanon work sites, no one pointed fingers at Jake. He prayed that never changed.

Allison's laugh came to him from the kitchen and suddenly she was there, her small hands on his shoulders. "Hey, cowboy. Ready to open presents?"

"I already have the only ones I ever wanted. You."

He jerked his chin toward the passel of family sprawled around the living room television. "Them. Home."

Her brown eyes softened. "Oh, Jake. This is the best Christmas ever."

"I can't argue that." Things weren't perfect. Problems remained with the mortgage and finances, but now that he was home for good, now that he had Allison at his side, he was confident something would work out.

In one corner of the large family room stood a massive Christmas tree trimmed in gold and red with a sprinkling of tiny football helmets and a lighted angel on top.

Someone flipped the television channel away from football and for once, no one complained as the sounds of the season came softly through the speakers. In a flurry of wrapping paper and ribbons, the family tore into gifts.

Jake and Allison sat on the floor in between Quinn and Jayla. Gifts piled into his lap, but his focus was Allison and her family, the hot air balloon feeling in his chest. He unwrapped a new wallet, a belt he and Allison had seen at the rodeo, a dinner for two at the Chinese restaurant. The pile grew until he was amazed.

"I can't believe this," he said, dumbfounded at what lay in the bottom of a small box.

Allison, deep in scarves and jewelry and books, looked up. "What is it?"

He handed her the card. "Did you have anything to do with this?"

As she read, Allison gasped, her expression turning from incredulity to joy. "The mortgage is paid in full."

"You didn't know?"

"No! This is wonderful. You won't have to sell your bulls. You can start your ranch."

Yes, and he could do something else, too. "But who?"

"Does it matter? This is the note, cancelled, fulfilled." Eyes dancing, she kissed the corner of his mouth. "The Hamilton debt is paid in full."

The wonder of the day overwhelmed him. "Kind of like Jesus, huh?" he said, softly. "He paid our debts when we couldn't."

"Exactly. Oh, I'm so happy for you. For us."

He caught her hand and drew it to his heart. Around them, paper flew and people talked while some kid sang about wanting a hippopotamus for Christmas. He didn't want a hippopotamus. He wanted her.

"I should have bought you a ring."

Allison froze in midchatter. "What did you say?"

"I thought we'd have to wait for years, but with the mortgage paid and the new job with Manny, we can make this work. Marry me, Allison. Be my Christmas present forever."

She opened her mouth, closed it, opened it again. Tears flowed down her cheeks.

"Don't cry. I love you." Jake's whole body quivered with the joy and hope she'd brought into his life.

Then surrounded by the awe and beauty of Christmas and the gift of family, Allison threw herself into his arms and through laughter and tears promised to be his.

And that was his best Christmas present ever.

* * * * *

A HICKORY RIDGE CHRISTMAS

Dana Corbit

To our firstborn daughter, Marissa,
who has been asking me to write
Hannah and Todd's story for four years now.
You already have so many wonderful stories in you.
I hope you find joy in telling them.

A special thanks to Monsignor John Budde for his
biblical research assistance; Michael G. Thomas,
CPA, for his knowledge of the accounting field;
and, as always, to my favorite medical expert,
Dr. Celia D'Errico, DO.

And be ye kind one to another, tenderhearted, forgiving one another, even as God for Christ's sake hath forgiven you.

—*Ephesians* 4:32

Chapter One

For the third time in as many weeks, Hannah Woods awoke smiling. She wasn't fully awake. Not really. For if she were, then the practical side of her mind would have insisted that she rein in those banned images. She was far too busy and far too focused to entertain little-girl dreams, at least in her conscious hours. She hadn't been a little girl for a very long time.

Just this once, though, in that private place between slumber and alertness, Hannah couldn't resist the temptation to let those pictures play out in full color.

Keeping her eyes tightly closed, Hannah let herself glance around in her make-believe world and take in sights and sounds so real that she could almost hear the organ prelude and smell sweet roses and pooling candle wax. Her heart warmed at the sight of her father standing at the altar, his Bible open to a familiar passage.

She couldn't picture herself, but she could almost feel tulle brushing her cheek and lacy bridal point, making her wrists itch. The last image, though, made her breath catch in her throat. Todd. Always Todd.

Standing across the aisle from her, he looked so handsome in his dark tuxedo. His shoulders had filled out the way she'd always imagined they would someday, but he still had the same boy's face she remembered, and his green eyes were as mesmerizing as ever. Those eyes still looked as sincere as they had when he'd told her he loved her.

When he'd lied.

As Hannah came fully awake with a start and sat straight up in bed, the twinkling lights of the miniature Christmas tree shifted into focus. They'd set it up the day before while still digesting their Thanksgiving turkey. This morning the tree's tinsel, garland and tiny red bows replaced all satin and pastel thoughts of the wedding that would never be.

What was she doing, anyway? She didn't have the luxury of indulging useless, adolescent dreams. And if she continued forgetting to unplug that little tree at night, especially with the apartment's wiring, they would be sifting through charred rubble before New Year's.

Clearly, she needed to get her act together. She was twenty-two years old now, not seventeen. She had responsibilities and obligations—things Todd knew nothing about and probably couldn't have handled if he knew. *You never gave him the chance to handle anything,* an unwelcome voice inside her pointed out with a punch she did her best to dodge. Forgiveness. She'd given that the old college try these past five years, but she couldn't quite get beyond the desertion part. Whether or not it had been his choice to leave with his parents when his father had been transferred to Singapore, the fact remained that he *had* left when she'd needed him most.

Perhaps only God could forgive and truly *forget.*

A litany of her own sins and failures played in her

mind as it always did when her thoughts turned to the boy she should have forgotten—the boy who was now a man. She would have allowed guilt to blanket her as she had so many times while the months stretched into years, but the squeak of her bedroom door offered a reprieve this time.

"I'm awake, Mommy," Rebecca called out as she bounded into the room, tucked something under the bed and then scrambled on top of the covers.

Though her child made that same announcement and followed the same routine every morning at about ten minutes before the alarm was set to go off, Hannah smiled. "Well, looky there. I guess you are."

"Is it Friday? Do I have my playdate with Max today?"

"Yes, sweetie, it's today."

Since Rebecca had been counting down the days until her playdate with her favorite friend, Max Williams, Hannah was pleased to finally say yes. Technically, the "playdate" was really only a day when Mary Nelson would be babysitting both Rebecca and Max while Hannah worked at the accounting firm and while Max's mother, Tricia Williams Lancaster, scoured Twelve Oaks Mall on the busiest shopping day of the year. Hannah didn't bother clarifying the point.

"Today. Today. Today!" Rebecca threw her head back on the bed and wiggled with the type of delight only a child could find before breakfast without a double espresso. Her fine towhead-blond hair stuck up every which way, and she squeezed her eyes shut tight, probably looking for the stars she liked to watch behind her eyelids.

Reaching down, Hannah brushed the hair back from

her daughter's fair-skinned face, all thoughts of obligations flittering away on a wave of pure adoration.

Rebecca opened her eyes and stared up at her mom. Hannah's chest tightened. It was probably the dream that made her react again to her daughter's green eyes when she'd been so proud of her ability to no longer notice them. Others probably hadn't found Rebecca's eye color remarkable since Hannah's eyes were a hazel-green shade—close but not the same. She saw it, though. Those were Todd's eyes that sometimes stared back when her daughter looked at her.

Clearing her throat, she gave the child a tight squeeze. "We'd better get up or we'll be late."

Rebecca lifted her head off the bed, and her bottom lip came out in a pout. "But…"

"Why? Do you have a better idea?"

The little girl pointed to the side of the bed.

"Is there something under there I should know about?"

Lying back and wiggling again, Rebecca nodded.

Hannah pressed her index finger to her lips as if pondering and then glanced down at her. "Is it bigger than a bread box?"

Rebecca's eyebrows furrowed. "What's a bread box?"

"A thing people used to use to keep bread fresh." Hannah gave the same answer she did every day.

"Nope."

"Is it smaller than an amoeba?"

"What's an amoeba?"

"A single-cell creature."

"Nope." A giggle erupted from the child's rosebud mouth. "Do you want to know what it is?"

"You'd better tell me. I just can't guess."

Rebecca climbed off the bed, peered under it and returned with the *surprise:* today's choice from their collection of Christmas storybooks they'd recently taken out of storage.

"Ooh, the manger story!" Hannah accepted the hardcover book, pleased with her daughter's selection with its quotes from the Book of Luke and Michelangelo-style painted illustrations. Hannah enjoyed reading all the festive stories to her daughter, but she was excited that Rebecca had chosen one that spoke of the true Christmas story instead of one about Rudolph and the rest of the holiday gang.

"There's baby Jesus." Rebecca pointed to the book cover, which featured a painting of the sweet infant, a halo of glory about his head. "And the sheep and the cows and the donkey."

"Looks like they're all there." Hannah opened the book to the first page, and Rebecca snuggled up under her arm. Only after they'd read the last page could they officially begin their day.

"The end," Rebecca announced with glee when they were finished.

Again Hannah smiled at her daughter. Rebecca approached everything with that same kind of enthusiasm, as if each hour was an uncharted land just waiting to be explored.

How could Hannah have forgotten, even for a minute, how fortunate she was to know this amazing four-year-old? How grateful she was to God for giving her the privilege of raising her. Loving Rebecca had nothing to do with obligation and so much to do with sharing in the joy and in the discovery.

During her conscious hours, Hannah didn't give herself time for regrets, not when she and Rebecca enjoyed so many blessings. If only she could rein in the images that crowded her dreams, as well. Those snapshots of the past hurt more than they healed, leaving her to awaken feeling empty and wondering whether something vital was missing from her life.

Todd took a deep breath as he stepped inside the church's glass double doors Sunday morning. If only he could remove the golf-ball-sized knot clogging his throat. He felt as queasy as an actor on opening night, only this wasn't a play and the only reviewer who mattered was sure to give him a scorching review.

Before he could even stomp the snow off his dress shoes and hang his coat on the rack that extended the length of the vestibule, an usher approached him.

"Welcome to Hickory Ridge Community Church," the man said as he gripped Todd's hand and pumped briskly. "Is this your first time visiting with us?"

Clearing his throat, Todd answered, "No—I mean it's been a long time, but—" he coughed into his hand and looked back up at the usher "—it isn't my first time."

"And we sure hope it won't be the last."

Todd tilted his head to indicate the crowded sanctuary, visible through a wall of windows. "I'd better get in there. I'm already late."

The man brushed away the comment with a wave of his hand. "Ah, they're just getting warmed up in there."

Todd thanked the man and continued past him. He'd hoped that arriving after services started would allow him to miss a formal greeting at the door, but he should have known better. Hickory Ridge had always been a friendly church on the "Bring-A-Friend Sunday" and the "Homecoming" events he'd attended with Hannah, and clearly that hadn't changed.

Plenty of other things were just as familiar, he found, as he peered through the windows into the sanctuary. Same stained glass window behind the choir loft. Same red carpet and red-padded pews. Same crowd of strangers. Same two guys sitting on the twin benches on either side of the pulpit.

Only the draped garland in the front of the sanctuary and the candles in the sills of the other stained glass windows even hinted at how long it had been since he'd visited. Those things suggested that months and seasons had sped by, but that mammoth second building behind the church where a field had once been, announced the passing of years.

The years scared him most of all.

Now that he was twenty-two, maybe it was too late. Maybe it had always been too late, and he'd only been deceiving himself, balancing on a tenuous lie of hope. The messages contained in airmail letters marked Returned To Sender and in the clicks of hang-ups for international calls should have been enough to convince him, but he'd refused to take the hints.

With his hand pressed on the door separating the vestibule from the sanctuary, he hesitated. His chest felt so tight that it ached to breathe. How could he move forward when it felt as if every moment of his life for half a decade had led him to this point?

How could he not?

Straightening his shoulders, he swung open the door and followed its path into the sanctuary. He slipped into the third pew from the back just as a music leader asked everyone to stand. Even as he turned pages in his hymnal, Todd couldn't help scanning the sea of heads. Where was she? Would he recognize her now? Even though he had it on good authority that she still attended Hickory Ridge, it didn't mean she wouldn't be sick this morning or out of town for Thanksgiving weekend.

Soon strains of "Just a Closer Walk With Thee" swirled around him, its lyrics celebrating the promise of God's presence. Warmth spread inside him, relieving some of the tightness in his chest. It was just like his God to find a way to remind him He was there, even when Todd was too preoccupied to sing the words.

As the song ended and the congregation sat, youth minister Andrew Westin stepped to the lectern. "Good morning, everyone, and welcome to Hickory Ridge. I hope you had a wonderful Thanksgiving."

Andrew's gaze settled on Todd, and a smile pulled at his lips. Of course, Andrew had been expecting to see him there. Todd should have known that he hadn't fooled anyone with his veiled questions when he'd called the church office a few days before. Especially not Andrew Westin. The Harley-riding youth minister never had struck Todd as any kind of fool.

As if Andrew recognized the question in Todd's eyes, he turned his head and directed his gaze toward a group of young adults sitting on the second pew. A couple of people on one end, a fancily dressed middle-aged woman on the other, and there she sat in the middle.

Todd didn't know if the world stopped turning or if time hiccuped, but for a few seconds or minutes, everything beyond her ceased to exist.

Even from behind that crowd of blondes, bru-nettes and silver-haired ladies, he couldn't imagine how he'd missed her before. He should have recognized that long, light blond ponytail anywhere, as it flowed down the back of her simple peach sweater. Hannah had often worn her hair just that way—smooth, neat and without fuss—and it was the feminine style he still found most attractive.

A piano introduction pulled Todd from his daze, but he couldn't wrap his thoughts around the words or the message of the second hymn. It shouldn't have surprised him. He'd always had tunnel vision when it came to Hannah, and that apparently hadn't changed. He couldn't remember a time when he didn't love her, and he couldn't imagine a future when he would be able to or even want to stop.

Around Hannah, Todd studied the group of young adults in her row and the one behind it, but none of them looked familiar. A tall, light-haired guy shared a hymnal with Hannah, but Todd couldn't remember seeing him, either, during his handful of visits. A few people were paying attention to the hymn, anyway. Todd was far too busy craning his neck and trying to get a glimpse of Hannah's face.

When the song ended, Reverend Bob Woods, who had grayed the last few years and now wore glasses, stepped to the lectern. He scanned the congregation, hesitating only briefly when he reached Todd. The minister's expression didn't change, but his Adam's apple bobbed. Guilt had Todd shifting in his seat.

Just because Hannah's father recognized him didn't automatically mean she'd confided in him about humiliating past events. Todd hadn't changed that much since they were next-door neighbors—at least, not on the outside. Anyway, it couldn't make any difference what Reverend Bob or Andrew Westin or anyone else knew about mistakes they'd made when they were still teenagers. He was here to make amends no matter what.

For a few seconds, the minister bowed his head as if in prayer, and then he looked up and smiled. "I'd like to add my welcome to Andrew's. We're so glad you're here. Whether you're longtime members or looking for a new church home, we're setting out the welcome mat."

Todd blinked. The minister probably offered that same greeting every Sunday, but this invitation felt more personal than that. For the first time since he'd pulled his car into the church parking lot and prepared for his past to collide with his present, he felt his confidence returning.

He did his best to focus on worship as Reverend Bob delivered a message on the birth of John the Baptist, that had taken place just prior to Jesus's birth, but no matter how hard Todd tried, he couldn't keep his attention from returning to Hannah. He'd waited so long to see her, had imagined this moment for what felt like forever, and here he was waiting again.

Please give me patience, Lord, and give me the words to make things right. Amen.

Hannah turned so that her lovely profile came into view. Her skin still looked as soft as he remembered, but the sprinkling of freckles across her nose appeared to have faded with time. Had her dimples, the tiny ones that only appeared when she really smiled, deepened as she'd entered her twenties? Did her eyes still crinkle at the corners when she laughed? Did those same eyes flood with tears whenever she spoke of her mother?

She tilted her head, appearing engrossed in her father's sermon. Todd hoped she'd had many reasons to smile and to laugh in the years since he'd left. More than anything, he wanted happiness for Hannah, who'd already known so much pain.

If only he could have been a better friend to her, could have provided a strong shoulder and a listening ear, instead of allowing his comforting touch to become something more. No, he hadn't been alone in that bed or alone in his decision to seek passion over purity, but he couldn't help believing he was more responsible than she was. He'd known how fragile Hannah was even so many months after her mom's death. Only one of them had been in any emotional state to put on the brakes in their relationship, and he'd ignored thoughts of sin and regret and gave into temptation anyway.

He'd known a lot of regret since then.

With effort, Todd set aside the emotions that threatened to distance him from his purpose. He glanced up at her again just as the congregation was singing the last chorus. The blond guy leaned close to Hannah and whispered something in her ear, and though she put her finger to her lips to hush him, her dimples appeared as she chuckled.

Todd's stomach tightened, and for the first time he gave the guy standing next to Hannah more than a passing glance. He'd worked so hard and had planned his return from overseas so carefully. Earning his engineering degree from Nanyang Technological University, targeting his job search to test engineering positions at General Motors Proving Grounds—everything—had been part of this long-term plan to work his way back to her.

He'd thought he'd looked at every obstacle. Clearly, he'd missed a huge one by never considering that Hannah might have dated other guys or even have found someone special in the last five years. Any man would have been crazy not to recognize Hannah for the amazing person she was and consider himself blessed to be with her.

The thought that Hannah might have dated others tore at his heart though he had no right to feel that way. Just because there had never been anyone else for him didn't mean she'd felt the same way.

What was he supposed to do now? No. He shook his head to clear his thoughts. He'd returned to Milford for two reasons only: to apologize to Hannah and to earn her forgiveness. Okay, he'd had secret hopes of building a life with Hannah, but he should have learned by now that he wasn't the type of guy meant for happy endings. Still, he was the type of guy who, just this once, would do the right thing no matter what it cost him.

By the time that Todd returned his attention to the front of the church, Andrew had stepped forward to pronounce the benediction.

"Father, lead us as we go out into Your world. Teach us to really love as You love and to forgive as You forgive. In the name of Your Son. Amen." After the prayer, Andrew ascended the aisle, waving at Todd as he passed.

Suddenly, a few things made sense. Was that what Andrew had really meant when he'd said some of the people Todd might know from the youth group had moved away? Had Andrew been referring to Hannah moving on with her life…without him?

Todd steeled himself again. It didn't matter. He couldn't let it matter. He'd waited an awfully long time and gone to more trouble than most men would ever consider to give this apology. Nothing, not even his owns fears, could stop him from doing what he had to do.

With resolve, he looked to the front of the sanctuary, past the other congregants who were chatting and gathering their coats. At first, he thought he'd missed her and that she'd left by one of the side aisle doors. Some of the people she'd been sitting with, including the blond guy, were already gone. But then she straightened from where she'd bent to retrieve her Bible.

Hannah turned her head to say something to the woman next to her, and then she stopped. He knew the minute she recognized him because her eyes widened, and her lovely mouth went slack.

For several seconds, neither moved. Todd felt like a spectator to his own life, unable to look away while the one woman he'd ever loved stared back at him as if he was the last person she ever expected to see again. Or maybe ever wanted to see.

As the Bible she held slipped from her fingers, its pages fluttering open on its path to the floor, Todd felt as if some small part of him—something elemental like hope—died.

Chapter Two

Todd.

Hannah's lips formed the word, but she couldn't summon the breath to give it sound. Her chest ached as fear and panic pressed down on it like a heavy hand.

She'd dreamed of him so often, with fondness and fury, and there he was. His presence seemed to fill the sanctuary from carpet to rafters. She'd tried so hard to forget those eyes, and there they were, staring back at her with that same unnerving intensity.

What was he doing here? What did he want? Why now? Why ever? Rebecca. What was she supposed to do about Rebecca?

Hannah didn't know how long she'd stood there staring or even that she'd dropped her Bible until her friend Steffie Wilmington pressed it back into her sweaty hands. She could barely hold on to its smooth leather cover.

She lowered her gaze to the Bible's gold lettering and then turned back to the college freshman stand-ing next to her. "Um…thanks."

Remembering where they were and how well attended

the Sunday service had been, Hannah glanced around, hoping none of the other church members had noticed her strange reaction. Could they tell who he was just by looking at him?

"Hannah, what's wrong…"

Steffie, who probably preferred "Stephanie" now but hadn't been able to squash the nickname, didn't even get the question out of her mouth before the source of Hannah's problem started up the aisle toward them.

Hannah couldn't answer. Her mouth was dry, and her heart raced. She felt this overwhelming need to run and hide. Why should today be any different? She'd been running and hiding from the truth since the second dot on the home pregnancy test had turned pink.

She stiffened, but she couldn't take her eyes off Todd's steady approach. He looked older than she'd imagined he would, his shoulders even wider than she'd predicted in the well-tailored navy suit he wore. He'd finally filled out his over-six-foot frame and could no longer be called lanky. His hair had deepened to a dark blond, but it still had that tousled look he'd never been able to control.

His face, though, had changed most of all. It was no longer sweet and boyish but was framed with the handsome, hardened planes of manhood. If he'd been smiling, his face probably would have softened and the dimple in his chin would have been more pronounced, but his expression was serious. Cautious.

"Who's he?" Steffie tried again, looking back and forth between the two of them. "Wait. He looks familiar. He looks like…"

The younger woman's words trailed away as Todd reached the front of the room and sidled into the pew behind theirs. Around them, church members continued to make their way toward the exit, but several glanced curiously at Hannah, Todd and Steffie.

"Hi… Hannah." His voice cracked, so he cleared his throat.

He expected her to say something; she knew that. The words just wouldn't come. Words couldn't squeeze past the guilt clawing at her insides. No matter what he'd done, no matter how hurt she'd felt, she should have found a way to tell him as soon as she knew. Or at least she could have found some occasion before Rebecca's fourth birthday. What was she supposed to tell him now?

"Look, I didn't mean to startle you," Todd told her. "I only wanted the chance to—"

"Sweetie, are you okay?" Steffie interrupted, reminding Hannah she was still there, observing en-tirely too much. "Do you need me to get your dad?"

Hannah shook her head and raised a hand to stop Steffie, but she still couldn't look away from Todd. He appeared just as frozen.

"Is there somewhere we can talk?" he finally choked out. "There are so many things I need to say."

Panic welled deep within her, its acidic tang bitter on her tongue. She couldn't tell him. Not now. Soon, but not yet. She jerked her head, breaking the cold connection of their gazes. Slowly, she started shaking her head and backing toward the aisle.

"I can't do this, Todd. I just can't. I have to go."

Turning, she pressed past Steffie and hurried up the side aisle.

"Hannah! Wait! Stop!"

His plea pounded in her ears, but she couldn't wait. She couldn't stop. She couldn't even look back as she rushed through the vestibule and into the hall leading to the Family Life Center. Rebecca would be waiting for her there in Children's Church.

Hannah could feel his gaze on her as she went, but she didn't hear his footsteps. If he followed her and tried to air out their past right now, he would find out the truth. He would know the secret she'd wasted so much energy trying to keep from him and everyone else. Part of her prayed he would do just that.

Todd watched her go, somehow managing to keep from chasing after her through the church and making a bigger fool of himself than he had already.

She hurried past the line of members shaking hands with the ministry team. Instead of continuing through the glass doors leading to the parking lot, she turned left and headed down a hallway toward the rear of the church.

Only after she'd disappeared completely from sight did Todd turn his attention to the young woman standing next to him. The tall redhead with a dusting of freckles on her nose was looking at him nearly eye to eye. She raised a delicate brow.

Finally, he remembered his manners and shot out his right hand. "Hi. I'm Todd McBride."

"Todd. Todd." She frowned while rolling the name around on her tongue as if she expected it to ring a bell. Then she shrugged. "I'm Stephanie."

He let go of her hand and then glanced at the sanctuary's rear door again. "I should go after her."

"She didn't seem all that thrilled about talking to you."

"Probably not." He ignored the hopeless feeling

threatening to resurface. "But she's going to have to anyway."

With a quick wave, he strode out the door. Finding only Andrew shaking hands and saying goodbye to the last of the stragglers, Todd assumed that Reverend Bob had slipped away to check on his daughter. As inconspicuously as possible, Todd started to follow the same path he'd seen Hannah take.

"Wait, Todd." Andrew caught up to him and gripped his hand in a firm handshake. "Glad you made it. You're probably looking forward to starting your new job. Did the folks at GM Proving Grounds give you a little time to get settled, or did they want you right away?"

"I guess they needed someone right away because I had to negotiate to wait until Tuesday."

"Isn't that just the way it goes? No rest for the weary."

"Guess so." Distracted, Todd cast a furtive glance down the hall. Was she still back there somewhere?

Andrew's gaze followed his. "So, besides Reverend Bob and me, did you see anyone you recognized at the service?"

Todd was barely paying attention, so the words took a moment to sink in. When they did, he turned back to the youth minister. "No disrespect intended, Reverend, but let's not dance around this anymore. We both know I came here to see Hannah."

Andrew nodded, the smile he usually wore absent. "And I noticed that you did see her."

"No one probably knew we were more than friends."

"I knew. Serena knew."

Todd's head came up with a jerk. "Oh."

"Remember that day all of us spent at the beach?"

"I guess so." Of course Todd remembered. It was

one of the memories he'd replayed in his mind in the last few years.

"We saw the way you looked at Hannah when you thought no one was watching."

Todd cleared his throat. He could only imagine the emotions that had been written all over his face. Because there didn't seem to be any way to respond to that comment, he changed the subject. "We built a sand castle with Serena's little girl…uh…"

"Tessa," Andrew said to fill in the blank.

"You had a thing for the single mother."

"Still do. But she's married now. To me. Five years." Andrew glanced down at the plain gold band he wore. "Tessa's got a brother now. Seth. We're having another one in March."

"Wow. Either a lot of time has passed, or you've been busy for a few years," Todd said with a chuckle.

Instead of laughing at his joke, Andrew became serious. "A lot of time has passed."

The words felt like weights being draped across Todd's shoulders. He stared at the floor and waited for whatever else the youth minister had to say.

"Hannah didn't seem happy to see you today."

"I suppose not." Todd reluctantly met the other man's gaze. "I didn't go about things the right way."

"It's hard to know the right thing to do sometimes."

Andrew now wore his concerned minister's face. Todd remembered Hannah once mentioning that Andrew had been a clinical counselor before entering the ministry.

"Apologizing to Hannah is the right thing to do," Todd said. "I know it. She just didn't give me the chance."

"I don't know everything that happened between the two of you or the full reason she ran out of here, but—"

"No," Todd said to interrupt him. "You don't." His sharp tone surprised even him. It wasn't Andrew's fault that Hannah had refused to talk to him. He had no one to blame for that but himself. Taking a deep breath to clear his thoughts, he tried again. "I've been waiting five years to talk to Hannah…about a lot of things."

"Have you ever considered that healing this relationship might not be as easy as you've imagined?"

"You mean that it might be too late? Sure, I've thought about it." *A lot.* He took a long breath and shook his head in frustration. "But I have to do the right thing. I've prayed about it, and I'm convinced it's what God wants me to do, so I'm just going to have to find a way to get Hannah to listen to me."

"You sound pretty determined."

"I am."

"I guess you'll be needing this then."

Andrew withdrew a pen and notebook from his pocket, wrote something on it and handed to him. It said, "Hannah," and it had a street address and an apartment number on it. Todd drew his eyebrows together as he looked up from it.

"You didn't think she still lived at home, did you?"

He answered with a shrug. As a matter of fact, he had. He'd already driven by his old home and that particular house next door several times since he'd arrived in town on Friday. He'd studied that familiar dwelling, wondering whether she was inside and hoping she would pick that moment to go out to her car.

Todd closed his hand over the slip of paper. "Thanks, Andrew."

"Will you do me one favor when you talk to Hannah?" Andrew waited for his nod before he continued, "When you're talking, will you be sure to listen, too?"

Of course he would listen, Todd thought as he climbed in his car and turned out of the church lot onto Hickory Ridge Road. He would listen, but he couldn't imagine what Hannah would have to say. She had nothing to apologize for; that was his department alone. Yet, an uncomfortable sensation settled between his shoulder blades. Why did he get the sense that Andrew knew something he didn't?

"What are you doing, Mommy?"

Hannah turned from the medicine cabinet mirror where she was repairing her makeup. Rebecca, dressed only in a pair of red cotton tights, underwear and a lace-trimmed undershirt, stared up at her from the bathroom doorway.

Quickly, Hannah turned her back to her daughter and brushed the last of her tears away with the back of her hand. "Nothing, honey. You go ahead and finish changing your clothes. Remember to lay your dress out on the bed so I can hang it up, okay?"

"Okay," Rebecca answered, though she would likely forget and leave the Christmas plaid dress in a pile on the floor. She started to leave and then stopped, turning back to her mother. "Are you crying?"

"No. Not really." Hannah pressed her lips together. Now she was even lying to her daughter. When would it all stop? "I guess I am a little sad."

"Don't be sad, Mommy." Rebecca wrapped her arms around her mother's thighs and squeezed.

"Go on now," she said, fighting back another wave of emotion.

As soon as Rebecca skipped down the hall, Hannah started swiping at the dampness again. She'd managed to hold herself together all through the ritual of collecting her daughter from her church program and through the drive home, but Hannah's control had wavered the moment she was alone, changing out of her church clothes.

Todd? In Milford again? Come to think of it, she didn't even know why he was in town. She might know that answer now if she'd given him a chance to speak. But how could she? Without any notice, she wasn't prepared to face him. Who was she kidding? Even with six months notice, she wouldn't have been able to come up with a valid explanation for what she'd done.

All of her excuses for not telling him—her anger for his leaving, her choice to never reveal the identity of her child's father, her rationalization that Todd didn't deserve to know—now sounded like the incoherent ramblings of a teenage girl.

That was what they were.

How could she ever have thought she had the right to withhold the information from him that he was a father? No one had that right to wield so much power over other people's lives.

She had to tell him; that was a given. And she would. Soon. She just needed a little time to regroup first. After that, she would ask around and find out whom he was visiting and how long he would stay. She would tell him everything then, but she would do it on her terms.

Hannah nodded at the mirror, her thoughts clear for the first time since Todd appeared at her church and tilted her world on its axis.

A knock at the front door, though, set her thoughts and her newly settled world spinning once again. Was it Todd already? No, it couldn't be. He wouldn't even know where she lived, although he would only have to ask her father to get that information. Reverend Bob, who still didn't know the whole truth, either.

Rebecca reappeared in the bathroom, this time wearing a reindeer sweatshirt with her tights. "Somebody's knocking on the door."

"I heard. I'll get the door. Why don't you go put your jeans on? Then go set up your dolls in the living room, and I'll be there in a minute to play."

Again, Rebecca scurried off, but this time, Hannah followed, turning down the hall to the front door. She stopped as her hand touched the wood. Without a peephole to check for sure, she could only hold her breath and hope she was wrong.

Lord, please don't let it be Todd. It's too soon. Please give me strength when the time comes. Amen.

Her hand was on the doorknob when his voice came through the door.

"Hannah, it's me. Todd. I know you're in there. I can see the lights."

Panic came in a rush that clenched inside her and dampened her palms. No. She couldn't tell him now. She wasn't ready. Not yet.

"Go away, Todd."

Though she recognized the voice as her own, the words surprised even her. She was taking the easy way out again rather than facing this mess she'd created, but she couldn't seem to help herself.

For a few seconds, there was no sound on the other side of the door. She almost expected to hear the crunch of snow as he trudged down the steps and away from her apartment, but instead there was a more insistent knock.

"You might as well open the door because I'm not leaving."

Hannah stared at the door. Todd sounded different. The laid-back boy she remembered had been replaced by this determined and forceful guy she didn't recognize at all, and yet she still found herself cracking the door open to him. *Whatever happened to your fear of strangers?* But irony encased that thought, for even this new Todd was in no way a stranger to her.

He stood on the porch, the collar of his wool jacket flipped up to shield his ears and his hands shoved in the front pockets of his slacks. Several years on an island off the southern end of the Malay Peninsula hadn't prepared him for a Milford December. She was surprised by the impulse to warm his hands with her own, but she remained behind the cracked door.

"How did you find out where I live?"

"Andrew gave me your address." He withdrew his hand from his pocket and held out a crumpled piece of paper.

"Why did Andrew—" she started to ask but stopped herself when the answer dawned.

Have you told Todd? Andrew's words from that long ago night flashed through her mind. The youth minister and his future wife, Serena, had counseled her when she'd first discovered she was pregnant. She'd denied Andrew's assertion that Todd was the father, and neither of them had pressured her to reveal her secret.

The secret that had come back to haunt her today.

Hannah sighed, suddenly exhausted by the energy it had required to keep the truth hidden. "Todd, what are you doing here?"

Todd's teeth chattered as he zipped his jacket higher. "I told you I want to talk to you."

She cocked her head to the side and studied him. Now that the shock of seeing him was beginning to wear off, old, mixed emotions began to resurface. Anger she realized she had no right to feel and long-buried hurt collided, leaving her insides feeling exposed. "After five years? Why would we have anything to talk about?"

"We do. I know *I* do."

Hannah stared at him. He'd surprised her again with his certainty when she felt so unsure. "Maybe in a few days but not yet. I'm not ready—"

As she spoke those last three words, she started closing the door. Todd pressed his foot into the space before it could close completely.

"Isn't five years long enough?" he said.

Staring at his dress shoe, Hannah waited, but he didn't say more, so she finally lifted her gaze to his. In his eyes was a look of anguish so stark that Hannah could only remember seeing an expression like it once before. She'd found it in the mirror the day that Todd's family left for the airport.

He glanced away and back, and the look was gone. "I've waited five years to apologize to you. I'm not leaving until you let me do it."

Hannah blinked, her mind racing. A million times she'd imagined Todd's reaction when she told him the truth. Now she only wanted to run and hide with her secret again, to protect her daughter from the fallout and herself from the blame she deserved.

But she couldn't run anymore. Todd was right. It was time.

"Then I guess I'd better invite you in."

Chapter Three

As Hannah pulled open the door, Todd released the breath he hadn't even realized he'd been holding. His foot ached, more likely from standing out in the cold than from where she'd squeezed it in the door, but he didn't care. He was here, she was here, and that was all that mattered.

"Nice place," he said before he even stepped on the mat and took a look around.

And it was nice. Though one of the four smallish apartments in a renovated older house, Hannah had made it look warm and homey with overstuffed furniture and soft pillows. It was decorated in earth tones and dotted with artistic, framed black-and-white photographs of children.

The Christmas tree he'd first glimpsed through the front window radiated warmth, as well, with its home-made ornaments, popcorn strands and spatter of silvery icicles. No hand-blown glass balls and fussy velvet bows for Hannah's apartment.

The woman herself looked as warm and casual as her house, dressed in well-worn jeans and a black long-sleeved top. She had fuzzy slippers on her feet. But her expression showed she was anything but comfortable with him in her space, and she looked as if she'd been crying.

"Yes, we like it."

We? The smile that had formed on his face slipped away as he turned to her. What had he missed? Hannah took a few steps into the living room and motioned for Todd to follow.

There in the corner that he couldn't see from the front door was a tiny blond girl, surrounded by baby dolls, blankets and play bottles. For several seconds, Todd stared at the child who was looking back at him with huge, haunting eyes. She looked familiar somehow.

"Come here, honey," Hannah called to the child. When the little girl stood under her protective arm, Hannah turned back to face him.

"Todd, this is Rebecca. She's my daughter."

Daughter? Hannah had a daughter? He looked back and forth between them, his thoughts spinning. Though their features were slightly different, they both had lovely peachy skin and light, light hair. They were clearly relatives.

When he glanced away to collect his thoughts, his gaze landed again on the amazing photos dotting the walls on either side of the Christmas tree. The subjects of those photos, taken in a variety of natural backdrops, weren't children, but rather one child—the same sweet-looking little girl standing right in front of him.

Clearing his throat, he turned back to them. "Nice pictures."

"Thanks."

"The photographer did a great job."

She nodded but didn't look at the portraits. Instead, she turned to her daughter. "Rebecca, this is Mr. Mc-Bride."

"Hi," she said quickly before taking refuge behind her mother's jeans-clad leg.

"Hello, Rebecca."

Todd shook his head, trying to reconcile the new information. Parts of this puzzle weren't fitting together easily. Was Hannah married now? Was that what Andrew had been trying to tell him when he'd suggested that healing the relationship might not be easy? If that was it, how could the minister have been so cruel as to let him go on believing…hoping?

His gaze fell to Hannah's left hand, the one she was using to lead the child back to her toys and out of earshot of their conversation.

Hannah wore no ring.

Suddenly all of Todd's other questions fell away as one pressed to the forefront of his mind: a question too personal for him to ask. Still, when she returned to him, he took hold of her arm and led her around the corner to the entry so he could ask it.

"Who's her father, Hannah?"

She shot a glance back at her daughter, as if she worried Rebecca had overheard. He couldn't blame her if she shouted, "How dare you" for the private question and more. He deserved it.

But instead of yelling, she began in a soft tone. "You have to understand—"

"Who is it?" He couldn't help it. He didn't want an explanation; he wanted a name. Jealousy he had no right to feel swelled inside him, burning and destroying. The thought of another man touching her left his heart raw.

If only he and Hannah had waited, their story might have turned out differently. Hannah might have been his wife. Her child, theirs.

Hannah stared back at him incredulously, as if she was shocked that he'd had the gall to ask. It wasn't about wanting; he *had* to know.

"Is it that blond guy from church?"

"Grant?" Her eyes widened and then she shook her head. "He's just a friend."

"Do I know him then?"

"Of course you do." She spat the words.

Strange, she sounded exasperated. She seemed to think he was an idiot for not knowing the answer. He stepped around the corner and studied the child again. She was so fair and beautiful, just like her mother. Rebecca must have sensed his attention on her because she looked up from her dolls and smiled at him.

And he knew.

His gut clenched, and he felt helpless to do anything but stare. Why it wasn't immediately apparent to him he couldn't imagine now. Her green eyes had looked familiar because he saw eyes like those in the mirror every morning.

Though he was no expert on children's ages and this particular child was probably small for her age, as her mother had been, he could see from her features that she wasn't a toddler. Rebecca looked about four years old, just old enough to have been conceived five years before.

"She's mine, isn't she?"

Hannah didn't answer, but her eyes filled and a few tears escaped to trail down her cheeks. She brushed them away with the backs of her hands.

"Tell me I'm right, Hannah. Am I Rebecca's father?"

Instead of nodding the way he was certain she would, Hannah shook her head. Her jaw flexed as if she was gritting her teeth.

"How could you have thought—" She stopped whatever she'd been about to say. Closing her eyes, she pressed her hands over her closed lids and took a few deep breaths before continuing. "If you're asking if you supplied half of her DNA, then you're right. But for her whole life, I've been both parents to Rebecca. She's mine. Just mine."

"Not just yours. She's mine, too."

Todd wasn't sure whether he'd spoken those words aloud or just in the privacy of his heart until Hannah stalked from the room and crouched down by her daughter. *No, their daughter.*

Maybe he hadn't said the right thing, but what did she expect when she'd just dropped a bomb like that? He didn't know what to *think,* let alone what to say.

How naive he'd been with his big plans to return here and to earn Hannah's forgiveness and her heart. He'd thought he and Hannah were the only two involved, that their old conflicts were only between the two of them, when a third person had been growing inside Hannah before he'd ever left.

Father. He couldn't wrap his thoughts around the title yet, let alone apply it to himself. Everything he knew about himself changed with that single admission.

"Why did you have to come back?" Hannah whispered when she returned to him, appearing more agitated than before. "We were doing fine. Just fine. Now you've messed all of that up. We'll never be the same."

"Come on, Hannah. We have a lot to talk about."

"I don't think so. You've got your answer now, so go."

"I can't leave now that you've told me this."

"Please go." Her eyes filled again.

Her plea tore at his heart. Clearly, they had more to say to each other, but maybe now wasn't the best time. He was still too shocked, too confused to make any decisions that would affect their lives. Three lives.

"I won't stay gone, you know. I'm living in Milford now, and I'm sticking around this time."

Either she didn't hear him or she refused to answer, but Hannah hurried him toward the door and closed it behind him. As the cold enfolded him, this time seeping to his very core rather than only touching his extremities, Todd realized that Hannah was right about one thing: None of them would ever be the same.

It wasn't until Todd was back at his Commerce Road town house and eating chicken noodle soup that refused to warm his chilled insides that he realized he'd never apologized to Hannah. After traveling from the other side of the world in miles and in years of effort, he hadn't even managed to do the most important thing he'd come to town to accomplish.

"You were too busy trying not to swallow your tongue to remember anything else," he said to the stacked boxes around him.

Sitting at the new glass dinette in the kitchen, he stared down into the soup bowl and stirred the noodles into a whirlpool. His thoughts traveled in a similar circular pattern, but unlike the liquid, they wouldn't stop spinning.

A child. His child. Of course, he should have considered the possibility that Hannah could have become pregnant. He knew the textbook mechanics of reproduction and the potential consequences of unprotected sex, but he'd never once considered that they might have made a child together. He and Hannah had only made love that one time. Apparently, it only took once.

The returned letters and unanswered calls made sense now. Not only had he left her alone with her guilt over what had happened between them, but he'd also left her alone with his child.

Alone. He felt that way now as he sat with only the bare walls and the truth to keep him company. He suddenly felt a stronger need to connect with his parents than he had at any time since he'd hugged them goodbye in Kranji a week earlier. But what would he say to them if he called? He could just imagine how that conversation would go: "Hello, Mom and Dad. Or should I say Grandma and Grandpa? I have just the best news."

He shook his head. No, that conversation would have to wait for another day when he was prepared to hear disappointment of that magnitude over international phone lines. He wasn't ready for that when he hadn't digested it himself yet.

But there was one call he could make now. He pulled out the phone book, looked up the name and dialed. He didn't even identify himself when the man answered on the second ring.

"Why didn't you tell me?" Todd said simply.

Andrew Westin sighed loudly into the line. "Todd. I had an idea I would be hearing from you."

"You could have saved yourself the call by telling me before."

"You make it sound so easy."

His jaw was so tightly clenched in frustration that it took Todd a few seconds to be able to answer at all and a few seconds more to answer civilly. "It was easy. The first time I called the church, you could have said, 'Hey, Todd, it's good to hear from you. Just thought you should know, you're a dad.'"

"Sure, I could have done that."

"Then why didn't you?"

"It wasn't my place. Then or now."

Todd stalked over to the tan striped couch, dropped onto it and sank into the backrest. "Then or now? What do you mean by that?"

"Hannah never told anyone who the father of her baby was. Until now."

"Until now?" Todd straightened in his scat. There could be no slouching after a comment like that, one that crushed as much as it confused. Hannah had been more ashamed of him than she'd been of being an unwed mother. He didn't know what to do with that information.

"Wait. Then how did *you* know?"

"I told you Serena and I had guessed you two were more than friends when we saw you together."

Todd swallowed. "Oh."

"So, when Hannah became pregnant, we suspected. Then when little Rebecca arrived, we…well knew."

The image of those pretty green eyes filled his mind again. If Andrew and Serena had already been suspecting, he could easily see how they'd connected the dots to solve the puzzle. They'd probably put it together faster than he had.

"What about Reverend Bob?"

"If he knows, he's never mentioned it to me." Andrew paused. "Bob was always more concerned with supporting his daughter than tracking down his grandchild's father."

"Another reason I never found out the truth."

"Todd, I always thought she would open up eventually, that *she* would tell you. But she didn't. So when you called looking for answers, I figured God was suggesting that I help the truth along."

"I don't know whether to say thanks or not." Todd shoved his free hand through his hair.

"But you know now, right?"

Todd blew out a breath. "Yes, I know."

"And how do you feel about that?"

"Don't use all that psychobabble on me, okay Reverend?"

"Fine. But she's a cute one, your daughter."

Emotion filled Todd's throat with a speed that surprised him. Rebecca was his daughter, and she didn't even know him.

"Yeah…she's beautiful," he choked out finally.

Andrew chuckled into the line. "Spoken like a true father. I do have one more question for you."

"What's that?"

"What are you going to do about it now that you know?"

What are you going to do? Todd didn't have an answer for the minister's question or for his own as they said their goodbyes. He clicked off the phone and laid it on the end table. It was a given that he would take some responsibility for the care of his child. His parents would expect that, and he expected that of himself. He didn't even want to remember all the other things he'd expected to happen when he returned to Milford.

Disquiet had him pushing off the sofa and crossing to the light wood bookshelf he'd just purchased and already had crammed with books. His fingers closed over a heavy cloth-covered album his mother had insisted he take with him on the plane at Changi International Airport. He took it back to the table and plunked it next to the bowl of soup that had already congealed.

He sat and opened it to the first page. It was as he predicted: a tribute to the lives and loves of the McBride clan. He would expect nothing less from Sharon McBride than a maudlin display, sure to cause more homesickness than to cure it.

The first few pages were all family pictures, both of the posed professional variety and informal shots taken in front of their homes in Milford and then in Kranji. His mother had a talent for pulling heartstrings.

Todd flipped through images of himself eating his first birthday cake, standing proudly on the first day of kindergarten and marching in the high school band. Then came photos of his friends in Singapore and even a few of Todd and Hannah hanging out at the Milford Memories festival. Because those last shots tempted him to feel sorry for himself, he turned the page.

The next pictures made him smile: first the wedding portrait of Roy McBride and the former Sharon Quinn and then a few other black-and-white snapshots of the two of them as children.

When Todd reached the last yellowing image at the bottom right, he stopped. He stared at the little girl looking out at him from the paper. In the white trim at the photo's bottom edge, someone had written in a slanted script, "Sharon, age four," but the picture could just as easily have been of Hannah's child. Not subtle like the similarity his daughter had to him, the resemblance between his mother and Rebecca was so obvious that at the same age they could have been twins.

Why that was the trigger—this mirror image—Todd couldn't explain, and yet he was suddenly furious. His hands clasped the edge of the table so hard he could feel the glass side imprinting on his palm. His jaw flexed, and he could feel his pulse beating at his temple.

How could Hannah not have told him? No matter what he'd done, no matter how angry she was with him or how much she wanted to cast him as the villain who deserved all the blame, he still had the right to know he'd fathered a child. The chance to *be* a father to his child.

He'd deserved the truth.

Would he have been a great father at seventeen? It was hard to say, but he'd deserved the chance to try. So much time had already passed. Rebecca was four years old. Whether she'd done it consciously or not, Hannah had stolen that time from them, time they could never get back.

The whole situation just didn't make sense. The Hannah he'd known could never have been so cruel as to keep this monumental secret from him. Then a thought struck him at his foundation. Maybe he hadn't known her at all. Maybe the girl he'd fallen in love with had only existed in his mind, and the future he'd planned for them was just as much of an illusion.

None of what he thought before could matter. Everything was different now that he knew about Rebecca. He still wanted to apologize to Hannah for past events, but the present was much more important. They needed to discuss Rebecca's care and to work out a plan for him to get to know his daughter.

Hannah would fight him on that, he was sure, but she didn't know him, either, if she thought that battle would be an easy one. Maybe he hadn't fought hard enough when Hannah had decided to eliminate him from her life five years ago, but he'd done a lot of growing up since then—physically and spiritually. Hannah had just better get it through her mind that he was here and he wasn't going away.

Chapter Four

"I'm hungry," Rebecca announced as she raced through the front door her mother had just unlocked. "When are we going to eat dinner?"

Hannah somehow managed to keep her sigh a silent one as she followed behind her with several plastic grocery bags draped over each arm. It wasn't Rebecca's fault that Hannah's day had been lousy, or even that they'd had to stop at the grocery store on the way home from Mrs. Nelson's because there wasn't any food in the house.

Hannah had no one to blame for either of those things but herself. When Todd had finally left Sunday, she'd been too exhausted to even think about grocery shopping for the week. She'd barely been able to just keep her promise and play dolls with Rebecca.

As they'd sat together on the floor, diapering, swaddling and feeding two hairless baby dolls with plastic milk and juice bottles, her thoughts kept returning to another baby and the father who'd just been blindsided by her existence. Would Hannah ever be able to forget the look of bewilderment that had strained his features? Even the fresh ache she felt every time she remembered that Todd hadn't immediately recognized Rebecca as his child couldn't compete with that. Still, it hurt her that he'd assumed she'd been intimate with someone other than him.

I won't stay gone. As they had several times in the twenty-four hours since he'd spoken them, his words echoed in her thoughts. Until the evening service and after it, she'd sat anxious and alert, waiting for him to make good on his promise.

All she'd gotten for her trouble was a sleepless night and a drowsy day at work when she needed to be sharp while doing year-end accounting for several small businesses. Too many more days like that and she could add joblessness to her list of problems.

"Mommy, didn't you hear me? I'm hungry." This time Rebecca said it in the woeful tone of the starving. She still hadn't learned that mothers often heard even when they didn't answer.

"Have patience, sweetie. Your chicken nuggets are coming right up."

At least they would come up as soon as Hannah preheated the oven and baked them for twenty to twenty-five minutes, but she didn't want to give Rebecca that bad news and risk a meltdown. That was the last thing she needed when her friend, Grant Sumner, would arrive at any time for the home-cooked meal Hannah had promised him weeks ago. She didn't even have the pork chops defrosted.

A bachelor who claimed an allergy to anything domestic, Grant already could recite every take-out menu in Milford verbatim. He didn't need her ordering a pizza on the one night when he could have been enjoying home cooking.

"But I'm hungry now," Rebecca whined. "Can I have a cookie?"

Irritation welled in her, but Hannah forced it back. "Maybe after dinner."

Already, Rebecca was cuing up the waterworks, so Hannah grabbed the first distraction that came to mind. "Why don't you watch your video until dinner's ready?"

"Yay, TV!"

Her daughter's glee came with its own sting of reproach. Hannah was convinced she was a bad mother now. She'd even started using "Aunt TV" as a nanny. "Just for a few minutes. Mr. Grant should be here soon for dinner."

Rebecca hurried off before the offer of the rare visual treat evaporated with the arrival of company.

As if he recognized his cue, Grant rang the bell, pushed the unlocked door wide and stepped inside.

"Hannah, you know better than to leave your door unlocked like that. Anyone can walk right in off the street and—"

"Yeah, yeah, I know," Hannah interrupted, smirking at her friend over the fact that he'd done just that.

Grant flushed in a way his fair skin failed to hide and shrugged out of his coat, hanging it on the coat tree next to the door. "You know what I mean."

"Of course I do. And thanks for worrying about me."

"Somebody's got to do it." As Grant started pushing the door closed, another pair of hands on the other side stopped it.

"Hannah, it's me." Todd's voice slipped through the crack.

"Me?" Grant yanked the door back open and came

face-to-face with the man a few years younger and a couple of inches taller. "Who are you?"

"Todd McBride." With that curt answer, Todd pressed past him into the entry. "Who's asking?"

"Grant Sumner, Hannah's—"

"Friend," she finished before Grant had the chance.

Hannah didn't miss the confusion in Grant's eyes or the irritation in Todd's, but she wasn't about to have a scene here with Rebecca in the next room. "Todd, this really isn't a good time."

Grant shot her a perplexed glance but jumped in with his support. "Yeah, sorry, buddy. We were just getting ready to have dinner."

Todd's jaw tightened, but he stood where he was. "It's never going to be a good time to—"

Hannah put her hand up to cut him off before he could say more. "I wish you would have called first."

"You mean so that you could *not* answer." Todd closed the door behind him and stood in front of it with his arms crossed. "Been there, done that. I'm over it. How about you?" His gaze locked with hers and wouldn't let go.

"What are you two talking about?"

At Grant's words, Hannah could finally pull her gaze away. Her friend was staring at them both by turns, and then he faced her alone.

"It's him, isn't it? He's the reason—"

Grant managed to stop himself before he said more, but Hannah ached for his hurt feelings. That she'd never led him to believe there could be more than friendship between them didn't seem to exonerate her for putting him in this awkward situation.

"I'm sorry, Grant," she found herself saying, though she couldn't imagine what she would say next.

Rather that looking at her for confirmation of his assumption, Grant turned back to Todd. "Maybe you'd just better leave right now."

Todd started out by holding his hands wide. "Look, friend, I don't have a problem with you, but—"

"I'm not your friend." Grant took a step toward Todd, but instead of holding his hands wide, he had them tight by his sides, fisted. "But I am Hannah's. And since she doesn't seem to want you here…"

Immediately, Todd's posture tightened, and he stepped forward, as well. "Don't you think that's her decision?"

"She already said this isn't a good time."

Hannah couldn't believe her eyes as she looked back and forth between them. With all this male posturing, they looked like a pair of gorillas, pounding their chests and announcing their dominance. The two of them standing their ground, just feet apart, would have been comical if the situation hadn't been so *not* funny. Her daughter was right in the next room.

Stepping to the side, Hannah peered into the living room. Rebecca was sprawled on the floor in front of the TV with her elbows jutting out and her head cradled between her tiny hands. Maybe "Aunt TV" wasn't so bad just this once.

When she returned to the front hall, Hannah stepped between the two men. "You know, maybe we should all just call it a night. Can I give you a rain check on dinner, Grant? I didn't get started the way I'd planned, anyway."

Grant gave her a distracted glance. "That's fine, Hannah. I'll just show him the door first." He pointed around her at Todd.

"I'm not leaving again until Hannah and I have some things settled, so you can go ahead."

Sidestepping Hannah, Grant faced Todd again. "Can't you see she doesn't want you here?"

"And can't you see this is between Hannah and me? I'm her friend, too—at least I was, once upon a time."

"Some kind of friend you were." Grant spat the words. "Friends don't take advantage of an innocent girl and leave her alone and pregnant."

"Stop it, you two!" Hannah looked around when she realized she'd raised her voice, but since Rebecca didn't scurry into the room, she figured she hadn't been as loud as she thought. Still, she spoke at just above a whisper. "I mean it."

Todd looked directly at Grant, not appearing to have heard Hannah at all. "It wasn't like that. I lo—" He stopped himself, waving his hand as if to wipe away what he'd almost said.

That nearly spoken word stopped Hannah when she should have been shoving both Neanderthals toward the door. After everything, Todd still claimed he'd loved her back then. Maybe he really remembered it that way, though it had probably just been infatuation, just a teen-age hormone-induced haze. She knew that feeling well. She'd made the same mistaken assumption in her own heart.

"You don't know anything about it," Todd said to Grant.

"I've been around for the last few years. That's more than you can say."

Todd tilted his chin up. "I'm here now."

"For how long?"

Grant posed the question, but Hannah was dying to know the answer to it.

"Not that it's any of your business, but I start a job at GM Proving Grounds tomorrow. I'm here in town. To stay."

"What if she doesn't want you here? What if *no one* wants you here?"

Todd raised his hands in surrender. "Resent me all you want. It doesn't change the fact that I'm Rebecca's father, and I intend to have some kind of relationship with her no matter what you think."

Hannah gasped and closed her eyes. *Please God. Please God. Tell me she didn't hear.* But when she opened her eyes again, the expressions on both men's faces told her the bad news before she could even turn toward the living room. In the doorway, Rebecca stared at Todd, her eyes wide with amazement. Finally, she turned back to Hannah.

"Is it true, Mommy? Is Mr. McBride my dad?"

Todd let the phone ring four times, waiting for the answering machine to pick up as it had each time he'd called Monday night and again since he'd been home from work that day. This time the machine didn't answer, which could only mean that Hannah had returned from work and had shut it off.

Too bad he couldn't turn off his guilt over last evening's events as easily as she'd switched off the power. If he continued to be as distracted at work as he'd been on his first day at the Proving Grounds, then he wouldn't have to worry about having a job for too long.

With the phone continuing to ring, Todd switched the handset from one ear to the other, as he shed his maroon-and-white pin-striped dress shirt. He was already sitting on the edge of the bed in his undershirt and trousers when something clicked on the other end of the line.

"Hello," a small voice said.

His breath caught, but he forced words anyway. "Hi, Rebecca. This is your— This is Mr. McBride."

"Hi," she said automatically. Then she added an uncomfortable "oh."

He frowned. After Hannah had insisted that both he and Grant leave, she had probably initiated a heart-to-heart talk with their daughter. What a four-year-old would be able to understand from this impossible mess, he hadn't a clue. He barely understood parts of it himself. Whatever else Hannah had told his daughter, he guessed from Rebecca's surprised reaction that her mother had also said they wouldn't be seeing him anymore.

That's where she was wrong. He hadn't just found out he was a father and then faced his parents' extreme disappointment when he'd told them know they were grandparents, only to be shut out of his daughter's life.

He was still coming up with something to say to Rebecca when he heard another voice in the background.

"Sweetie, do you remember that I told you not to answer the phone?" Hannah said.

"But it's... Mr. McBride."

After some muffled voices and footsteps, Hannah's voice came on the line. "Would you please stop calling here? I had to unplug the machine."

"I'm sorry about yesterday."

"You and Grant—what you did was unforgivable. This time you hurt my child."

"*Our* child," he corrected, though he couldn't argue

with the rest of what Hannah had said. "I didn't want Rebecca to find out that way any more than you did."

"So why'd you tell her?"

"You were there. You know I didn't intentionally—"

"Anyone who knows the first thing about parenting knows that children hear and see everything that's going on around them."

"Whose fault is it I don't know —" He managed to stop his retort before he said, "How to be Rebecca's father." Hannah was at fault for that, but as far as he could tell, there was plenty of blame to go around. He wasn't going to make any progress by pelting her with accusations.

After counting from ten backward, he tried again. "Okay, this isn't about fault, but she knows now. We have to deal with that…together."

"I've already dealt with that." Her voice screeched at the end of her sentence. "Just like I've dealt with everything else in her life. Neither of us needs you or your help."

"Hannah, I might have let you do it before, but I'm not going to allow you to cut me out this time."

"Me cut *you* out?" She became quiet for a few seconds, as if she realized she'd said more than she intended. Finally, she sighed. "Don't you think you've done enough?"

"No! I haven't done enough."

What happened to that patience he'd just found? But the fact remained: He hadn't done anything to care for Hannah or to provide for their daughter's needs. That he hadn't been given the chance didn't change the bottom line.

"Don't call anymore, Todd. I won't answer."

The connection went dead as she clicked off the phone. He didn't bother dialing again. She would probably just leave it off the hook, anyway, and even if she didn't, she would be screening his calls.

Todd ignored the hopelessness threatening to take hold in his heart. He couldn't give up, not when there was so much at stake—more now than even a teen romance that had seemed so real at the time. This was about their daughter, and Rebecca deserved to have a father in her life.

A week before, Todd never would have imagined himself admitting this, but he wasn't sure he even wanted a future with Hannah. At least not this Hannah. She was cold and selfish and spiteful. *Is she also hurt and scared?* Todd wanted to ignore that charitable thought. He didn't want to forgive her yet, and that appeared to be just what his heart was tempted to do.

"Lord, why do I have to be the one to keep taking the first step?" he whispered.

But the answer was so clear in his thoughts it was as if God Himself had spoken the words. *Because she can't.* For whatever reason, Hannah couldn't be the one to offer an olive branch. Though his hurt was new, his wounds fresh, Hannah had been harboring hers for a lot longer, allowing them to fester instead of heal. Forgiveness was never easy, but he guessed that it became harder to give over time.

Still, he couldn't allow Hannah's problem with forgiveness to keep him from knowing his daughter. Every day that passed with Hannah nursing her resentment was another day he and Rebecca couldn't be together. That was as unacceptable as Hannah avoiding him by refusing to take his calls.

Suddenly, an idea began forming in his thoughts. Once before, Hannah had been able to avoid him when she'd wanted to, but this time there were no parents, oceans or continents separating them. Just a few traffic lights, the Huron River and a tiny, down-town shopping district.

Since the choices of destinations were limited in Milford, even outside church and school, friends crossed paths whenever they bought a quart of milk at Breen's IGA, picked out end tables at Huron Valley Furniture or even grabbed a Coney dog or some Thai food from one of those new joints on North Main.

If seeing friends and neighbors regularly was so easy, he imagined that the opposite was true, as well: Avoiding someone a person didn't want to see would be almost impossible. Because Hannah was on a tight budget, she probably wasn't in the market often for new end tables, but she needed milk frequently, and she probably craved a good Coney once in a while.

Todd finally understood John Mellencamp's 1980s anthem, celebrating life in a "Small Town." Milford was a small town, all right. Hannah was about to find out just how small.

Chapter Five

Hannah had tried her best to make it as normal a Sunday morning as possible. She'd hurried Rebecca through their morning routine, and she'd actively contributed to the discussion in her young adult Sunday school class. Even now she was chatting with several women in the vestibule as she usually did, but nothing about this morning or the last few days had felt normal—not with Todd appearing like a case of indigestion everywhere she went.

The conversation continued around her, but Hannah couldn't help but divide her attention between it and the door where Andrew Westin greeted mem-bers and guests. She expected one of them to be Todd, and she couldn't decide whether she would be more disappointed if he showed up or if he didn't.

"Hannah, are you with us?"

She turned back to catch Julia Sims grinning at her, excitement dancing in her dark, heavily lashed eyes.

"You're missing the news."

"What news is that?"

Charity McKinley, Julia's half sister, who was the

golden opposite to her raven-dark looks, wore the expression of the cat who had swallowed the canary. Charity reached out her hands to Steffie Wilmington and Serena Jacobs, encouraging those two and several others into a tight circle.

"It's finally happened. I'm pregnant," she said in the quietest voice possible for someone fairly bursting with excitement.

"Congratulations," Hannah said, stepping forward to hug Charity. She was thrilled that God had blessed her friend, who'd longed for a child since she and Rick had married four years before.

"That's wonderful," Serena agreed. "Rick must be thrilled."

Though it seemed impossible, Charity's smile widened. "That and he's turned into this broccoli-and-whole-grains-toting drill sergeant. 'Here, sweetheart, eat wheat germ. It's for the baby.'" She imitated her husband's deep voice but she finished with a laugh.

"Was your mom thrilled with the news?" Hannah asked her.

"She's already knitting booties."

"I'm happy for her, too." It was great to see healing in Charity's relationship with her mother, Laura Sims, after their painful rift from a few years before. But rather than dampen Charity's excitement by mentioning difficult memories, Hannah changed the subject. "Looks like our church is having a population explosion."

"Look what you started," Julia said, shaking an index finger at Serena, whose swollen belly announced her new arrival, expected in March.

Serena rested her hands on her stomach. "I love being a trendsetter."

"I don't know about the rest of you," Steffie said, pausing for effect before she added, "but if I was newlywed, I wouldn't be drinking the water here."

Immediately the other women turned to Tricia Williams Lancaster. Married just over a year to Michigan State Police Trooper Brett Lancaster, Tricia definitely still qualified as a newlywed, though she already had three children with her late first husband, Rusty.

"I'll be sure to keep that in mind," Tricia said.

Tricia turned her head as if in search of a new topic, and her face brightened as a square-jawed man with a military haircut and a football player's shoulders squeezed through the doorway.

"If that's not Trooper Joe Rossetti in the flesh and in a *church* on a Sunday morning," Tricia said with a grin. "God does work in mysterious ways."

"Brett's friend?" Julia craned her neck for a better look at the handsome State Police trooper. "I thought you said Brett had been inviting him for months. How'd he get him here? Tell him there was an illegal arms sale in the church basement?"

"No, even better. We promised to stuff him with Sunday dinner after church. What starving single guy can resist that?"

They were all having a laugh over that when Serena suddenly stopped. "Uh, Hannah…"

The youth minister's wife was staring at the entry where her husband had kept his post, and Hannah didn't have to stretch her imagination to guess who'd just come through the door. She spun around in time to see Todd shaking hands with Andrew, but he barely glanced at her before opening the side door and entering the sanctuary.

"It's the guy from last Sunday," Steffie exclaimed.

"What's the story—" she began again, but one of the others cleared her throat to interrupt her.

Slowly, Hannah faced her friends, bracing herself for their questions. Though they couldn't conceal the curiosity in their expressions, no one spoke up, and the one who might have asked was discouraged by Charity's staying hand on her shoulder.

They knew about Todd—at least they had to suspect by now. Serena knew far more than the others, and Andrew had probably discussed Todd's arrival with her, as well. Of the others who hadn't witnessed the scene in the sanctuary last Sunday, they surely had heard about it. Unfortunately, scandalous information sometimes traveled faster than the *Good News,* even in churches.

Still, her friends didn't ask. She should have expected as much. God had blessed her with true friends. They wouldn't pressure her. They would simply wait until she was ready to tell them.

The first notes of the organ prelude saved her from having to decide whether or not she was ready today. Certain rules of etiquette applied to the preacher's daughter, and one of them made it a no-no for her to race into services late.

"I'd better get in there," she said, clasping her Bible tightly under her arm to keep from fidgeting.

"I'll go with you," Steffie said. "Where's Grant this morning?"

Hannah stiffened as she pulled open the sanctuary door. "I'm not sure."

Some amazing friend she was. Hannah hadn't even noticed that Grant was absent, even though Steffie and she usually sat with him during Sunday-morning services. She hoped he wasn't staying away from church because of her and the events of the other night.

It certainly hadn't kept Todd away.

He was already camped out in the center of the third row—right behind her usual spot every Sunday. Though he was studying the church bulletin as if it contained the great secrets of God's universe, Hannah was convinced she could see him smirking.

"Brendan's looking especially nice today," Steffie whispered after they passed him on their way to the front of the church.

He was also looking taken, given the presence of the striking blonde gripping his hand, but Hannah noticed his deep blue dress shirt and slightly darker tie for Steffie's sake. "Blue is definitely his color."

"It brings out his eyes."

Unfortunately for Steffie, she'd only had eyes for Brendan since junior high, and he'd only thought of her as a friend.

"Well, Olivia's here bright and early on this first Sunday of Advent," Steffie whispered.

As glad as she was that they were finished talk-ing about Brendan, Hannah wished Steffie hadn't switched to that topic. "Now be nice."

Still, she couldn't resist taking a peek at Olivia Wells. Every Sunday for the last six months, Olivia had sat in coiffed blond perfection on the aisle end of the second row that marked her position as the widower minister's lady friend. The attractive widow had dressed in one of her trademark prim suits—this time red for the holiday season—and her makeup was flawless as always.

"As nice as *she* is?" Steffie asked.

"Nicer."

That wasn't fair, and Hannah knew it. Maybe she wasn't the woman Hannah would have chosen for her father, but still she had to admit that Olivia had been perfectly pleasant to her and Rebecca as well as the rest of the congregation. Because she felt guilty for suggesting otherwise, she stopped to greet Olivia warmly and gave her hand an extra squeeze before slipping past her to the center of the pew.

"Do you think she and your dad will get married?" Steffie whispered once they'd taken their seats.

"I don't know what I think."

Both became quiet as the service began, but her answer to Steffie's question continued to roll through her thoughts. It felt like the most honest thing she'd said all day and for reasons beyond her father's romantic life. Her equilibrium was as fragile as blown glass, susceptible to shattering into tiny shards with the littlest provocation.

Just over her shoulder was the man whom she couldn't seem to escape lately, when once she'd wished away the ocean that had divided them. He'd told her he wouldn't make it easy to cut him out of her life again, and his methods might have been unconventional, but he'd been doing just what he said.

The question at this point wasn't whether he would continue trying; it was why Hannah was trying so hard to prevent him from keeping his word. Why was she fighting so determinedly against what she knew in her heart to be right? Rebecca deserved the chance to know her father.

But then this wasn't about Rebecca, and she knew it. Fear paralyzed her every thought, tainted her every move. What was she afraid of? That she would feel guilty every time she saw Todd and Rebecca together? That he would love her again? Or that he wouldn't?

Hannah managed to make it through the opening hymn and the offertory, singing the notes even if their message couldn't penetrate the guilt and uncertainty crowding her heart. But as Reverend Bob stepped to the lectern, she straightened in her seat and concentrated on the sermon. Since Hannah's childhood, the melodic sound of her father's voice had always made her feel God's presence. She really needed to feel it today.

Reverend Bob began his usual first Sunday of Advent sermon on preparations for the birth of Jesus. "When Gabriel appeared to Mary to tell her that she'd been chosen to give birth to God's son, how did she respond? Did she say, 'Not now, God, I'm betrothed to this really great guy, and an unexplained pregnancy will mess up my plans'?

"No, she answered in Luke 1:38, 'Behold, I am the handmaid of the Lord; let it be to me according to your word.' Her dutiful answer becomes even more amazing when we consider several biblical scholars' assertions, based on cultural norms of the period, that Mary was probably only a girl of about thirteen at the time."

Though Hannah was certain her father had included that information in his sermons before, that detail suddenly struck her. Jesus's mother had been younger than Hannah had been when she'd delivered Rebecca.

She could just imagine the disapproving glances— Hannah remembered a few of those, as well—that Mary must have faced though she wasn't guilty of any sin. And the fear—had Mary been afraid about becoming a mother first and then the mother of God's only son?

"Did Mary hesitate, though in her time a man who

found his betrothed to be with child from another man could easily have had her stoned?" Reverend Bob continued and then paused, shaking his head. "No, she simply submitted to God's will. She was an example to all of us. How will we answer when God asks something of us?"

Hannah swallowed. The words seemed to speak to her alone. What would she do? Would she stop and act or keep running? Until now, it had always been easier to run, but she was tired. Bone tired. Now she only needed to find the strength to do what God had been telling her to do all along.

Hannah drove into the nearly empty parking lot at Hickory Ridge Church, surprised that her father had demanded a meeting with her on a Thursday night and commanded her to ask Mary Nelson to babysit Rebecca. As a rule, Reverend Bob never demanded or commanded anything, rather made suggestions and let the Lord do the rest.

She pulled to a stop under one of the streetlamps that cast a yellow haze over piles of plowed snow on the parking lot's perimeter. With daylight saving time in full force, those lights were already illuminating a midnight sky at just after the dinner hour.

Leaning her forehead on the steering wheel, Hannah took a deep breath and prayed a quick plea for fortification. Dad had probably put together the puzzle about Todd, and now he would expect to hear the truth from her. Just like Todd, her father had deserved to know everything years ago, but that didn't make facing this conversation any easier.

At the sound of a car engine, Hannah lifted her head and caught sight of another pair of headlights. She glanced to Reverend Bob's regular parking place near the main entry, but the black sedan he'd been driving for years was already there. A mini SUV pulled into the parking space next to hers. It wasn't until the driver opened the door and light flooded the interior that she recognized him.

"Not now. Not now." She threw open the door and stepped out into the slushy snow.

The subject of her frustration climbed out, as well, and waved a gloved hand as he closed his car door.

She marched around the car to face him, lifting on her toes to look larger than her usual five feet two. "Okay, I get it that you're not going away. Will you stop following me already? Stalking is a crime in Michigan."

Todd only smiled as he pulled his stocking cap down over his ears. "Really? I'll be sure to keep that in mind."

"And I know the Milford Police Chief, too."

"Oh, you mean Pete Conyers. Saw him at the Rite Aid yesterday. What are the odds that we would both run out of toothpaste the same night?"

Hannah frowned. Of course, Todd knew Pete. He'd been a young cop in the village while Todd and Hannah were still at Milford High. She would have trumped his comment by saying her good friend was a State Police trooper, but Todd would only have said how nice it was to meet Brett Lancaster when Todd had moved his church membership to Hickory Ridge on Sunday.

With a sigh, she asked, "What are you doing here, Todd?"

"It's a command appearance." He raised an eyebrow, lifting the same side of his mouth with it. "You?"

Hannah didn't even answer him. She turned away and squeezed her eyes shut instead. She'd always thought of her father as a purposeful man, a man of God who had clear-cut views on sin and consequences, but she'd never before thought of him as cruel. Was Dad really going to make her confess everything in front of Todd?

Because her eyes were burning as she opened them, she didn't turn back to Todd but trudged to the main church entrance. Footsteps crunched behind her.

Reverend Bob met her at the door.

"Hannah, you're looking lovely." He bent to drop a kiss on top of her hat-covered head. "I trust that Rebecca is doing well."

You saw her yourself at Wednesday prayer meeting, Hannah was tempted to point out, but she doubted it would do anything to make this conversation more comfortable. Why didn't he just forget all the niceties and get on with the interrogation?

As Todd came in the door behind her, Reverend Bob greeted him with a handshake. "Todd, it's good to see you again. I hope you're settling in well at the Proving Grounds."

"You know how new jobs go, Reverend. The learning curve is pretty steep right now, but hopefully I'll get to the bend before long."

Bob laughed at his comment as he pulled the glass door behind Todd into place and turned the lock. "Are you at least getting to take the new prototype cars for a spin on the test track?"

"I might eventually, but I haven't yet. As a test engineer, most of my work is using a computer to monitor data about things like temperature and voltage as the vehicle is operated under various conditions."

"Well I hope you get to test-drive one eventually." Hannah's father patted Todd on the shoulder of his heavy coat—just a mutual admiration society. She'd stepped outside of reality, Hannah decided. Whatever happened to her father toting a shotgun or whatever dads did to defend their daughters' honor?

Finally, Hannah had had enough. "Dad, what are we all doing here?"

The minister turned back to her, his expression carefully blank. "Todd thought the two of you might have some things to talk about."

Hannah shot a venomous look at Todd. "Com-mand appearance, huh?"

"Your father set the time and the place."

"I guess it wasn't enough that you hired Harold Lasbury—my boss—as your new accountant on Friday when there are three CPA offices in Milford. Then you moved your membership to Hickory Ridge on Sunday, made an appearance at Faith Singles United on Tuesday and attended Wednesday prayer meeting last night."

Todd shrugged without remorse. "Guess not."

"I can't imagine what would have been enough."

Todd had even asked Harold if Hannah could personally handle his tax return, and he'd managed to somehow be at Breen's IGA the night she stopped in for milk, eggs and that popping rice cereal Rebecca loved so much.

It was as if he'd been watching her every move, waiting for a chance to pounce, and now he'd made her father an accomplice in his plans to get under her skin. Well, he was there, and his presence itched.

"By the way," he asked, "don't you ever go to the post office or the video store or the library?"

He met her frown with an amused expression that had her hands fisted at her sides.

"How dare you follow me! You're stalking me! What right do you have to invade my life like that?"

Todd stretched up and towered over her. "What right do you have to keep me away from my daughter?"

Hannah's retort died on her lips at Todd's announcement, and she turned wide-eyed to face her father. Reverend Bob didn't wear the compassionate minister's expression she'd come to expect from him. His was the face of a furious father.

"Enough," he said in an even voice but with enough finality to strike silence on the other two people in the room. "I need to see both of you in my office immediately."

Chapter Six

Without another word, Reverend Bob turned and strode to the stairway leading to his second-floor office. The look Todd captured her with had to be as cold as the one Hannah had trained on him, but both looked away quickly and headed in the direction the minister had taken.

When they reached his office, Hannah's father was already seated in his executive chair. He gestured to the pair of chairs opposite his desk. Never before this moment had Hannah felt her father's disappointment in such a profound way, even on that awful day when she'd had to air her humiliation in front of the whole Deacons' board.

"Dad, I'm so sorry—" Hannah began as she stiffly lowered into the chair, but her father raised his hand to stop her.

"I'm sure there's a lot of blame and guilt and apologies to go around." He first trapped Todd and then Hannah in his direct gaze.

Hannah stiffened but couldn't look away from her father. Would his disappointment spoken aloud be worse than his silent displeasure? Without looking at Todd, she sensed that he sat as straight as she did, his hands gripping the chair's arms.

"But that's not why the three of us are together tonight, is it?" He paused, crossing his arms over his chest. "We're here because of your daughter, and Rebecca deserves better than this."

Hannah opened her mouth to say something, anything, but the words wouldn't come. The thoughts wouldn't even come. She hated it that Todd found his voice first.

"I know you're right, but—"

"Todd." Reverend Bob's voice held the warning of a man—even a man of God—whose patience had worn thin. "Both of you have had plenty of chances to talk. Now it's time for you to listen."

With a curt nod, Todd sat back in the chair and rested his hands in his lap. Hannah settled back, as well, trying her best to relax when her thoughts and pulse were racing at competing speeds.

"You two are behaving like children, especially you, Hannah." He paused to focus pointedly on his daughter, making her squirm. "You are children no longer."

She straightened in her seat again, glancing sidelong at Todd. He sat stiffly, but he nodded, his Adam's apple shifting. Was this the uncomfortable way he would have looked if he and Hannah had faced her father together when she first learned of her pregnancy? She suspected the discomfort would have been the same, but she would never know how that confrontation might have gone or where the four of them might have been today.

"Selfishness is a privilege of youth," Bob began again, as if he was gearing up for one of his best sermons. But a small smile appeared where his tight expression had rested. "You two lost that privilege when you made a child together. God has entrusted Rebecca into your care, and your daughter's needs must always come first."

Hannah couldn't help shaking her head. "But Dad, I do put Rebecca first. She's everything to me."

"I know you love your daughter. I see that every day. But in this instance, you've been very selfish. This child needs a father. You know how she longs for someone to fill that role in her life."

Her breath hitched because she did know. Her sitter, Mary Nelson, occasionally repeated parts of conversations she'd overheard between Rebecca and Max Williams, who'd lost his father to an accident and then found a great stepfather in Brett Lancaster. Rebecca had been asking questions about her father long before she'd overheard Todd and Grant batting around her paternity like a weapon.

Since that horrible night, Rebecca had been asking even more difficult questions: "Why don't some daddies live with their kids?" and "Why are some mommies and daddies mad at each other?" How could Hannah explain anything to her daughter when her thoughts were muddy waters that refused to clear?

Because she didn't answer, Reverend Bob continued. "Unlike some unfortunate unwed mothers, you have a young man who is interested in, even adamant about, taking responsibility for his child. No matter what your feelings are regarding Todd, you must put them aside and allow Rebecca to have a relationship with her father."

The minister stopped then, as if he'd said his piece.

Hannah let her gaze fall to her gripped hands. He was right, of course, but that didn't make it any easier to accept.

After five years of fighting for every miniscule amount of self-sufficiency, it wouldn't be easy to hand over part of the responsibility for Rebecca's care to anyone, let alone Todd. At the thought of him, Hannah couldn't help glancing his way. Todd had his gaze trained on her, a tight expression on his lips.

"And you, Todd."

At the sound of Reverend Bob's voice, both turned back to face him.

"You could have approached this situation with a lot more maturity, as well."

Todd sat forward in his chair and gripped the edge of the desk. "Now wait a minute. I tried everything—"

"Should everything have included the post office, video store and the library?" he asked, repeating Todd's own admission that he'd staked out those places.

"I suppose not."

"You suppose then that following my daughter everywhere she went wasn't the best idea?"

The side of Hannah's mouth pulled up at the sight of Todd facing her father's questions. It was just like Reverend Bob to call each of them out on the carpet by turns.

"No, not the best," Todd said, shaking his head. "But I was desperate. Five years of planning, of taking the right classes, of imagining apologies, of predicting possible outcomes and of praying, just so I could come back to…here."

Hannah blinked. It wasn't so much what he'd said, although the words he'd spoken aloud were shocking enough. But what she suspected he'd almost said was even more disquieting. *Her.* He'd done all those things, not to come back *here* but to *her*. Even though it was much too late to consider "what might have beens," she couldn't help feeling a begrudging respect for his effort. When she glanced up at her father, she caught him studying her. Had Dad read the confusion, or, worse yet, the respect, in her expression?

Without commenting on anything he'd seen, Reverend Bob turned back to Todd.

"You could have contacted me sooner." He waited for Todd's nod before he added, "Just as you could have come to me five years ago, when my daughter first locked you out of her life…and your daughter's life."

"You knew!" Hannah's question came out as a shriek, and she didn't even care. She stared at him, incredulous that her father could have kept a secret like that. Better, obviously, than she'd kept hers.

"I would tell you that fathers aren't as oblivious as you think, but I have to admit the hints were hard to miss," he said, as he leaned forward, resting his elbows on his desk. "First, your best friend moved across the globe, and you didn't hear from him. Ever. Then you started rushing to beat me to the mailbox, even when your morning sickness was so bad you could barely get out of bed.

"And finally, I picked up my bedroom extension and heard a familiar voice and the sound of you hanging up the phone on him. I didn't even need to see Rebecca to confirm what I already knew."

"But you never said anything," Hannah said.

"What was I supposed to say?"

Todd looked back and forth between the two of them, amazed that both could so easily miss the point. "Oh, I don't know. Perhaps you could have insisted that she tell the baby's father, or at the very least you could have told me yourself."

He still couldn't get over the fact that Reverend Bob had known all along. No wonder he hadn't gone ballistic when Todd, finally desperate after trying everything else, had gone to him, confessed that he was Rebecca's father and begged for help in reaching Hannah.

"I was waiting."

"For what? Rebecca's high school graduation?" Todd's voice grew louder with each word, but he couldn't seem to be able to contain his anger. Bob, Andrew, Serena—everyone, it seemed—knew but him, and no one had bothered to give him a simple heads-up.

The noise Reverend Bob made sounded like a chuckle, but his expression held no mirth.

"I deserve that. But I was waiting until I wasn't so angry anymore. No matter how hard I tried, I couldn't be neutral in this situation. I'm Hannah's father. I was furious. It was hard to feel any obligation to the young man who stole my daughter's innocence and her childhood."

Todd gripped the side of the desk as old guilt re-emerged from beneath the surface of his anger. "That wasn't fair."

"I never said it was, but it was human." Reverend Bob leaned back in his chair and crossed his arms again. "Don't get me wrong. I wasn't blaming you alone, Todd. If I remember correctly from my marriage, sexual intimacy requires two partners."

The skin on the back of Todd's neck suddenly became hot. Were they really discussing such private matters with Hannah sitting next to them? In his peripheral vision, he could see her shifting in her seat.

Reverend Bob waved his hand as if to brush away that

topic as water under the bridge. "But the reason I didn't tell you was more than my anger about sin and the consequences it had on my daughter's life or even on behalf of my grandchild, who wouldn't know the security of a loving two-parent family. I was waiting for one of you to take responsibility."

"You've got to be kidding, Dad." This time Hannah came out of her seat and paced toward the window, where the cloudy night sky stretched in endless blackness, striped with gray. When she turned back to them, her hands were fisted at her sides, but her eyes appeared damp.

"For five years, I've done nothing *but* take responsibility. I've diapered and burped and laundered and skipped sleep to study so I could support my family. I've earned a bachelor's degree in less than four years and have begun my one-year apprenticeship period in public accounting so I can take the CPA exam."

Reverend Bob studied his steepled hands before he met her gaze and spoke again. "Hannah dear, if you had owned up to *all* of your responsibilities, then we wouldn't be having this conversation right now."

Her shoulders drooping, Hannah returned to her chair and slumped into it. She pressed her lips together as if she wanted to say more, but she wisely held back. It wasn't an argument she could win, anyway, just as Todd could no longer continue to play the victim. He could have done just as the minister had suggested, moving past his fear and embarrassment over their sin and asking her father to intercede for him with Hannah. His cowardice had cost him more than he'd even known.

When father and daughter continued to eye each other in a silent standoff, Todd couldn't help but to speak up.

"I'm sorry it took so long." At Hannah's surprised expression, he continued, "Sorry for both of us. And for all of us."

For several long seconds, she said nothing, but then she nodded almost imperceptibly, the tiniest motion for what had to feel like a huge act of surrender. Hope, as fragile as a seedling sinking its roots in sandy soil, threatened to find a place in Todd's heart, but he was careful to contain it. He could hope for a relationship with his child and nothing more.

Reverend Bob brushed his hands together to suggest the matter was settled.

"Now that we're all on the same page, let's discuss a few things about Rebecca." He leaned forward and rested his elbows on the desk. "As Todd mentioned when he came to me, he would like to establish paternity through the courts so he can set up a plan to pay child support. If I'm correct that will mean submitting to a paternity test. Hannah, will you allow Rebecca to be tested?"

"Yes."

The minister nodded at her softly spoken answer and turned back to Todd. "After paternity is determined, you'll be able to set up a regular visitation schedule. I would like to recommend, though, that the two of you work out a temporary schedule right away."

Todd watched Hannah, dreading the moment when she would object. They'd come so far, and he hated to see all that progress wiped away because they were moving too quickly. He couldn't help backpedaling. "Well, maybe not right away, but—"

"No," Hannah said to stop him. "That's fine."

"Good." Reverend Bob opened his desk drawer and withdrew a pad of white paper and a pen. "Rebecca already knows Todd is her father, and she's very curious about him. I think it's time for the two of them to really get to know each other."

The tightening around his heart surprised Todd. With all of the opposition Hannah had given him, he had focused on the battle rather than just how important it had become to him to have a chance to be with his daughter. Gratitude filled him that he would receive his most precious gift weeks before Christmas.

He opened his mouth to thank the minister, but Hannah spoke first.

"I agree." She paused as if the next words came hard for her. "She needs to know her father."

Reverend Bob watched from his upstairs office window as his daughter and the young man who had broken her heart entered their cars and turned on the engines. Hannah and Todd might have agreed to a truce for their child's sake, but they hadn't made any grand gestures of civility as they left the building.

What had he expected, that they would shake hands and be talking again in "friendspeak"—that combination of half-finished sentences and inside jokes that had marked their friendship in their teens? As a minister, he'd been in the heart-healing business too long to believe in Pollyanna thoughts like that. Healing took time, work and a whole lot of conversations with God.

As the cars backed out of the parking places, Bob's chest tightened. He pressed his fingers into the achy place and then moved his hands to rub his temples. His body seemed to be telling him he'd just made a big mistake in getting involved in the situation between Todd and Hannah. His mind had announced the same thing the minute he'd agreed to participate with Todd in this intervention.

At least they'd agreed to seek further counseling with Andrew instead of him. Too close to the situation, he felt incapable of providing an unbiased opinion. Even agreeing to help Todd in the first place had felt like conspiring with the enemy.

Bob shook his pounding head and kneaded his aching shoulder as he returned to his desk and settled in his well-worn executive chair. That young man wasn't the enemy any more than Todd alone was to blame for what had happened between himself and Hannah. Todd had even proven his integrity as a man by his determination to be a good father to his child, despite Hannah's unwillingness to let him.

Still, there was a difference between recognizing that Todd had grown into a decent man and encouraging Hannah to let him back into her life and into her daughter's life. Bob should have protected his own child in the first place. He should have—

Bob tried to stop himself from listing again the parental failures that he'd enumerated so many times before. The series of what-ifs when history and circumstances had made them moot. If he'd been there more for her. If he'd been able to see past his own grief to help Hannah face hers. If his wife hadn't died.

"Oh, Deborah, why'd you have to leave so soon?" His words came on a sigh. He continued whispering, as much to himself as to his wife's memory. "I feel so ill-equipped to help her sometimes. You would have known."

Turning in the chair, he glanced down at the three portraits on his desk and sought out the one with the gilded frame. The image that smiled out at him was of

Deborah, the first woman he'd ever loved and the one who still held his heart. Yes, his late wife would have known what to say to their daughter during the dark times over the last few years. She would have directed Hannah with her quiet dignity and inherent grace.

His gaze lingered on Deborah's smiling face and then moved to the other portraits: Hannah and Rebecca. Would Olivia's face ever look out at him from a frame on this desk? Would there come a time when he would put away Deborah's photo as a sign of his moving forward? He shrugged. Maybe not today, but perhaps one day soon.

If he did decide to move on and choose a wife, Olivia was the kind of woman who would make any man proud. The lovely widow had so many fine qualities: from her warmness and caring spirit to her generosity and steadfast faith. He'd witnessed these qualities and more since he'd helped her to secure the job in the church office the year before.

Olivia was such a wonderful addition to the downstairs office, and to his personal life, as well. He hadn't even realized there was an empty place inside of him until she'd stepped inside to fill it. And the way she looked at him sometimes, as if he held all the answers to her questions—what middle-aged man's ego wouldn't glory in that?

Would he ever be able to love Olivia, or any woman, the way he'd loved Deborah? He shook his head, not only because he was convinced he couldn't but also because it wasn't a fair question to ask. If given the choice, he always would have chosen a life with Deborah, one where their years together would have been chronicled in lines on their faces and the gentle aging of their bodies. But that choice wasn't his. Deborah was gone, and a part of his heart had died with her. Still, God had a plan for him, and that meant continuing his life on earth for now.

He had told the widows and widowers of his church this so many times before. If God wished them to love again, He would open their hearts to the possibility and give them a different love, worthy of the special individual He'd sent their way. Bob wanted to believe the words he'd said were true in his own life.

Bob had noticed that Hannah hadn't warmed to Olivia the way he had hoped she would over these last months. No one could ever replace her mother, he understood that, but he didn't believe Hannah would want him to be lonely, either. Sometime soon he would have to discuss this matter with his daughter, especially if he decided to form a closer relationship with Olivia.

Maybe a discussion would be unnecessary after they had all spent Christmas together this year. Hannah would have a better chance to get to know Olivia, and his lady friend would have the opportunity to see how she might fit in the Woods family.

The Christmas dinner was Olivia's idea. He wasn't exactly at peace with the idea of having another woman cooking in Deborah's kitchen and serving at the table where Deborah had lovingly set so many wonderful holiday meals over the years. Since her death, Bob and Hannah hadn't once eaten a Christmas, Thanksgiving or Easter dinner at home, always accepting gracious invitations from other church members.

So for him, this dinner was a significant first step in his personal life. He would simply have to pray for the strength to push aside feelings that allowing someone else into his life was abandoning the memory of his wife.

Changes. There were certainly a lot of them in his family this holiday season, beyond this first Christmas dinner at home in years. For the first time since Rebecca had been born, she wouldn't wake up Christmas morning in her grandfather's home. He knew how important it was for Hannah to make this statement of her independence by spending the morning in her new apartment, but he knew how much he would miss watching Rebecca's joy as she opened her presents.

Hannah would deal with some sadness of her own, as, for the first time, Rebecca would spend at least part of the holidays with her father. If loneliness filled him at the thought of his adult daughter being away from him Christmas morning, he could just imagine how Hannah would feel without her child.

Would they find a way to focus on the glory of the Christ child's birth when they were all so caught up in the drama of their own lives? Bob hoped so. He also hoped he would have the right words for Hannah if she came to him and asked his advice about dealing with Todd.

He sensed that the young man might still have feelings for his daughter, but would those feelings be enough to erase all of the pain and sorrow between them? Or would Todd's reappearance only result in more pain for all of them?

All the questions only made Bob's body ache more. He held his head in the cradle of his hands and closed his eyes. Slowly, a realization awakened in him: Why, when his world felt so heavy, had he been trying to bear it alone? Strange, if one of his church members had been feeling this same weight, he would have suggested that she turn it over to God. What made it so hard for him to follow his own advice?

Father, I'm entrusting all of these questions to Your capable hands. You've known the answers all along. Please share them with us in Your time. Amen.

As he ended his prayer, words from one of his favorite passages, Psalm 27 filtered through his thoughts. He whispered the words in the room's silence. "'The Lord is my light and my salvation; whom shall I fear? The Lord is the stronghold of my life; of whom shall I be afraid?'"

Bob felt relief for that first time since he'd called Hannah and insisted on her presence at the church that night. Everything would be fine, he suddenly knew with certainty. The situation was safely in God's hands.

Chapter Seven

Hannah lifted her collar to block the wind, wishing she could as easily warm her insides, but that was unlikely on this night of firsts. Around the three of them, the display windows of Milford's downtown shops were dressed for the season with miniature Christmas trees, garland and twinkling lights. The wind caused the outdoor displays to jiggle and sway as if adding its own layer to the season's air of anticipation. Christmas was only nine days away.

Strange how all of that gaiety seemed distant to Hannah, as if she was extraneous to it, just as she was to tonight's father-daughter outing. Though she understood that this was a good thing, she couldn't help feeling as if she was looking at Todd and Rebecca from outside the glass.

Todd had suggested that Hannah join him and Rebecca on their first outing, even though she'd been at home both times he'd visited in the last week. He thought Rebecca might be more comfortable with Hannah there, and she'd agreed. Now if she had to spend the night walking on eggshells—or crunching over snow on Main

Street as the case appeared to be—she would do what it took to make the night go smoothly for her daughter.

Still, needing something to do with her fidgety hands, Hannah reached down to pull up Rebecca's hood, but her daughter picked that moment to race ahead. The child's unzipped red parka flapped behind her like the cape of "Amazing Rebecca," out to save humanity once again.

"Look at me. Look at me."

Hannah was looking, all right, and choking back mom panic regarding slippery ice, strangers and fast-moving cars. "Rebecca, slow down."

Oblivious to the danger, Rebecca looked back at them and ran even faster, past shoppers with armloads of packages and lighted trees in the downtown sidewalks. Hannah shot a worried glance Todd's way, but he only gave her a mischievous grin before shooting out after their daughter.

"You can't escape me," he called in his best monster imitation as he captured Rebecca in his arms. He swung her around and around, eliciting giggles though he had effectively ended her escape. When they finally stopped spinning, Todd lowered the dizzy child to the ground and knelt in front of her to zip her coat.

"It's cold out. You need to keep this zipped." He pulled her hood up over her ponytails and then dug her mittens from her pockets and slipped them over her hands.

Amazingly, Rebecca didn't even fight his efforts, though as an independent preschooler, she usually refused all assistance with winter wear on principle. Todd appeared more like a relaxed veteran than the inexperienced father he was. His ministrations lacked the efficiency of movement Hannah had learned with four years of practice, but what he lost in style, he made up for in humor. Finally finished, he stood and patted Rebecca's head.

"There. Now doesn't that feel warmer?"

Taking her hand, he strode back to where Hannah stood watching them. He glanced down at the child looking up at him. "You don't want to scare your mother again by running off like that. You could fall on the ice or get hit by one of those cars. They go really fast."

Hannah couldn't help smiling at the back of his head as Todd stood and turned away from her. *Scare your mother.* Rebecca had worried one of her parents, all right, but for this one, the experience was new and intense.

"Okay, Daddy. Can we look at the toy store now?"

They'd stopped in front of the Village Toy Shoppe's brightly decorated display window, but no one except the child took notice. Hannah's breath caught. *Daddy.* The new title flowed so naturally from Rebecca's lips. How quickly she'd adapted to Todd's arrival and his new place in her life. Todd had heard it, too. Hannah could tell by how stiffly he stood. He glanced sidelong at Hannah, his eyes a little too shiny in the streetlamp's glow.

Hannah's own eyes burned as she lowered her gaze to the child standing between them. If bliss had a face, it would have been the one looking up at her. A wave of emotion rolled over Hannah, the last of her reluctance floating back to sea with the frothy tide. This was the right thing for Rebecca.

"Can we go?" Rebecca repeated, drawing her eyebrows together.

"Of course we can look," Hannah answered when it appeared Todd wasn't ready. She used the same phrasing she always used when the two of them entered toy stores. Browsing was usually all the two of them could fit into the budget, except for Christmas and birthdays, and even then extravagant gifts were out of the question.

They took a few steps toward the entrance of the small mall where the toy store was housed.

"Wait." Todd stopped and turned to Rebecca. "Does this mean you think you might be getting toys sometime soon?"

Rebecca giggled again. "Santa brings me toys for Christmas…if I'm good."

"Oh, really? You're probably good all the time then."

Her tinkling little-girl laughter flitted through the crisp air.

"Most of the time, anyway," Hannah assured him.

"Then let's hurry. We have a lot of toys to pick out."

"Mommy says it's not nice to ask for too many. God and Santa wouldn't like that."

The side of Hannah's mouth pulled up. At least her daughter had mentioned God first. She didn't mind Rebecca enjoying the fantastical celebrations at Christmas as long as she knew the real reason for the season.

Todd swung Rebecca's arm as he started again toward the shopping center's door. "Your mom's right. You don't want to be greedy. But that doesn't mean we can't look at every single toy before you pick a few special ones to put on your Christmas list."

"Will you look at *every single toy,* too?"

"Absolutely. I love toys." Todd glanced back over his shoulder. "What about you, Mommy? Are you ready to look at more toys than any kid should own?"

"I'm right behind you." Hannah shook her head, but she couldn't help smiling at the merry prattling of her companions about baby dolls, race cars, plastic dinosaurs and building sets as they stepped inside the mall entrance and continued into the specialty toy shop.

Rebecca and her father were so at ease with each other, no longer strangers, as they'd been a week before, but fast friends. They seemed to share a comfortable, private rhythm, a sign that they were building a foundation for a relationship between just the two of them.

Hannah waited, expecting jealousy to squeeze inside her and to strangle all the magnanimous feelings she'd been experiencing tonight. Todd was an interloper; before, Rebecca's heart had belonged to her mother alone.

To her surprise, Hannah felt only warmth. Her eyes were wet as she stared at the blur of bright colors from games, toys and puzzles stacked high in the tiny shop. Strange how she didn't feel cramped herself in this new relationship. There seemed to be plenty of room for both Todd and her in Rebecca's heart.

She'd been naive to believe Rebecca didn't need a father in her life. Now she wanted that for her daughter. It had become intrinsically tied to all the hopes and dreams Hannah had for her child: for a strong relationship with God, for a good education, for love, adventure, dreams and joy.

"Mommy?"

Hannah glanced down at the little love of her life, who was pulling on the hem of her parka to get her attention. A packaged collector's doll in a satiny, pink dress rested in her daughter's arms.

"Do you think Santa would mind if I asked for just one doll this year?"

"Sweetie, that isn't really the kind of doll that you would play with." Or one her mother could afford. That familiar disappointment pulled at her spirit, a reminder of the way that tight budgets warred with Hannah's need for independence in caring for her child.

"But she opens and shuts her eyes and everything." The child shifted the box to demonstrate before hugging the package to her chest.

"She sure does, but this doll—" Hannah paused to read the name printed on the box "—Miss Gabrielle is the kind of toy you put up on your shelf to look pretty."

"She is pretty, Mommy. Look, her hair's just like Tessa's."

Hannah glanced down at the doll's collection of dark curls, all tidily collected with a bright pink ribbon. That hair would look *exactly* like Tessa's unruly mass of springy curls before they could finish Christmas breakfast.

"You mean Andrew and Serena's little girl?" Todd asked as he came closer to study the doll.

"She's a big girl. Tessa's nine."

"Ooh, I stand corrected." Todd said seriously.

"But the doll…" Hannah began again.

"Okay, Mommy. I'll put her back." Rebecca returned the toy to the shelf with her sister pricey dolls but only after several hugs and a promise to visit. Even after Miss Gabrielle was standing tall next to her sisters, Rebecca stood looking up at her with longing.

Hannah peeked over at Todd, who appeared to be fighting back a smile and losing the battle. He crooked his index finger to call Hannah over to him. Her stance stiffened. He wasn't going to question her parenting, was he? She jumped in before he had the chance.

"Look, Todd, no child should ever have everything she wants. Even if I could afford it." She glanced around, hoping Rebecca hadn't overheard, and lowered her voice. "I've had to explain this to Dad and to my child-care provider, Mary, but I don't want everyone overindulging Rebecca. They need to understand that I'm the parent."

"Rebecca has two parents now," Todd pointed out softly.

Hannah blew out an exasperated sigh. "I know, but…" She let the words trail off because even she didn't know but *what*. Todd kept a solemn expression when he could have given her the condescending smile she deserved. She appreciated that.

"I know I'm new at this parenting thing, but I just want to be a part of the team, okay?" He squeezed her shoulder and released it quickly.

"I promise not to buy things for Rebecca every time I take her anywhere. And I won't ply her with treats. Buying someone's love dooms a relationship as much as it does a wallet."

Hannah's body relaxed from the battle that would be unnecessary. Rebecca continued to stare at the doll, having a tough time saying goodbye to her dream. At least this coparenting thing might not be as difficult as Hannah had first imagined.

Todd was a reasonable person. She'd forgotten that about him. His reasonableness had been one of the things she'd liked about him. One of many.

"That said," Todd began, but stared into her eyes as if gauging her reaction before he continued, "it's Christmas. Can *our* daughter, this one time, have something utterly impractical, just because her daddy wants to indulge her?"

Again, that word. *Daddy*. Images of Hannah with her own father flooded her mind. But those memories of normal activities—of unwrapping presents and removing training wheels—transformed into stark thoughts of a teenage girl and her father standing next to a casket in the snow.

Todd tilted his head to the side and studied her quizzically when she didn't answer. "Please, Hannah."

Hannah was weakening—she could feel it, but that didn't stop her from pressing her argument once more. "You saw it. That doll is ridiculously expensive."

He nodded, his gaze never leaving hers. "Ridiculously. And Rebecca will want to play with it instead of leaving it on a shelf to collect dust. Miss Gabrielle will probably be naked and have messy hair before Christmas day is even over."

When she glanced at him sharply, Todd shrugged. "I've seen her other dolls. She seems to prefer them au naturel."

"If you know it's too expensive and even that she won't care for it the way she should, then why do you still want to buy it for her?"

"It's my first Christmas as a dad. I want to make it special."

Hannah had opened her mouth to try again, but her teeth clicked shut. Her heart squeezed. For the last few weeks, she'd thought only how their lives—hers and Rebecca's—had changed. Todd's life had been altered just as dramatically, and yet he was relishing the newness. No matter what the difficult circumstances of her birth, Rebecca was blessed to have a father like Todd.

"I'm sure she'll be pleased," Hannah said finally. "When would you plan to give it to her?"

Todd sent a quick glance Rebecca's way and then turned his sheepish expression on Hannah. "Well, I've already bought a few Christmas presents for her—just a few books, games and stuff. I wouldn't want to give her too many presents, so I was hoping that this one could be a present she finds under the tree Christmas morning. From Santa."

From Mommy and Daddy, he might as well have said. How easily he'd bypassed the delicate subject of affordability. As much as she appreciated that, she didn't want his thoughtfulness to go unrewarded.

"Are you sure you don't want her to know? Each time she plays with the doll, she would remember that it was a gift from you. She'd know you were thinking of her."

"That doesn't matter." He glanced up as a very solemn Rebecca made her way back to them. "I just want to see her smile."

"Look at this one, Mommy."

In her palm, Rebecca proudly held up a tiny star-shaped sugar cookie. Well, it was almost a star, though one of its five points was missing, and the remaining four were far from even.

"That's really nice, honey." Hannah bent to brush some of the flour off her daughter's face. She didn't know why she bothered. Only a bath could remove all the batter, frosting and colored-sugar sprinkles that had decorated Rebecca along with the cookies.

"Nice? Nice, you say?" Todd wore an incredulous expression as he looked up from the table where he and Rebecca sat, cutting the shapes and putting them on baking sheets. "Now that cookie is amazing."

Setting his own cookie cutter aside, Todd moved the newest creation from Rebecca's hand to the pan among the other stars, Christmas trees and Santa shapes. On his black turtleneck and black jeans, he wore nearly as much flour and sprinkles as his daughter did. Hannah's fingers itched to grab her camera again, but she'd already taken several pictures, and even Rebecca was sick of posing.

"What color frosting are you going to put on it after it's baked?" Todd asked her. "Green, white or red?"

Rebecca squinted and studied the cookie for several seconds before coming to a decision. "Blue."

Todd nodded as if seeing the finished masterpiece the way Rebecca envisioned it. "Blue sounds great."

"You mean we need to make *more* frosting?" Hannah put on her best stern expression when she asked it. Really, she didn't mind a bit that they would use up all the flour, confectioner's sugar and food coloring in the house and that she would be scrubbing cookie dough off the tabletop, cabinet doors and laminate kitchen floor for days.

"More frosting. Yum!"

"You were right, Becca." Todd nuzzled his messy little girl under his chin. "This was a better idea than sledding."

She poked his nose playfully and squirmed out of his grasp. "You wanted to make cookies, Daddy."

"But you were the one who thought it sounded like fun."

Hannah swallowed a chuckle as she took the three-step walk back to the counter where she'd been whipping frosting of various colors. She'd suspected that cookie making had been Todd's idea, but now they'd confirmed it. Rebecca and her father could have gone sledding together as they had on Sunday, but he'd made a point of including Hannah this time in the fun. Gratitude filled her that he had. Maybe someday she would learn to enjoy the solitude while her daughter spent time with her father, but at this point, the apartment felt too empty, her heart too lonely.

To keep her hands busy, Hannah pulled her last mixing bowl from the cabinet and measured one-third cup of butter for her fourth recipe of buttercream frosting.

Rebecca must have recognized that the new project left the other bowls unattended because she slipped over to the counter, pulled a bowl down to her level and scooped a dollop of green frosting with her finger. She had that finger in her mouth before Hannah could turn off the mixer.

"Rebecca Faith Woods." Hannah pretended to threaten her child with the business end of a rubber spatula and earned a round of giggles for her trouble.

Todd glanced over from the table, but his mouth was tight. At first, his reaction confused Hannah until she realized she'd spoken their daughter's last name aloud. That name wasn't McBride.

She was beginning to imagine how uncomfortable that had to make Todd and how important it would be to him for his child to carry his name. Hannah met his gaze and smiled at him tremulously, hoping it reassured him. The name would be another thing they would discuss in the weeks to come.

Todd smiled back at her, and the strangest thing happened. Oh, she remembered it, all right. Knees like gelatin without a proper mold. Pulse pounding out a Latin beat. With Todd, she'd felt this strange sensation so many times—a tickling electricity, a sense of being more fully alive. In the last five years, she hadn't felt anything like it.

Not until Todd came back.

Hannah drew in a sharp breath that she covered by clearing her throat. As a distraction, she flipped the mixer back on and whipped the butter until it was fluffy.

But the spinning beaters only seemed to underscore the thoughts whirling through her mind. When had her anger against him cooled? When had she come to see him as anything besides an obstacle to her independent life with her child? She couldn't say. More disconcerting than that, now that the first of these unacceptable thoughts had escaped her tight hold, she couldn't make them stop.

As if he was unaware of the battle of wills inside Hannah and the wide berth he should give her because of it, Todd leaned close and nabbed the container of red frosting off the countertop.

He shrugged when Hannah batted her spatula at him. "I have to make sure the red tastes okay, too." He popped a fingerful into his mouth and made a humming sound of approval low in his throat.

"It's good, isn't it, Daddy?" Rebecca said.

Hannah grabbed the bowl of white frosting before either of them decided to double-dip with their germ-covered fingers. She frowned at Todd.

"Some example you are."

Perhaps he wasn't a great example for healthy baking techniques, but he was a really good dad. He seemed to have donned the role so easily, and he wore it well. In one side of the strong, confident man he'd become, Todd had maintained a childlike sense of play and an ability to laugh at himself.

Hannah couldn't help watching him with Rebecca, as he laughed genuinely at jokes from a four-year-old and made a game out of creating the ugliest cookies ever.

In a tender moment, he brushed Rebecca's gummy hair back from her face, the flour on his hands only adding to the mess.

"I do my best."

Hannah shot a sidelong glance at him as he returned to the table and helped Rebecca back into her chair. He was responding to her remark about his eating the frosting, but it almost felt as though he'd read her thoughts and had answered them instead. Without looking up, Todd rolled out another ball of sugar cookie dough. His daughter stuck a bell-shaped cutter right in the center, just as she had done the last three times, and still he laughed.

Todd covered his daughter's tiny hand with his, her fingers so dwarfed by his that they seemed to disappear. Hannah found she wasn't jealous of that special touch between father and daughter. No mother would deny her child the opportunity to smile like that.

Still, Hannah couldn't help remembering the warmth of Todd's hand when he'd covered her fingers with his own. She'd felt safe and precious in his arms. Would it ever be possible for her to be on the receiving end of his caring again? And, more importantly, would she ever want that?

Returning her attention to the bowl in front of her, Hannah mixed the confectioner's sugar into the butter and added vanilla and milk before squeezing in about half a tube of blue gel food coloring. The result was a bowl of cornflower-blue frosting—not a color she would normally have associated with Christmas.

"How many more days until Christmas, Mommy?"

Hannah took a few seconds to calculate. "Just five. It

won't be long now." She smiled, knowing full well that to a four-year-old, five days was a lifetime.

"Can Daddy come to our house for Christmas?"

Hannah's cheeks grew warm. "We've already discussed this, sweetie. You're going to your daddy's apartment for dinner on Christmas Eve, and then we'll all go to the service together Christmas morning. It's Sunday this year."

She glanced at Todd, realizing suddenly that she didn't know what further plans he had. With no family around and no time to have made close friends, Todd would probably be spending the holiday alone. No one should be alone on Christmas, and her heart squeezed with the sense that Todd might be.

Rebecca was shaking her head when Hannah looked back at her. "No, Mommy. When I get up. Can Daddy come when I open my presents from Santa?"

Hannah paused, waiting for the bite of jealousy to sting. This would be their first Christmas in their own apartment. Hannah had looked forward for months to having this private morning to mark their move to independence—just the two of them. But the only thing that struck her was a sense of rightness. Of course, Todd should be there when Rebecca opened Miss Gabrielle, for so many reasons beyond his special gift.

"Sure, he can…if he wants to." After washing her hands, she wiped them on a dish towel and turned back to him. "Todd, would you like to join us for Christmas morning and breakfast before church?"

He didn't hesitate. "That sounds great."

"You could come to Christmas dinner, too, if you like. It will be at my father's. His…friend is cooking dinner."

"Thanks, but I've already agreed to have dinner with the Westins."

"Oh, you'll enjoy that. We've spent several holidays with the Westins."

Her disappointment was as quick as it was bewildering. She turned back to the sink to rinse blue frosting off the beaters. It should have come as no surprise that Andrew and Serena had extended an invitation to Todd. They usually planned a big celebration, inviting all those who might otherwise have a lonely holiday.

She was disappointed for Rebecca's sake, she tried to tell herself. It was too difficult to admit that at least part of her frustration had nothing to do with her daughter.

Over her shoulder, Hannah found herself saying, "Well, maybe you could drop by for dessert then."

When Hannah turned back from the counter, Todd had stood up from the table and was studying her, his eyebrows drawn together. His gaze found hers and held it. So many emotions danced in his eyes, and he seemed willing to bare them all—regret, frustration and hope.

Rebecca, oblivious to the unspoken conversation, stood up, as well, and slipped her sticky hand into her father's.

"Please, Daddy. Please eat dessert with us."

Todd glanced down at her and smiled. "For you, sweetheart…anything."

Chapter Eight

Christmas dawned clear but frigid as rare, winter sun-shine glinted off ice-covered branches and snow-flocked evergreens. Todd didn't even mind that he could see his breath inside his car as he drove to the morning festivities at Hannah's apartment. He hadn't been this excited for Christmas morning since he was a little boy.

He had only parked his car by the curb and stepped out into the snow when Rebecca threw open the door.

"Merry Christmas, Daddy. Look, Mommy curled my hair." She shook her head, sending the cascade of tight blond ringlets flying.

"Merry Christmas. I like your hair."

"I have a new dress, too."

Rebecca spun in the doorway, making the full skirt of the velvety red dress pouf out around her.

"It's very pretty."

She wrinkled her nose. "It itches."

Before his daughter could run out into the snow and launch herself into his arms, fancy dress, black buckle shoes and all, Todd hurried up the steps. Balancing the shopping bag filled with gifts in one arm, he nabbed Rebecca and propped her on his hip.

Todd pressed his cheek to hers, breathing in the clean, baby shampoo scent that he'd come to associate with his daughter. She looked so sweet and pretty this morning. If only his parents could have come for Christmas. He would have loved to have the chance to introduce his daughter to them today, but part of him was equally glad that it was just the three of them this special Christmas morning.

"We've been waiting all morning for you, Daddy."

Todd closed the door, setting the shopping bag aside. "All morning? It's only seven-thirty."

"Yes, *all* morning," Hannah called from down the hall. Her tired voice suggested just how early Rebecca had awakened for Christmas morning.

Lowering his daughter to the floor, Todd hung his coat on the coat tree in the entry and waited. He expected to see some of that exhaustion on Hannah's face as she entered the room, but she looked serene in an elegant black dress that smoothed over her trim figure and fell nearly to her ankles. She'd worn her hair long today, the tresses turned softly toward her face, and around her neck she'd draped a strand of shimmering pearls.

Time paused for a few seconds as Todd forgot to breathe. Hannah was so beautiful. Her hair, that skin, those lips—he'd tried so hard these last four weeks not to see, not to remember. But here she stood about eight feet from him, giving him one of those smiles that used to take him down like a bat to the back of the knees. Clearly, it still could. All those feelings he'd worked so hard to bury came flooding back.

He needed to look away from her, but he couldn't help

watching for a few seconds longer. Hannah continued to watch him, too, though she blushed prettily just as she had so long ago. Maybe he hadn't imagined the connection he'd thought they'd made the other night at Hannah's apartment. Maybe…no he had no business going there. It was reckless to hope.

"Can we open presents now, Mommy? Please."

Startled, Todd and Hannah glanced down at the child now standing in the space between them, looking back and forth and wearing a confused expression.

Hannah was first to recover. "I did tell her she could open her gifts as soon as you got here."

"It's Jesus's birthday, but we get presents, too," Rebecca told him.

"Oh, really. Why do you think that is?"

Rebecca pursed her lips and squinted her eyes in concentration before answering. "Because God wants us all to have fun."

"It's really more than that," Hannah began, but then she stopped. "Maybe I should wait for a more teachable moment on that one."

"Why? Does someone want to open gifts right away?"

"I do! I do!" Rebecca chimed.

"Are you sure you don't want to wait until after breakfast, Becca? Maybe some pancakes or eggs and bacon?"

The child's sunny expression fell. "No, thank you."

"Well, since you said it so politely…" Todd looked to Hannah for confirmation.

Instead of answering, Hannah lowered her gaze to the shopping bag by the door. "More presents?"

"I held back last night."

"Not enough when you were shopping, apparently."

"Guilty." Todd raised his hands, palms up, but he refused to be sorry. "I couldn't help myself."

"Oh, well." Hannah frowned. "Rebecca, do you want to hand out the presents?"

Their daughter didn't waste any time rushing into the living room and digging several packages from under the tree. The collection wasn't large, but Hannah had made each package special by adding curly ribbons, bows and candy canes to the bright holiday wrapping paper.

Hannah crossed the room and sat on the sofa next to her camera bag. Todd sat in the recliner opposite her.

"This is mine." Rebecca set a small package in the center of the floor before retrieving another from the tree. She went back to the tree several times and returned to add packages to her little pile.

"She's reading already?" Todd asked, his chest puffing up with fatherly pride.

"A little. They learn to recognize their names from their badges at preschool."

Glancing back from the tree, Rebecca grinned and held out a small package wrapped in homemade paper that was covered with Christmas stamps. "This one says 'Mommy.'"

"She made that at preschool, too."

Rebecca scrambled over to hand the present to her mother and then rushed back to the tree. The next package she lifted was identical to the other. "This one says 'Daddy.'"

"Oh. Wow."

"Rebecca asked her teachers if she could make two gifts. Wasn't that nice?"

Todd could only nod. His throat became dry. His eyes burned. It wasn't as if he hadn't considered that his daughter might give him a Christmas gift, courtesy of her mother. But this was special. It was Rebecca's idea.

"Put your dad's pile right by his feet."

Having missed her father's strange reaction and her mother's effort to cover for him, Rebecca continued happily digging behind the tree and pulling out the last few packages. After asking her mother to read the name on the two final boxes, including one that she struggled to carry, Rebecca placed them next to Todd. He peeked at Hannah, who only looked away shyly.

"What about those presents?" Rebecca pointed to the bag by the door.

"How about I pass those out?" Todd stood and stepped over to the door to retrieve the bag.

The first two he placed in Rebecca's pile, and the remaining four he set at Hannah's feet.

"You weren't supposed to do this."

"Why? You did."

Her gaze fell on the two presents in Todd's pile. "Mine were just— Oh, never mind."

Twin pink spots appeared on her cheeks again, but a small smile lifted her lips, as well.

To Todd, her reaction felt like a gift in itself. This was the Hannah he remembered: the girl who got a kick out of sunsets, who could be excited about a gift box without even caring what was inside. That Hannah had been open to the world's surprises without constantly guarding herself against its pitfalls. He was so pleased to know a part of that girl remained in the woman she'd become.

"I'm youngest," Rebecca announced. "I get to go first."

When nobody argued with that, she tore into the first package. Soon the floor was littered with paper and ribbon, and a felt board play set, a princess dress-up outfit and a doll diaper bag were piled next their daughter.

Though Todd had wisely saved only the less-glamorous gifts of books and a puzzle for Christmas morning so as not to rain on Hannah's parental moment, he couldn't wait for Rebecca to choose the big package on the bottom of her stack. She saved that one for last.

"Mommy, Daddy!" she shrieked. "Santa brought Miss Gabrielle!" She hugged the doll to her, box and all, and posed for the camera with her new best friend.

"Oh, Rebecca, she's so pretty. Santa has good taste." Hannah exchanged a secretive glance with Todd and nodded her approval, as if she'd decided the doll wasn't such a bad purchase after all.

"Well, look at that." Todd realized his smile was probably bigger than even Rebecca's, but Todd didn't care. He loved seeing her this happy and knowing he'd had a part in this wonderful surprise.

Everything about his being a father had been a surprise, from the reality of it to the joy he'd found in it. He'd known Rebecca for such a short time, and yet he couldn't imagine his life without her.

Though he had no doubt she was her own person and would flex the muscles of her independence more and more as she grew, Todd was pleased to know that she demonstrated the best in both of her parents: her mother's spirit and enthusiasm and her father's dry wit. Rebecca made him proud and humbled him at the same time. God had given them all a special gift when He'd brought this child into their lives.

"Mommy, can you help me open it?"

"I just don't know why she didn't ask me for help," Todd said with a feigned frown.

"From what Rebecca told me, her new fashion doll lost most of its hair last night when you took it out of the package." Hannah knelt next to Rebecca, opened the box and made quick work of removing the plastic ties that held Miss Gabrielle captive.

He stepped behind her and examined her work over her shoulder. "Hey, you got the easier packaging. Houdini couldn't have escaped from the one I had."

Hannah straightened, taking on an air of superiority. "Maybe I just make it look easy." She held the straight face for several seconds before it folded into a grin. "It gets easier. Really. But you've already figured that out all on your own."

After her last words, Hannah looked up at him, making it clear she meant more than just the parental headache of wrestling with toy manufacturers' packaging. She seemed to speak of parenting in general, and, unless he was mistaken, she had just encouraged him and maybe even complimented him on his growth as a dad.

Todd cleared his throat and looked away to fight the emotion building inside him. "You go next, Hannah. We have to hurry. If you don't mind, I have a story I'd like to read before breakfast."

"Sounds great."

Hannah unwrapped the giant white-chocolate candy bar, the leather-covered journal and the Detroit Pistons plaque, inserting an embarrassed "you didn't have to" right after each "thank you."

"You see? I couldn't help myself."

It had been a balancing act, choosing inexpensive gifts that wouldn't seem too personal for their tentative relationship but would be symbolic to Hannah. Todd could tell from the way she chewed her lip and didn't make eye contact with him that the favorite things of her past still meant something to her now.

As she opened the last gift, a Christmas ornament for the collection she'd been amassing since she was a little girl, Todd wondered if he'd gone too far. It was a simple glass ball ornament with a painting of the Madonna. Why hadn't he considered that the token he'd purchased as a tribute to both Hannah's late mother and the mom Hannah had become might just be a stark reminder of all she'd lost?

For a few seconds, Hannah covered her face with her hands, but then she spread them aside. Though her eyes were shining with tears, she was smiling. Pain did fade, it appeared…over time. Perhaps, just perhaps, anger faded, as well.

"Thanks, Todd." She tilted her head to the side and coughed into her hand. "That was sweet."

"It's your turn, Daddy."

Rebecca scrambled over to the pile of gifts next to him and lifted the smaller of the two packages up to him. Inside it was a navy wool scarf.

"It's to keep you warm," Rebecca explained.

"The winter's going to hit you pretty hard after a few years near the Equator." Hannah indicated with a nod of her head for their daughter to hand Todd the second, much heavier gift.

As Todd pulled a thick photo album from inside the box, he glanced over at Hannah.

"I thought you deserved your own copy of history."

On the first page were the words "Rebecca's Birth Day." In one picture, Hannah stood in a hospital gown, her hands resting on her full, rounded belly. Those that followed were the first pictures of a wrinkly and bald baby being cradled by her mother, grandfather and a woman Todd recognized from church.

A few pages further into the book, the photos began to change. Instead of snapshots alone, there were incredible black-and-white images—of the baby sleeping under a spray of sunlight, a toddler splashing water at the beach. Todd turned a few more pages, but those obviously professional pictures continued to be mixed among the candid shots.

Remembering, Todd glanced over to the Christmas tree and the framed artistic photos on the wall behind it. He shot a glance back to Hannah.

"They're yours, aren't they? You're the photographer."

She nodded, smiling. "It's a hobby mostly. A photographer and an accountant—a strange combination, don't you think?"

"Not strange. Anyway, you're a great photographer."

"It brings in a little extra money."

He studied the framed photos again as his thoughts were drawn to another place, another time. "You used to take pictures all the time. I hated it."

He chuckled with the memory of the wrestling matches that had resulted from his efforts to remove that camera from her hands…and the embraces that usually ended the game. Hannah must have remembered, as well, because she suddenly looked away, embarrassed.

"Thank you." He waited for her to look back at him before he continued. "It's great. I love it."

"I'm glad." She cleared her throat.

"Do they have Christmas at your old house, Daddy?"

Todd glanced up from the photo album. "You mean in Singapore?" At her nod, he continued. "It's an island, you know. Some people there celebrate Christmas just like us. But they don't have snow like we have here. It's very hot, and it's rainy sometimes."

"Are they sad that there's no snow?"

A smile pulled at his lips. "Maybe some are, but many like the warm weather, too."

Her attention span filled with all the geography she could handle for one day, Rebecca turned back to her toys and immediately began undressing her doll.

"Didn't you say something about a story?" Hannah reminded Todd.

Rebecca looked up from the floor. "Yeah, Daddy, will you read us a story? Please."

"I can do that." He reached one last time into his shopping bag and produced his worn, brown-leather Bible. Opening it to the passage he'd already marked, Todd made room for Rebecca to squeeze in next to him in the recliner. "I thought this would be a perfect occasion to read from the Book of Luke. It's about Joseph and Mary's trip to Bethlehem.

"'While they were there, the time came for the baby to be born, and she gave birth to her firstborn, a son. She wrapped him in cloths and placed him in a manger, because there was no room for them in the inn.'"

"Mommy said a manger was a eating trough for animals. Why did they put Baby Jesus there?"

"Joseph and Mary were away from home and didn't have a bed for Baby Jesus. At least the hay in the manger would keep our Lord warm. There he was, the Son of God, sleeping beside the farm animals."

Todd hoped Hannah would pipe in with her opinion on the subject, but he only caught her staring at him strangely. "What? What is it?"

Instead of answering immediately, Hannah continued to stare at him, looking perplexed.

"Is something wrong, Hannah?"

She shook her head. "No, not wrong."

"Then what is it?"

"I thought I knew you so well," she said with a shrug. "I never really knew you at all, did I?"

At first her words made no sense to him, and then realization dawned. Though years ago Hannah had heard him speak of so many things, he'd never spoken so openly of his faith. Or had a whole lot of faith to speak of.

"You knew me. You still do." Though he itched to touch her hand, Todd reached out to her with his smile alone. "I've changed some. But some changes are for the better."

Chapter Nine

"Are you sure you don't want another slice of pumpkin pie, Todd?"

Olivia Wells already had the pie plate in one hand, the server poised in the other. Sitting across from Hannah at the Woods family's formal dining room table, Todd appeared almost the sage color of his sweater. He'd already eaten large servings of Olivia's apple pie, cherries jubilee and Black Forest cake, even after consuming his share of the massive Christmas dinner at the Westins'.

"Come on, Todd. One more couldn't hurt," Reverend Bob prodded, holding back a smile.

"Except that it might make me explode right here on Mrs. Wells's heirloom tablecloth."

Hannah shook her head. "Ew, that wouldn't be pretty."

"Now, Todd, didn't I tell you to call me Olivia?"

"Sorry. But no, thank you, Mrs.— I mean, Olivia. Your desserts are amazing, but I couldn't eat another bite."

Reverend Bob pushed back from the table and patted his full belly. "I believe I've had enough, as well, though the meal was wonderful." He flashed a grateful look to Olivia before turning back to Todd. "Did you get the chance to talk to your parents today?"

"I called them this morning, which was already tonight, their time. Mom said the day was sunny and eighty-five degrees."

"Did you tell her you'd build a snowman for her?" Hannah asked.

He nodded. "She told me she'd make a sand castle at the beach for me."

"When do you think they'll return stateside?" Bob sat back with his hand pressed to his stomach.

"Dad already took an extension, so he should be returning soon. They've been talking about wanting to come back a lot lately." He didn't have to mention the current development that probably had inspired their interest in moving back soon.

"It's too bad they couldn't come just for the holiday," Bob continued. "We would have loved having them here, and I know they would have enjoyed Olivia's cooking."

Again, Bob smiled at his guest, and Olivia beamed. If this woman could make her father that happy, Hannah decided she could at least try to make an effort.

"Uh, Olivia, I just wanted to tell you that you really outdid yourself with Christmas dinner. Thanks so much for planning this."

She meant it, too, even though initially she'd felt strange seeing her mother's good china paired with Olivia's lace tablecloth and linen napkins. The turkey had been golden and juicy, the side dishes, scrumptious. Olivia's ham with honey-apricot glaze even had finicky Rebecca returning for seconds.

Although Hannah had been uncomfortable with the idea of sharing Christmas with her father's lady friend, the celebration had been lovely. It was another great addition to the day that began with the private gift exchange at her apartment and continued through Reverend Bob's inspiring holiday sermon at church.

Olivia stood up from the table and started stacking dishes. "It's unfortunate that Rebecca fell asleep before dessert. Should we wake her?"

"No, that's all right," Todd said, shaking his head. "She has to be exhausted by now." As he stood, he raised a hand to stop Olivia's movement. "Here, let us get those. You have to be exhausted, too."

Hannah stood next to him. "Yes, why don't you and Dad go in the living room and relax. We'll finish up in here." Strange, the thought of being in a room alone with Todd didn't make her feel uneasy the way it would have a few weeks before.

"Sounds good," he said. "Just let me go check on Rebecca, and I'll be in to help."

Her heart warmed as she watched his retreating form. He was such an amazing father. How could she ever have questioned whether he would be? She listened to the sound of his footsteps as he climbed the stairs and then stopped in the doorway of her childhood bedroom. Soon she heard footsteps on the stairs again.

"Boy, she's dead to the world," he said as he reentered the kitchen through the swinging door.

"I wonder why. It wasn't as if she woke up—and woke me up—at five-thirty or anything."

Todd stepped next to her until they were standing nearly shoulder-to-shoulder at the sink. Hannah rinsed the dishes and passed them to Todd to put in the dishwasher.

"Just five-thirty? I thought you said she got you up really early."

"It's early enough."

"So you still get grouchy when you miss your beauty sleep."

Hannah turned to give him her best evil eye, but Todd's silly grin made it impossible for her to hold the glower. "I guess some things never change."

"Some things do. I was glad to see Reverend Bob dating again. How long have he and Olivia been together?"

Hannah shrugged. "I don't know. Several months."

"You don't like her, do you?"

"I like her just fine."

His expression told her he didn't believe her. "But you don't think she's right for your dad."

Again, Hannah shrugged. "I don't know what I think."

"Would you think *any* woman was right for your dad?"

"Probably not."

"But you want him to be happy, don't you?"

Out of her side vision, she caught him watching her, waiting, expecting her to tell him what he already knew to be true. Reluctantly, she nodded. Of course, she wanted her father to be happy again. Maybe he would even be blessed to find someone with whom to share his life. She could still remember her father's devastation after her mother died. Todd was there. He remembered, too.

Todd poured the automatic detergent into the dishwasher and closed the door. "Olivia seems to make him happy."

"I know. I keep telling myself that. She's not all that

bad really, even if I don't feel comfortable around her. She can't help it she's not—"

"Not your mother?"

"No, silly. Not Mary Nelsen."

"Who? Your babysitter?"

"Mary's great, and I think she's been in love with Dad for years. He doesn't have a clue. Mary loves Rebecca, too." She paused, the memory of her child-care provider with her daughter bringing a smile to her lips. "She's the closest thing to a grandmother Rebecca's ever had."

"She has another grandma…and another grand-pa," Todd said in a quiet voice.

"Sorry. I didn't mean—"

He waved away her apology. "Don't worry about it. My parents are dying to meet her." He shot her an embarrassed look. "Well, they're excited now that they've gotten over the shock of learning about her. They hope to visit in February."

"I'm sure Rebecca will love meeting them." For now, Hannah was just relieved that they'd changed the subject.

"You know you can't choose for your father, right?" Todd said, dragging them back to the old subject.

"I know."

A knock at the kitchen door ended the conversation. Reverend Bob stuck his head inside. "Oh, you are finished. We wondered what was taking you two so long."

Hannah shifted, worried her father had overheard, though she doubted he would have been smiling like that if he had. Grabbing the dishrag, she started wiping down the counter. "We were just finishing up."

Bob continued to stand holding the door open. He was wearing his long overcoat to cover his slacks and sports jacket.

"Olivia and I thought we'd take a stroll to work off our dinner. We would invite you two to join us, but we didn't expect that you'd want to wake Rebecca."

He probably wanted to be alone with his lady friend, too, but Hannah refrained from mentioning it.

"No, that's fine. We'll stay here," Todd told him.

"Why don't you two start a fire? Olivia and I will probably want to warm ourselves by it when we get back."

"Sure, we can do that."

With a wave, Bob backed out of the door.

Todd wiped his hands on a towel and crossed to the kitchen door. "I can't believe they would go out into that weather on purpose when they could stay inside and keep warm."

"Don't worry. You'll get used to the Michigan climate again. You did last time." She followed him down the hall to the family room where five stockings dangled from the mantel—three embroidered ones for Bob, Hannah and Rebecca and two red felt socks, purchased just for this occasion.

He turned back to her. "The last time we were only moving here from Tennessee. This move has been much harder coming from a tropical climate."

"Maybe it's an age thing. You are a whole lot older this time."

"Speak for yourself, sweetheart. Isn't it great that we're the same age?"

She wrinkled her nose at him. "Well, anyway, we still need to build that fire. You know how to do it, right?"

"I was hoping you knew."

"Never a Boy Scout, eh? Well, allow me to demonstrate for you." Hannah crouched in front of the fireplace, opened the glass doors and twisted a black control just beneath the pile of logs. Golden flames leaped out and licked over the faux wood.

Todd broke out in a round of applause. "Okay, you got me. I didn't remember you having a gas fireplace."

"Dad had it put in a few years ago." She stood and warmed her hands near the fire before partially closing the doors.

Staring into the flame for several seconds, Todd approached the mantel and smoothed his index finger over the tiny Baby Jesus in the crystal crèche arranged on top.

"That belonged to my mother." Hannah stretched up to the mantel and ran her fingers over the sloping shape of one of the crystal Christmas trees that marked both ends of the display.

"I remember it. There are several things still in this house that remind me of her. She's been gone for seven years, and her fingerprints are still everywhere here."

Hannah's heart squeezed. It was just like Todd, the Todd she remembered, to reassure her that her mother's memory would be preserved. How had he known just how much she'd needed to hear that today when another woman's touches filled the kitchen and dining room?

"I wish you could have known her better."

"Yeah, me, too. She died about six months after we moved in."

"By the time you met her, the uterine cancer had already taken so much of her spirit." The flames drew Hannah's attention as she settled on the sofa and drew her stocking-clad feet up under her dress. "Sometimes it seems like so long ago that she died, and other times it feels like just yesterday."

"Yeah, I know what you mean."

His words drew her out of her haze. When she looked up at him, Todd's face was hidden in shadow.

"You know, I probably never would have survived those first few months, the first few years even, without you. So if I didn't remember to thank you then, I want to do it now. Thank you."

"You didn't need to thank me, then or now. I wanted to help if I could. You just didn't realize how strong you were. You would have found your way eventually on your own."

"Fortunately, we never had to know that for sure."

Todd watched Hannah closely as he tried to absorb what she'd just said. Her comment was as strange and unexpected as so many of the things she'd done lately, from including him in her private Christmas celebration to spending hours making that incredible photo album for him. What message was she trying to give to him?

"Have you ever wondered 'what if'?" The second the words were out of his mouth, Todd regretted speaking them. Why couldn't he just enjoy the moment? This was the first time since he'd moved back that Hannah had allowed him to get this close, and he had to sabotage it.

Todd rested his elbow against the mantel and waited. Instead of striking back as he expected she might, Hannah simply stared at him from across the room.

He rushed to backtrack. "I don't mean what if we hadn't made— Or if you didn't get—" Finally, he stopped himself, staring at the floor. "I don't know what I mean."

"Yes," she whispered.

His head jerked up, and he searched her face for whatever she wasn't saying.

Her eyes were shiny, and her tongue slipped out

to moisten her lips. When Todd was convinced she wouldn't say more, she cleared her throat and began.

"I've wondered what if. About a lot of things."

"But not about having Rebecca." He didn't even need to pose it as a question. He knew what her answer would be.

She used the back of her hand to swipe at her eyes. "No. Never Rebecca. I've never even questioned my decision to keep her, though a lot of people thought I should have considered adoption."

Something cold gripped his insides. He'd always believed adoption to be a great thing—still did. Many strong families were built by the selflessness of birth mothers' difficult decisions.

But if Hannah had made that choice, he might never have known that their child existed. He wouldn't even have known to mourn the empty place in his life that would have been there without Rebecca.

The thought weighed so heavily on his mind that he crossed to the sofa where Hannah sat and slumped onto the opposite end.

Hannah turned so she faced him and leaned her back against the sofa's armrest. "I sometimes wonder what our lives would have been like if I'd told you as soon as I knew I was pregnant."

He'd wondered the same thing so many times himself and had blamed her for guaranteeing that neither of them would ever know. But now he couldn't work up the energy to continue holding a grudge.

"If only I'd told my father the whole story," Hannah continued, staring at her hands. "Dad would have convinced me to tell you." She lifted her head to meet his gaze. "You had the right to know."

"It's all in the past now." He leaned back and popped his feet on the box-shaped footstool next to the couch. "Anyway, I can't promise I would have come off as a hero back then. We both know I didn't make the best decisions at seventeen."

It was good to see her stark expression soften even though her eyes still looked damp.

"My decisions weren't exactly stellar, either."

Todd smiled, his memory of that teenage girl and the woman she had become melding. Her sweetness and vulnerability—things he'd loved about her but believed she'd lost—were still there, just buried beneath layers of self-protective armor.

"Whatever mistakes you made, you've done an amazing job with Rebecca. She's an incredible kid."

"She is pretty great, isn't she?" Hannah settled back into the sofa again, some of her tension from moments before seeming to ebb.

Todd found himself relaxing, too. "She's happy and kind and well-adjusted. You see, God always had a plan for her—for all of us."

Tilting her head, Hannah studied him, drawing her eyebrows together. "There it is again. You lived next to me for two years. You went to church every Sunday with your parents and even with me a few times. In all that time, I don't remember you talking about your faith."

"I didn't have much faith to speak of at the time," he said with a chuckle. "Oh, I believed in God and all. I'd heard the message from the cradle. It all seemed reasonable enough. I just didn't see any reason to take it as personally as you did."

Hannah suddenly straightened and lowered her feet to the floor. "Personally? If I'd been focused on my personal relationship with God, then— Oh, I don't know. But we weren't talking about me, were we? This was about you."

Todd shrugged. "The story of my faith journey is pretty pedestrian. Unoriginal. I had to hit rock bottom before I looked up."

Her front teeth pressed into her bottom lip, and for several seconds Hannah said nothing. But, in a whispered voice, as if she didn't want the answer but had to know, she finally asked, "When was that?"

"When I was ten thousand miles from here, on one of the most beautiful tropical islands in the world and so lonely that I thought I might die. It did no good to call. My letters just came back unopened. It felt as if someone had carved my heart out and left it beating outside my body."

Hannah squeezed her eyes shut and covered them with her hands. "Now that was graphic." When she lowered her hands, she crossed her arms over her chest in a nervous self-hug.

"Okay, it came from a teenager's point of view. One who'd been playing too many video games. But those were stark days. I'd been so stupid that I ended up losing everything that mattered. That's when I hit rock bottom."

"Then what happened?"

"I turned to God, and He came alive for me." Todd held his hands wide to show how obvious that answer was. "He was there, showing me that I wasn't alone. I didn't realize until later that He'd been there all along."

"I'm glad."

Todd drew his eyebrows together. "That I found faith?"

"That, too, but more than that." She paused to study

her hands and push back the cuticles on two of her nails. But finally she looked back at him. "I'm glad you weren't alone. I know what's that's like. To feel alone."

"Is that how you felt?"

She didn't answer right away, but her eyes looked shiny in the firelight and then a single tear traced down her cheek. "More than just alone, I felt abandoned. Even before I took the pregnancy test."

You abandoned me. She hadn't phrased it that way, but he felt the condemnation of it anyway. Closing his eyes, he could picture Hannah as she must have been then, sitting by herself in her room, keeping a terrifying secret locked up inside.

Of course, she felt abandoned, whether he'd intended it or not and despite that he'd had the argument of a lifetime with his father for taking the foreign assignment. He couldn't change the fact that she'd been alone, perhaps even more alone than he'd felt without her.

"I'm so sorry I wasn't here."

"Yeah, me, too." She gazed into the fire for several seconds. "I'm sorry about a lot of things."

"Then we have something in common. I've been trying to apologize to you ever since I came back to town. Since before I even knew about Rebecca."

"There's no need for you to apologize."

"But could you do me a favor and let me anyway?"

At first she shrugged, but she finally nodded.

"I'm sorry about pressuring you into— Well, you know. A sexual relationship. You were only looking for comfort, just someone to talk to in those months after your mom died, and I read something more into it. I wasn't thinking about you, or consequences or sin. I thought only of myself."

Todd had always wondered how Hannah would react when he finally apologized, but her nervous laughter he definitely didn't expect.

"Pressure?" Hannah said when she finally stopped chuckling. "It wasn't like that, and you know it. You can try to take all the blame. For a long time, I would have been more than happy to let you.

"But it wasn't all your fault. I was there, too. We just became too close and got carried away."

"Thanks for saying that." Todd blew out a tired sigh. "We've caused each other so much pain. Do you think we can ever get past it?"

"We have to…for Rebecca's sake."

"What about for *our* sake, Hannah? Yours and mine?"

At first Hannah appeared confused. They hadn't spoken about anyone's needs but their daughter's since Todd had returned to town. It was probably a mistake to do it now, but Todd couldn't help himself.

"A long time ago you and I were friends. Good friends. We were good together."

Hannah started shaking her head. "It was a long time ago. Maybe we really can't go back."

"Can't? Why not?" Then he stopped himself. He couldn't push, or he might frighten her away. "We don't have to go back. But I would like to go forward. This is my what if. I think we owe it to ourselves to explore it."

"What are you saying?"

"I'm saying that I would be honored if you would consider going out to dinner with me one night this week."

"A date?"

The word seemed to clog her throat. Todd's throat tightened, as well. Had he asked too much too soon?

Had he become too anxious to reach his ultimate destination and messed up the journey?

He would have backtracked again, perhaps even assured her that their date would only be as friends, if he hadn't heard the squeak of the front door from the other room.

"Hannah, Todd, we're back," Reverend Bob called out, as if he thought it necessary to announce himself.

Though they were adults and simply sitting on opposite ends of the couch, they both straightened and planted their feet on the floor. Sounds of the rustling of outerwear and then approaching footsteps followed.

Their moment, their sweet cocoon of time alone together, was ending, and Todd worried that his chance with Hannah was coming to a close along with it.

"Yes, a date. Well, what do you say?"

The wait for her answer seemed to take hours instead of seconds. She glanced at the doorway through which her father and Olivia would come in only seconds. Was she gauging the amount of time she had to put him off completely?

But then she turned back to him, her lips curving into the most beautiful smile in the world. "Yes, Todd, I'd love to have dinner with you."

Chapter Ten

"Are you sure this place isn't too expensive?" Hannah glanced around nervously, first at the crisp, white tablecloths and crystal stemware and then at the candles that cast the whole restaurant in a golden glow. At least he'd warned her the place would be dressy, or she might have worn jeans instead of the long, black-velvet skirt, cream sweater and the dress boots she'd chosen.

This place—maybe her accepting Todd's invitation altogether—might have been a mistake. He'd made reservations less than twenty-four hours after she'd agreed to have dinner with him, not even giving her time to change her mind.

"Well, I might be a little short. Do you think you can pick up the difference?"

Todd gave that mischievous half smile that had always made her feel light-headed and made her stomach tickle. "I can afford it. Maybe not every week, but I can afford it. I have a job now, remember?"

"But Five Lakes Grill? It's so extravagant." She glanced out the restaurant's front window that faced Main Street. Garlands still wrapped the streetlamps and holiday lights still glimmered in the store across the street, but she could see a few signs in the windows that read After-Christmas Sale.

"You finally agreed to go out with me. I wanted to impress you. Did it work?"

Hannah glanced around the room again and then back at Todd. He'd impressed her, all right. Dressed all in black, from his wool sport coat to his turtleneck and trousers, he'd never looked more handsome. Even the candlelight seemed to give him special attention, dancing over the blond highlights that remained in his hair.

She cleared her throat. "You didn't have to impress me."

"But I did, didn't I?"

She nodded, pressing her hand over the flutter in her stomach. Though she glanced away from his intense gaze, she could still feel him watching her. Why was she so nervous, anyway? During the short span of their friendship, she'd gotten to know this man better than most people ever knew each other. They'd shared their deepest thoughts, their failures and their fears.

Todd had borne the pain of her mother's death as if the loss had been from his own heart. How could she have forgotten all those stolen hours of intimacy that had nothing to do with the physical and everything to do with why she'd fallen in love with him?

Then the idea struck her that although they'd shared food and conversation together so many times, they'd never gone on a real date before. Dating had seemed extraneous to the relationship they'd already built together.

"Can you believe this is our first date?"

Hannah stiffened at his words, and her cheeks warmed. She shouldn't have been surprised that his thoughts had traveled the same path as her own, but she was.

Either the candlelight hid her discomfort or he pretended not to notice, but he continued as if she'd already answered him.

"I don't know about you, but I'm really nervous."

An ironic chuckle bubbled inside her throat. "It doesn't seem right, does it?"

He shook his head. "We know each other too well for us to be nervous." His eyes took on a faraway look as he lifted a hard roll from the bread basket and buttered it. "Or at least we used to."

"We still do," she assured him, not because she didn't share his uncertainty but because she wanted so badly to erase that sadness from his eyes. She set a slice of nut bread on her bread plate but didn't take a bite.

"It's okay if we don't know every little thing about each other today," he said.

"What do you mean?" Unable to meet his gaze, Hannah looked down and traced spinning circles on the tablecloth with her fingernail.

"At one time, we knew each other better than anyone. We finished each other's sentences. Before I sneezed, you'd pass a tissue into my hand."

Her fingers calmed against the cloth as she allowed the memories to blossom inside her thoughts where she'd once held them in perpetual winter. "It *was* like that with us, wasn't it?"

"I want it to be different this time."

As Hannah looked up from the table, Todd reached across it and covered her left hand with his right. How opposite their hands looked—hers finely boned and pale from the long Michigan fall and his hand, broad and strong, still clinging to its island tan. His skin felt so warm, his touch as sure as the man he'd grown to be.

It would be best for her to pull away discreetly—she knew that. Then both of them could pretend nothing had happened. But how could she pull away when the connection felt so right?

They stayed like that for a few minutes, just touching. Todd probably expected her to move her hand, but when she didn't, he finally spoke again.

"This is our first date. We've had many experiences together, but this is new. I want it all to be new like this."

Hannah gently removed her hand from his this time, and he lifted his fingers to let her go. Immediately, her skin felt cold.

"As nice as all this sounds, Todd, we can't rewrite history."

He nodded as if to concede that point. "But we can add new pages to our history. I know it—*we*—can be different together this time."

"Can there be a chance for us after all that's happened?" Even as she said it, she felt a wave of loss thinking that the past might need to remain the past and the future only an unattainable dream.

"Maybe this is a mistake. Maybe I shouldn't have agreed to come. If you want, we could leave instead of ordering. We're only ripping open old wounds and taking the chance that we'll create even deeper ones. Wounds that won't heal."

"We're doing all of that?" Todd held his finger to his lips as if in deep concentration. "I thought we were just having dinner."

Despite herself, Hannah laughed. Seconds before

she'd been contemplating pain and loss, and now he had her laughing again.

Todd laughed with her, his deep baritone turning the heads of a few other restaurant patrons before he lowered his voice. "Now are you sure you're just a photo-taking accountant? I see a future for you on the stage. You have a flair for the dramatic."

"I like to keep my professional options open."

He smiled at first, but then his expression turned serious. "I know a lot has happened between us, but can't we think of tonight as just dinner? We can pretend we're just two single adults getting to know each other better. We'll keep all our baggage carefully hidden the same way everybody else does on first dates."

When Hannah paused for a moment to digest Todd's suggestion, the waiter must have seen the break in conversation as his chance because he approached the table to take their order. The parchment-style menu still rested on the table where she'd laid it earlier. She'd been too busy talking to even decide what she wanted to order.

She met Todd's gaze across the table. If she ordered, it would be admitting that she'd decided to stay after all. After a quick look at the menu selections, she turned back to the waiter and ordered a puree of butternut squash soup and roast duck in a bread pudding.

After Todd gave his order of potato-crusted Lake Superior whitefish and the waiter left the table, he turned back to Hannah, who was watching him.

"You sound as if you have a lot of experience in the first-date department." She shouldn't have brought it up again, but she couldn't help being curious.

Todd raised an eyebrow, "If a lot means the three times in the last five years that my mother insisted I attend this or that function with the daughter of some executive in dad's company, then I'm a first-date expert."

"You are an expert compared to me," she said with a grin. "This is my *first* first date. I haven't had much interest in socializing with members of the opposite sex in the last few years."

"But you had a lot of offers, didn't you?" he said, though her comment appeared to surprise him.

Again, her cheeks felt warm, but she told him the truth, anway. "Yes, I've had some offers."

"Especially from that one guy at your house. That Grant or somebody."

The way he avoided her gaze suggested that his memory of Grant Sumner wasn't as foggy as he would like her to believe. He wasn't immune to a little latent jealousy on the matter, either.

"Yes, Grant was one of them."

"What's the story with that guy, anyway?" he asked too casually.

"Grant's a great guy, a good friend, but he wasn't the right person for me." Hannah braced herself for Todd's knowing glance that would suggest he knew just who that right person was, but he only nodded. "I tried not to encourage him, but I guess he thought someday…"

Hannah took a deep breath, still wishing she'd handled the situation better. "Well, anyway, I wish he would come back to church. I've missed him lately."

"He's probably having a tough time letting you go. I know from experience how difficult that is."

She blinked. A jealous comment she would have expected, but Todd's compassion surprised her. Many things about this adult Todd surprised and pleased her. Still, the conversation had become too serious, so she decided to lighten the mood by adding, "A few others asked me out, too."

"You sure know how to kill a guy."

Hannah chewed her lip, trying not to smile. "The infant safety seat in the back of my car probably discouraged a few of them, but I still had some calls."

"I'm sure you did. Who could blame them?"

Soon they were both grinning, the discomfort that had been between them evaporating as their natural banter reemerged. They discovered that they did know each other, and what they didn't know about their current lives they began to learn.

They traded samples from their dinners as they joked about old times and shared stories from the more recent past. Often, the conversation would sneak back to their daughter's antics, and they laughed about those, as well.

Hannah felt more at peace than she'd been in a long time. She might have attributed it to the restaurant's ambience—the candlelight, the murmur of quiet voices, the sense of romance blossoming at nearby tables—but she decided not to lie to herself this time. Her feelings had nothing to do with the atmosphere and everything to do with the company.

She'd caught Todd watching her a few times when he'd thought she wouldn't notice. How could she not? The yearning in his gaze was strong enough to have awakened her from a sound sleep. Did Todd see a similar expression when she looked back at him?

No, she couldn't have thoughts like that—thoughts of any future beyond tonight. Not yet. Maybe not ever. The risk was too great. The prospect of another loss too terrifying. Would she ever be able to recover if she lost him again?

"What time did you tell Mary Nelson you would pick up Rebecca?" Todd asked, drawing her from the abyss of her dark thoughts. "I was surprised you took Rebecca there instead of having Mrs. Nelson come to your apartment."

Hannah set her fork aside and wiped her mouth with a napkin. "Oh, didn't I tell you? Rebecca gets to spend the night at Mrs. Nelson's. Mary insisted, and Rebecca was thrilled about sleeping in Mary's big guest bed."

"She'll really sleep there?"

"No, she'll be crawling into Mary's bed before the night is out. Mary doesn't mind."

"That's good news."

Hannah tilted her head to the side and gave him a quizzical look. "That Rebecca will be sneaking out of her bed in the middle of the night?"

Todd choked on the drink of water he'd just taken and coughed into his napkin before he could answer. "No. The good news is that you don't have to rush right home. We can have dessert and coffee."

"I don't know…" Hannah said, a smile pulling at her lips. Strange, as confused as she was about the two of them and what the future might hold, the one thing she did know for certain was that she wanted to stay right where she was. With him.

"Come on…tiramisu, chocolate mousse, sorbet…"

"Well, when you put it like that…"

Todd wiped his forehead with his napkin as if he'd just survived an ordeal. "Whew, you're a tough negotiator. I didn't think I'd make it through that one."

"I went easy on you that time."

"I appreciate that."

Hannah was rolling the last bite of the creamiest

lemon tart she'd ever tasted around on her tongue when she caught Todd staring at her again. Her face felt warm under his regard, but she had to attribute at least part of the heat to the frothy cappuccino she'd been sipping.

Around them, the waitstaff had already begun clearing the tables and setting up for the next evening. Only one other couple remained at the corner table, probably newlyweds from the private glances they were exchanging.

"We should be getting home," Hannah told him.

"Why? Do you have a curfew? You said Rebecca was settled for the night."

Hannah wiped her mouth and set her napkin aside. "I have to work in the morning. Some of us don't have the week between Christmas and New Year's off each year. Some of us are just entering tax season where we'll barely be coming up for air until after April 15, and that's if we don't file a bunch of extensions."

"Oh, sorry. I forgot that you had to work." He studied his dessert plate for several seconds before his head popped up again. "But you could take just a few minutes longer…so I could walk you home, right?"

"Walk me home? Won't your car start?"

"It had better. It's only a month old. I just thought that it looks like the perfect night for a walk. It will be good for us, especially after that dinner."

Outside the restaurant's front window, dozens of snowflakes were skittering toward the ground, but trees planted in the Main Street sidewalk weren't swaying, so the wind from earlier in the day must have died down. She looked back at him.

"Then I'm glad you didn't pick a restaurant in Novi

or Northville. I don't know if I would have been up for that hike."

"But you can handle the three blocks to your house, right?"

Hannah let her shoulders slump and tried to look exhausted. "Barely. But I'll make it."

She glanced out the window again. Huge, perfect snowflakes continued to twirl as if to a symphony of silence. The sky appeared clear and bright with the sliver of a moon towering above it all. Hannah was tempted to let herself believe that God had staged the whole setting just for the two of them, their own private glimpse of His amazing firmament.

It wasn't like her to give in to such romantic notions, but just this once, just in the expanse of time it took to reach her house, she wished for the freedom to be that young girl who still believed in happily ever after.

The wind picked up the minute they stepped outside, so Todd worried he might have made a tactical—and chilling—mistake. He tucked the scarf Hannah had given him more tightly around his neck and tugged his hat lower on his ears. Beside him, Hannah pulled the hood of her long dress coat up over her hair.

But the wind gust was only a long sigh before stillness resumed. He'd wanted a few more precious minutes with Hannah, and the car ride home would have been too short. He still had so much to say.

"I'm sorry this was our first date."

Hannah turned toward him, her face peering out from the hood's edge of faux fur. "What do you mean?"

"I should have taken you on dates when we were younger. You deserved to be treated to nice dinners, movies and shopping trips. You deserved to be cherished." She had always deserved someone better than him, but he couldn't bring himself to say it aloud.

"We never needed anything like that. Everything between us was so simple. We were...just us."

"That's because I never had the guts to ask you on a real date. You had to settle for just watching TV or playing foosball in the basement."

"We had a great time."

"You deserved more."

They walked side by side in silence for a few seconds before Hannah started chuckling. "Even if you had asked me out, I'm not sure I would have been able to go. Dad and I never got around to the discussion of when I would be allowed to date. He always thought of me as his little girl."

The image of Rebecca immediately appeared in his mind. He could relate to Reverend Bob's feelings on that subject. He didn't even want to think about someday having to let some good-for-nothing teen-age boy take his little girl out to the movies. That had to be the hardest thing for any father—to realize he was no longer the only love of his daughter's life.

Hannah continued as though unaware of how many years forward Todd's thoughts had traveled.

"When I wouldn't give the name of my baby's father, I thought I was keeping this huge secret," she said with a chuckle. "It wasn't as if I had tons of opportunities to sneak out with boys. Not everyone would have known immediately, but for those close to me, their list of possible candidates was short."

"I'm probably the only one who thought it could have been someone else."

Hannah lifted a shoulder and let it drop, but she didn't say anything.

"I'm sorry I jumped to the conclusion that anyone else could have been Rebecca's father. All I had to do was look at her to know the truth. And I should have known you wouldn't—" Todd cleared his throat. This subject matter was nothing if not delicate. "That was just my stupid jealousy talking."

"There never could have been anyone but—"

Though Hannah stopped herself, Todd realized what she'd almost said: *you*. She'd already told him she hadn't dated in all these years, but was she really saying there was no one else for her? Just as he'd always known that Hannah was the only woman for him?

Before he could stop himself, Todd reached over and closed his gloved hand protectively over Hannah's. He felt that same wave of wonder, of rightness that he'd experienced when he'd touched her hand in the restaurant. The sense was so powerful that he wondered if she could feel it, too.

But insecurities immediately invaded his peace. Would she pull away as she had earlier? Maybe she'd only been talking about her intention to avoid sexual temptation until she was married, and she hadn't been indicating anything about her feelings for him.

He waited, his heart pounding, his palm damp under the glove. He didn't even realize that they'd stopped walking until Hannah looked up at him and then down at their joined hands. Instead of pulling away, she shifted her hand until their gloved fingers laced.

Neither said a word. Neither had to. With her simple movement, like a tacit agreement made with touch, everything changed. They had so many possibilities, when not long ago there had been so few.

With the wider-spaced streetlamps to guide them and the occasional passing vehicle and the crunch of snow beneath their feet as the only sounds, they continued up Commerce Road, turning left on Union Street to reach Hannah's apartment.

The wind picked up again, but Todd barely felt the chill. Hannah was this warm presence beside him, her hand fitting comfortably in his. The delicate, floral scent of her hair drifted into his nostrils, and he wanted nothing but to inhale the sweetness.

At her front steps, they paused, their hands unlacing and falling back to their sides. The temptation to draw Hannah into his arms was so overwhelming that Todd shoved his hands into his pockets to prevent it.

Hannah turned toward him, her face peeking out from the furry hood, but she stared at the ground and chewed her lip. He could just imagine what she had to be thinking. Did she dread the moment he would kiss her, or did she worry he wouldn't want to? The irony tempted him to smile. He couldn't imagine a time when he would be near Hannah and not want to kiss her, to hold her, to claim her as his own.

But now wasn't the time for any of those things. This moment was too important. He had too much to show her.

Finally, Hannah glanced up at him. "Thank you for dinner. I had a really nice time."

"Me, too."

"Well, I had better..." She let her words trail off, her gaze darting to her front door.

Todd jutted out his right hand and waited.

Hannah drew her eyebrows together and tilted her head to the side.

He only smiled, lowering his hand. "In case you're worried, I don't plan to kiss you tonight."

"I wasn't worried," she said, though everything about her tight demeanor suggested she was—either pro or con.

"Now don't get me wrong. I'm not opposed to the idea."

An embarrassed grin settled on her lovely mouth. "I'm not sure I understand."

"This is a first date. I wouldn't want to offend you by kissing you on our first date, so…" Again, he extended his hand, and she accepted it. The gesture felt surprisingly intimate because of the promise inherent in it. He would show her more respect this time. He would treat her the way she deserved to be treated.

Clearing her throat, Hannah stepped to the door and unlocked it. "Thanks again. I'm glad we did this."

"Me, too." He had descended the porch steps when he stopped and spoke over his shoulder. "You see, Hannah, everything will be different this time."

Chapter Eleven

Different. Todd had warned Hannah to expect that, but he hadn't prepared her for just how wonderful spending time with him would be. He'd proven both of those things so many times in the past three days as she'd seen almost as much of him as when he'd lived next door. Who could blame her for enjoying every minute of it?

Even as Hannah's fingers clicked across the keys of her office computer late Friday morning, she could still picture Rebecca's smiling face and hear her laughter as they'd taken her skating for the first time on the tiny ice rink at Central Park.

She touched her left hand with her right, remembering how nice it had been to hold hands with Todd on the couch after they'd put their daughter to bed. She needed to concentrate on the figures on the screen in front of her, but it was too tempting to remember the funny things he'd said and the way he looked at her that warmed her all the way to her heart.

"What are you smiling about? I thought you said those year-end figures were a mess."

Hannah jerked her head to see her boss, Harold Lasbury, standing in her office doorway looking at her with one of those strange expressions he reserved for anyone who wasted too much time laughing or smiling. Her cheeks burned.

"Oh, they were, but I'm finally whipping them into shape. I've already reconciled the bank statement and have posted the cash disbursements and cash receipts."

He cleared his throat. "Well, that's good. You'll want to compute the annual depreciation of equipment after lunch."

Hannah nodded, though she already knew well what was necessary to finish the client's year-end accounting. Sometimes Harold seemed to forget that she already had an accounting degree.

He started to leave but stopped and turned back to her. "Oh, you have a…guest in the waiting area."

Guest? She'd never heard her boss refer to a client that way before, and she certainly hadn't scheduled any client appointments the last workday before the new year. That her boss raised an eyebrow before continuing to his own office only confused her more.

Tightening the hair clip at her nape and straightening her suit jacket, Hannah headed to the waiting area, preparing herself mentally to welcome an additional client on a day when she was too busy to even take a lunch hour.

But the sight that greeted her when she reached the cramped room, with standard-issue waiting chairs and salmon-colored wallpaper, made her smile again. Todd sat in one of the cushioned seats, a picnic basket taking up most of the seat next to him.

"What are you doing here?" she asked. "I told you I couldn't have lunch today." She wondered if it was okay for her to be secretly pleased about a visit that would put her behind for the rest of the afternoon.

He indicated the basket next to him. "No, you said you couldn't *leave* for lunch today. I just wanted to make sure you wouldn't go hungry."

"Thanks."

He stood and grabbed the basket handle. "Let's go in your office and eat so you can get back to work."

"What do you have in there?"

"Only the best impromptu picnic fare that money can buy." He followed her into her office and set the basket on her desk. "Sandwiches from Village Deli with cherry turnovers for dessert from Milford Baking Company."

"Boy, you had to work to get this stuff. Crossing Main Street at the lunch hour is like taking your life in your own hands."

"I do think some of the drivers believe those pedestrian crosswalks in the middle of the street are just suggestions." Todd set three sandwiches and two cans of soda on the desk and then pulled out a white bakery bag.

"Are all three of those for me?"

"You always did have an appetite twice the size of that tiny frame of yours." He paused, chuckling. "But I was hoping to eat at least one of the sandwiches."

In the end, they each ate a turkey sandwich and tore the ham down the center. Together, they demolished the pastries until there were only flaky crumbs.

Hannah licked a drop of tart cherry filling off her thumb and wiped it with her napkin. "I guess I was hungrier than I thought. Thanks for doing this."

"An early New Year's present. So how come you're working so hard when the rest of the world is kicking back for the holiday?"

"We have the year-end accounting to do for several of our corporate clients. That means year-end corporate tax returns and year-end payroll. We have to analyze and post the cash disbursements, which means figuring out which accounts they belong in. Then we have to go through the cash receipts, making sure they're all for sales. After that, we compute annual depreciation of equipment and do comparative analysis with figures from prior years."

"So in other words you're just sitting around waiting to ring in the New Year."

Hannah raised her hands in a mock surrender. "Oh no. You caught me."

"Well, I don't want to keep you from your afternoon nap, so…" He was grinning as he cleared away the empty wrappers, shoving them back into the basket. "We sure can put the food away. We don't need to wonder where Rebecca got her healthy appetite from."

"Or her strange sense of humor."

"Or her beauty."

"Are you complimenting yourself there?" she asked, though she felt warm inside.

"One of her parents, anyway."

Instead of waiting for her to find some clever retort, Todd took his basket and headed toward the door. "I'll call you tonight, okay?"

"Okay."

Todd had called three nights in a row, and she found she could get used to the regularity of it. She could get used to a lot of things about the last few days, but she didn't allow herself to dwell on them.

"Thanks again for doing this."

"Anytime."

With a wave, he was gone. Hannah couldn't help feeling the acuteness of his absence. It was as if all the laughter in the room had left with him.

Yes, they were different together this time but not in the way Todd must have meant with his promise. He'd always treated her as if she were someone precious to him. That hadn't changed with time or distance. But they were different people now. They'd made mistakes and had learned to live with their consequences. They'd wounded and been wounded. Yet somehow they'd found a way to continue on despite their scars.

Hannah stared at her computer screen, but she kept imagining Todd's image in the pattern of numbers—as the boy he'd once been and as the man he'd become.

She'd loved that boy; she could finally admit that to herself. Did she feel the same thing for him now that he'd emerged from the milieu of youth as this amazing, strong man? She shook her head, the incongruity so clear in her thoughts. If this scary, thrilling feeling was love, then it wasn't the same at all. It was stronger. Deeper. Emotional and spiritual in a way that only came with maturity.

She was so tempted to give in to the feeling, to let it soothe and heal. But she had to think this time. More than just two hearts were involved now. She had Rebecca to consider.

And even if she were certain that this was the best thing for all of them, would love be enough to make her forgive and forget, or would the seeds of distrust hidden just below the surface still linger? Would she ever be able to trust Todd fully with her heart?

The sounds of someone clearing his throat brought Hannah back from her dark thoughts. Harold stood in her office doorway with his arms crossed over his rounded chest. Hannah straightened in her seat. It was the second time her boss had caught her daydreaming in one day. She really was trying to begin the New Year in the unemployment line.

"Staring at the computer screen is not going to get those forms completed by five o'clock."

Hannah shook her head to expel the last of the errant thoughts. "I'm sorry, Harold. I just need to get focused."

"Too much picnic food?"

"No, it's not that."

"Big New Year's plans distracting you?"

Well, there was a certain church service that was taking on an extra significance this year, but that wasn't her current distraction, so she shook her head.

"Then I trust you'll expend the extra effort to ensure that our paying clients have their year-end reports completed correctly?"

"Yes, sir."

Her ringing desk phone saved Hannah from any parting comment from her boss. "Harold Lasbury and Associates. How may I help you?"

"Is this Hannah Woods?"

She started. Callers didn't usually ask for her first but more often were transferred to her when she had been assigned their year-end reports or 1040s. "This is she."

"This is David Littleton."

"Oh. Deacon Littleton, what can I do for you? I can schedule your appointment for filing your personal tax return, but I don't have any available until mid-January."

He cleared his throat. "Um…no…this is another matter."

An unsettling feeling crowded Hannah's insides. Deacon Littleton was always direct, not one to mince words in order to protect feelings.

"Is something wrong?"

"Oh, probably not. I've probably just made one of those bookkeeping mistakes we volunteers do on occasion, and I was wondering if you might take a peek at the church books for me."

"Well, today I am really swamped, but—"

"Oh, there's no real rush." He paused as if considering. "In fact, don't worry about it. I'm sure I can find the mistakes."

"You're sure? I don't mind looking over them at all. I even have a day off Monday since New Year's is on Sunday."

"No. That's all right. Enjoy your day off. If I can't find them, I'll be sure to ask for help."

"You do that, okay?"

"You're the professional."

Hannah ended the call, feeling relieved that she didn't have to add another task to her growing to-do list. But something about the call still didn't sit right with her. Why had the deacon asked for her help if he was only going to retract his request?

Another thing, Deacon Littleton had been keeping the church's books for as long as Hannah could remember, and the paperwork he kept was impeccable. He never made mistakes. What was different this year? And what had the deacon so worried?

Hannah shook away the uncomfortable thoughts and focused on the form on the screen. If she had the choice, she would just give up and call the day a wash. First, questions about Todd and now concerns about church.

The owners of Village Gifts and Milford Beauty Supply had the right to expect her total attention on their business accounting. Maybe her boss had the right idea. Harold loved crunching numbers to the exclusion of everything else. She needed to follow his example, at least during office hours. She would have to figure out her love life and the puzzle at church on her own time.

"Daddy, why are you and Mommy not married?"

Todd jerked, an unfortunate reflex given he was sitting cross-legged on the floor, balancing a wiggly Rebecca, a messy-haired Miss Gabrielle and a copy of *Alice's Adventures in Wonderland* in his lap. The child's backside, the doll and the book's hard cover hit the floor before Alice could even attend the Mad Hatter's Tea Party.

"Oh. Sorry, kiddo," he said, pretending not to notice the other adults in the children's department at the nearly new Milford Public Library. They'd heard the question as clearly as he had and were trying not to get caught staring.

"Ouch, Daddy. That hurt." Rebecca frowned at him, rubbing the offended part of her before climbing back into his lap. All trespasses forgiven, she situated Miss Gabrielle, which was discreetly covered in her dress that day, and collected poor *Alice,* returning it to her father's hands.

But instead of opening the book and continuing reading Lewis Carroll's classic story, Todd set it aside. How could he explain something so complicated to a four-year-old? He was tempted to distract her, to offer to find more books or to go eat ice cream, but Rebecca deserved better than that. She deserved a straight answer given at a level she would understand. It was his turn to answer their daughter's questions. Hannah had been answering them for a long time.

"How about we find a different place to sit so we're not on the floor?" They didn't need an audience for this conversation, either, but he didn't mention that.

Taking her hand, Todd led her into one of the tiny glass conference rooms and shut the door behind them. Setting the book they'd been reading on the table, he sat in one of the chairs. Instead of sitting in the other, Rebecca scrambled up into his lap.

"Why did we go in the room?"

"You asked me a question, and I wanted to answer it."

She seemed to consider and then nodded. "Okay."

"I wish your mom and I had been married when we were younger." He brushed his hand over her tiny blond pigtails. "Before we had you."

"Why didn't you?"

"Because we made too many mistakes. And then I lived too far away. I didn't know you lived here." He couldn't see any reason beyond payback to tell Rebecca he hadn't known she existed, so he kept that knowledge to himself.

"You don't live far away now."

"No, I don't." Todd couldn't help smiling. His little girl just might have a future in law given the way she could already argue her case.

Rebecca lay back in his lap until her head hung upside down over the side of the chair with her pigtails drooping toward the floor. "Daddy, are you and Mommy still mad at each other?"

The question surprised him, but it shouldn't have. Did he really think that Rebecca, who rarely missed anything, would have been oblivious to the tension that had been stretched tight between Hannah and him in the beginning and the gradual loosening of the rope?

"No, honey, I don't think we are."

Her head popped up, and she scrambled down from his lap.

"Then you can get married."

"You see, it's not that simple." But even as he said it, he wished it could be.

"Then we could all live in the same house, and you wouldn't have to live in your apartment, and we could get a dog."

"A dog?" Todd threw his head back and laughed. "That's what all of this is about? A dog?"

Rebecca slumped in the chair next to his and crossed her arms. "At Max's house, they got a puppy for Christmas. His name is Rudy. Max's mommy got married last year…" She let her words trail off to signify that she'd made her point: marriage first, then dog.

"Honey, even if your mother and I did get married, that doesn't mean we could get a dog." When those eyes started to fill, he considered telling her that even kids who lived with one parent sometimes had dogs. Still, realizing that a comment like that might make Hannah angry enough to remain a single parent indefinitely, he kept that bit of trivia to himself.

"But I *want* a dog."

A giant tear rolled down her cheek until Todd reached over and brushed it away. After a few more followed it, he pulled her from the other chair back into his lap.

Was this really about a dog or about other things in her life that were just as out of her control? If only he knew. This feeling of helplessness was a part of the parenting experience. Hannah had explained that much to him. Would he always feel the need to hang the moon for his little girl and be frustrated when he couldn't?

Well, he would never be able to guarantee that life was perfect for Rebecca, but the one thing he could do for her was to love her mother. He was becoming really good at it. And if he had anything to say about it at all, he would make sure that Rebecca's parents were married, and they were all living together—with or without a dog—by next Christmas.

Chapter Twelve

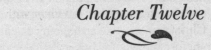

The scents of pine and melting wax wafted through the darkened church sanctuary as candlelight cast the bowed heads in shadow. Todd realized he should have been praying, too, spending some time in quiet meditation as a brand-new year approached, but he couldn't keep his eyes closed while the woman he loved sat next to him, already an answer to his prayers.

In the candlelight, Hannah looked so beautiful and serene as a strand of her hair that she'd worn loose fell forward over her cheek. It looked like spun gold, and he knew if he brushed the hair back from her face, it would feel like it, too.

He shook his head. He shouldn't be thinking thoughts like these, especially here in church. But then where could he go that he wouldn't think of Hannah? She lived with him at home, at work, in his dreams, even in his prayers. He had to tell her that, to make her understand that they were meant for each other.

Nervous tension flooded his system, making him shift in his seat. What if after all the time they'd spent with each other, she didn't agree that they should be together? Still, his need to connect with her was stronger than his misgivings, so he closed his hand over hers.

Without opening her eyes, she leaned toward him. "You're supposed to be praying in the new year," she whispered.

"I pray better this way."

He laced their fingers, resting their hands on the pew between them. It felt like such a significant statement to hold hands with her in church—like an announcement of their connection before the whole Hickory Ridge community. Already they'd stood sharing a hymnal, which he'd always considered a statement in itself.

Because he expected her to pull away, to be uncomfortable with the message they telegraphed to the rest of the congregation even in the low lights, his heart warmed as her long, elegant fingers pressed into the back of his hand. It made what he intended to say later tonight seem even more right.

"Amen," Reverend Bob said into the sound system on the lectern, ending the period of quiet meditation. "Now that we've prepared our hearts and minds, please file forward to accept Communion in silence."

Todd leaned close to Hannah. "Do you think Rebecca's asleep by now?"

"Mary promised she would put her to bed by ten."

"It was nice of her to take Rebecca overnight again so we could attend the service."

"She's like that." She glanced up at her father and back at Todd. "Now hush, will you?"

After the solemn service and Andrew Westin's inspiring closing prayer, the holiday event ended just after the stroke of midnight. Church members filed silently out of the dark sanctuary into the lighted vestibule before sharing cheer and good wishes to celebrate the arrival of the new year.

While the church building emptied, Todd retrieved both of their coats from the rack. A gray-haired man approached them, already wearing his coat.

"Todd, have you met David Littleton?" When he shook his head, Hannah turned to the other man. "Deacon Littleton, this is Todd McBride."

The two men shook hands, but the older man kept his gaze focused on Hannah. "I'll let you know about that other thing, okay?"

"Call any time if you need help. I mean it."

Deacon Littleton nodded and continued past her.

"What was that all about?"

"Oh, tax season begins. The questions come from everywhere." But she continued to watch the older man as he left, a perplexed expression on her face.

When Hannah reached for her coat, Todd rested a hand on her arm to delay her. "Can we go somewhere? I'd like to talk to you about some things."

Her eyes widened, and she glanced through the glass doors into the night. "You want to go somewhere in that? It's New Year's. It's probably crazy out there."

As if to punctuate her comment, the multiple pops of firecrackers being set off in a nearby neighborhood drifted in as someone opened the church door. Somewhere in the distance, someone shot a rifle into the air.

Standing next to them in his Michigan State Police jacket, Brett Lancaster grumbled. "Let the 9-1-1 calls begin. When will people ever realize that firearms, illegal fireworks and holiday celebrations don't mix?"

His wife, Tricia, came up beside him. "Don't mind

him. I just have to go home and relieve the sitter, but he has to go into work tonight."

"Sorry to hear that, Brett." Todd patted his shoulder. "Stay safe on patrol, okay?"

"Better pray that the rest of the drivers on the road will stay sober and safe."

"I'll pray for that, buddy."

Todd was relieved when the other couple continued past them to shake hands with Reverend Bob and Andrew. Making polite conversation was difficult when he was anxious to get Hannah alone and say things that needed to be said.

Turning to Hannah, he gestured toward the sanctuary, still illuminated only by candlelight.

"You want to talk in *there?*" she asked.

She chewed her bottom lip in the nervous way he'd come to recognize. If she was flustered at the prospect of a serious conversation with him, he could just imagine how she would act if she knew what he was going to say. He did know, and he was nervous enough for the both of them.

"I doubt we'll get in trouble for talking in there since the service is over."

"I didn't mean—" She rolled her eyes yet seemed to relax a little. "Okay."

He led her past several stained glass windows with candles in their sills and past the candelabras near the rounded stage platform and the altar. In the front pew, opposite the organ, he sat and motioned for Hannah to join him.

Her gaze darted toward the lighted vestibule. "Dad will want to lock up soon."

"Hannah, don't worry. There are still a few people out

there. And even if there weren't, Reverend Bob would give us a few minutes to talk." He patted the seat next to him. "Please sit."

With a sigh, she lowered herself into the seat. "You sure are persistent."

"You bring that out in me."

Hannah wore a small smile, but she focused on her wringing hands. "I'm sorry about that."

"You bring out all kinds of feelings in me."

Her hands stilled, and slowly she looked up at him, her eyes searching for answers.

He didn't know how to phrase it, where to start, but he couldn't keep it bottled up any longer, either. "You know how much you matter to me, don't you, Hannah? You understand that I returned with this grand scheme to win you back."

He didn't even pose the last as a question. If she'd been watching or listening to anything he'd done or said in the last few weeks, she had to know. "And then you told me about Rebecca."

Hannah lowered her gaze to her hands. "We don't have to do this. Rehashing it isn't going to change history."

"I'm not talking about history." He paused, the sound of his heartbeat so loud that she had to hear it. "I'm talking about the future."

"Future?" Her head lifted slowly.

He couldn't decipher her tight expression, but he couldn't stop now. She needed to know how he felt. He desperately needed her to know. What she did with that knowledge was up to her.

"I told you once that I loved you, and then I promptly disappeared from your life."

"Todd, what you are trying to say?"

"Oh, right. I said I wasn't going to talk about the past." He paused long enough to take her hands. "This isn't *in* the past. I care so much about you. I always have. And I'm not going anywhere this time."

Slowly, he returned her hands to her lap.

"I just wanted you to know that."

"That's it?"

Hannah looked as shocked as he was that she'd spoken those particular words.

"What were you expecting? A proposal?" He couldn't help it. A chuckle bubbled up in his throat, deflating the air of romance he'd hoped to build with all that candlelight.

"Yes. No. I don't know." She turned and covered her face with her hands, but pretty soon she chuckled, too.

It felt so surreal, the two of them sitting shoulder to shoulder with Hannah in the front pew of the darkened room, laughing until their eyes grew damp. But then he and Hannah had never been about candles, flowers or greeting cards with someone else's flowery words on them. They'd always written their own poetry of simplicity, a natural accord that couldn't be squeezed into a box of chocolates.

Laughter was intrinsic to the time they'd spent together, years ago and today, so it was only right that it would echo off the walls at a moment like this. Still, the melodic sound in her throat stopped the moment he slipped his arm around her shoulders.

"Now don't misunderstand me. I have every intention of asking you to marry me someday soon, when the time is right. We belong together…as a family." He tried not to notice how her shoulders tightened slightly under his touch.

"You can think of this as fair warning. I'd like to think of it as my commitment for the new year." He held his breath, waiting for the answer that could bolster his hope for the future or dash it before they'd really even tried.

"Don't you worry…that it's too late for us?"

The catch in her throat startled him as much as what she'd said. She hadn't begged him to propose today and be done with it, but she hadn't told him to forget asking, either. It was something.

When he turned to face her, he saw something more. Tears glistened in her eyes, and one traced down her cheek. The tears were his undoing. With his thumb, he wiped her cheek, and then he cradled her face in his hands.

"No, it's not too late. It can't be."

Two more tears escaped her stronghold, but she didn't answer. Maybe she couldn't. As Todd brushed the tears away with his thumbs, he couldn't help reaching slightly farther to feather a touch across her lips. They were just as smooth as he remembered. Just as perfect.

"I would really like to kiss you right now, but I want it to be your decision, too. May I kiss you, Hannah?"

For several heartbeats, she said nothing, did nothing. Dread clawed at the edges of his consciousness. Would now be when she told him that it would never work between them? Would he have to continue facing her every week while he planned outings with their daughter, knowing she would never be his?

She nodded, and his whole world shifted.

With utmost gentleness, he drew her to him and

pressed his lips to hers. He remembered this—the softness of her lips, their sweet taste—but his memories paled in comparison to this moment. Kissing her here in church felt like a promise before God, a preview of the day, if she allowed him to, he would finally make her his wife.

Todd lowered his hands to her shoulders and touched his lips to hers a second time, just a brief caress but one with which he offered his heart as a gift. "Happy New Year, Hannah."

"Happy New Year."

And it would be a happy one. He just knew it.

The flash of the overhead lights coming on in the sanctuary caused the two of them to jump apart. Reverend Bob stood just inside the door, his hand on the switch.

"Oh, you two are in here?" the minister asked too innocently.

"Yeah, Dad, but we were just leaving."

"Oh, no hurry. I just need to put out those candles before I lock up."

Todd popped up from his seat. "Here, we'll help with those." He climbed the steps to the platform and lifted the brass snuffer to extinguish the flames in the candelabra.

"Yeah, we can help," Hannah said as she stood.

"Thanks, you two, but Hannah, it would help me more if you could go out to the Family Life Center and check the locks on the rear doors."

She shot a nervous look at Todd, but she nodded and ascended the side aisle to the exit.

Todd didn't waste any time waiting for the minister

to approach him. His crossed to the row of stained glass windows where Reverend Bob was working.

"I take it you'd like to talk to me."

"You'd be right." Bob turned to him and met his gaze directly.

"I have an idea what you saw, but I can explain."

"Do you have something you feel guilty about?"

Todd shook his head. "No, sir, I don't."

"Good. I'm glad."

"You have to know that I love your daughter." He waited for the minister's nod before he continued. "I came here planning to win her back—even before I knew about our child."

Bob extinguished another candle before he turned to him. "What are your plans now?"

"My intentions? They're honorable, I assure you. I'd rather die than hurt her or Rebecca."

"You've done it before."

"I never will again."

"See that you don't."

"See that he doesn't do what?" Hannah called out from the door at the rear of the room.

Both men turned to look at her guiltily, but neither answered.

"All right then," she said, wearing a frown that said it was anything but all right. "If you two are finished discussing me behind my back, I'm ready to leave now."

Todd moved up the aisle toward her. "Don't get mad, Hannah. Your dad's just concerned about you."

Still, she turned away from him to focus her frown on her father instead. The minister shrugged, unrepentant.

"I'm not a child anymore, Dad."

"You'll always be my little girl," he said simply.

"You think he's bad. Your dad's a pushover compared to what I'm going to be like the first time some teen-age boy asks Rebecca out. I'll put a little fear in him."

Bob chuckled. "I feel sorry for that young man."

"Me, too," Hannah agreed. Her expression had finally softened. "Rebecca and I don't need any pity, though. I think we both have pretty great dads."

Twenty minutes later, Hannah stood on her front porch with Todd, nervousness and anticipation com-bining with the brand-new January chill. Would he kiss her again? She hoped so. She'd never felt so safe as she had tonight in his arms. If only she'd been brave enough to tell him the feelings in her heart. But, as always, she'd been a coward.

"This was the best New Year's I've ever had," Todd said as he shifted his position so he could block the wind from reaching her.

The gallant gesture made her smile. Not so long ago, when he was fresh from balmy Singapore, Todd would have been suggesting that they both go inside, out of the wind.

"I agree. It was the best."

"It's going to be an even better year for us." He drew her into his arms, holding her tightly against his thick coat.

As she rested her head against his shoulder, Hannah closed her eyes and breathed in his musky cologne. It felt so right that it should have frightened her, but for once she just let herself enjoy the wonder of being with him.

After a few seconds or minutes, Todd drew away from her and rested his hands on her shoulders. "I love you, Hannah. I've wanted to tell you that for so long."

Hannah's chest squeezed, and her eyes burned. Until that moment, she didn't realize how much she'd longed to hear him say those words, as well. It wasn't the first time he'd spoken them, but this time meant so much more.

He smiled at her and traced his gloved thumb along her jawline. Placing his fingers beneath her chin, he lifted her mouth toward his, but he paused as if again asking her permission. She nodded and closed her eyes, waiting.

His kiss was soft and unhurried. Hannah had never felt so cherished as she did at that moment in the shelter of his arms. When he finally pulled away, he squeezed his eyes shut and leaned his forehead against hers.

"Why do all my purest intentions flee the moment you're in my arms?" he said with a chuckle. "Sorry."

"Why are you sorry? You only kissed me."

He took a deep breath and shook his head as he took a step back from her. "I can't ever imagine kissing you and not wishing for more."

Hannah stared at the ground. Even in the wind, her cheeks felt warm. But somehow his confession made her feel more treasured. "I guess I shouldn't invite you in then."

"Probably not a good idea." He smiled. "I want to do this right this time. I can wait."

They stood there in silence as the chill seeped through their outerwear. Hannah tightened her jaw to keep her teeth from chattering.

"You know, I loved you even then," he said quietly, drawing her attention back to his face. "Even when I wasn't mature enough to know what to do with all those feelings."

"I knew, even then." The time had come; she could

feel it. Could she finally confess aloud what had been in her heart all along? Clearing her throat, she whispered, "I love you, too. Then and now."

Hannah waited, expecting the panic inspired by the words to settle in, heavy and immovable. Instead, her heart felt light, as if a weight she hadn't even known was there had been lifted.

On a sharp intake of air, Todd drew her into his arms again, cradling her head against his shoulder. "I've waited so long to hear you say that. I thought you would never forgive me. I thought—"

He stopped himself, but Hannah heard the thick emotion in his voice. "You do forgive me, don't you?"

"Of course, I do," she heard herself assuring him. And she had, really. She couldn't continue to hold him accountable for leaving her when it wasn't his decision. Todd so clearly trusted her with his heart. Maybe one day she could learn to trust that way, too. Completely. For now, loving him would have to be enough because it was all she had to give.

Chapter Thirteen

"Happy New Year!"

"Happy New Year to you, too, Mom." Todd pressed the portable phone to his ear and peeled open his eyes one by one. The only light filtering into the room came from a streetlamp outside his apartment, and his bedside clock read six forty-five.

"You didn't happen to check the time before you called, did you?"

"Of course," Sharon McBride said. "It's nearly eight. I just cleaned up the dinner dishes. We had pot roast with red-skin potatoes."

"Sounds delicious," he said, though he doubted he could have eaten even that at this hour. "There's a thirteen-hour time difference, remember?"

"I never can remember how many hours it is." Her chuckle filtered through the phone line along with some intercontinental static. "But you need to get up for church soon, anyway."

He could have slept two hours longer, and he'd been too keyed up to close his eyes before three o'clock that morning, but he kept that information to himself. Flipping the light on, he climbed out of bed and padded into the kitchen. He wouldn't be able to go back to sleep after this conversation anyway.

Sharon cleared her throat audibly. "Todd William McBride, are you going to tell me or not?"

"Tell you what?" Todd couldn't help smiling because he knew exactly *what*. Finally he took pity on her. "No, I didn't propose to Hannah yet."

"Why not?"

"It was too soon."

When she didn't say anything Todd knew from experience that his mother expected him to explain. "I don't know. I'd even bought the ring and had it with me, but I felt like God was telling me to wait."

"Can't argue with that." Though her tone made it sound as if she wished she could. "You did send Hannah our love, didn't you?"

"Yes, I did. Don't worry, Mom. I'm going to ask her." He poured himself a bowl of cereal and opened the refrigerator for the milk.

"Well, don't wait too long. Your dad and I are looking forward to coming back for the wedding. And I can't wait to get my hands on my grandbaby."

"Remember, Mom, Rebecca's not a baby anymore."

"Then you'd better marry her mother and give her your name before my granddaughter is a teenager who doesn't want to be spoiled by her Nana McBride."

It was such a relief to hear his mother talk that way, showing that she was ready to accept her grandchild with open arms.

"Rebecca will let you spoil her even before we get married. She's very generous that way."

"I'm sure she is." She chuckled for a few seconds and

then became serious again. "Still, don't you think it's time for you to bring your family together? Past time?"

Todd nodded though she couldn't see him. "That's what I plan to do, and it's going to be perfect."

"Remember, honey, perfect is an awful lot to expect from anyone. We're imperfect people. We're just loved by a perfect God."

"She forgave me, Mom. For leaving her behind. For... everything."

"That's wonderful, honey. Now don't you think it's time you forgave yourself?"

His mother ended the conversation soon after, but her question followed him while he finished breakfast and showered for church. Why had it been so easy to forgive Hannah, even for keeping Rebecca from him, when it was so hard to forgive himself for the sins of his past?

What if God was so selective with His forgiveness? Todd shook his head over the ludicrous idea. God always forgave, and Todd knew he'd been forgiven from the moment he'd first repented his sin with Hannah. And yet he couldn't let it go. Even when he'd opened his life to God, he'd clung to this tiny part of him, holding on to his guilt so tightly that he'd denied himself the intimacy that he craved with the Father.

He didn't want that distance anymore. *"Forgive, and you will be forgiven."* He'd understood that much from the Scripture in the Book of Luke. But now he finally understood that to have the kind of relationship he longed for with God first and then with the woman he loved, he had to finally forgive himself.

Half of January had already ticked away and tax season was in full force by the Monday morning when

Hannah received a strange summons for a meeting at Hickory Ridge. It had to have something to do with Deacon Littleton's question before the holidays, she surmised. Otherwise, they never would have called on her.

Still, she'd been unsettled by the odd sound in her father's voice when he'd phoned, asking her to join the meeting. Was the discrepancy more serious than the head deacon had let on?

Unbidden, her thoughts flashed to another time and a different meeting in the church conference room. Andrew and Serena had been there, facing down the Deacons' Board and accusations of sexual impropriety, all to protect Hannah's secret a few days longer. Though she had no sin to confess this time, a sense of foreboding tripped up her spine.

Nothing appeared too out of the ordinary at first, even the Michigan State Police patrol car that sat in the parking lot alongside several other cars. Trooper Brett Lancaster occasionally stopped through while he was patrolling the perimeter of GM Proving Grounds where they connected Livingston and Oakland Counties.

But the second police car, this one from the Milford Police Department, gave her pause. Something was very wrong, and from the tone of her father's voice, it had something to do with him.

Call Todd, a voice inside her immediately suggested, but she pushed aside the thought. She didn't know anything yet, and even if she did, her only reason to phone him would have been to lean on him, and she had to believe she was stronger than that. She was probably just being silly to consider calling him.

A rumble of voices emerged from the conference room as soon as she passed through the church entrance.

She knocked on the door before pulling it open. A sense of déjà vu struck her like a sudden wave of nausea.

The painting of Jesus surrounded by children still hung above the fireplace in the room where, to describe the lighting as poor would be considered an understatement. All nine deacons were in their regular places along the long dark wood conference table. Reverend Bob and Andrew were seated at the end of the table on metal folding chairs.

The cast would have been the same as from that play five years before except for the addition of building contractor Rick McKinley, who'd recently filled the vacancy on the Deacons' Board, and two uniformed officers, representing different police agencies.

"Oh, Hannah, we're glad you're here."

The greeting came from Deacon Littleton, but Hannah couldn't help glancing at her father instead. Reverend Bob had folded his hands in a prayerful pose, but his eyes were open. Though his glasses had slipped down his nose, he made no effort to push them back in place. How old and pale he looked, as though he'd battled the world and lost.

Her pulse raced, and it was all she could do not to rush to her father and demand to know what was wrong.

"Hannah," Deacon Littleton said to draw her attention back to the center of the table.

"What's going on?"

The head deacon glanced around the room before he spoke. "Do you remember the bookkeeping problem I mentioned to you a few weeks ago? Well, my mistake didn't turn out to be a mistake."

"I don't understand." Thoughts rushed at her in a hailstorm that allowed no time for weighing conclusions. What did this have to do with her or her father?

Deacon Littleton gestured toward Milford Police Chief Pete Conyers, who picked up the conversation from him. "Hannah, there appears to be a widespread case of embezzlement involving several of the church accounts, including the building fund for Hickory Ridge's Family Life Center."

She shot another glance at her father, who still stared at his gripped hands. Panic tasted acidic in her mouth. Could her father have— No. She dismissed the thought before it had a chance to fully form.

"There has to be some mistake."

"Unfortunately, there isn't." Brett spoke this time, his expression grim. "My gut told me something was wrong. I should have listened…"

Hannah drew her eyebrows together as another thought struck her. "You don't think I—"

Andrew came to his feet, shaking his head to stop the direction of her question. "No, Hannah, we don't. Look, we're not making ourselves clear. We've asked you here for two reasons—your familiarity with the church accounts and your acquaintance with Olivia Wells."

"Olivia?"

"Also known as Olivia Wilson, Olivia Wilder and Olivia Whiting," Chief Conyers said, looking up from the spiral-bound notebook in his hands.

"Are you serious? What kind of money are we talking about?"

Deacon Littleton glanced down at the printed list of figures in front of him. "As close as I've been able to tally it so far, about twenty-five thousand dollars."

Hannah blinked. To some families in the wealthy

suburbs of Detroit, a figure like that was a nice bonus after a healthy sales season, but to a small church, where every dollar had to be stretched to keep the black columns from becoming red, it was a fortune.

"She is also wanted for questioning in connection with embezzlement cases at the Presbyterian church in Brighton, a Methodist one in Okemos and a tiny Baptist congregation in Dansville," Chief Conyers continued.

"I knew she looked familiar that first time I saw her at Bible study," Brett said, shaking his head. "But I just couldn't connect the sweet lady at church with the police sketch on the bulletin board I passed every day at the *Brighton Post*."

Andrew lowered into his seat next to Reverend Bob. "Come on, Brett, give yourself a break. She fooled us all."

Several of them glanced at Reverend Bob then, but if he noticed at all, he didn't give any sign of it. He was the one who had been fooled most of all, and Hannah wished with all her heart she could take away her father's pain.

Brett, clearly in his role as Trooper Lancaster now, stood and paced the room.

"Hannah, when is the last time you saw Olivia Wells?"

"Uh, it must have been at church yesterday." She thought for several seconds. Come to think of it, Olivia hadn't been there. If she'd noticed it at the time, she would have thought it odd. Olivia had become one of the most regular attendees in the last several months. "No, that isn't right. I think it was a week ago Sunday."

Brett cleared his throat. "And what about you, Reverend?"

The minister started at being addressed directly. "I'm sorry. What did you ask?"

"When is the last time you saw Olivia Wells?"

"At church on January eighth. She said she would be away a few days visiting some extended family."

Brett wrote something down in his notebook. "Did she happen to mention where these family members lived?"

"Outside Lansing, I think, but that could mean anywhere, couldn't it?"

"Yes, it could, but it could also mean that Olivia hasn't skipped the state yet."

"And that she really might be from Michigan," the police chief chimed in. "The suspect certainly tried to stay close to home while committing her alleged crimes. All the embezzlement cases occurred within a fifty-mile radius. We'll check the NCIC database—that's the National Crime Information Center—and see if we come up with any hits."

Andrew, who had stepped to the rear of the room to refill his foam coffee cup, turned back to the rest of them. "That one's simple. She took a chance that leaders of the different churches in the region didn't hang out together and share notes, and she was right."

All those in the room nodded and murmured over that, probably feeling by varying degrees guilt over the lack of ecumenical fellowship that had allowed someone to continue these crimes for so long.

There would be more questions to follow: how much they knew about Olivia Wells outside church, where she lived and who else resided with her, what she did during her off-hours from the church office. The last question turned back to the man who had remained strangely quiet throughout the meeting.

"Bob, you will make yourself available for further questioning, won't you?"

Reverend Bob nodded to Chief Conyers but didn't meet his gaze. The whole situation struck Hannah as terribly unfair. Olivia had been the first woman her father had taken any interest in since her mother's death. How cruel she had to be to take advantage of struggling churches and a man who'd done nothing but give of himself to those who needed him.

When the meeting was finally over and most of the others had filed from the room, Hannah turned back to her father, who sat staring out one of the room's two narrow windows. Andrew paused at the doorway and caught Hannah's attention, but she motioned for him to go ahead without her.

As she approached her father, he smiled up at her, but the expression didn't reach his eyes.

"Are you okay?"

"I wouldn't call it my best day."

"What would you call it?"

"A day when I'm glad God is here to catch me."

He reached his right arm across his body to rub his left shoulder.

"Here, let me do that." She kneaded his shoulders that felt frailer than she remembered. Was it a sign of adulthood to realize her father was just a middle-aged man rather than some larger-than-life hero?

"Thanks, honey." He shifted so that her hands fell away from him.

"This could all be a big misunderstanding, you know."

"It could be."

But they both knew it probably wasn't. Olivia's absence was at the very least suspicious.

Instead of saying more, Bob glanced at his watch. "Shouldn't you be getting back to work?"

"Is that an excuse not to talk about it anymore?"

"Possibly."

"But you'll call me if you need anything?"

"Of course."

As reluctant as she was to leave, Hannah crossed to the door she'd entered. Her father returned to gazing out the window or, as she suspected, talking open-eyed to his God.

From the pulpit and in his home, Reverend Bob had always taught Hannah not to hate, but she was having an awfully hard time following his example. If Olivia Wells was guilty of the crimes they suspected, she'd hurt Hannah's father in ways beyond his social life. She'd attacked the church community he'd loved and nurtured. She'd struck him right in the heart.

With her arms stretched like an airplane, Rebecca took timid, wobbly steps along a balance beam that rested squarely on the gymnastics center's padded flooring. Todd willed her on each step as he watched through the window of the viewing area. Her parents cheered when she reached the end and took the six-inch jump to the ground.

Their little girl beamed, looking like a true gymnast in that sparkly little leotard she'd been begging to wear every day until her gymnastics class began. At least one of them was having fun.

He glanced sidelong at Hannah, who had pasted on a smile and was giving their daughter the two-thumbs-up.

"You can tell me what's wrong now," he told her.

"There's nothing—"

"And you can stop denying it, too."

Hannah opened her mouth and then closed it again. Her shoulders slumped, and she covered her face with her hands, exhausted eyes peeking out between her splayed fingers.

"There was a problem at church today. It's a mess, and it involves my dad."

"Yeah, I heard."

Dropping her hands, she turned her head to face him. "You knew?"

"Brett wanted to know the last time I'd seen Olivia. He filled me in on the details."

"If you knew what was wrong, then why have you been pressing me from the moment you picked us up?" She straightened in her seat and turned back to stare through the window into the gym.

"I wanted to hear it from you. We've seen each other every day since New Year's, and we talk on the phone at least once a day while we're not together. With something as important as this, you might have called."

If she'd noticed the annoyance in his voice, Hannah pretended she hadn't. "I just didn't want to bother you at work. I planned to tell you about it tonight." She pointed to the glass. "Oh, look what Rebecca's doing now."

His jaw tight, Todd turned his head back to look through the window. Their daughter was standing on top of a cube-shaped foam form, while her instructor helped her into the correct position to do a forward roll down the incline of the triangular-shaped form next to it. With assistance, she managed the move on the first try.

Rebecca lifted both arms in the air, having mastered a gymnast's "ta-da" bow just as easily. Again, her parents clapped, presenting the perfect, happy fan club.

As soon as they stopped applauding, Todd leaned in close to Hannah. "You know I would have come."

"I know. That's why I didn't ask."

Couldn't she understand that it was exactly why she should have asked? *Need me,* he wanted to shout, and yet he hated how pitiful that sounded. Hannah's family was in crisis. She had enough to worry about without having to balance on eggshells not to hurt his feelings.

"How's your father doing?"

"Probably better than I would be in the same situation." She paused to glance at Rebecca, who was taking her turn swinging on the thick rope that dangled from the ceiling, before she turned back to him.

"For Dad's sake, I hope this turns out to be a mistake. If it's true, if Olivia really did this to him and our church, I pray that she's arrested and convicted."

"I hope your dad isn't hurt by the scandal. He helped Olivia get her job, didn't he?"

"Yes, he did," she said, her hands coming up to rub her temples. "I don't know what Dad and I will do if…" She let her words trail away as if she couldn't bear to complete the thought.

"You mean what *we* will do, as in all of us, right?" Todd didn't realize how harsh his comment sounded until she drew her eyebrows together and stared at him.

"What?" She shook her head as if to clear it. "Oh. Right. That's what I meant."

"Of course."

Hannah turned her attention back to the class, but Todd couldn't stop replaying the conversation in his mind. She planned to *tell him about it,* but he wasn't invited to get involved. Maybe her comment wouldn't have bothered him so much if distance weren't so endemic to their relationship. He was allowed to spend time with Hannah and Rebecca as long as he stayed at arm's length. He could love them as long as he didn't get close enough to hurt them.

Chapter Fourteen

Hannah frowned at Todd's profile as they went through Rebecca's bedtime routine two hours later. He'd been brooding all night, through the ride home from gymnastics, their daughter's bath and her bedtime prayers. Hannah had tolerated his moodiness at first, but now she'd reached her limit.

She dropped a kiss on Rebecca's brow, tucking the blankets under her chin. "Sweet dreams, honey."

On the other side of the bed, Todd snuggled up to his daughter, cheek to cheek. "Sleep tight, Becca."

Their last smiles of the night were for their daughter as they shut off the light. As soon as they closed the bedroom door, Hannah tugged on Todd's arm, directing him toward the kitchen. Once inside it, she pulled the pocket door closed and whirled on him.

"What in the world is the matter with you?"

"Were you really going to *tell me about it* tonight?" He slumped into the seat at the kitchen table where he'd hung his coat earlier and stared up at her, accusation in his eyes.

"What are you talking about?"

"You would tell me, but you never had any intention of letting me help you or your dad."

She blew out an exasperated breath, dropping into the seat across from him. Usually, she would have sat next to him so he could reach for her hand, but she wasn't in the mood to be touched. She could tell by the way he studied her chair that her move hadn't gone unnoticed.

"It's not that big a deal. We didn't need—"

"That's right. You don't need me or want to need me. That would be too much risk for you."

Hannah blinked, startled by his accusation. "I don't understand you. Don't you think I have enough to worry about right now without you bringing this up?"

His gaze narrowed, making him look far angrier than he should have been for something as trivial as her neglecting to call him after the meeting at church.

"When do you suggest I bring it up?"

"Sometime when my family isn't in an uproar."

"Your family? *Your* family?" His voice had climbed an octave by the second time he said it. "You're *my* family. Can't you see that?"

She shook her head, exasperated. "Of course I see that."

"Then would you finally let me in?"

It was Hannah's turn to be angry. "Let you in? That's all I've been doing since you came back here. First, into my house, then into our lives and into my heart. What more do you want?"

"Ever since I came back, you've been holding me just out of reach. The thing at church today is just the symptom of a larger issue. It's just like before, when you were pregnant. You wouldn't let me help then, and you won't let me now."

"This situation isn't anything like before. It isn't really even about me."

"Isn't it?"

"No. And besides, I haven't been holding anything back from you. I even told you that I love you." She heard the sharp, accusatory tone in her voice, but she couldn't help herself. Didn't he realize how much that admission had cost her?

"But you don't trust me."

She opened her mouth to dispute his words, but he raised a hand to stop her.

"Sure, you trust me to show up for dinner on Friday and not to be late when I have plans with Rebecca, but when it comes to your hopes and your fears, you're not willing to let yourself fall into my arms. You're afraid I won't catch you." He gripped the edge of the table with both hands. "You don't trust me at all."

"Can you blame me? You left!" she shrieked. "I'll probably never be able to trust you completely."

The second the words were out of her mouth, Hannah was sorry she'd spoken them, even sorrier that she'd ever thought them. But she couldn't take them back now that the words hung between them, heavy and permanent. Worse than what she'd said, no wishing could change the fact that she'd spoken the truth. He would have to understand that, but they could find a way to work past it, couldn't they?

Todd flinched as if she'd struck him with her hand rather than her words. The wound, she surmised, would have been less grievous if she'd just hit him.

Planting his elbows on the table, he leaned his head against his folded hands and squeezed his eyes shut. He stayed that way for what felt like an eternity. Though a few minutes before she'd avoided touching him, she longed to reach across the table, squeeze his hands between both of hers and tell him they would find a way to make everything all right. They had to.

Only when he looked up at her again, pain and resignation so clear in his eyes, did she begin to realize what she'd lost.

He shook his head, a self-deprecating laugh emanating from deep in his chest. "I had all these great ideas when I came here. I would win you back, and we would begin the life together that I had imagined before you'd even realized we were more than friends."

Hannah drew in a sharp breath. "We can still have all that…in time. That doesn't have to change."

He lifted his gaze to meet hers but only briefly before he reached back for the coat hanging on the chair behind him. Out of the pocket, he produced a satiny white box. "I've been carrying this ridiculous ring around in my pocket since before New Year's."

Turning it toward her, he popped open the box, revealing a sparkling marquise solitaire diamond. Hannah coughed, swallowing the sob that scaled her throat with angry claws. He stared at the ring, the fluorescent kitchen light fluttering over its facets, before he snapped the box shut and stowed it in his pocket.

Todd smiled, perhaps at a pleasant memory, though certainly not at her. "I even had it with me during that New Year's Eve service at church. I knew it was too soon, but I had to buy it anyway. It was this silly, romantic notion that I'd be beginning the new year with our future all planned out."

Without looking at her, he continued, perhaps as much to himself as her. "That night, I was so tempted to slip off the pew and propose right then and there in the candlelight. The only thing that stopped me was this sense that God was telling me to wait."

He reached behind him again, his hand closing over the pocket where the tiny box rested. His lips formed a grim line. "I wonder what the return policy is on engagement rings."

Hannah's eyes burned, and her chest felt as if a horrible weight had been placed on it, cutting off her oxygen, her hope. "Please don't give up on us, Todd," she begged, hearing the desperation in her own voice.

"But don't you see? I have to. For my own survival." Todd reached across the table and squeezed her hand just once before pulling away. "You never really forgave me for deserting you, even though we both wanted to believe it when you said you had. You aren't able to forgive me, and I can't live with the truth that you can't."

"But, Todd, I have..." Hannah let her words trail away, surprised by how unconvincing she sounded.

"I know you tried. Just as I tried to earn your forgiveness. But I finally realized something." His smile was a sad one. "Forgiveness from someone you've hurt is like God's forgiveness. It isn't earned. It's a gift."

Tears filled Hannah's eyes and spilled over before she could control them. "I'm so sorry."

Again, he touched her hand, just a brief squeeze of comfort that he might have offered any friend who mourned as she did now. "I'm sorry, too. But I can't marry you. We'll always have some kind of relationship as Rebecca's parents, but I can't build a life with you."

"I...love...you... Todd." Each word seemed to emerge on its own wave of agony. Impotent words, their message moot.

He covered his face with his hands, and when he pulled them away, his eyes were damp, his raw pain visible.

"And I love you. Until a few weeks ago I believed that knowing you loved me would be enough for me." He shook his head as if to emphasize how wrong he'd been. "But now I realize that I have to have your forgiveness, too. I have to have your trust."

Todd backed his chair from the table and stood. Clearly, he recognized as she did that there was nothing else for them to say. Hopelessness filled her at the thought of the impasse they'd reached. Loving Todd wouldn't be enough to keep him with her. Another truth, though, produced a fresh ache inside her: Her heart had been broken by her own unwillingness to bend.

Reverend Bob stared at the computer screen the following evening, Sunday's sermon still no more than a title on the screen. "The Tithe." But how could he give the annual message to his congregation about sharing their financial gifts and talents with the church community when he was responsible for bringing in someone who'd stolen from them?

He had a headache and his shoulder was hurting again, but neither of those things should have surprised him after the day he'd had. Even though no one had mentioned the investigation since yesterday's meeting, he could think of nothing else.

He'd been holed up in his office all day with the intention of writing his sermon, but he'd gotten no further than looking up the word "tithe" in his concordance and searching for fresh Scriptural references in what church members often considered a tired topic. Already, it was past five, but he wasn't in any hurry to leave the security of his office and to face the uncertainty of his life.

The sound of a file drawer closing in the next office told him that Andrew was making a long day of it, as well. The youth minister wouldn't press him, but Bob felt comfort in knowing his friend was there if he needed him.

"Lord, what am I to do?" he whispered. "How do I make this right?"

It wasn't as if he expected an immediate answer. God always answered prayer in His own time, and His answers were perfect. Still, the tick of the flashing curser on the computer screen seemed to taunt him like a series of questions marks with no answers in sight.

His office suddenly felt so warm. He peeled off his gray wool sweater and unfastened the top button of the shirt he wore beneath it. With his handkerchief, he dabbed at the perspiration dotting his brow.

This crime, and he was beginning to be convinced that a crime had been committed, would hurt the Hickory Ridge community so deeply. Where would they come up with another twenty-five thousand dollars to replace the missing funds?

He would claim responsibility for the fallout. He was the one who'd introduced Olivia to the Deacons' Board and convinced its members she would be a good candidate for the church office position. Her résumé had been solid, but he'd been too distracted by her physical beauty and her passion for God to check her references. That beauty had been on the surface only, and even her faith had probably been only a masquerade.

Had he helped her at least in part because he wanted to impress her so she would see him socially? He shook his head. No, Olivia had definitely been the one to pursue him from the day she'd first shown up at the church's Christian Singles United program and then at morning Bible study.

At the time, he'd found her interest flattering. Now that he knew her real motivation for visiting Hickory Ridge, it only compounded the humiliation he felt for letting the whole church community down. Perhaps he deserved the shadow of suspicion this case would cast on him and on the ministry he'd built at Hickory Ridge over the last fifteen years.

He would probably be forced to resign now. Who could blame the deacons for making that decision? Would he ever be called as a head minister of a church again?

The last thought was too much for him to take. His eyes and nose burned as emotion clogged his throat. He removed his glasses and would have wiped them with his handkerchief, but his left hand felt strangely numb. No rubbing seemed to awaken his slumbering fingers. He was still staring down at it, still wondering at the sensation when he felt a strange pressure, like a weight, on his chest.

Realization settled just as heavily as that weight. He clutched his chest. *Lord, help me.*

"Andrew." He couldn't tell if he'd yelled or only whispered, but he tried once more. "Andrew…help."

The computer screen, the unfinished sermon and the portraits on his desk wavered in and out of focus. He had to get help…reach the door…call to Andrew. Bob struggled to his feet, holding himself steady by gripping the edge of his desk. He could do this. He was close to the door. So close.

Turning away from his desk, he took that first step toward the door. There wouldn't be a second step as darkness swept up from the floor and swallowed him whole.

The phone rang the moment Hannah entered her kitchen with four plastic grocery bags slung over her arms. She planned to let it ring and deny yet another telemarketer the opportunity to invade her home during the dinner hour, but Rebecca got to the phone first.

"Hello." The little girl shook her head. "No, this is Rebecca….My mommy?… Yeah, she's here."

"Here, honey, let me talk, okay?" she said, making a mental note to warn her daughter about answering the phone, and especially about identifying herself to strangers. She accepted the handset, mentally preparing herself for the sales pitch about a great new long-distance plan or a low rate on a home-equity loan, but the voice on the other end of the line startled her.

"Hannah, it's Andrew."

She drew in a breath. Had Olivia been arrested? Had the embezzlement been more far-reaching than they'd first imagined?

"What's wrong?" she immediately asked, though Andrew had phoned to check on her and Rebecca many times over the years. His tone didn't suggest a social call.

"It's your dad. We think he's had a heart attack."

"Heart attack?" A million thoughts—all dark and devastating—slammed through her mind at the same time. "Is he—"

"No, he's alive, but I think it's serious."

"Is he conscious? Is he asking for me?"

"He's been going in and out. Before the ambulance

arrived, I had to use that portable defibrillator we had installed at the church last year."

"Andrew, does that mean—"

"Now, Hannah, we don't know anything yet. You just need to get to West Oakland Regional Hospital as soon as possible. The ambulance just left to take him there."

"I'll be there." Either she was experiencing an overwhelming sense of calm or she was in shock, but she suspected the second. She backed to the kitchen table and slumped into one of the chairs. She couldn't just sit there. She needed to move, and yet she felt paralyzed. Details needed to be handled, but for the life of her she couldn't list them in her mind.

"Hannah, do you want me to have Tricia take Rebecca? Or do you need me to call Todd for you?"

"No, I'll phone him, but thanks."

Only after she ended the call did she realize she'd answered only one of Andrew's questions, and it should have surprised her which one, but it didn't. Without bothering to wonder whether after last night she should ask, she dialed his number. She had to. She needed him.

He answered on the second ring.

"Todd."

"Hannah, is that you?"

"Yeah, um, I have some bad news."

"Tell me. What is it?"

"It's Dad. They think it's a heart attack."

"Oh, I'm sorry, honey."

"This can't be happening. He's only sixty."

"He'll probably be fine," Todd tried to assure her.

"I have to leave for the hospital. Do you think you could—"

"Are you at home?"

She glanced at the bags of groceries still sitting on the counter, the ice cream already beginning to melt. "Yes, but—" She didn't even know *but what*. Her whole world was cloudy, and the only thing that seemed clear was that she'd made the right decision to call him.

"Stay where you are. I'll be there in five minutes."

Chapter Fifteen

He'd made it in four. Hannah smiled at the thought when little else had given her any cause for happiness since she'd arrived at West Oakland Regional four hours before. Todd had driven her to Commerce Township after showing up at her house so quickly that she'd only had time to toss water on her face and wrestle Rebecca back into her boots and coat.

He'd insisted that Hannah was in no shape to drive, and only now did she realize he was right. She couldn't have navigated the village streets and twenty-miles-per-hour zones on the way to the hospital without him.

In fact, she couldn't have handled any of the details without him—from registering her father in the emergency room to contacting relatives to plan-ning for Rebecca's care.

She hadn't thought about any of those details again until now, not since she'd glimpsed her father in that hospital bed with so many tubes and wires and monitors attached to him. Not when the hours that followed were filled with tears, prayers and uncertainty.

But in this moment of clarity, she allowed herself to

recall all of the help Todd had given her, even after all the awful things they'd said to each other the night before. When the ground had seemed to be shifting beneath her, he'd been a solid rock, calmly suggesting that she give him her keys so he could take Rebecca home where the child could sleep in her own bed.

Todd's help and her silent admission that she couldn't handle the situation alone would have terrified her a few months ago—or even a few days ago. Self-reliance had once mattered more to her than self-respect. But she felt a strange sense of relief in accepting Todd's help. It felt good to leave the details in his capable hands.

She couldn't allow herself to read too much into Todd's kindness. Just because he'd reached out to her didn't mean he would be able to accept her on her terms—conditions that even she could no longer justify. Todd was a good man. He would probably have done as much for anyone in need, but still her heart squeezed with gratitude. He'd caught her when she was falling, despite the fact that she'd hurt him in ways she couldn't even imagine. If only she could be the kind of woman Todd deserved.

A creak from the door at the back of the chapel drew Hannah from the lonely place her thoughts had ventured. Mary Nelson stood in the spray of brightness seeping into the softly lit chapel through the open door.

"Hannah, sweetie. The nurse was looking for you. She said you could go back in and see Bob."

"Is he conscious again?" Hannah asked as she straightened in her seat and brushed at the smeared mascara beneath her eyes.

"She didn't say. They only give reports to family members."

Those words drew Hannah's gaze back to the woman standing just inside the door. Mary was watching an arrangement of lighted candles on the far wall. She looked so sad. Standing up from the short pew where she'd been sitting, Hannah crossed to her dear friend and placed her arm around her shoulder.

"That nurse obviously doesn't know us then." If anyone was family to her father, Rebecca and her, it was Mary. No lack of blood ties could change that.

"I'll let you know as soon as they tell me anything, okay?" she said as she stepped back from her.

"Thanks. I'm sure the others will want to hear, too. Nearly twenty church members are in the waiting room."

"Dad would be so embarrassed by the fuss." She paused before adding, "And humbled by the concern."

Mary's smile couldn't quite take the sadness from her eyes. "He's too used to being the one in the hospital waiting room, drinking bad coffee and leading the prayers." She pointed to the door. "You should go on now. He shouldn't…be alone."

Her voice broke then, anguish she'd been holding back all evening breaking through the cracks of her control in a near-silent sob. That hopeless sound tore straight to Hannah's heart, and she gathered Mary into her arms.

"Why didn't you tell my father?"

"Tell…him…what," Mary asked in a muffled voice into her shoulder.

"Oh, come on, Mary. That you love him."

Mary pulled back and gripped Hannah's forearms. Behind her glasses, the older woman's eyes were red rimmed, their usually shiny brown color had lost some of its luster. "How did you know?"

Hannah chewed her lip. Perhaps this wasn't the best

time to mention that anyone paying attention—clearly her father couldn't be counted in that number—would have noticed how Mary lit up the moment Reverend Bob walked into the room. Her interest hadn't been as obvious as Olivia's, but then Mary's affection was more sincere.

"Maybe people carrying around secrets have a special connection with others who have secrets," Hannah told her.

"Maybe."

Hannah watched as Mary tightened her tan cardigan sweater around her body and retied its belt at her waist. She could relate. Hannah hadn't been warm since the moment Andrew had called her with the news.

"My father is blind if he doesn't see how wonderful you are and how wonderful your lives would be together."

"Thanks, sweetie."

"He's going to be okay, you know," Hannah said, surprised to find herself reassuring the other woman when she wished she could be that certain.

Yet Mary nodded as if she had enough confidence for the both of them. "God and I have been talking about that all night."

Arm in arm, the two women moved down the hall to the waiting room. Several church members came to their feet as they entered the room. Andrew was the first to reach them, but others—Rick and Charity McKinley, Charity's mother, Laura Sims and Deacon Littleton gathered around them.

"You'll want to check at the nurses' station," Andrew said. "They're looking for you. I think they're ready to give you an update."

He indicated for Hannah to wait for a second while he helped Mary settle back into her seat, and then he went with her to the nurses' station. She wouldn't allow herself to think that the youth minister was there to support her in case she had devastating news.

"Miss Woods?" the nurse asked when they reached the desk. At Hannah's nod, she continued, "I'll page the doctor if you can wait here for a minute."

"I'm sure he's going to be fine, Hannah," Andrew told her while they waited.

She smiled at having received the same assurance she'd just given Mary, but something from earlier struck her, and she studied Andrew. "You said before you had to use the portable defibrillator on my father. Did his heart stop?"

"No, but his heart rate went crazy. The defibrillator did what it was supposed to do, though. When I put those pads on his chest, the machine said he had an irregular heartbeat, and then it shocked his heart. After that, the EMTs arrived." Andrew stared down the empty hallway, appearing lost in his thoughts.

"Thank you for saving my father's life."

He turned back to her. "God just made sure I was in the right place at the right time."

"Then thanks for listening to Him."

The doctor arrived with an update. After a string of four-syllable medical terms, Hannah managed to gather that her father had been given a "clot buster" drug and was heavily sedated. Though he would soon be moved to the Cardiac Care Unit, Hannah was allowed a few minutes with him in the Emergency cubicle.

Leaving Andrew to update the others on his condition, Hannah passed beyond the locking metal doors leading into the E.R. Inside the curtained cubicle, she found her father much as he'd been when she'd seen him briefly hours earlier.

It was so strange to see her big, strong daddy reduced to merely human under the hospitals unforgiving fluorescent lights.

"Oh, Dad…"

Again, heat rose behind her eyes. She'd already watched one parent die, had sat back as a helpless spectator while her mother wasted away, her sweet spirit losing its battle before her body succumbed. Hannah couldn't imagine how she would survive if her father died, as well.

She shuffled to the chair across from the narrow hospital bed that looked like a heavily padded ambulance stretcher. Pulling the chair close to the bed, she sat and reached over to lay her hand atop her father's.

"Come on, Dad, wake up."

Hannah waited, expectant, but this was real life, not the movies. Reverend Bob's eyelids didn't even flutter. Then her gaze moved to the IV stand and the morphine drip, and she remembered. At least he wasn't in pain. The monitor next to the bed showed the zigzag evidence of his heartbeat, and his chest continued to rise and fall in a steady rhythm.

The tiny room blurred. She didn't bother brushing away the tears that trailed down her cheeks. Without closing her eyes in case her father chose that moment to emerge from unconsciousness, she whispered a prayer.

"God, please lay Your healing hands on my father. Please heal his heart and send him home to us." She couldn't bring herself to pray for God's will in the situation when she feared that His will might have been something very different from her own. "His work here isn't finished yet, and we don't know what we'll do without him."

She hadn't breathed the word *amen* yet when the words from Philippians 1: 6, one of the many Scriptures her father had encouraged her to memorize over the years, drifted through her thoughts. "'He who began a good work in you will carry it on to completion until the day of Christ Jesus,'" she recited softly, hoping her father would hear the Scriptures he loved and open his eyes.

His chest continued to rise and fall in its steady rhythm. Hannah shrugged and shook her tired head. It had been worth a try. Coming up from her seat, she leaned over her father and kissed his lined forehead.

She stepped to the edge of the curtained area and glanced back at her father once more, but she felt none of the earlier anxiety at having to leave him for the short while until he could be moved to Cardiac Care. He was only resting, and the doctors were making sure he wasn't in too much pain. *He who began a good work in you.* The Scripture gave her comfort when everyone's platitudes, including her own, hadn't helped. It felt as if God was telling her that her father's work here really wasn't finished. Finally, she felt some cause to hope.

Hannah stumbled into her apartment Friday night, operating on only the fumes remaining after a three-day adrenaline rush. As she shrugged out of her coat, several snowflakes broke away from her scarf and fluttered to the floor. Strange since she hadn't noticed it was snowing. The roads were probably slick tonight, but she hadn't noticed that, either. God's hand must have been on her car for her to make it home at all.

Her back ached between the shoulder blades from too many hours spent keeping vigil next to her father's bed, but the rest of her body felt numb. She could barely distinguish the first day from the third in her memories as each worry, each prayer and each moment of foreboding melded with the ones before.

She would have been there even now if Mary hadn't promised to stay with her father through the late-night hours and insisted that she go home and get some sleep.

Hannah wondered if she would be able to sleep, anyway. After all the nightmares she'd witnessed while wide-awake, would she be able to take a chance at succumbing to her dreams? She'd witnessed too much of life's frailty and fleetingness not to wonder what would happen when she closed her eyes.

Hannah glanced around the empty rooms of the apartment. It felt so small, so unwelcoming, when a few days earlier she'd thought of it as home. In the corner, Rebecca's dolls, except for Miss Gabrielle, sat too neatly atop the toy box, awaiting the girl's return. The special doll had served as their daughter's companion all week while she'd spent her nights with her father and visited with other church members while Todd worked during the day.

She wondered if she should have asked Todd to bring Rebecca back tonight instead of waiting until morning, but then she worried if that would have been more for her benefit than her daughter's. And she suspected that even if Rebecca were in the next room sleeping, Hannah would still have been prowling around the dark apartment, trying not to crawl out of her skin.

Guessing that she might feel better if she ate, she shuffled to the kitchen and pulled open the refrigerator door. Eggs, lunch meat, fresh vegetables and milk lined the shelves. Todd had put her groceries away that first night and had been adding items to the refrigerator since then. Once again, he'd handled the details when she'd been too overwhelmed to do more than put one foot in front of the other.

Too bad her stomach was rolling so hard that she couldn't consider eating any of the food he'd supplied. She couldn't pull her thoughts away from her father, who was still battling his way back to health, though he'd already made it through the darkest hours.

For his part, Reverend Bob had dozed away most of the hours of his crisis under sedation, only occasionally having a few lucid moments to hear of the clot busters and the angioplasty that had cleared the blockage in his heart and the life changes that would be necessary to continue forward.

Perhaps more distressing than watching her father had been serving as witness to Mary's silent vigil. Each time Reverend Bob had awakened, Mary had been among those nearby, but she'd taken care to stay on the periphery.

What did it feel like to have that kind of regret? To love in secret, to pine alone? The ironic thought wedged a new ache inside her heart. Hannah knew that regret intimately. She'd lived that secret love, she'd pined, and when she'd had the opportunity to live that love out in the open, she'd been too scared to risk her whole heart. For that, she'd lost everything.

Hannah tried to push those useless thoughts aside as she changed into a pair of oversize sweats and climbed into bed. But her thoughts chased her in the darkness.

She'd made so many mistakes out of anger and fear. Though the anger had faded, she'd clung to the fear.

She was so tired of being afraid. She was tired of letting that fear run her life.

Hannah sat straight up in bed and climbed out from beneath the sheets. She wouldn't be getting any sleep anyway. Straightening her sweats, she threw her hair into a ponytail and pulled on her coat. In the bottom of her purse, she dug around for her keys. She knew it was late, but it was long past time to set things right.

Chapter Sixteen

A knock at his front door awakened Todd, but that wasn't saying much when he'd done no more than toss and turn for the past three nights on the lumpy sofa in his town house apartment. He'd even sacked out early tonight, hoping to catch up on his sleep, but that only gave him time to count every paint drip and shadow on the ceiling and to notice how bare and pitiful his walls looked.

After untangling himself from his makeshift bed, he staggered toward the door in his Detroit Tigers sweatshirt and plaid lounging pants. He rubbed his aching neck and wondered why he'd ever bought that couch. It made a better torture device than a cozy place to kick back and watch TV—and an even worse bed. But he'd given up his bed to his little girl.

When he opened the door, Hannah stood on his stoop, her pulled-up hood keeping her face in shadow. His thoughts and his pulse raced.

"What is it, Hannah?" He shook his head, trying to find some clarity. "Is your dad okay? Did something happen? I thought he was doing better."

She pushed past him into the apartment. Until she swept the door closed behind her, Todd hadn't even noticed the snow blowing in on his bare feet.

"Dad's fine," she assured him as soon as she'd pulled off the hood. "Well, as fine as someone can be with a damaged heart and bruises all over his legs from doctors routing catheters through his arteries."

"Remind me to never have a heart attack."

"Never have a heart attack."

"Thanks."

"You're welcome."

Hannah smiled as she removed her coat, but her effort couldn't quite brighten the exhaustion dulling her eyes. She looked bone-weary, with blue-gray crescents beneath her lower lashes. At least she looked comfortable, dressed in sweats just like the ones she used to wear when they were teenagers.

"Why are you here, Hannah?" As soon as her eyes widened, Todd was sorry he'd asked. She would probably leave now, and no matter what he'd said before, that was the last thing he wanted. "Did the police catch up with Olivia? Or did you want to see Rebecca? I can wake her up if you want me to."

She shook her head, not indicating which question she was answering. "No new news that I'm aware of. Oh, I wanted to thank you for taking care of Rebecca and for the food. For everything." She leaned her back against the door, folding her arms and rubbing her hands over her upper arms.

"That was nice of you to call Grant. He came by the hospital to see Dad and me."

"He's your friend" was all Todd was able to say. He'd known Hannah needed a friend these last few days, and he'd wanted to make sure someone was there for her if he couldn't be.

Hannah nodded. "He said you were really nice to him and invited him to come back to church." At his shrug, she continued, "Grant said you're a nice guy."

Todd could only imagine what those kind words had cost Grant, but the blessing of Hannah's friend didn't matter now that everything had changed.

Stepping farther into the living area, she lowered her gaze to the sofa, covered with a tangle of blankets and bedsheets. "Oh, I woke you. I'm sorry. I can go."

"I don't want you to go. I just want you to tell me why you came."

"To talk," she said finally.

She glanced at the couch again. He'd made sure Hannah hadn't seen it messy like this each morning when she'd picked up Rebecca. But he hadn't been prepared for her visit this time.

"That had to be so uncomfortable. You gave up your bed for Rebecca?"

"She's my child."

She nodded, as if she, too, understood that no sacrifice was too great for their daughter.

"Anyway, I was planning to buy a bed for Rebecca's room when she visits, but I didn't get the chance before…"

Hannah met his gaze, obviously not missing that he'd referred to his guest bedroom as Rebecca's room.

"Are you sure you don't want me to get her up? She'd probably love to see her mommy."

"I don't want to wake her, but I would like to look in on her if you don't mind."

Waving his hand for her to follow him, Todd led the

way down the short hallway past the spare room that would soon be their daughter's to the slightly larger master. In the center of the big bed that had been his one self-indulgent purchase—aside from the big-screen TV in the living room—Rebecca looked so tiny, so young and precious. She lay with her knees tucked under her body and her backside pressed up in the air.

"She used to sleep like that when she was a baby," Hannah whispered in the doorway.

"You probably loved watching her sleep."

"I did." Hannah slipped inside the room and dropped a kiss on their daughter's silky head. Then she followed him out of the room.

"Why didn't you just sleep in there with her?" Hannah said as they reached the living room. "There's certainly room."

"I didn't want to wake her by coming in later. I did lie down with her each night, just until she got to sleep."

An unsettling silence fell over the room then, while Todd held back his questions and Hannah didn't offer any answers. Their lives had changed over the last few days since Reverend Bob was hospitalized, but nothing could change the things they'd said to each other before all this happened. They couldn't take those things back.

"You said you wanted to talk," Todd said when he couldn't stand to wait any longer. "Here, let's sit."

He hurried over and ripped the sheets, blankets and pillows off the sofa, dropping them unceremoniously in a pile on the floor. He lowered himself onto the cushion, and Hannah followed his example, but instead of beginning, she sat gripping her hands together.

"Do you want me to take Rebecca for the rest of the weekend?" he prompted. "I can take her next week, too, if that will help you out. I don't have any vacation yet, but I can probably work something out. Whatever you need—"

"I need my best friend."

She said it so softly that Todd wasn't sure he'd heard her right at first. A lump suddenly filled his throat. He coughed into his hand. What was she saying? He needed to be cautious for his self-preservation. Could he be only a friend when his heart wanted to be all things to her—a husband, lover and a friend?

But even his misgivings couldn't stop him from drawing the only woman he'd ever loved into his arms and offering her whatever comfort his sturdy shoulders could provide. She didn't sob as he'd thought she might, but she held on tightly, her fingers pressing hard into his back.

It felt so good holding Hannah in the circle of his arms. He'd thought he would never hold her again, and his arms had ached from the loss.

He couldn't help himself. As he breathed in the floral scent of her hair and felt her clinging to him as if he possessed all the answers to her life's questions, he couldn't help wishing for impossible things, things he'd told himself he could live without.

For the longest time, neither said anything, and they simply rocked back and forth on that lumpy sofa.

Though he longed to hold her just like that forever, Todd forced himself to set her back from him. She'd clearly come with something to say, and he wanted to give her the chance to say it.

"I've had a lot of time to think lately," Hannah said when he was convinced she would never tell him what was on her mind. "Though I spent time praying for my father's recovery, there were still plenty of empty hours for me to get my head on straight."

"I always thought it looked pretty straight before." Even now, even in this quiet, serious moment, he couldn't help teasing her. Humor was part of who they'd always been together.

She rolled her eyes at him, but she still smiled. "Thanks. Watching my dad go through all this was like a roller-coaster ride. First, the heart attack. Then the clot buster drug opened the blockage. Just when everything seemed okay, it reclotted, and they had to do angioplasty to break it up again.

"It was hard enough for me to watch my father in pain that way. But then seeing Mary going through it was worse. I don't know…" She let her words trail away, shaking her head.

Todd sat back in his seat and crossed his arms as he tried to follow along in her story. Clearly she wanted him to read between the lines, but he was missing the point.

"Mary Nelson was there?" Come to think of it, other church members had been watching Rebecca when Mary was her regular sitter.

Hannah nodded. "I felt so badly for her. It was so sad. She wouldn't leave Dad's side. She just sat there regretting the things she'd never said and wondering if she would ever have the chance to say them."

"That had to be tough."

Todd understood what it was like to second-guess decisions. *If I knew then what I know now…* But he decided not to lie to himself. He would have chosen to return to Hannah every time, and he always would have risked any pain for the chance to know his daughter.

"I don't want to do that," Hannah said, drawing him back from his thoughts.

"To do what?"

"I don't want to live with that kind of regret. Not anymore."

Todd shook his head with more sorrow than determination. "Hannah, so much has happened be-tween us. A lot of things we can't change no matter how much we wish we could."

"Please," she said, turning her shoulders so she faced him as they sat. "Please let me try."

Todd braced his hands on the edge of the sofa, his chest feeling tight. Though he wished it were different, nothing had really changed between them. She needed him to hear her, so he would listen, but he couldn't allow himself to settle for less than his heart needed to survive. "Go ahead."

"I've thought a lot about what you said about God's forgiveness and our forgiveness. You're right. It is a gift. One I never gave you."

As she spoke, Hannah gripped her hands together and squeezed her left thumb so tightly that it turned red at the tip. "I never really forgave you for leaving me, though I told myself—and you—I had. I was lying to us both."

"No, Hannah. You believed it, so it wasn't a lie."

"But you saw right through me."

One side of his mouth lifted. "Well, not at first, but…" He was tempted to say *not soon enough,* but he couldn't wish away a single minute of the sweet hours of his oblivion. Knowing was better, he kept telling himself, hoping he would eventually believe it.

"I just couldn't see it. And I couldn't forgive the way

God forgives. Completely. He doesn't hold a grudge, but I did. I was wrong."

Todd couldn't stop himself from reaching for her hands and curving his fingers over her clinched grip. "We both were. About a lot of things. But we were just kids. We made mistakes."

Hannah gently pulled her hands from his, tucking them under the sides of her legs. "Even if we could have used that as an excuse then, it doesn't work now. For me, it was more than just not forgiving. Blaming you was easier than facing the truth that most of the misery in my life I'd brought on myself."

Todd opened his mouth to interrupt her, though he wasn't sure what he would say to defend her when she'd spoken the truth. His instinct was to protect her even if she was wrong.

"No, let me say this. It's long past time."

Closing her eyes, she held her index fingers together like a church steeple and pressed the bridge of her nose to the point at the top. Finally, she spoke again. "I was wrong to keep Rebecca a secret from you. At first, I did it because I was angry, and then the secret became like a trap I'd built and then couldn't escape from it."

"Once everything was going smoothly again, it was probably just easier not to make waves," he said.

"I kept waiting for the right time, and I know now that if you hadn't returned, that *right time* would never have come."

Though Todd had often suspected that was the case, he still ached inside having heard it spoken aloud. "I can't imagine not knowing her."

"And her life would never have been the same if she

hadn't gotten to know her daddy. She…loves you." Her voice broke as she spoke the word *love*.

He could still hear Hannah's timid voice when she'd confessed that she loved him, and it still hurt to realize that love wasn't enough.

"I'm so sorry, Todd. And I'm proud of the father you've become. All those hours and minutes I've stolen from the two of you I can't give back." Tears were tracing down her cheeks unchecked.

"Honey, thank you for saying it, but I forgave you a long time ago."

Though she'd been staring at her hands in her lap, Hannah lifted her gaze to meet his. "It took me a lot longer than you to reach that place, but I want you to know that I'm finally there. Forgiveness is a gift, and I'm giving you mine right now. All of it."

"Are you sure?"

"I'm sure."

If he questioned at all whether she was sincere, he had only to look in her eyes. Her pain and regret was clear.

Todd drew in an unsteady breath. He'd waited, he'd hoped and he'd mourned when hope had disappeared. And now Hannah sat there before him, the woman who'd possessed his heart since before he'd even become a man, offering him the thing that mattered most. She'd gift wrapped her promise for him and tied it with a bow.

Without hesitation, he leaned forward and folded Hannah in his arms again. It felt like coming home, holding her there, with her cheek resting against his shoulder, her tears dampening his sweatshirt. He sensed that God had formed his arms at least in part for the honor and responsibility of holding her.

For several seconds, they clung together, giving and

receiving comfort. Finally, Todd pulled away and looked into her tearstained face. He slid his hands down her arms and then reached up and brushed away her tears with his thumb.

"I love you, Todd. Do you think there's a chance for us…after everything?"

His heart squeezed as he stared into her pleading eyes. Even after all this time she still didn't know how deeply he loved her. Wordlessly, he showed her, first by gently taking her hands and pulling her to her feet and then by pressing his lips to hers.

Never had a kiss felt so perfect. He didn't know if it was possible to squeeze a lifetime of hopes and dreams into a single kiss, but he tried to convey it the best he could.

"I love you," he breathed against her skin.

Tracing her hands over his shoulders, Hannah clasped them at his nape. She smiled up at him, her eyes shining, and then stood on tiptoe to kiss him. It felt as if she was giving him a message of her own—one of promises made and promises kept.

When the kiss ended, he touched his cheek to hers. A chuckle bubbled from deep inside him. "Look at us. We've had to travel so far to get to each other."

Hannah pulled her head away so she could look up at him. "Some of us farther than others."

"At least we can tell our grandchildren I flew around the world to win you back."

"Grandchildren?"

Todd couldn't help grinning. It was so nice to lighten the mood after the intensity of the conversation they'd just had and the week they'd just survived. "You think we should worry about raising the children before we make plans for the grandchildren?"

"Children? As in plural?"

"Is that a problem?" He waved his hand to dismiss the subject. "We don't have to make decisions about the future right now. It's too early for such serious discussions."

Hannah shook her head, looking at him with a confused expression. "Too early for what?"

"Too early Saturday morning." He pointed to the wall clock that read half past midnight.

"Oh, I should be getting home," she said, taking another step back from him.

Automatically, both of them turned to look at the door, and just as quickly Todd realized he wasn't ready for her to leave. If she left now, he would wonder if her visit tonight had just been the one pleasant dream on his uncomfortable couch bed.

"I don't know about you, but I'm starved." He waited until she looked back at him before he spoke again. "How about I make us some breakfast?"

She lifted a shoulder and lowered it, probably preparing to decline, when her belly growled. Pressing her hand against her stomach, she gave him an embarrassed grin. "I wasn't hungry earlier."

"Sounds as if you are now. Besides, are you in a hurry to go out in that?" He stepped toward the front window and gestured for her to join him.

Outside, a new blanket of snow had transformed Milford into one of those scenes on a Christmas card, and the snowfall didn't appear ready to taper off anytime soon.

"I guess I'm not in a rush. It's pretty out there, though."

Todd slipped his arm around her shoulder, and they

watched the snowflakes flutter to the ground for a few minutes longer. The snow was pristine, still unmarred by foot traffic or turned to gray sludge by automobile tires and exhaust. Under the streetlights, some of the flakes on the ground sparkled like diamonds.

That fresh snow reminded him of the new, tentative relationship they were forming inside the glass. Without the stains of past mistakes, everything felt new.

Chapter Seventeen

Reverend Bob blinked a few times before finally opening his gritty eyes. The space around him blurred first and then settled into an equally confusing clarity. It was dark outside his low-lit patient room, and several snowflakes clung to the window.

He wasn't sure how long he'd slept this time or whether he was better off now than he'd been the last time he'd awakened. Now that the medication was wearing off, his body felt as if he'd experienced the unfortunate end of a battle with a steamroller. At least the doctor had warned him to expect some soreness.

Turning his head slowly toward the side of his bed where his IV stand rested, he was surprised to see he wasn't alone. Mary Nelson slumped in a chair next to the bed rails, her head at an awkward position on the backrest. She would be sore when she awoke, but she dozed so peacefully that he hated to awaken her.

He reached for his glasses from the bedside table and glanced at her again. She was a handsome woman with a youthful face, an ever-present smile and a contagious joie de vivre, but there was an extra sweetness about her while she slept.

Come to think of it, Mary had been around a lot the past few days, always seeming to be with Hannah when he'd awakened. He couldn't have been more grateful to her and the other church members for helping Hannah.

Suddenly, her eyes fluttered open.

"Hi," he said when her gaze came to rest on him. "You again."

She straightened in her seat and patted her dark hair nervously though its no-nonsense, short style appeared tidy as always. "Yes, me."

"Where's Hannah?"

"I sent her home for some sleep."

"Thanks. You look like you could use some sleep, too."

Mary waved away his suggestion with her hand. "I'm fine. I just wanted to help out."

"You've been hanging out at the hospital a lot this week. You must really like the antiseptic smell."

He'd meant it as a joke, but she looked embarrassed, refusing to meet his gaze. Bob drew his eyebrows together. Maybe the painkillers hadn't worn off as much as he thought, and he was still under a medicated haze.

"I just couldn't leave, not when you were lying there, when you still didn't know."

"Know what?" As soon as the words were out of his mouth, he realized he knew the answer to his own question. A hundred tiny things—inconsequential things like an offer of help on the church Christmas Decorating Committee and kind words after some of his sermons—added up in his thoughts. Though not overt like Olivia's attention, Mary had shown her affection in simple ways, and he'd been oblivious to it all.

"I'm sorry. I didn't realize."

She smiled. "People are blind sometimes."

"I suppose they are." He smiled back.

Strange how he knew Mary so well, as a church member, a friend to his daughter and to him and a childcare provider to his granddaughter, but until now he'd never seen her as a woman. A kind and compassionate woman. She'd fit so seamlessly into their lives that he'd never noticed.

He noticed now.

"In all these years, you've never told me about your late husband," Bob began, suddenly wanting to know everything about her.

"George has been gone ten years now."

Mary's eyes took on a faraway look that Bob recognized. Others probably had read it in his eyes hundreds of times over the past few years. Clearly, Mary remembered her late husband the way Bob cherished his memories of Deborah. Mary would understand that a part of his heart would always belong to his late wife.

They continued talking in hushed voices for another half hour, sharing stories of Bob's daughter and the happy life Mary and George had lived together though they'd never been blessed with children. Occasionally, Mary would offer him ice chips or a cup of water. The conversation was simple and unrushed as the two of them got to know each other for the first time…all over again.

Hannah followed as Todd led the way to the kitchen. She should have gone home, especially with all that snow blowing around outside. But she couldn't bring herself to leave him now, not when they had just found hope for a new beginning. Besides, it was only breakfast. She would leave right after they cleaned up the dishes and after she cleared the snow off her car.

"What are you hungry for?" Todd said as he peered into the shelves of his refrigerator. "Eggs? Pancakes? I make a mean omelet."

"No Belgian waffles or a soufflé?"

"You're testing your short-order cook's abilities here." His head popped up from behind the refrigerator door. He kicked it closed, balancing eggs, a stick of butter, green peppers, mushrooms and tomatoes in his arms. "The fridge is looking pretty bare except for these."

"What a coincidence. I just happen to have a craving for scrambled eggs with tomatoes, mushrooms and green peppers."

"Then we're set." He lowered his collection of food to the kitchen counter and gestured for her to sit at the glass dinette.

"But I can help."

"You can also sit there and watch me."

Todd collected a mixing bowl, cutting board and frying pan from the cabinet and pulled a knife and a whisk from the drawer next to the stove. He seemed utterly focused on his culinary duties, as if their conversation from twenty minutes before hadn't fazed him a bit.

How could he concentrate on dicing vegetables and melting butter when their relationship had just taken a huge step from impossible to probable? Hannah was glad she wasn't cooking because she would have sliced off a finger or two along with the tomatoes.

"You're awfully quiet," he said, not looking up as he poured the egg mixture into the pan.

"Just thinking."

"Care to share?"

"Not especially.

He shrugged, but even in profile, she could tell he was smiling. Though she suspected he was enjoying her discomfort a little too much, she couldn't help smiling with him.

Just as the toast popped and Todd moved the frying pan from a heated burner to a cold one, Hannah heard a sound behind her. Rebecca stood in the doorway wearing her yellow, footed pajamas and a frown. She rubbed her eyes and squinted under the fluorescent kitchen light.

"Daddy? Mommy? Is it morning time?"

When her daughter crossed the room and climbed into her lap, Hannah brushed Rebecca's messy hair back from her face. "Hi, sweetie. Did we wake you up?"

"It smells funny," Rebecca said, wrinkling her nose.

"Green peppers. I guess a smell like that is better than an alarm clock." Todd grinned when he turned back from the stove with two filled plates in his hands. He set one plate in front of Hannah and the other at the empty space beside her.

"Honey, we'd better get you back to bed. It's too early for you to be up."

Rebecca pointed to the dark bread sticking out of the toaster. "I want to eat breakfast, too."

Todd pointed to his colorful egg dish. "Want some?"

"Yuck."

"We like it." He looked conspiratorially at Hannah. "Do you think we should share some of our toast with her?"

Hannah squinted her eyes, trying to appear deep in thought. "I don't know. Only if we put jam on it, I guess."

"Ooh, jam."

Soon the three of them were seated around the table, enjoying an early-morning, family breakfast. Hannah found herself memorizing the sights, sounds and tastes of it. This was what she'd hoped for. This was how she'd always imagined family life to be, and if it wasn't really like that, she hoped she wouldn't wake up from her dream.

When they had taken the last bites of eggs and Rebecca had enough jam on her face to spread on a third piece of toast, Todd cleared away the dishes, refusing any help. He made quick work of loading the dishwasher and then opened a cabinet to put away the spices he'd used.

Sitting opposite Hannah, on her knees so she could reach the table, Rebecca planted her elbow on the table and rested her heavy head on her hand.

"Do you want me to carry you back to bed?" Hannah's heart warmed as she watched her sleepy little girl. In another couple of years, she wouldn't even be able to carry Rebecca to bed. She hoped that time passed as slowly as possible.

"Can Daddy carry me?" the sleepy voice asked.

Quickly, Todd turned his head back from the sink where he'd returned to wash his hands. He appeared startled that Rebecca had chosen him over her mother, even for this small privilege. His gaze met Hannah's, and he waited.

In the span of a heartbeat, she smiled. His expression softened, as well.

"Sure, I can take you, honey." He turned away from

them, digging his hand into the spice cabinet once more. "But I need to do one more important thing first, okay?"

"Okay, Daddy."

Hannah turned back to the counter, not seeing anything left to finish. Then Todd approached the table with a satiny white box in his hand, and she knew. She drew in an unsteady breath. But when his lips curved upward and his gaze connected with hers, all of her nervousness drifted away.

Never breaking eye contact with her, Todd lowered himself on one knee and opened the box in his hand. Again, the lovely solitaire winked out at Hannah, not long ago a painful reminder of broken promises and now a symbol of a lifetime commitment.

"Hannah, I've loved you ever since I can remember."

"Daddy, are you and Mommy going to get married now?" Rebecca asked, suddenly bright-eyed instead of drowsy.

Hannah started, having forgotten momentarily that this tender moment was for a crowd of three rather than two.

Todd looked up from his position on the floor and held the white box high enough for Rebecca to see. He lowered his voice and winked as if he were sharing a big secret. "I'm getting ready to ask her."

The preschooler grinned as if she'd had her second Christmas in a month. Hannah looked back and forth between the man she loved and their child. Perhaps it wouldn't be as private as some proposals, but it certainly would be as memorable.

"As I was saying," Todd began again, "I've always loved you, even before I understood what love was and what it meant to put someone else's needs ahead of my own. Though our mistakes pulled us apart, God has led us back to each other and given us the most awesome responsibility of raising our child.

"I would love to do that with you, side by side. Will you please be my wife and finally make our family complete?"

"Please, Mommy, say yes." Rebecca had climbed down from her chair on the opposite side of the table, and now she knelt by her father on the linoleum floor.

"Yeah, please, Mommy, say yes," Todd chimed in with a grin.

"Well, you two are pretty persuasive. I think I'll have to say…yes. Definitely. Absolutely. I want more than anything to spend the rest of my life with my best friend. How's that for an answer?"

"Good enough for me."

Todd pulled the ring out of the box and, taking her hand, slipped it on her finger. Still holding that hand, he leaned forward and touched his lips to hers in a kiss of commitment.

"Me, too." Rebecca snuggled between them.

Todd stood and, with one arm, scooped up a giggling Rebecca, while extending his other hand to pull Hannah to her feet. For several seconds, the three of them stood there in the kitchen, in a tight group hug.

Hannah inhaled the sweet scents of the two people in the world she loved most. Her feelings must have shone in her eyes because Todd smiled down at her. "You see, I told you I would ask when the time was right."

She reached over and brushed Rebecca's hair back from her face. "I think you picked a perfect time."

When Todd released her, Hannah glanced down at the blindingly beautiful ring on her finger and then up at him. "I thought you said you were planning to return the ring."

"It's a better story to say that I decided not to return it, knowing that in the end we would be together, but the truth is this week was so crazy for all of us that I didn't get around to taking it back."

"Go with the first story. The grandkids will like it better."

"Grandkids?" He glanced at the child still propped on his hip.

"Ah, but we should probably focus on our children before we worry about that next generation."

"Children? As in plural?" he said, repeating her words from earlier.

"We'll have plenty of time to discuss that later."

But Rebecca, who had rested her head against her father's shoulder, once again close to dozing, suddenly straightened. "I want a baby brother."

"Is that so?" Todd tweaked her nose.

"And a dog," Rebecca added.

"Oh yes, the dog." He turned back to Hannah to explain. "Max got a dog after Tricia and Brett were married."

He ruffled Rebecca's hair. "How about we worry about that after your mom and I are married? But first we get to plan a big church wedding."

Rebecca was cheering, the baby brother and the dog forgotten for now, but Hannah stared at Todd in shock.

"A big church wedding? Don't you think it would be inappropriate—"

Instead of answering her, Todd gave his daughter a conspiratorial glance, the side of his mouth pulling down in a frown. "I'm going to have to convince your mommy to have a big party, so I'm going to take you back to bed first, okay?"

Rebecca didn't argue with that, so he washed her face and left the room with her, staying gone only long enough to tuck her in and kiss her good-night again. But that was plenty of time for Hannah's secret dreams of a perfect, elegant church wedding to resurface. She'd understood that they were just dreams, each time she'd awakened from them, still humming the organ postlude. Was it right for a young mother to still wish for all that pomp and ceremony?

When Todd returned to the kitchen, he jumped back into the conversation before she had her argument ready.

"Are you saying it's inappropriate for me to marry the woman I love in front of God and all our friends?"

"Maybe something small and in the parsonage would be better. It wouldn't be so—"

"So what?" Instead of waiting for her to answer, he pressed forward again. "Is that the wedding you've always dreamed of…at the parsonage?"

She shrugged and then finally shook her head. "But it's different for us—"

"Is it?" He reached for her hand on the table. "Aren't we a young couple in love, ready to make lifetime vows before God?"

She wanted to believe, wanted to smell the floral scent filling up the sanctuary, wanted to speak those precious words and feel her Lord's blessing on their vows. "I just don't know if we should."

"Can you name a single member of Hickory Ridge who would object to us making our wedding a big celebration for the whole church?"

Hannah said nothing, only pressing her lips together and trying not to smile.

"Okay, I take that back." There wasn't a church around that didn't have a judgmental member or two, and he'd already met Laura Sims at Hickory Ridge. "Would *most* of the members of our church be thrilled to celebrate with us?"

"Yes, but—"

"Then we should give them a reason to celebrate."

"I don't know."

"Sure you do. What would Reverend Bob want you to do?"

"He would tell me to follow my heart."

"Are you going to?"

And suddenly Hannah realized that she was going to do just that. She knew deep in her heart that Todd was the man God intended for her. She wanted her whole church family to be a part of the beginning of their life together. Love like theirs deserved to be celebrated.

"We'd better get busy. We have a wedding to plan."

Chapter Eighteen

Hannah stood outside the glass separating the vestibule from the sanctuary on the first Saturday after Valentine's Day. On the other side of the glass, a wedding scene very different from the one she'd pictured in her dreams was unfolding. Different but just as nice.

In keeping with the season of love, the church was adorned with red and white roses and white tapered candles. Small red hearts blended with the fluffy bows on the ends of the pews.

She brushed an unsteady hand down the front of her ivory satin wedding gown, her fingers smoothing over the stitching from one of the appliqués just below the fitted waist. It was a beautiful dress, and she should have been feeling like a princess wearing it, but the band around her neck felt too tight and the seams on the bodice itched.

"Do you need some sneakers? Are you going to make a run for it?"

Hannah looked up to find Serena Westin standing before her in her crimson-colored bridesmaid gown. The dress had been let out to allow for Serena's advanced pregnancy, but she still looked darling in it, her skin rosy and glowing.

"I'm not running anywhere. But you can if you need the workout." Hannah fussed with her veil, only managing to make it go cockeyed on her head.

Tricia Lancaster stepped forward to right the thing, resecuring the headpiece with the bobby pins Hannah had pulled loose. "What are you so nervous about, anyway? This wedding has been a long time in coming."

"Too long, but this isn't exactly how I pictured it." She pointed to the glass doors leading to the outside, where a mid-February snowstorm raged. Though most of the guests had arrived only in the last fifteen minutes, their cars were already covered with a thin layer of snow that would build during the next few hours of the wedding and dinner reception.

Steffie Wilmington looked up from where she was adjusting the strap of the satin sling-back shoe that matched her bridesmaid's dress. "Look in there. This storm didn't stop anybody from getting here."

"At least Roy and Sharon got here a few days early," Hannah said. "I would have hated it if their flight had been delayed and they'd missed their son's wedding."

"Are you kidding?"

Hannah turned to see the woman she'd just spoken of had come up behind her. "Oh, hi."

Her future mother-in-law leaned close and air-kissed Hannah so she wouldn't muss her hair. "We wouldn't have missed this for the world." She scanned the vestibule, looking past three of Hannah's bridesmaids. "Where is that beautiful granddaughter of mine?"

Hannah looked around, for the first time noticing her daughter's absence. "Oh, no, where is she?" Wedding or no wedding, she should have been watching. What if something happened to their little girl all because she was distracted?

"Relax, sweetie," Charity McKinley called out as she emerged from the ladies' room in her bridesmaid's dress. Charity stood holding hands with Rebecca, in her frilly, crimson flower girl dress, and Max Williams, in his tiny ring bearer's tux. "Remember, I was supposed to take the junior members of the wedding party for a last potty break before the ceremony."

"Oh. Right."

"Hi, Nana," Rebecca called out, rushing into Sharon McBride's arms, as if they'd known each other years rather than days.

Sharon gave her granddaughter a squeeze. "Oh, it's time for the usher to seat the mothers—" She wore a pained expression when she turned to Hannah. "Oh, I'm sorry, sweetheart."

"It's all right." But that wasn't completely true. Hannah hadn't realized how putting on this gown and preparing to stand before these people with her own daughter would make her miss her mother more intensely than she had in years. Her father was here and she should have been satisfied with that, especially after how close she'd come to losing him, too, but part of her still longed to share her wedding day with her mother.

Sharon cocked her head and studied Hannah for a few seconds as Tricia handed her son, Max, his ring bearer's pillow and gave Rebecca her basket of flowers. Finally, Sharon drew Hannah aside, and lowered her voice.

"You have to be missing your mother a little today. I didn't know her well, but she seemed like a kind woman. I would never want to try to replace her, but I want you to know that I would feel privileged if you would think of me as a mother to you as much as to my son."

Hannah's eyes burned, and she sensed her nose was in danger of dripping right on her wedding gown. Still, she pressed her cheek against Sharon's. "Thank you."

Because she couldn't say more and not be the first to cry at her wedding, she left it at that. The organist chose that moment to begin playing "The Wedding Song," by John Lennon, and she had to hold her breath to keep from smearing her makeup.

"Well, ladies, how about we get started with this little shindig," Andrew said as he came out to be with the wedding party. He indicated for Sharon to go with the usher waiting to escort her down the aisle.

At the same time, the door at the right front side of the sanctuary opened, and Reverend Bob, Todd and his father, whom he'd chosen as his best man, filed out and took their positions at the front of the church.

And suddenly the day became perfect after all.

Todd. Always Todd.

In his black tuxedo, he looked more handsome than in her best dream, though he was already tugging at his tight collar. He turned toward the back of the church, seeking to see her face from behind the crowd in the wedding party.

She was so grateful to him for seeking her out in the first place, even when she'd been perfectly content to hide behind her wall of anger and secrets. He'd given his heart to her, and she felt so unworthy of the gift.

Her gaze drifted to the other man she loved most. He still looked frail, far from the robust hero of a father she'd either known or imagined. But it warmed her heart to see him standing there in front of the altar, his well-worn Bible clasped between his hands. First, he stared down at the book as if in prayer, and then his gaze traveled up and off to his right. Hannah didn't have to look far to discover who held his attention. There'd been a lot of secretive glances lately.

Mary sat discreetly in the fifth row, needing no place of honor as the minister's lady friend. Hannah didn't even have to worry that her dad would overdo on her wedding day, not with Mary keeping a careful watch over him. Like Todd and Hannah, her father and Mary had been given another chance at love, and Hannah was so pleased to see that they saw it for the gift it was.

As the music changed for the processional, groomsmen Roy McBride, Grant Summer, Rick McKinley and Brendan Hicks took their places next to the bridesmaids. Hannah couldn't be more pleased that Todd included her friend in the wedding party. It was another reason to love Todd, as if she didn't have enough already.

Andrew stepped next to Hannah and tucked her hand in the crook of his arm.

"Thanks for standing in for my father, Andrew."

He smiled down at her. "I'm honored." He helped her lower the blusher of her fingertip veil over her face.

Hannah watched as her sweet little girl traveled down the aisle, scattering flowers from her basket and somehow managing not to run to her daddy as he stood near the altar. She was pleased that the paperwork had already been filed for Rebecca to eventually carry her father's name.

"Doesn't it seem like we've traveled an awfully long journey to get here since that night when you and Serena let a scared, pregnant teenager cry on your shoulders?"

"Sometimes the best destinations are found at the

end of long journeys." Andrew turned back to watch little Max and the rest of the wedding party proceed down the aisle.

Again, the music changed, and the crowd rose and turned back to the entry where only Hannah and her escort stood.

Hannah turned to her friend once more before she took her first step toward the man she loved. "And sometimes that end is just the beginning."

Todd's heart squeezed and his throat clogged as he watched his bride marching to him in a lovely gown that still paled next to her beauty.

To him. He loved the way that sounded. After all this time, after all the emotional miles she'd traveled away from him, they were there together walking toward their future.

Hannah smiled at him, her gaze never leaving his, as she continued down the aisle. As much as he'd longed for the years they could already have spent as husband and wife, he wondered if he would have cherished the gift of a life with her if it had come easily.

When they reached the front of the aisle, Andrew placed Hannah's hand in Todd's, and they turned to face Reverend Bob. Instead of beginning with the "dearly beloved" speech they'd all come to expect, the minister stopped and lifted the front of Hannah's veil to kiss her on the cheek.

"Over the years, I've married dozens of couples," he said, slipping one hand inside his Bible to hold his place. "But this is a once-in-a-lifetime experience for me as a father. I get to marry the daughter of my heart to the young man who claimed her heart so many years ago."

Reverend Bob turned his attention to his Bible. Soon Todd found himself speaking the words he'd only dreamed about in the five years he'd waited to return to Milford and to Hannah. She smiled at him, love so clear in her eyes that Todd could barely recite his vows without his voice breaking.

So this was what it felt like when a man received everything he'd ever wanted. He was amazed and humbled by it.

Todd turned to his father, who lowered the wedding band with five tiny inset diamonds into his hand. Holding her left hand, Todd slipped the ring on her finger.

"With this ring, I thee wed."

Once she'd slipped the plain gold band on Todd's finger, Reverend Bob told him he could kiss his bride. As Todd touched his lips to hers, he felt a wonderful peace of completion, as if God's will finally had been done.

"I love you," he murmured against her mouth.

Hannah's lips turned up. "Right back at you," she whispered.

The minister motioned for Rebecca to join her parents before the altar. "I would like to present to all of you for the first time, Todd and Hannah McBride and their amazing daughter, Rebecca. And I'm not the least bit partial here, either."

Applause and laughter broke out in the auditorium, and even a few whoops could be heard coming from the back of the room. For a relationship that had borne its share of sadness, it was only right that its new juncture would begin with cheers.

Hannah wiped the last bit of white buttercream frosting off her cheek from the smear Todd had given her when he'd fed her their wedding cake.

"Sorry about that," Todd said, using a napkin to help her. "I didn't know you were going to turn your head."

"A likely story," she said with a grin.

All across the open area of the church's Family Life Center, guests sat at tables eating huge quantities of homemade dishes that church members had provided for the reception. Indulgence was the order of the day, and that was even before they reached the cake with its white roses and intricate piping. Of course, there were several heart-healthy selections for her father to choose from, and he had been allowed the tiniest sliver of wedding cake.

"Are you sharing any of that cake?" Brett Lancaster asked as he swiped three plates from the table. The state trooper took a few steps away before turn-ing back to Hannah.

"Did Reverend Bob tell you the good news?"

"What news?"

"Police caught up with Olivia yesterday in Jackson. She'd already picked a little Friends church there as her newest target and had just started a job in the church office."

Hannah shot a worried look at her father who was sitting at one of the red cloth-covered tables next to Mary. News of Olivia's arrest hadn't been too hard on his heart apparently if he could find that much to laugh about this afternoon.

Todd came up behind Hannah and dropped kiss on top of her head. "Did I hear someone say good news?"

"They've arrested Olivia," Hannah explained before turning back to Brett. "Any word on the missing money?"

Brett shrugged. "We're unlikely to recover much of

it for any of the churches. Olivia apparently had a gambling problem, and she was always looking for a new mark to pay her debts."

"That's too bad," Todd said.

"Are you serious?" Hannah asked, but then she shook her head. "Sorry. Forgiveness is a bit tough for me. I didn't know whether you knew that about me or not."

Todd stepped up beside his wife and took her hand. "I've heard tell."

Several members of the wedding party crowded around them then.

Julia Sims was the first to speak up. "Brett, are you sharing your good news with everyone who will listen?"

Hannah looked at the other church members quizzically. She felt guilty enough about her eye-for-an-eye reaction to news about Olivia's arrest without having to see her fellow church members have a veritable celebration over it. "He's already told us about the arrest."

Brett shook his head, drawing Tricia under his arm when she came near him. "We have more good news. We're expecting!"

Hannah looked back and forth between them. "You, too?"

Todd stepped forward and shot his hand out to Brett. "Congratulations, buddy. What do the kids think about it?"

Tricia shrugged. "Rusty Jr. and Lani are pretty excited about it, but Max isn't sure how he feels about giving up his position as the youngest."

"They're all excited that we're going to have to move to a bigger house, though," Brett added.

Steffie seemed to be getting a big kick out of the announcement. "You see, I told you not to drink the water."

"I know," Tricia said, shaking her head and feigning a sad expression. "I should have listened."

"You two," Steffie said, pointing to the church's newest pair of newlyweds, "had better watch out. There's something in the water at Hickory Ridge."

Hannah scanned the crowd standing around her. At nearly full-term, Serena rested her hand on the small of her back and had removed the shoes from her swollen feet. Charity and Rick were standing next to them, and unconsciously Rick's hand had moved to splay across his wife's slightly rounded tummy. Tricia didn't show at all yet, but a new life grew in her womb, as well.

"Okay, I'd better avoid all the church water fountains," Hannah said, trying to keep a serious face. "Should I worry about the water we use to make the coffee, too?"

"I say bring on the church's water." Todd didn't even bother to hide his amusement. "I want to fill up our house with babies, and we should get on it as soon as possible."

As if he hadn't realized how the comment would sound until it was out of his mouth, Todd ended his statement with an awkward "oh." He covered his eyes with his hand.

More laughter filled the room.

"All-righty then," Rick said with a mischievous grin. "Sure glad we got the Family Life Center finished. It sounds like there's going to be a population explosion at Hickory Ridge, and there would be no place for all the Sunday School classes."

Finally, the party began to wind down. Hannah allowed Todd to draw her into one of the classrooms for a quick kiss. She was nervous, but she couldn't wait to be alone with her husband, consummating their life together, this time with God's blessing.

As the kiss ended, Todd pressed his forehead to hers. "Are you happy, Mrs. McBride?"

"Very."

"Are you sorry we waited so long?"

She shook her head. God's timing was perfect, and this was the perfect time for her family to be together.

Todd bent to kiss her again, but a passel of children zoomed through the room, playing hide-and-seek as they often did in the classrooms with their removable room dividers.

"Mommy, Daddy, why are you in here?" Rebecca stopped long enough to ask.

"Just taking a minute to be alone."

That seemed to satisfy her, so she ran off again.

As soon as the room was empty, Todd sneaked another kiss.

"We'd better get back to our reception," Hannah said finally. Hand-in-hand they returned to the main room, earning a round of applause from their guests.

When Hannah looked over at her father, he was smiling.

"Does this seem like a dream to you?" Todd whispered in her ear, his warm breath tickling her neck and ear.

Hannah nodded, smiling. "If it is, I don't ever want to wake up."

"We'll keep dreaming together," he promised.

"I don't have to dream anymore, when all of mine have already come true."

* * * * *

SPECIAL EXCERPT FROM

LOVE INSPIRED
INSPIRATIONAL ROMANCE

*An Amish man gets more than he bargained for
when he moves next door to a large spirited family
during the holiday season.*

Read on for a sneak preview of
The Amish Christmas Secret
by Vannetta Chapman.

"Get back!"

Definitely a female voice, from the other side of the barn. He walked around the barn. If someone had asked him to guess what he might find there, he wouldn't in a hundred years have guessed correctly.

A young Amish woman—Plain dress, apron, *kapp*—was holding a feed bucket in one hand and a rake in the other, attempting to fend off a rooster. At the moment, the bird was trying to peck the woman's feet.

"What did you do to him?" Daniel asked.

Her eyes widened. The rooster made a swipe at her left foot. The woman once again thrust the feed bucket toward the rooster. "Don't just stand there. This beast won't let me pass."

Daniel knew better than to laugh. He'd been raised with four sisters and a strong-willed mother. So he snatched the rooster up from behind, pinning its wings down with his right arm.

"Where do you want him?"

"His name is Carl, and I want him in the oven if you must know the truth." She dropped the feed bucket and swiped at the golden-blond hair that was spilling out of her *kapp*. "Over there. In the pen."

Daniel dropped the rooster inside and turned to face the woman. She was probably five and a half feet tall, and looked to be around twenty years old. Blue eyes the color of forget-me-nots assessed him.

She was also beautiful in the way of Plain women, without adornment. The sight of her reminded him of yet another reason why he'd left Pennsylvania. Why couldn't his neighbors have been an old couple in their nineties?

"You must be the new neighbor. I'm Becca Schwartz—not Rebecca, just Becca, because my *mamm* decided to do things alphabetically. We thought you might introduce yourself, but I guess you've been busy. Mamm would want me to invite you to dinner, but I warn you, I have seven younger siblings, so it's usually a somewhat chaotic affair."

Becca not Rebecca stepped closer.

"Didn't catch your name."

"Daniel...Daniel Glick."

"We didn't even know the place had sold until last week. Most people are leery of farms where the fields are covered with rocks and the house is falling down. I see you haven't done anything to remedy either of those situations."

"I only moved in yesterday."

"Had time to get a horse, though. Get it from Old Tim?"

Before he could answer, a dinner bell rang. "Sounds like dinner's ready. Care to meet the folks?"

"Another time. I have some...um...unpacking to do."

Becca shrugged her shoulders. "Guess I'll be seeing you, then."

"Yeah, I guess."

He'd hoped for peace and solitude.

Instead, he had half a barn, a cantankerous rooster and a pretty neighbor who was a little nosy.

He'd come to Indiana to forget women and to lose himself in making something good from something that was broken.

He'd moved to Indiana because he wanted to be left alone.

Don't miss
The Amish Christmas Secret *by Vannetta Chapman,*
available October 2020 wherever
Love Inspired books and ebooks are sold.

LoveInspired.com